The Convert

(A Fiction)

The Convert
(A Fiction)

K. P. RATH

KALPAZ

ISBN: 978-93-5128-166-5

Price : ₹ 190

First Published, 2016

Published by

Kalpaz Publications
C-30, Satyawati Nagar,
Delhi – 110052
E-mail: kalpaz@hotmail.com
Ph.: 9212142040

Printed at: G. Print Process, Delhi

Cataloging in Publication Data—DK
Courtesy: D.K. Agencies (P) Ltd. <docinfo@dkagencies.com>

Rath, K. P., author.
The convert : a fiction / by K.P. Rath.
pages cm
Novel.
ISBN: 9789351281665

1. Indic fiction (English) I. Title.

PR9499.4.R38R38 2015 DDC 823.92 23

Contents

Acknowledgements

I am deeply indebted to my wife Gita and daughter Ruma who stood like sheet anchors behind all my efforts to write this Novel. My special thanks are due to my grandsons Sruti Sagar and Devi Dutta for their introducing me to the wonder world of Mcrosoft Office Word, which made my writing and rewriting so easier.

I am thankful to my mother-in-law Rama Devi who is a well known writer and a winner of Odissa Sahitya Academy award, for her appreciation of my earlier works.

I thank all those, specially my friends and dear ones, for their good words and good wishes, which prompted me to write and write, to mention a few Indira, Basanta, Saraju, Niranjan, Ashok, Purnendu, Amar, Kabita, Sucheta, Mamata, Dharitri, Sanjukta, Nalini, and Swagata.

CHAPTER 1

It was a cold dark night in Kiderpore, Calcutta. All were asleep in their *Jhumpdis.* The narrow lanes between the huts were deserted, except for a few street dogs, out in search of shelters to save them from the biting cold. A dim street lamp at a corner was the only source of lighting in the area. It showed the filthy lanes littered with garbage, left to be cleaned by the sweepers in the morning. The silence of the night was broken by the shrill sound of a whistle of the Police, followed by heavy footsteps and shouting, 'Stop or we will shoot'. More sound of running. This time, a person was seen running towards the *bustee.* The Policeman chasing, takes out a revolver from its holster and fires a shot. There was a sharp cry, mingled with pain and fear. The person disappeared in the enveloping darkness of the *bustee.* The policemen gave chase for some time and then left.

Ranee finished her daily chore of washing of the household utensils and arranging them on the shelf. She lay down, covered herself with a quilt and was about to go to sleep, when she heard the blowing of the whistle and afterwards the crack of the gun shot. She sat upright on the mat, thoroughly shaken. Then, she heard someone entering and running across towards their backyard. She waited for some time, breathlessly. Her brother and sister-in-law were already asleep. She did not want to wake them up. When every thing was quiet except for a distant barking of a dog somewhere down the street, she mustered courage and slipped out of the hut to explore. It was dark outside and the cold was biting. She covered herself with a blanket and stealthily inched her way to the backyard. The backyard was fenced off by placing used asphalt drums on the ground, which sloped towards the main drain. There was a small enclosure inside, which served as a store for fire wood and coal. A screen stitched out of gunny bags was hung at the entrance. With thumping heart, standing outside, she tried to peep in, but could not see anything. She shivered in the cold. At last, she summoned courage and asked, 'Is anybody there?' No answer. Then she distinctly heard, someone whimpering inside. This time, she did not hesitate to lift the screen and look inside. In the dim light thrown by the street lamp, she could discern a man sitting on the floor, clutching his hand, from which blood dripped. The man looked at her with pain and appeal in his eyes. Obviously, he was hurt. Ranee was a brave girl. She had undergone a short course of training in nursing and was employed in a local dispensary, run by missionaries. She asked the man to keep quiet, rushed to her room, to fetch a First Aid Kit. The man was evidently shot at, luckily the bullet grazed his hand tearing off a little skin. She washed the wound, applied an antiseptic and dressed it, expertly. Now Ranee had a good look at the man, he appeared to be twenty or there about and had a boyish face. He managed to smile and said, 'Thanks. I will have to move now.' He tried to get up, staggared and might have fallen had Ranee not steadied him and said, 'You seem to be weak and tired, let me get something for you to eat.' She made him sit on a log of wood and removing her blanket, covered him with it. Asking him to sit quietely, she rushed back to her room and returned with a few slices of bread and a cup of milk and asked him to eat. While the young man was gulping the food, as if he was starving, she looked at him and asked, 'What is your name?'. 'Raja', he said. 'And yours?' 'Ranee.' He laughed, even in that hopeless situation and said, 'God must have sent you to come to my aid or else I was done for. They have been chasing me for the past one hour and I was running for my life, giving them the slip every now and then. But they seem to know all nooks and corners in this area. They kept doggedly following me and forced me to run into this *bustee*. I just ran wildly, they following closely till some one took a shot at me. I might have been killed or injured seriously, had that fool of a policeman, toying with the gun, not slipped over a puddle of water and fallen. The bullet hit me, but only grazed my little finger.' 'What were you running from?' 'That is a long story. This is not the time for telling you that. I must get away from this place soon.' 'But you are too weak, you need rest. You are safe at this place. No body comes here except for me, not even my sister-in-law because she is carrying. No body will come to know of your presence here. You may leave this place after daybreak.'

'Okay. So be it. Will you please keep this packet with you, till I ask for it?'

He handed over a packet to her.

'Alright, I will see you in the morning. Now you better take rest and try to get some sleep.'

Casting a glance at him with concern, Ranee returns to her room. She could not sleep that night and was worried stiff, about what she did, was it proper? Should she not tell her brother that she provided shelter to a fugitive? Gradually sleep took over and she slept. Before day break, she woke up with a start and the entire episode of the night, came back to her, as in a dream. But, the thick envelope, lying under her pillow, belied her thoughts; she got up from her bed and rushed to the back yard. There was a thick fog in the air, hovering above the drain, making everything on the ground hazy. She groped her way and reached the hideout of Raja. Putting aside the screen, she looked inside and found to her great surprise and dismay that the shack was empty. There was no sign of Raja. She was greately perturbed and also angry at his behaviour. *'How ungrateful'*, she hissed. *He could have told her, that he was leaving. Is this the way of repaying one's kindness? Let him go and get caught in the net of Police or whosoever he was running from. Why should she bother?'*. She was bitter. At the next moment however, she was sad and worried. *Where could he have gone and where does he live?* She had no idea. She intended to talk to him in the morning and find out. She prayed God to protect him from the evil. *In the morning, before she leaves for her job, she would visit the temple and light a 'lamp' before the deity, seeking Her Blessings.* Her resolve comforted her.

Returning to her room she slipped into the bed silently. There was an hour to go before daybreak. She tried to forget the incident but the face of Raja with his impish grin came back to her time and again. If he was to go away from her life, he would not have left that money with her, she thought. Sleep came over and she slept.

Her *boudi* stirred in her bed. Day was breaking. Gopi, her husband was still sleeping soundly on the floor beside her, wrapped in a blanket. *Why Ranee has not yet lit the chullah? There was no smell of smoke. Usually she was not late.* She was running seven months and felt heavy to move. She raised herself slowly and managed to sit with the support of a pillow. She called Ranee, without raising her voice, lest it might wake up Gopi, which he resented. *He should have his full quota of sleep, he said. After all, that was the only time he rested his tired limbs, after his day long toil, pulling a rickshaw*. She managed to raise herself with the support of a cloth stand nearby and walked up to the next room. She found Ranee still sleeping. She prodded her to wake up. Ranee got up with a start and seeing *boudi,* by her side, was worried. The doctor madam, who visited the *bustee* every week advised her to lie down on the bed and not to get up without someone's support. She did'nt breath a word of the incident of the night, to her and supporting her carefully, helped her to the bed.

* * * * *

Raja looked at his watch, it was *three* in the morning, not a soul any where in sight. Fog was thick and it obscured every thing from one's view. With difficulty, he leaves the *bustee* and arrives at the main road. To any body observing, he might appear to be a ghost, floating in the fog. Guided by the dim glow of the street lamp, he reaches the Railway Yard, his destination being, an empty goods shed, normally used by the homeless as a night shelter. He entered the shed and lay down on a heap of rags at a corner. Others had already occupied their preferred places. He brought the blanket given to him by Ranee. When she would find him gone, in the morning, what she would think of him, nothing short of a common thief, he was sure. But he had no intention to put that sweet and brave girl in difficulties by over stepping on her generosity. He tried to hold the blanket tight against his body to keep the biting cold off, but could not succeed. Finding a heap of half burnt logs in a corner, still giving rise to smoke, he kindled the fire and warmed his hands and feet. He was more comfortable. The throbbing pain in his little finger, where he was hit, was almost gone. Dressing of the wound by Ranee *(yes, that was her name),* had done wonders. He could not see her face in the darkness clearly, but was aware of her sharp features. Little did he know, how important she would be to him, in his life.

* * * * *

Raja managed to reach Bombay safely. He was a small operator in the bottom rung of the organization, without even knowing from whom he received his orders. His job was confined to running small errands such as giving information about movement of Police and transfer of cash from one fund collector to the other. He did his job diligently and was never caught by the Police. He received a commission for each of the transactions, which was sufficient for his needs. He survived because he was not ambitious. But jealousy and ill will prevailed in the organization, amongst its associates. Raja's honesty and sincerity paid dividends, he was assigned with more responsible jobs, which earned him good money. Unknowingly, therefore, he caused heartburn in others and became a victim to their evil designs. Usually he travelled by public transport in rush hours and used different disguises for different occasions and wore at times wigs and dark glasses. Today he wore only a *kurta* and *pyjama*. As he sat in the rear in the tram clutching a bag, he looked tired and exhausted and to a casual observer, was nothing other than an ordinary trader returning home after a busy day. Someone had betrayed him and Police kept watch over his movements. The minute he stepped into the tram at Esplanade, Police in plainclothes followed him. At that hour of the night there were few passengers. The weather being cold, everybody sat huddled in their seats. Raja had a sixth sense, which told him that there were two policemen in plain clothes in the carriage. He had spotted them from their ways of looking at him furtively from time to time. He made his plans. The next stop would be the Tram Depot, the terminus, where he was supposed to alight. He knew from his previous rides, that the tram would slow down, because of a bend before the Depot. He got ready and as the tram slowed down to negotiate the bend, he jumped clear of the car and merged into the darkness. He knew the locality and sprinted till he came to the first lane which was lighted. He could see the Police men coming after him, blowing their whistles. He was forced to enter the *bustee* area, which was semidark. Taking advantage of the darkness and the thick fog he ran ahead and was about to enter inside a green fence when he was shot at. Writhing in pain and clenching his teeth he bolted inside like a frightened hare. The Policemen missed him and blowing whistles went ahead.

* * * * *

Raja had only his bag, to carry. He hoisted it on his shoulders and walked out of the Railway Station, in search of his destiny. He was young and full of hope and vigour. He had no address to call upon. He walked aimlessly along the road keeping to the left and took a turn into the first lane on the left. Bombay was different from Calcutta. Skyscrappers filled the horizon wherever he looked, people rushed by and nobody noticed him. Pedlars and hawkers did brisk business, goods were thrust at you, whether you wanted them or not. A boy, hardly twelve years old carried hankies displaying them on a wooden cross and yet another tried to sell perfumes and that too '*Evening in Paris!*' He moved on, as long as his legs carried him, till he felt tired and hungry. He must have been walking for an hour, by now. He found himself, opposite to a restaurant. He entered and sat at a table. The place was crowded, mostly serving to office goers and factory workers. A boy, wearing a cap and a dirty towel thrown over his shoulders, comes over, puts a glass of water on the table and looks at him with his eyebrows quzzically raised, he asked him what was available. The boy let out a stream of words, perhaps giving out the menu for his benefit. He could not make anything out of it.

'Do you have *samosa?*'

'*Samosa mangta, aisa bolo na seth*'. The boy goes inside, brushing aside a thick curtain which had not seen a laundry in its life and comes out after few minutes, balancing a tray holding a plate of *samosas* and a bottle of sauce, which he puts on the table and asks, 'Tea, coffee?' 'One tea, please.'

He munched the hot and crisp *samosa*, took a sip of the tea, which the boy had brought, in the mean while. He noticed that tea at Calcutta was sweeter. He wanted to ask for a little more sugar, but let it go. '*While in Rome, behave like a Roman*'. Raja observed that the man at the cash counter looked at him intently. He knew the type, a customer wary. Perhaps, Bombay is crawling with such customers, who at the earliest opportunity would slip away, bypassing the cash counter. *A lousy set up*, he said inaudibly. With a smile in his face, he picked up the scrap of paper which was left by the boy, one rupee scribbled on it. Carrying his bag, he sauntered towards the cash counter. His worries never showed in his face. That was his characteristic. He carried a smile in his face permanently, as if he was happy and contented. That, forty eight hours before, he was being chased by Police and shot at, inside a non descript *bustee* at Calcutta, nobody could guess by looking at him. His features were such, that every body would look at him twice before throwing his image in the dustbin. With his curly dark hair, angular face and steel grey eyes it was not easy to ignore him.

The proprietor at the cash counter kept on looking at him, as Raja approached to pay the Bill. While receiving cash, the proprietor tried to hold a conversation with him.

'Aap kahanke ho babujee, surely, not from here?', he asked showing interest.

Raja directed his bewitching smile at him and said, 'No, any problem?', he waited with a questioning look in his eyes. The proprietor thought this man was not only smart and handsome but also clever. He said, 'Definitely not sir, definitely not. You are always welcome. I have a proposal for you sir, would you step into the office, for a minute please?' He showed the way and Raja followed him, amused. The office room, he noticed, was lavishly furnished, quite distinct from the area, he just left. It had an aura of wealth and sophistication. Thick cushioned velvet lined sofas, wall to wall carpets, brightly painted walls, concealed lighting and above all, central airconditioning, confirmed the same. Cinema posters, filled one of the walls. He was impatient to know his interests in him. Having asked him to sit down he said, 'Let me introduce myself, sir, I am Mahesh, the proprietor of this joint. I also work for the film industry, I run an agency to hunt for new talents and introduce them to the film producers, for selection and audition. You may not believe me Mr…', he paused.

'I am Raja.'

'Yes, Mr. Raja, as I was telling, you may not believe, if I say, famous film personalities such as Shantaram, Mehboob, Modi have honoured me, by visiting this place in their times.'

Raja said, 'I do believe, but where do I come in?' He glanced at his watch and said, 'I have to go. I must find a place to stay. '

'Raja ji, if I may call you so, you need not worry about that. We will take care of that. But please listen to me. From the moment you entered this place, I have been watching you, I told myself, *here is a man who is not only handsome but has personality. Look! How he holds himself, how he walks with confidence, as if he owns the place.*'

Raja smelled danger and braced himself to meet the situation. Mahesh continued, 'You have all the get up to become a film star. But you require a little grooming, our man here, will take care of that. We have experts here, they will start working on you and your training starts from tomorrow. You are our guest from now on.'

Raja thought only for a moment and said, 'Yes, why not, I agree.'

Mahesh showed him a room which was well furnished and comfortable. Telling him to relax, he leaves. Raja throws his bag on a table, lies down on the bed and closes his eyes. What is this set up? He is virtually held up, as a prisoner. '*Okay, enjoy the situation*', he speaks to himself and smiles.

Originally, he is from a village near Bhadoi, a busy town near Banaras and belongs to a family of farmers. His father and uncles still lived in the village, tilling land to support their families. He alone, from the family, left the village for Calcutta with a relative who worked as a mill worker. He has come through the mill alright and now grown up. He is no longer a boy, to be duped. He can take care of himself. He knew Bombay *thugs* and probably he is caught in the web of one. He got up, went to the door and tried the door knob, found it locked. *Very interesting, the way these thugs operate*! He glanced at his watch, it was already noon. Time for a little nap, he decided. He bolted the door from inside, had a look at the bathroom, found it clean and hygienic, took a shower, dried himself with a towel from the rack and went to sleep without a care. He must have slept for an hour, when there was a knock at the door. Suppressing a yawn he gets up and opens the door. He finds a man standing at the door with a food tray. 'Your lunch sir', he says, and brushes past him and puts down the tray on the table, putting aside his bag in the cupboard. While he arranged the dishes on the table, another person enters with a package in his hand. He says, 'Your clothes sir, Maheshji said, you may get ready by three O'clock, he would come to pick you up.'

When both the characters left, Raja sits on the bed and contemplates. He looks at the food, neatly served on the table, napkins, spoons, forks all arranged in their places. As he was not feeling hungry, he took only some salad, a little rice and a piece of chicken and downed them with a glass of fruit juice. He opens the packet and finds a good brand of readymade dresses, a suit, complete with shirt, vest, tie and under garments. Sizes suited him, they must be expecting from him, a lot. Play with them well, he said to himself and got busy dressing. He looked at the mirror and whistled at the handsome young man, smartly dressed, looking back at him.

There was a knock at the door, it was exactly three pm, he said, 'Come on in'. Mahesh, accompanied by another person, entered. He said, 'Raja ji this is Raman, he is to accompany you to a film personality of yester years, who still calls the shots, and if she is impressed, the going will be easy for you; she has made the career for many. Wish you good luck, I'll be seeing you in the morning.' With these words, he left.

Raja was not happy with the set up, yet he wanted to give it a try. *No doubt, this Raman is a dalal. If he keeps his eyes open, no harm will come to him, he is sure*. He was new to Bombay, which is different from Calcutta in size and glamour. Through the window of the taxi, he noticed high rise buildings, wide roads bustling with rapid moving traffic, long bodied imported cars overtaking them. Then he noticed the blue ocean, yonder. Raman pointed out that to be the Juhu beach, lined with spacious bungalows belonging to film celebrities and industrialists. An imposing structure painted in white, glistening in the sun came into his view. Raman said, that was the ISKCON temple, a new addition to Bombay's landmarks. Finally, the taxi stopped in front of an apartment block in Andheri East. For the first time Raja was seeing a twenty storeyed building, rising sky high. The name NANDIGHOSH engraved on a marble plaque with golden letters lent character to the building. Raman gave an address and the *security* let in the car. Far from feeling nervous, Raja enjoyed the situation. Using one of the lifts, they reached the 7th Floor, where the lady had her apartment. A maid servant answered the bell and asked them to wait in the lounge. The room was cool and furnished with thick drapery and carpets. Raja observed that flower vases were kept at every corner on tall mahagony stools. There was a faint smell of jasmine in the air, ostensibly, a feminine touch. Then the curtains parted and a lady entered. She was the most beautiful woman Raja had ever seen. He expected to see an elderly woman past her prime, with heavy makeup and gorgeously dressed. But this woman whom he was staring at, was nothing like that. With her wheatish complexion, without any makeup or facials, she looked as fresh as a morning lily dressed to kill. Wrapped in a plain bluish original chiffon saree which accentuated her curvaceous body, she looked a Greek goddess. She was definitely no ordinary woman. So this is how film stars look like, from close quarters. He stood still gaping when the goddess addressed, 'Why Raman, you have not introduced your friend'.

'I am so sorry, Saralajee. Meet Raja, he is from Calcutta', he said. 'Quite new to Bombay', he added. The goddess then extended her hand, Raja was enchanted when she addressed him, 'Hello Raja, how are you?' He appreciated the courtesy and took her hand. It was soft like a rose petal, the grip was infinitesimal, he felt as if her hand would slip away, he had to hold it tight. Did he feel a response? His voice failed to reply her. The maid then brought tea and snacks on a tray. The maid served them tea, he furtively looked at her. There was more than, that met his eyes. Are they planning something sinister for making him a scape goat? But as '*inquisitiveness killed the cat*', he was ready to bite the bait. Whenever she looked at him, he smiled. At last the cat was out of the bag. Saralaji suggested, since she was going to dine outside, would they join her, she would be pleased. Raja waited for Raman's reaction. As he expected, Raman excused himself saying, since he had an appointment to keep, it would not be possible, for him to join and asked Raja to accompany her.

She said, 'No problem, you need not worry Raman, your guest is my guest. I will take care of him and see that the baby reaches home safely.' Thus the numero one scene was over and the curtain was drawn with the exit of Raman.

No sooner Raman left the room, Sarlajee got up and went to a cupboard to bring out a bottle of coagnac and two glasses on a tray. When she started pouring out the drinks he interrupted her saying, 'Not for me please, I do not drink.'

She said, 'This is no drink my dear, but a tiny bit of appetizer. It will not cause any harm. Are you afraid of your *mommy*? No body will come to know of it. Come on, be a sport.' She pressed into his hand the glass with a bit of sparkling liquid in it.

Why not make the best use of the situation? In the process of accepting the drink from her hand, he gets up, puts his hand on her slim waist and presses her close to him, unconcerned of the consequences. And before she could know what was happening, with a quick twist of his hand he touched the glass with his mouth and emptied the contents into the nearest flower vase. Sarala was not prepared for such a turn of the event and taken aback, enjoyed the situation. She felt the muscular arm of Raja encircling her and the masculine smell of his body enthralled her. *Well. So here is the man, from whom much more could be expected.* Her face was so close to Raja's, separated only by inches, that she felt their breaths mingled with each other raising the warmth, which was engulfing them. She, with misty eyes/remained looking at him and waited for the next step, he would take. While Raja who engineered the motions, for a moment, thought that his feet were being swept away by waves and waves of her body warmth and fragrance. Before he was lost totally, he recovered his composure and steadied himself. He loosened his grip over her waist and stood apart, mumbling excuses. He was not sure whether he had overacted. But the effect was not lost on Sarala, who was an experienced woman and not new to such advances before.

She began liking this young man, so fresh and daring. She straightened the wrinkles off her saree and sat down. As a friendly gesture, she pulled down Raja to sit by her side and rewarded him with a smile. After a while she said, 'Let's leave now. '

She pulled him by his hand and both of them proceeded towards the lift, hand in hand. The lift whirred and down they went. Her chauffeur waited at the porch with the car. Respectfully, he opened the door and they sat inside. He seemed to know, where her employer wanted to go. He manoeuvred the car expertly through the crowded streets and came on to the ring road. Born and brought up in poverty stricken areas, Raja had no idea what luxury, money could not buy. Every city seemed to have its quota of rich and poor. Though covered under the same sky their worlds were different. From a footpath to a lavishly furnished mansion is a far cry, a dream which perhaps was never achieved. His mind revolted against this discrimination and injustice meted out to millions of his country men. Why some are born rich and some poor, how one can expect the poor to race against the rich? He may achieve success but the odd is one in ten thousand or even more. Being born poor they are handicapped in every sphere. They are the ones who are down-trodden. All development schemes, progress over their bodies. Throughout their lives they are hunted and displaced in the name of urbanization and development. If the roads are to be widened, it is they who suffer, their *bustees* are razed to the ground. If a dam is to be built, their lands and homes got submerged.

No where they are secure, but they are very much wanted in the society, however much they are scorned and hated by the rich, simply because they till their lands, they carry their loads, they clean their filth and above all they constitute a sizeable portion of the electorate in a democratic country such as India. If they remain poor, remain uneducated and unemployed, so far so good, it would serve better the interests of the cream of the society. While Raja was engrossed in such thoughts, Sarala inched towards him and sat close to him, having her own dreams. This man was not only handsome but seemed to possess brains. What if, he is not sophisticated and may not measure up to the standards of her friends at the club. The club was exclusive and only meant for people of her class, rich, modern and fun loving. She decided to introduce him as her special guest, Kunwar Raja Saheb, a scion of a royal family of Rajasthan. She was pleased at her innovative idea. It would give her an edge over that pompous and obnoxious *buchee,* Mrs. Suleman who boasted that her grand parents were direct descendants of *Nawabs of Oudh* and scoffed at others telling that she was doing an honour for visiting their club, otherwise she belonged to clubs, normally frequented by Royal personalities. She would dump her husband, an old man, already bent, at the bar and rove with darkened eye lashes, to locate available young men and pick one of them as her dancing partner for the evening. She nudged Raja softly and said, 'Where are you lost my dear, we are almost nearing our destination. I am taking you to a very elegant club, as my guest. But I warn you that you must behave properly and should not give away, that you are not, what you are supposed to be.'

Raja said, 'What does it mean?'

Sarala said, 'It means, that you are not simply Raja, from a middle class family. You are Kunwar Raja Saheb from a princely state of Rajasthan, on a pleasure trip to Bombay. I am going to introduce you, that way at the club. I take it, you may not be knowing much of English and you would rather reply in monosyllables, the rest I will take care of.' She straightened his tie, looked at him appreciatively and said, 'That would do, you look like a born Royality.'

Raja smiled to himself, that he was a graduate in Commerce from Calcutta University, he did not want to disclose to the lady and preferred to keep quiet and let things take their own course. Meanwhile the car had entered a drive and stopped under the porch. Raja was about to open the door but the hands of his companion stopped him from doing so. She hissed at him, 'Sit quiet, the chauffeur will let us out.'

Hand in hand they proceeded up the steps and reached the Hall, where Raja found himself in a different world. *'What sort of a club is this*?' he wondered. It looked like a fairy land, he read about. There was glamour and opulence, wherever he looked. He felt the grip of Sarala tightened, she was whispering, *'Do not look lost, you fool, bear a non-chalant appearance on your face as if you are accustomed to such things*.' A girl scantily dressed, came holding a tray towards them. Sarala accepted a glass and signalled with a flicker of her eyes to Raja, to pick one. While picking up the glass from the tray, Raja could not help to glance at the swelling of the half covered bosom of the girl who stood close to him. Raja had never seen the breast of a woman before and his face reddened. All this did not escape Sarala's eyes. She pulled Raja away from the spot and guided him to a corner where several men and women had clustered around and were busy in small talks. Almost everyone had a glass in his or her hand. Seeing Sarala approaching them, they broke conversation and welcomed her.

'Hi Sarala, how're you? Long time no see', said one of the ladies who separated herself from the crowd and came forward to greet them. The lady was far from slender, gorgeously dressed and with her heavy make up, looked grotesque to Raja who just stood there with his arm linked with Sarala's.

The lady said, 'And who may be this handsome prince you have hooked today?' Sarala's eyes were blazing fire but her words were sugarcoated. She said, 'Hi, Mrs. Suleman, glad to see you all. I was busy. And meet my guest Kunwar Raja Saheb, the first cousin of Maharaja of Alwar.' Hearing his name announced, everyone turned to look at him in awe and wonder and greeted him. Raja bowed and accepted their greetings switching on his bewitching smile at them. Soon he became the darling of the group. Almost all the ladies surrounded him, wanting to be close and more intimate. Sarala felt proud in the beginning, as if her prize pet was being patted, but when the goings went too far and particularly few amorous ones tried to engage him with libidinous talks, she came to his rescue and pulled him out, mumbling excuses, that they have to leave soon.

Smiling and saying, '*Hello*' to acquaintances, she came across, she led him to the dining hall. After they were seated at a table, Sarala heaved a sigh and said, 'What a frightful scene you created, you were almost being mobed. You seemed to be enjoying it.' Raja said, 'Saralejee, what were I to do, I never expected such behavior from ladies.'

'Ladies, my foot', she said, 'slut is a better word they deserve,' she fumed for some time, then she calmed down. The dining hall was slowly getting filled up, couples were seen entering and the atmosphere buzzed with laughter and small talks. Waiters and waitresses were seen moving around the tables taking orders for drinks. When one approached their table, Sarala ordered some wine. This time Raja did not desist. The drinks came. She gulped it without so much as asking him to take a sip. It was better that way or else she might have created a scene. Raja observed that her mood was spoilt as she took another drink. Raja never took drinks but he knew the symptoms of getting drunk. Saralajee was behaving like one. What was he to do? How could he tackle her? A crooner began singing a melody with the accompaniment of a guitar. It was a dance tune. The DJ was inviting the couples to take the floor. Now Sarala got up as if she was waiting for the signal, and taking the hands of Raja brought him to the dance floor, other couples took the cue and joined. When Raja hesitated, she started dancing holding the hand of Raja in one hand and putting the other hand around his waist. He had to hold her by the waist to keep his balance. They danced to the music. Raja looked over and saw that everyone was engaged with his or her partner. Whirling and stepping they moved round and round, their faces touching each other, their bodies pressing each other. Suddenly Raja felt the whole body weight of Sarala, she was almost leaning on him and to his consternation, he saw that she had gone to sleep over his shoulders. *To hell with it!* He slowly carried her, without anyone noticing, and slumped her in the nearest chair. Did she pass out? He was alarmed. She was now his responsibility. What was he supposed to do? Suddenly he remembered the chauffeur, who must be waiting with the car outside. He rushed out and located the man. He accompanied him to the dining hall and between them managed to bring her out through another exit and safely deposited her in the back seat of the car. By way of explanation the faithful chauffeur said. 'No need to worry *Babujee*, she will be alright in the morning and most probably forget the entire episode, that she ever met you and took you with her to the club and danced with you.' Raja was aghast, he said, 'What do you mean?'

During their ride back to home the chauffeur related this srange story to Raja.

'Madam was one of the glamorous heroines of the yester years. She was the most sought after heroine of the films and worked for a decade beginning from 1955. Film producers lined up at her Juhu residence to get bookings. She became a trademark for successful films. Any film she acted in, was a box office hit. That was Reshma. She was called Sarala when she arrived at Bombay with her uncle from Punjab, the riot torn state after independence. She was only thirteen years old, when her uncle, the younger brother of her father had to leave his ancestral home in Punjab, after the death of his elder brother, and he had to take Sarala with him, the only child left by his brother. Uncle and niece arrived at Bombay, almost penniless. They lived on the footpath. The girl knew how to sing and her uncle had brought with him an old harmonium, the only legacy he inherited from his brother. They performed on the roadside, entertaining passers by and earned a little money to sustain themselves. It was sheer luck, that one day, when she was singing a *sufi bhajan*, a film producer was passing by and got attracted by her voice. He stopped his car and came over to the spot where people had gathered. He saw a lanky girl in ill fitted dirty clothes, singing in a melodious voice with the accompaniment of harmonium played by a young man, hung from his shoulders. Somehow the quality of her voice and her features appealed him. He waited till the performance was over and the crowd dispersed. He approached them and learnt, how they were driven away from their home and hearth and came to Bombay to earn a living. He brought them, to his bungalow and accommodated them in an outhouse. The benevolent person was none other than Shorab Modi. From that day, Goddess fortune beamed on them and Sarala was groomed and trained to be an excellent singer and actor, At that time, Shorab Modi was making the famous cinema, "*Rani of Jhansi*" featuring himself and his wife Mehtab, the first Technicolor film. Sarala's voice was recorded for one of the songs and as luck would have it, the girl who was to act as the child '*Rani of Jhansi*' fell ill and Shorab Modi decided to give that role to Sarala, the poor girl from Punjab. That was how the actor Reshma was born, Sarala not only had a musical voice, she possessed acting talents too. She grew up to be a beautiful young woman and her demands in Hindi films grew. In a year or two she built up her career under the care and patronage of her mentor. Gradually she became a household name and people thronged the cinema halls to see her films. In 1960, she was at the pinnacle of her career, when tragedy struck. Her uncle died in a road accident, she suddenly found herself alone in this world. She was totally dependent on him and could not cope with her affairs in his absence. Without him, her finances were in shambles. Before things turned worse, she decided to marry. When a film producer proposed to marry her, she consented, even though he was thirty years older.

It was a marriage of convenience and there was no love between them. She endured and pulled on. This film producer was basically an industrialist and a very rich person. He was a widower and had several children by his first wife. In the interest of family peace, he purchased a luxurious independent flat for her, where she continued to live. It was then, I came to work for her as a chauffeur. Since then, I have been with her. I have seen her from very close quarters. Sethjee, her husband, used to come to her flat not very often, but mostly remained busy in his business affairs and stayed with his family. She served him with all humility and respect, while he stayed with her. Sethjee was sorry for her and made all provisions for her future needs.

One day the inevitable happened and Sethjee succumbed to a heart stroke while at work in his office. His family did great injustice to her and did not inform her even of her husband's death. She came to know of the loss of her husband from the morning newspapers. More shock for her awaited at the residence of Sethjee, where the body was laid at rest for the mourners to pay their last respects. She was debarred from attending the ritual, by Sethjee's family members. She broke down and I had to bring her home. She locked herself, and did not come out from her room for the entire day. We were all worried and waited outside anxiously. When she came out, we saw her completely changed. Gone was the beauty and vigour of the cinema lovers' darling Reshma and in her place, stood a dishevelled woman with sunken eyes and cheeks, clothes disarranged. She had aged overnight. She was given such a beating by the fate that it took months for her to recover. Meanwhile the lawyer who was in charge of her estates paid a visit to her and gave her the list of assets and property bequeathed to her by

Sethjee, as his legal wife. Reshma, who adopted her original name Sarala, was now a rich lady by her own rights. But something had snapped within her and her old staff including me were aware of it and took care of her with all tenderness and care. She did not encourage any visitor male or female. She had not developed any intimacy with anybody while she was in her profession. Her lawyer Mr. Sampat thought, perhaps she needed medical care and consulted a psychiatrist, who suggested that she must preferably go out to a club and mix with people and share their joys, which will make her forget her own sorrows. After leading a life of recluse for several years, she began visiting the club, which became a ritual for her. We noticed improvement in her health and appearance and she began taking interest in life. Gradually her mood became jovial and the atmosphere in the household became lively. I used to drive her daily to the club in the evening and bring her back home before Ten in the night. Sometimes she used to dine in the club itself and on such occasions, I found her tipsy and a lady accompanied her, whom I used to drop at her residence on the way. One day the lady came to fetch me and told me, that Saralajee got a little drunk and would require help to come to the car. So I went in and found her slumped in a chair. My heart sank, seeing her in this plight. We brought her to the car. At home, her maid took charge of her and put her to sleep. The doctor was consulted and cautiously dropped a hint to her *'ayah'*, who was with her for the last fifteen years, that perhaps a male companion would make her a little happy. I would hate to tell you Babujee, that it was you, who was sent by the Agency to fulfil that role this evening.'

Raja was aghast to hear this strange tale. *So, he was being used as a gigolo! Well!* He cast a look behind. Saralajee was sleeping soundly in the back seat. He had full sympathy for her. They had arrived at her apartment.

Back in the hotel, he made up his mind. He must get out of this hopeless situation, immediately. He manipulated the lock so that the latch would not hold. He calculated that the safest place to spend the night would be the Railway Station. He neatly folded the clothes that he was wearing and put them in the cupboard. He put on his own clothes and silently slipped out of the hotel in the dead of the night. He took a rickshaw and came over to the Railway Station. He slept inside the waiting room without a care in his mind. In the morning he had tea and *pao bhaji* from a stall and came out of the Railway Station. His wandering, took him to Juhu and then to the ISKCON temple. The grandeur of the temple attracted him, as he entered. There was a morning crowd, offering prayers before the Lord, he joined and prayed, '*Oh! Krishna, You have brought me thus far, where to now?*' When the crowd pushed him from behind he came out to the courtyard and sat beside a wall where there was a little shade. From this point, he looked around. Devotees arriving with *puja thalis* and garlands in groups and singles, met his eyes. Suddenly, there was a commotion and people rushed towards a spot, he heard some one yelling that a child had slipped through a gap in the railing. He got up and rushed to the scene. Pushing through the crowd he came to the spot where the child fell down. Miraculously, the child's dress was entangled with a projected bar and he saw the child hanging in the air twenty feet above the ground. He realized, any moment the dress would give under the strain and the child would fall. Amidst all shoutings and wailings, he jumped over the railing, went down the drain pipe, caught hold of the child and slided to the ground below. The crowd which had gathered, cheered. The child's parents rushed and took him from the arms of Raja. The mother wept and held the child, a boy six years old against her bosom. The child's father was, however, on the lookout and spotted Raja in the crowd. Approaching with folded hands, he expressed his gratitude for saving his son from certain death and broke down in tears. Raja tried to pacify him and said, 'Now that your son is safe by Gobinda's Grace, you need have no worries, Sir. In the sacred home of the Lord nothing untoward can happen. May Lord bless your son.'

Ram Gopal, the father who was in tears said, 'Truly, you have saved our child. When you handed over the child after rescuing him, I had a vision as if Gobinda gave back our child.' He, then took him to his wife Maya and his sister Jaya, who were still pacifying the child and said, 'Look Maya, this is the youngman who rescued our child.' Raja paid his respects to them.

'What is your name *beta*?', Maya asked.

'It is Raja, *maa jee*', he said.

'Will you not join us and have *prasad,* in the temple? We are celebrating the sixth birth anniversary of Ganesh, our son', Maya said.

'It will be a pleasure, may the Lord, give him a long life, *maa jee*.'

As they were coming out of the dining hall, Ram Gopal said, 'Are you new to this place? If you need any help, you are welcome at my house, any time. Here is my business card.'

'Thank you very much, *babu jee*, for your kindness and giving me an opportunity for having *prasad*, in the temple. Something tells me that we may meet again.'

'Why not, *bhaiya,* a good deed begets good results', Jaya said and to the boy, she said, 'Ganesh, say *Namaste*, to uncle.' Raja fondly ruffled Ganesh's hair and said, 'Bless you *beta*, I have something for you, I picked it up at the Railway Station.' He gave him a key ring with a small plastic attachment with a picture of Lord Ganesh. The boy took it and said, 'Thank you, uncle. I should have a box now, with a lock, so that I will put the key in this ring.' Everyone laughed at the child's spontaneity. At the parting, Maya said, 'Raja, we will always remember you with gratitude'. Jaya thanked him again and they parted.

* * * * *

Raja learnt from someone, that if he was looking for a place to stay, he might try at Dharavi. He boarded a train towards Dharvi, one of the largest ghettoes of the country. Artisans, craftsmen, workers and all those who toiled to earn their livelihood, lived in this area in *Kholis*. Bombay being the financial capital of the country, thousands thronged this area in search of jobs and accommodation. It is a city within a city, but with no resemblance. The demarcation between rich and poor was complete and shamelessly projected in this place. People from different walks of life, from film producers to tourists, thronged this place in large numbers, for different purposes, but mostly to see and commercialise their findings, about how these people lived in the most unhygienic conditions, bereft of road, drainage, swearage and water supply facilities, yet striving to have modern ameneties enjoyed by their rich brethren, such as, electricity, fridge and cable T. V. connections in their *kholis*. Even though a million people lived in this area, it was not provided with a railway station. There was a network of streets lined with huts on either side. The taxi dropped him at a junction. An aweful stench pervaded the area, caused by human faeces and garbage dumps. He entered the nearest tea stall, to escape the stench and was welcome with a smell of burnt milk and deep fried *pakodas*. At the entrance sat the proprietor, busy in fiddling with a radio, trying to tune in *Bibidh Bharati*. The city's two faces became clear and loud to him. While one face depicted wealth, riches and comforts, the other face exposed the dirty facet of raw poverty, with a will to live and endure.

While sipping the pungent *masala* tea with cream, Raja learnt from a snooty fellow, that there were enough job opportunities in the area. Eyeing the mascular build of Raja, he dropped a hint that he could get him a job, in a local garage, at a consideration. Raja knew the type, they are the scum of the society who live on others. Many a hapless men and women, would fall in their snare and come to grief, even before they begin their livelihood. After saying good bye to the fellow, he came out of the stall and surveyed the scene outside, which was anything but serene. Over the din of wrangling of women at a water tap, he saw street urchins playing some sort of cricket with sticks and a *desi bullah* in the street and clamouring over recovering the ball from an open drain into which the ball had fallen. People did'nt seem to bother all this hullabaloo and went about their way. Raja began walking away from the spot towards a field with a compound wall, on which was written 'Private Property, No Tress Passing'. The wall, cast long shadows on one side, where he saw a group of people huddled together and busy over something. No sooner he began walking towards them, they looked at him and bolted, collecting their things. Strange; in their hurry, they, however, left one thing behind, which spoke of their engagement. It was a pack of cards, old and discoloured. So, they were gambling and seeing a stranger must have dispersed, taking him to be a policeman. A little beyond, he came across a garage, which boasted of few vintage cars, Ford, Austin, Hillman etc, which had seen their heydays and now lying discarded. A garage in this God forsaken place!The owner must have been an adventurous type to have risked the investment, no doubt. When the city grew, prime land must have become scarce and the land sharks supported by *muffia* must have eyed marshy and low lands and filled them up with garbage, to be leased out. That is how slums develop. He, also saw cars of recent brands such as Fiat, Ambassador and even few imported cars, inside the garage, undergoing repairs. He located the owner, a burly *sardarjee*, shouting in filthy *Punjabi,* at a mechanic for messing up the tuning of the engine of a Ambassador. Raja approached the *sardarjee* and said, he could fix up the tuning, if permitted. Seeing, he was dressed up like a *babu,* he said, '*tusi ki gal karte ho babu jee, ye gaddi di kam hai ga–*' He cut him short and said, '*han, han*, I know this is *gaddi di kam*, but, I am a motor mechanic, *sardarjee* and I can fix up this engine.' '*Mannu ki patta hai jee, ki tusi motor mechanic ho*?' A man who stood, by the side of the car, so long, with a worried expression, now opened his mouth and said, 'I am in a hurry, *sardarjee,* if he says, he can do it, why don't you let him try?

'*Thik hai, tussi* try *karlo*', he said to Raja.

He asked for a tool box, rolled up his sleeves and set to work. As a matter of fact, Raja did a course in Automobile Enginering from an Industrial Training Institute at Calcutta and was engaged in an auto workshop for two years, before he decided to study in the college for his B. Com. degree. Aligning the cam shaft sprocket mark with the Top Dead Centre of the crank shaft, was child's play to him. Once that was done, valve tappet adjustments with feeler gauge and cleaning of carburettor ports and valves, followed. When the engine was started thereafter, the running and pick up was so smooth that, *sardarjee* thumped him on his back and said, '*badda chunga yaar.* 'After the car owner left with his car, satisfied, the garage owner took Raja inside his cabin and had a discussion with him. He was pleased to know that Raja was unemployed. It took no time to settle the terms. At the end of the day, he had a job and also an accommodation in the *bustee*. When *sardarjee* wanted to know his name, at the time of opening an account for him, out of an impulse, he told that his name was '*Shekhar*'. Why he did that, he did'nt have an explanation, at that time. He had no idea, how that single irrational act of his, would save him from great perils in future. To his new acquaintances, , therefore, Raja came to be known as Shekhar, from that date. The garage owner was impressed with his skill and sincerity and above all, with his charming personality. Shekhar managed to get a small *Kholi* with only one room, with his help, for his accommodation. The good wishes and prayers of the family, whose child's life he saved in the morning did miracles, he believed, or how else, he could get a job and also an accommodation in Bombay on his first day. His first thought, when he lay down on bed, centred on Ranee, the brave girl of the Kiderpore *Bustee* in Calcutta, who threw all dangers aside, to come forward to help him, that frightful night. In the crowded hours of the day, he did not have the time to think of her. The last thought before sleep overcame him, was, what Ranee would be doing at that hour, thousand miles away.

Ranee was tossing on her bed without sleep in her eyes. It was only at night, when she was alone, she thought of Raja, the mysterious stranger with curly hair and grey eyes who had taken shelter in her backyard one night, and vanished in the morning. Would he ever return? She felt the bulge of the packet under her pillow, to be reassured, that he would, because she was holding his trust property. Reassured with this thought she went to sleep.

In a few days Shekhar's importance in the garage grew because of his expertise, particularly in Fiat cars. Thousands of this make of cars plied on Bombay roads and almost all the taxi cabs were Fiats. One day Shekhar was busy in tuning the engine of a car, a boy came and told that *Sardarji* wanted him in the office. The so called office of the garage owner, was a cabin, built out of wooden planks, the only room in the garage which also served as a store. An old calendar with a picture of *Guru Nanak* hung on the wall along with a picture of *Ganapati Bappa.* Shekhar on entering saw a person sitting across the table facing the owner.

He overheard his employer, saying, 'You need not worry *sirjee*, he is an excellent mechanic and he would set the engine, in no time.'

On seeing Shekhar, he said, 'Here he is, *sirjee*, you may hand over the key of the car to him. He will deliver the car at your bungalow by tomorrow evening, after repairs.' The person turned to look at Shekhar. It was now Shekhar's turn, to stare. He saw a tall and fair looking man with greying hair near the temples, with a strong jawline speaking of stubbornness. He wore dark glasses but Raja was sure of being X-rayed with two piercing eyes. The man did not speak to him, he handed over the keys and left. After his departure, the owner mopped his forehead with a hand kerchief. He said, 'Be quick with that car, Shekhar *puttar*, if you do a good job, you will earn accolades, if you fail, it will bring misfortune to me.' Shekhar said, 'I will do my best *sardarji.*'

The car was parked alongside the road, it was a Mercedes, a black one. Raja was somehow averse to that colour. He brought the car inside. The garage boy handed him a cup of tea. Tea in this area was really good, but nothing like Calcutta tea, which has real *Darjeeling* flavour.

He yearned for it. He lifted the bonnet and kept the engine, running. A cursory examination revealed that this was no ordinary car. The upholstery was regal and of shining leather. Inside, it was soundless and cool, the A/C functioned well. It was a priceless car no doubt, may be the rich man's prize possession. He concentrated on the engine, everything looked spick and span. The complaint was—the engine had stopped, accompanied by a splutter. It was a diesel engine and he knew, that diesel engines were sturdier and did not suffer from the unpredictable defects as in the electrical circuits of cars with petrol engines. The engine was already running, for perhaps five to seven minutes, when it suddenly stopped. He checked the pump, it was okay. He brought the Fuel Injection Testing Kit and zeroed on the fuel injection and found that the fuel supply was sometimes erroneous. Mercedes spares are not esily available. He thought, if it was a choked filter, definitely it would be corrected. With great care and finesse, he removed the filter and found the thin mesh of copper wire strainer was covered with a layer of brown sediments, may be the tank filter was not functioning at all. He cleaned both the filters and started the motor. The engine was running smooth. He checked the sound, it was okay. He kept the engine running idle for twenty to thirty minutes. Satisfied he took out the car on a test drive. It was a pleasure to drive the car, it was a giant of a car. The moment he stepped on the accelerator the car jumped forward with unbelievable acceleration and he was touching almost 100 kmph within seconds, wonderful. He brought back the car and asked the garage boys to give it a wash and a polish.

When he reported his employer that the car was ready for delivery, he was pleased and gave him the address of the owner. It was an address in Colaba. He wondered what brought this man to Dharavi. Anyway that was not his concern, he was merely a garage mechanic. Once he delivers the car his job will be done. He had a long way to go. He got into the driving seat and brought the car on to the road, he loved this machine. It sprang to life at his touch and raced forward as a horse would do at its rider's commands. He drove through the entire city, stopping only at a place for tea and snacks. He was still in garage overalls with grease stains on his clothes. He drummed his fingers on the wheel and hummed a tune, at times he whistled. He must have touched a hidden switch or something somewhere, a little drawer noiselessly slided out from the dashboard all of a sudden. He looked inside, there was a yellow flannel cloth, used for wiping and cleaning. There was something else, underneath. He uncovered and stared. It was a gun. He had never seen a gun before, except in films. He slowed down the car and brought it to the kerb, and killed the engine. The sight of the grey steel chilled him. Suddenly, it dawned on him that this object lying before him looking so inert would have been the cause of death to several, at the hands of this *Sir jee.* Yet, he was tempted to touch the deadly weapon. He wanted to hold the gun and feel it. He did not want to let go the opportunity. Next moment he was holding the gun. It was heavy, beyond his expectation. He was imagining wildly. Sitting motionless, he thought over, he didn't give it a damn. Rich people always need weapons to defend themselves and their wealth, why he should bother. There was no need for panic. He put back the gun in the secret chamber. His immediate concern was to push back the drawer, it did not budge. Obviously, it was operated by a mechanism, triggered by a switch, he must find it. It must be on the right side, he reasoned, to be easily accessible, in case—. What other secrets this car possessed, he wondered. He was certain that the switch was camouflaged. He looked over intently, without sparing a inch of space. There was no sign of any switch or lever whatsoever. He was really worried now. He perspired. It was getting hot inside, he lowered the glasses. Then he noticed for the first time some thing, it was really strange. The key, the ignition key, was it not peculiar? He removed it and looked at it with growing interest. It was not the key which interested him, it was the ring and particularly the miniature Barbie doll attached to it. It was no ordinary doll. Could it be the key to the secret switch operating the gun's chamber? May be, why not try ? He was holding the key on his palm, the doll with its tiny blue eyes stared at him. Intution no doubt, he pressed the protruding breasts, nothing. What an idiotic hunch ! Exasperated, he inserted the key, turned and pressed again. He couldn't believe what he saw, the hidden drawer was closing noiselessly and in few seconds merged with the dashboard and was out of sight. He was sure that Ali Baba couldn't have been happier when the cave door was closed at the magic words. So that's it. Quite ingenious indeed, a tiny remote control, cleverly and perfectly hidden.

After few minutes, he reached the place. It was a huge mansion, the security checked him and let him in. He was asked to wait under the porch. Then *sirjee* came accompanied by another person who looked like a bully. The ripples of his muscles showed under his clothes and he had a perpetual grin on his face. Shekhar disliked the man, at first sight. *Sirjee* went to the driving seat and asked Shekhar, to sit by his side. The bully took the back seat. Now what was this setup? He did not like the gorilla sitting behind him. Are they going to knock him out? *Sirjee* took the car along the drive and then out of the gate. He raced it, Shekhar looked at the speedometer. It was doing 100 kmph. He slowed it down, looked at him and said, 'Do you know, I like this car so much, that when it started behaving badly this morning, I really got worried. I was there on business. I usually drive this car myself.' *'No wonder'*, Raja thought, '*How else you would take out the gun, you big man*?'

He brought back the car to the house. They got down, 'You have done a good job', he said and gave him a thousand rupee note. Shekhar had never seen a thousand rupee note, before. *Sirjee* was saying, 'Keep it and get in touch with me, I may need you sometime.'

Shekhar *salammed sirjee* and came away pocketing the thousand rupee note. The parting words of the big man kept him, worrying. What would he need him, for? Not, for any respectable job indeed? He reached his *kholi* late in the night. He was tired and went to sleep as soon as he struck bed.

The morning was no different. He went to the garage and reported to *Sardarji.* He was pleased and said, *'khush kar di puttar*, now get on with the job.' The garage boy brought him his tea and while sipping it he put his hands inside his pocket and felt the crisp *thousand rupees note*. He decided to keep it and not spend it. He must have impressed the big man in some way, because the next day a man came to his *kholi* and told that the *boss* wanted to see him immediately. Now what was this? It was already late in the evening, the watch indicated *seven*. The man said it was urgent, he had a car with him. He thought for a moment and then accompanied the messenger. *Boss* was waiting for him in the hall. The messenger was asked to leave. He was a man of few words. Without beating around the bush he said, 'I have a job for you, it is not difficult but requires guts and good driving. You will drive a vehicle. My men will be on it. They will ask you to drop them at a place and then pick them up a little later. You will be following their directions of course, and be watchful, nobody should follow the vehicle during this period. You will be paid for the same.' Shekhar realized, that he was in, for trouble. But discretion was the better part of valour. He kept quiet.

They drove for some time on a lonely road running parallel to the sea. There was a waning moon in the sky. He was asked to drop them at a spot near the sea shore. He drove the vehicle away from the spot and parked it near a decrepit warehouse. He sat in the vehicle with the engine running. It was pitch dark and silent outside. A wind had started blowing, He was not happy about the situation. He should not have agreed to. If he wanted he could drive away, but where to? He did not know the way out. He might be caught in no time. The men might go to any length, if necessary. His weakness had always been to run after danger and adventure. That gave him pleasure and if he earns a little money in the process, what is wrong? He was about to kill the engine, he noticed in faint moon light, the men were sprinting towards him. Then he saw, they were given chase by two persons. What frightened him was, that they were policemen. He kept the engine running and as soon as the men came nearer he put the vehicle in gear and put it in motion, the men jumped into it and they sped away with crunching sound of loose gravels under the wheels. There was a gunshot but, they were out of reach. Raja had enough for the night. What sort of job was this? *Sirjeee* had told him that it was not difficult. Definitely these men were upto something illegal and he was dragged into it. The men told him to take the road on the left and drive as fast as possible. The vehicle roared, when the gas pedal was pushed down and went speeding like a rocket. He was asked to drive the vehicle through a gate into a compound, which looked like a barn. Men were guarding it and it seemed that they were expected. The vehicle was parked near a farm house. A man came and got busy in changing the number plates. They got down, one of the men handed him a packet saying that it was meant for him and he was advised to take a late night train and check into a hotel near the railway station. He might spend the night in the hotel and leave for his place in the morning, they said.

In the hotel room, Shekhar opened the packet and could not believe his eyes at what he saw, it was a wad of one thousand rupee notes. There were fifty of them, a sum of fifty thousand, a fortune ! So much money for a little driving, of course it was fraught with risk. Having paid this amount, the *boss*, virtually purchased him. May be he would require more of his services, in which case he would have to let go the mechanic's job in the garage. Two days later, Shekhar received a message from the *boss* that an accommodation has been arranged for him and he must leave Dharavi and accompany the person who would be calling on him the day after.

His new home was within the precincts of the farmhouse which he had earlier visited, after his wild drive to escape from the clutches of police. Though small, it had all the comforts, it had a kitchen and a bathroom. No sooner he saw the room his mind traversed to the girl, who had come to his rescue in Calcutta. He could not brush away her, from his memory. At times he dreamt that he had gone back to her and wandered hand in hand in the lush green expanse of the *maidan*. But these sweet dreams never lasted long. The dark shadow of *Sirjee* would loom large across his path and shatter his dreams. One night, in one of his semi wakeful states, he heard footfalls outside. He got up with a start and went to the door, which opened to the corridor. Pressing his eyes over a slit in the door, he tried to see. Nothing met his eyes. It was only darkness. Suddenly, there were knocks at the door. Somebody at the door and at this hour ! He was fully awake by now. There were knocks once again. Now, they were insistent. He unlocked the door and held it slightly open and before he could see who was knocking, the door was pushed and some one came inside. To his great consternation, the intruder closed the door shut. All in few seconds. It was a girl, he could see.

'What the—', before he could say further, the girl clamped his mouth shut with her hand and said, 'Shh, keep quiet. I don't have much time. I have to go. Listen carefully, what I have to say. This place is a shit, I saw you being brought in. I wondered, how such a nice looking young man like you was roped in. You cannot move out without their will. This is a prison and worse than that. See, what they have done to me.'

Next moment, the girl had taken off her robe, which was a shawl wrapped around her body and underneath she was naked.

'Oh! No.' He shut his eyes.

The girl was saying', The black spots, you saw on my body are burning cigarette marks, I was branded with, whenever I resisted. Even my breasts and those parts were not spared. There is a rapist and sadist person around here. I have taken a vow to kill him, come what may. Will you help me?'

He got his breath back and said, 'I cannot believe this, they are rogues. What are your plans, tell me. I am with you.'

'Spare your anger and listen. Twice I tried to escape, they caught me and tortured me with double vengeance. Now I want to hit back. This is my plan.'

He listened with quietude and before he could say something, the girl opened the door and melted into the darkness. Inspite of the cold, Shekhar sweated, he sipped some water and sat upon the bed, burying his face between his hands.

'Oh! God, where have I landed myself ?', he muttered.

Next morning, he was asked to come down to the guards room, which was near the gate. He had company. It was the girl of the previous night looking smart and beautiful in her nurse's uniform. She behaved as if she did not know him. There was another guy, mean looking, with packed muscles under his shirt and a bulge under his pants. The girl motioned him with her eyes towards the man. So, this was the scoundrel, he thought. Already horny, rascal. Before long an ambulance was driven in, with a Red Cross sign and a Hospital's name painted on it. The man at the guards room handed him a packet and asked him to change. Shekhar went to the wash room for changing. A little later, he came out dressed in a driver's uniform, with cap and all. He saw the man ogling at the girl as if he would eat her up. Now, another person walks in. He recognized this man, he was the same man, who was sent to fetch him from his *kholi.* But now dressed in a medical attendant's uniform. What a lousy set up ! This odd group now proceeded towards the Ambulance led by the *thug,* showing off that he was the *boss.* The girl and the *thug* went to the rear and closed the door shut. Shekhar was asked to drive the vehicle, the fake medical attendant moved to the cabin and occupied the seat next to him. He brought the vehicle out and was asked to drive straight to Mazagaon. The man beside him looked straight; outline of a gun was distinctly visible from his side pocket. He was getting nervous. The success of their plan depended on the girl, he did'nt know how such a frail girl could tackle that gorilla.

There was a small window in the partition between the cabin and the rear. Shekhar's attention was glued on to the road ahead. The man beside him peeped through this window, from time to time and had a lascivious smile on his face. He was enjoying the scene behind and had his hand rubbimg his crotch, over the jeans. Shakher could well imagine what was happening over there and was worried.

As soon as the rear door was shut on them and locked from outside, Rohini, the girl prepared herself for the ordeal, she was to tolerate the monster for few more moments. To divert his attention, she opened the top two buttons of her starched coat so that her breasts would be uncovered. Not mindful of his stare, she looked at the hapless girls. There were seven of them, thrown on the floor like trussed chickens, their lips sealed with tape. She controlled her emotion and turned her attention fully to the uncouth man, who was about to rip open her dress and had already cupped her breasts and brought his mouth close to her face. His breath was reeking of beer and his eyes red shot. She felt his calloused hand, pulling at her panties. She allowed him a moment more to feel her soft mound and then erupted into action. She pinned him in a tight embrace for support and thrust her knee with a tremendous force against his crotch. He yelled in pain and kneeled down clutching his parts. Rohini waited for this moment and with all her pent up anger brought up her pointed shoes to kick him in the chin. Something snapped and the man doubled up with a scream. Without wasting time, she released him of his gun and stood there, pointing it at him breathing heavily. The scene inside the cabin was one of confusion. The fake medical attendant heard the screaming of his accomplice and looked behind, through the little window. He gaped at what he saw. The indefatigable Khan, the hero of many missions was cowed down by a mere girl. He shouted through the aperture, 'Hey! You fucking bitch-'. The distraction was enough for Shekhar to spring into action and grapple the neck of the man in a tight grip, incapacitating him. He brought the vehicle to the road side and switched off the engine. It took only a moment for Shekhar to disarm the man and ask him to get down at the point of the gun. He forced the man to proceed to the rear and unlock the door. As soon as the door was open, he gave him a kick at his butt, he fell face downward and then he shoved him inside. The other *thug* was still writhing in pain. He sized up the situation at a glance, he climbed into the van and with the assistance of Rohini, tied up the *thugs* securely back to back with a rope.

They heaved a sigh of relief and then paid attention to the captive girls. All this took hardly few minutes. The girls were freed of their bindings and the adhesive tapes were removed from their mouths. They stood up in a body and rushed to Rohini and clasped her wailing. It was a heart rending scene. They were seven little girls looking utterly lost, unfed and uncared for, being taken perhaps to be transported to some Arab countries for commercial exploitation. They pitied them. Perhaps Police will be able to send them back to their homes. He addressed the little ones and told them not to worry as they were free now and the Police would take care of them.

He drove the vehicle to the nearest Police Station. They had shed off their uniforms, underneath they wore their own dresses. They jumped off from the van and before anybody could spot them, ran away to safety, firing few shots in the air to attract attention and dropped the guns in a thicket after emptying them.

They merged in the crowd and walked away hand in hand, looking like two tourists enjoying the scene. Rohini asked, 'What will they do with the guys,'

'Trafficking of children is a serious offence you know, and these guys may also have previous Police records. No doubt, they will face convictions with all this evidence. What is your plan Rohini? We must leave this place quickly and be away from this gang as far as possible. If you have no place to go, you can come with me to Calcutta, because that is where I am going.'

'Thank you *bhaiya.* You have already done enough for me. I do not want to be a burden on you any further. I have saved some money, it is with me. I will go to Poona, they will not find me there.' He found tears in her eyes, as she spoke these words.

'If God wills, we may meet again some where *bhaiya.* May God bless you, I will remember you always.'

'Not so soon. As it happens, you are coming with me. At least, we will be travelling together up to Poona. We will bid farewell to each other, there.'

Parting from Rohini at Poona was really sad. The poor girl had suffered terribly at the hands of the gang, that was her destiny, she said. She had come to Bombay in search of a job and fell into the web of tricksters. Without his help, she could not have escaped, she said. The train moved on. With a heavy heart and pity for this brave girl and wishing her all happiness, he continued his journey.

The moment, he stepped on to the Howrah railway platform, the familiar crowd of passengers, red shirt porters, blaring of loud speakers announcing arrivals and departures of trains and the posters of Bengali films greeted him. It was home coming almost. The first thing he did on arrival was to rush to a tea vendor for a cup of tea. Ah! Wonderful, to sip tea in a earthen cup at Calcutta, at last. He got hold of a News Paper and scanned the head lines. One item caught his eye. He read-

CHILDREN TRAFFICKING IN BOMBAY

'Bombay Police succeeded in bursting a children trafficking racket. Two accused have been arrested, under mysterious circumstances, as reported. Horrific tales were told by the girls rescued. A farm house, supposedly their operational headquarters was raided and incriminating papers were recovered, Police investigation continues. From the recorded statements of the girls, Police came to know about two persons, a man and and a woman, who helped to apprehend the culprits and rescue the children, but later disappeared from the scene mysteriously. Police is on the lookout of these persons and believe that they will be able to provide crucial information in this case.'

Shekhar *alias* Raja, however, was not sure whether they would ever succeed. When he came out of the Railway Station and had a view of the Howrah Bridge, he felt that he was really home. He liked the view from the Bus, the sight of boats on the river Hoogly ferrying people across, old ware houses on the Strand road and children jumping into the river from the bank, refreshed him.

He can assume his own name 'Raja' now. He had got a foothold on a bus to Kidderpore; the morning fresh air blew over his face tingling his cheeks. While in Bombay, he grew his hair and sported a French beard, with dark glasses covering his eyes, it was hard to recognize him as the same Raja who was being chased by the Police in a Kidderpore *bustee*, a year back. He checked in a nondescript hotel, where nobody bothers about others, as long as the bills are paid. After changing his dress and having a hair cut and a clean shave, and after a good breakfast, Raja walked the distance towards the *bustee.* He found it more or less deserted at this hour of the day. It was not difficult to locate the *jhumpdi,* where he had taken shelter on that cold night. He reached the place and was debating whether he would knock at the door and ask for Ranee, when the door abruptly opened and she stood there with a baby in her arms. He was dumbfounded, she gaped at her with shock stamped on her face. Moments passed, they woke up when the baby started wailing.

'What happened Ranee ?', a voice spoke from inside.

'Nothing, *boudee,* it is some one asking for an address.'

'Raja it is you! I thought you would never return. Wait for a moment.'

Before he could say something, she was gone. He was bewildered and remained there standing, looking at her receding figure. She came after a little while, this time a *dupatta* thrown over her shoulders.

She said. 'That wailing brat is my brother's son. I am her *pisima* now, how respectable it sounds, is it not?' Where were you all these days? You look so thin.' She went on gibbering as if she had known him for years. He simply said, 'Can we go somewhere out, where we can talk?'

'Yes, of course. Let us go to the park, nereby.'

They crossed over the *nala* on a wooden foot bridge and reached the park which was almost empty at that hour of the day. Ranee led him to a cement bench under a tree and they sat down. No sooner they had settled, a hawker came forward selling *moong phalli* in paper cones, they could'nt wish him away and had to purchase two cones. The place was cool. Raja wondered at this girl, who sat close, almost touching him. She is so young and brave, this was the girl, who gave him shelter and food that night, when he was running away from the police. She had looked older and commanding, inside the dimly lit shed. But today in the day light, she looked very young and frail, and yet, she possessed enough courage to come with him, alone.

Why did he come to her actually ? Definitely not, for the money, he left *with her? He looked at her and met her searching eyes scanning him.*

Ranee said, 'How long will you take, to tell me where you were these days?'

'I have been to Bombay, in search of a job, Ranee. You know how difficult it is these days, to get a job.'

'But why at Bombay, you can try at Calcutta. *Dada* could help you to get a peon's job for you, in some office at Behala. I hope, you have gone to school. He knows the *babus* there, he will try for you. Then you can settle here. *This girl is already talking of settling in Calcutta. What she is up to? He will not be surprised, if she is dreaming of a home and children, running around.*

Aloud, he said, 'What! at Calcutta?'

'Why, what is wrong?'

'Bombay is the place for me.'

'Oh!', she didn't say anything further, but Raja was startled to notice tears in her eyes. She has already started behaving as a typical housewife.

Raja held her hand and asked, 'What is the matter Ranee?'She withdrew her hand and said, 'Leave me, let me go, *boudi* may be needing me, and here is your money, for which you came here, I suppose.' She took out the packet from inside her *kurta*, gave it to him and got up to go. Raja didn't let her get up, he pulled her down, beside him and said, 'What has come over you? I came for some thing, more important and valuable, to ask for, from your *dada.*' 'What do you mean?

'This time, I am not going to Bombay alone, you are coming with me. Of course, with your brother's consent.' Ranee looked at him with surprise, in her eyes.

'Oh! You stupid girl, how am I to tell you ?' He held her hands, looked into her eyes and said with all earnestness, 'Will you marry me?' The moment he said this, Ranee blushed and hid her face in both of her hands. She ran away to her home and hugged her *boudi*, who was putting the baby to sleep. Caught unawares, she turned her face and seeing Ranee in a great excited mood, asked her what was the matter. 'He has come', she said.

'Who has come, Ranee ?'

She was out of her breath, and had difficulty in speaking.

Slowly she spelled out, 'It is Raja'.

'That boy, you told me about ? I completely forgot that incident. I never expected to hear of him again. You know, what your *dada* said, when I told him of your adventure that night? He laughed and said, *most probably, Ranee had a dream.*'

Then, she related the conversation, she had with Raja, in the park.

'But my dear, you cannot probably think of marrying him, we do not know him yet. Where from he comes, what is he doing etc. I do not think your brother will approve of that.'

Ranee did'nt say anything for few moments, she looked down and said with conviction, 'I like him and I am sure he will take care of me. I have seen in his eyes a spark of honesty and integrity. Please *boudi,* you tell *dada,* that I am willing to marry him.'

CHAPTER 2

They were duly married, few days later, with the blessings of her *dada* and *boudi*, in a temple sanctified by a priest. Gopi had invited few of his friends and well wishers to a feast for the occasion. He presented a gold chain and a pair of ear rings to Ranee which belonged to her mother. When he wanted to present something else to Raja, he declined and said, 'Gopi *dada*, you have gifted me your sister, what more do I need from you.'

Gopi accompanied them to the Railway Station to see them off. Raja said, before boarding the train, '*Dada* please accept this as a token of my love. On reaching Bombay, I shall post you my address. Please keep in touch with us.' He pressed a thick packet in the hands of Gopi, as the train left the platform. The train gathered speed, Ranee kept looking through the window at the receding figure of her brother, till the train took a bend. She could not control her tears and sobbed. Raja let her shed the tears. To leave one's home permanently and settle in the husband's home, must be very painful for the girls, he reailised. But that is the custom, world over. A woman's place is always by the side of her husband. Male dominance is apparent in every society. He became thoughtful. Take the case of Ranee, his wife. She was born and brought up in Calcutta, grew under the care of her brother, having lost her parents in childhood. He could visualize a pair of children, brother and sister, roaming the streets, doing odd jobs to fill their stomach and sleeping at times on the foot path, braving cold and rains. Adversity must have made them stronger and resolute to face the world and find a niche in life, never losing faith in God and hard work. The country is teeming with millions of such people. They are virtually the backbone of the country, they keep the wheels running with their toil and honest work. Greed and deceit have not corrupted them. Ranee helped her *boudi* and *dada,* in running their house hold. Their's must have been a colsely knit family. And yet, she had to leave her family and home behind, to join hands with him to set up a new home at a new place, hitherto unknown to her.

His simpathy was all for Ranee. At that moment, he decided, to keep her happy, come what may.

They regaled each other with stories of their childhood as the train rushed past many places, dropping and taking in passengers, noon came, evening set in, meal vendors supplied meal trays and gradually the day wore off, giving way to the night. Finally they were at the end of their journey and the train blew its whistle and steamed into VT, Bombay. The coach which was home to so many, ultimately became an empty shell after the passengers got down. Raja and Ranee alighted and came on to the platform.

While Ranee was veiwing the new place with anxiety and hope, Raja rummaged through his pockets and got the card on which the address of Ram Gopaljee was printed. He went to a telephone booth and called a number. Someone lifted the telephone at the other end and said, 'Hello',

'Nameste jee, may I speak to Ram Gopal jee?'There was a gap and a voice came on,

'Yes?'

'Nameste jee, this is Raja, I hope you remember me, sir, you met me at ISKCON temple, last year, when you were celebrating the birth day of your son……'

'Yes, of course Raja, how can we ever forget you. Where from you are speaking?'

'I have just arrived from Calcutta, sir, I am at the Railway Station.'

'You have my address, you come straight to my place, everything will be taken care of.'

An hour later, a taxi dropped them at Ram Gopal's residence in West Malad. It was an impressive building with a drive way and an expanse of lawn with lush green hedgings and colourful flower beds. A middle aged person received them at the porch introducing himself as Ramu *dada*, Raja and Ranee bowed before him. He led them to an adjoining verandah and asked them to take their seats on sofas placed at a corner. Minutes later, Ram Gopal came out to see them. On seeing him, Raja abruptly stood up and motioned Ranee to touch the feet of *babujee*, she paid her respects by touching his feet.

He said, '*Jite raho*, who is she Raja?'

'She is Ranee my wife, *babujee*', Raja said.

'Our blessings to her, why did'nt you tell us before, that you were married.'

'When I met you at the temple last time, I was not married. Afterwards, I returned to Calcutta and got married.'

'Good choice, congratulations, let me call Maya, she must take her inside and properly receive her', he called Ramu and asked him to inform *choti ma.* Moments later, Maya came and was very glad to see Raja, then she looked at Ranee, Ram Gopal hastened to explain, 'Do you know Maya, Raja has married in the meanwhile, she is Ranee, his wife.'

Ranee stood up and paid her respects to Maya. She took her in her arms and said, 'Come let us go inside, let them sit outside and talk.'

'But don't detain her too long, they must be tired after the train journey, let them refresh and take rest', Ram Gopal said.

'*Babujee,* I do not see Jaya jee and Ganesh *baba,* where are they?'

'Jaya has gone to the college and Ganesh to school. They will be too glad to see you. You know, after that incident, Ganesh kept talking of you for days and always carries that key ring you gave to him. It proved lucky for him, he got a good grade in the examination.' Maya said fondly.

'*Achha,* Raja, tell me what are your qualifications and what you have been doing so far?'

Raja didn't want to disclose, that he was a commerce graduate and so far not been employed. It would be safer, to tell that he had been working in garages.

'So you are a mechanic. That is good. I am a transport and a building contractor and have to maintain vehicles, for my business. I depend on other garages for their repairs, now that you are here, we may have our own garage. We will talk about it later. Ramu will show you, your quarters, you may go and take rest now.'

Ramu *dada* showed them a lodge inside the compound where they would stay and told that he would be sending food for them. After he left, Ranee exclaimed, 'Raja, you didn't tell me that your *babuji* is such a rich person. *Choti ma* is so affectionate and kind, she treated me as a daughter. One good deed brings a lot of good fortune, in return.'

'So it has been proved in your case.'

'What do you mean?'

'Had you not helped me that day, you would not be with me today.'

'Now that you mention, may I know, what you were running from, that day?'

Raja cursed, he was in for trouble. He said, 'You go, wash yourself and change, Ramu *dada* will be coming any moment with our food'. He almost pushed her into the bathroom. Raja felt sorry for Ranee, he should'nt be hiding things from her. There should'nt be any secret between husband and wife. He decided to tell her his past life, and face the consequences.

When Ranee came out of the bathroom, she saw him in a thoughtful mood and said, '*Ogo,* What happened? Food is getting cold, go and wash yourself, I am feeling hungry'. It was her turn, to push him into the bathroom.

Once they were in bed. and alone, Raja said, 'I have to tell you some thing, which I can no longer hide from you.'

'What is it Raja?', there was panic in her voice.

'It is about certain dangerous people, I got associated with, before I met you.'

Raja told her about the nature of works, he handled at Calcutta and how, while trying to escape from the police net, he met her, accidentally. '

'But the end result was good, wasn't it?'

'Yes, we must thank our stars for that, but at Bombay it was a case of *from frying pan to fire.*'

'How so?'

'I succeded in getting out of Calcutta without notice of police and the people I worked for, but how I was to know that my handsome features would have dragged me into the net of a psychotic film heroine.'

'How romantic it sounds, please tell me what she did to you.'

'You seem to be enjoying every bit of it, I thought you would be cross with me for having cheated you.'

'Did you?'

'Of course not, I ran away and straight fell into the company of really dangerous people. Smuggling, murder, drug trafficking and what not, they were involved in.'

'Don't tell me, Raja, that you were part of this gang.'

'I could not escape, the situation was like that. I can never forget the *boss*, his eyes are like a cobra's, steel grey. If he ever finds me, he is sure to kill me.'

'Oh, Raja why did you mix up with such a gang?'

'It is again, due to my being a good mechanic. I fixed the car of the *boss* and he took me into his gang. When I gave them the slip, he must have been furious and issued orders to kill me, because I have seen him and pose a threat to him. Usually, few of the trusted ones only see him. But don't you worry, Bombay is a very big city, it is easy to lose one's identity, here. More over, they do not know me as Raja. I let them call me Shekhar while I worked for them and I kept long hair and sported a beard. With close cropped hair and clean shaven face, now, no body can mistake me for Shekhar.'

Ranee took the face of her husband in both of her hands, looked deep into his eyes and said, 'I am very much afraid Raja, why did you come back to Bombay, let us return to Calcutta.'

'Bombay is the place for me to prosper my dear, I will be careful, we are safe at this place. We have *babujee*'s protection.'

* * * * *

In Ram Gopal's garage, there were two cars. There was already one driver; Raja was asked to drive the second car, which was exclusively used by Ram Gopal jee on outside trips. Within a week Raja was able to organise a small workshop, where day to day maintainence and minor repairs of vehicles could be attended to. Raja used to drive Jaya to the college, wait there and bring her back. Ranee was happy in her new home. Throughout the day she remained busy as a bee, in setting up the kitchen and keeping the house tidy. She had pleanty of time at her disposal and used to go to the main house and assist *choti ma* in her works. Maya liked the girl who was of the same age as Jaya. In a matter of few days, Ranee endeared herself to the family and became very friendly with Jaya who frequently came to Ranee's place to gossip, whenever she found time.

One afternoon, while Raja was driving Jaya back home from the college, she wanted him to stop near the Central library. She got down and asked him to wait for her in the parking lot. Raja saw her entering the library, he took a turn and parked the car. After some time, he saw Jaya coming down the steps of the library and when she had almost reached the road, and Raja was about to bring the car to pick her up, another car with tinted glasses suddenly appeared, screeched to halt by her side and he saw to his horror, that she was pulled inside and the car drove away before anybody else could notice it. By the time he reached the spot, the car was speeding away and disappeared before his very eyes in the maze of lanes. Before he lost sight of the car, he had a glimpse of the number plate with prominent letters BMW 11—. It was a silver grey car. He was in a shock and failed to think, everything seemed to be lost. His heart was sinking. Before his mind became blank and he collapsed, it appeared suddenly from a side lane ahead of him and took to the highway at a reckless speed. He gave chase and almost caught with it, but maintained a distance. He followed for some time and even allowed the car to gain speed. He was making 50 mph. When the traffic thinned out, he decided to close in. He put the accelerator down and sped up. He came close enough, but could not see anything as the glasses were raised. At the first opportunity, he swerved to left and gave the car a brush. It's driver did not expect it and lost control, for a moment Raja thought it would leave the track and crash. *Oh! God, what is he doing?* The car skidded and turned in the opposite direction and went down the slope and miraculously stopped before reaching a ditch. In agony, he closed his eyes for an instant. He took a U turn and rushed to the spot. Thank God, all the passengers were safe. In the front seat, there were two boys hardly nineteen or twenty years old, sitting completely dazed, the boy driving, still had his hands on the steering wheel and Jaya sitting in the back seat gripping the front bucket seat, her knuckles white and veins showing. Boiling in anger, he dragged out the boy and threw him out, reached behind and unlocking the rear door pulled out Jaya. The other boy opening the door on his side ran away into the field, to escape the wrath of Raja. He lifted the boy, who was still lying on the ground frightened out of his wits and rained blows at him. He wanted to hand over the boy to the Police, the boy trembled at the name of Police and fell at the feet of Raja, begging to let him go. Jaya had recovered her composure, in the meanwhile and asked Raja not to report the matter to Police and let the boys go. He wanted to say something but she stopped him saying, 'We will talk later, let them go first.'

After the boys had left, leaving their car behind, Raja said, 'Why did you let them go free, they deserve severe punishment. After all what they did, amounted to kidnapping, it is a criminal offense.'

'I know, but think over, how my *bhaiya* will react. No doubt the culprits will go to jail, the news will spread and he will not be prepared to expose me to any further danger. The net result will be, I will have to stay back at home and bid good bye to my studies and my career. Would you have preferred that? More over, I am okay, I am not harmed, so why bother?'

'Okay, Jaya jee, if you say so.'

'Promise that you will not breath a word to any one about this.'

'Okay Jaya jee'

'What is this 'Jaya jee', can you not address me simply as 'Jaya', after all I am like your younger sister.'

Next day, he was to drive *babu jee* to Poona on a business trip. Ram Gopal had a farm house at Poona, which was a sprawling building surrounded by a mini forest close to a Marahattan fort. Next to Bombay, Poona was fast developing to be an industrial hub. Many industrial houses were busy in setting up their factories. Once a hilly town, known only for its hills and streams, attracting Government pensioners and business tycoons to set up rest houses and Holiday Homes, was now a scene of frantic activities of construction. Ram Gopal had come to settle a deal for acquiring land in the out-skirts with an eye to build a hotel. In the course of his visit to Poona, RamGopal once caught Raja scanning a copy of the Economic Times in the car, while he was busy at the site.

He asked, 'Raja do you know English?'

'Yes *babu jee, I* am a graduate in commerce', Ram Gopal was dumbfounded.

'Why, you never told me, I would have found for you, a better job.'

'It is alright *babujee,* this suits me, it gives me an opportunity to be with you most of the time. When I arrived from Calcutta, with my newly wed wife, I had no where to go, you gave me a job, accommodation and above all love and affection. I am grateful to you, *babujee.*'

'Okay, we'll talk it over later. You may drive me, I have no objection, but not as my driver, henceforth you will be my assistant and assist me in my office work. Maya will be glad to hear of your educational qualifications; since the day you have saved our son, she is all praises for you and treats you as her brother.'

* * * * *

Jaya spent a sleepless night, she had no appetite to eat and feigning a head ache she had retired to her room early. How could she forget the event, that she had virtually been abducted. She could never imagine, that such a thing could happen to her. She knew her brother; if he ever came to know of this, he would raise hell and leave no stone unturned to bring the culprits to books. She could not face the publicity. Now that, she escaped unscathed, it would be better to dismiss the entire event from her mind as a bad dream, and she could absolutely rely on Raja's discretion.

She reflected on Kamal, to meet whom, she went to the library, that day. Kamal is one of the brilliant students of the college, where she studied. She came to know of him in the course of a debate competition, which she attended. She marvelled at his command over the language and debating skill. Not only he out shone the other competitors and took away the prestigious award, but left a lasting impression on Jaya who studied in B. A. She gathered from Seema, her best friend, that Kamal was in B. Sc final year and tipped to come first in the University examination, that year. Being a bright student herself, she admired him and was on the look out to get an opportunity to talk to him. She overheard one day, while at the college office, Kamal enquiring from the cashier, whether his scholarship amount was credited to his account, so that he might withdraw some money. The cashier shook his head. Kamal beseeched him to check again because his mother was hospitalized and he was in dire need of the money. Jaya wanted to help him, but how could she? He did not know her. She devised a plan. She managed to deliver a slip of paper through an office boy, asking him to meet a friend at the Central Library immediately, after college hours.

The library was close to the college and she hoped that Kamal would keep the appointment. She was not sure, whether he would accept the money, she was going to offer him. She checked her purse and found that she had one thousand rupees with her, she hoped, that would be sufficient for his immediate needs. Fortifyed with this thought, she entered the library on her way back to home and found him sitting at a snacks bar near the entrance.

Approaching him, she said, 'Hi, I am Jaya, of third year. I attended the debate competition, that day and heard you. It was superb, simply marvellous, the way you put forth your views. The judges had no alternative but to declare you the best. My congratulations.' She extended her hand in a gesture, to shake hands with him.

Kamal was aghast and did not find any words to reply. He stared at this girl so bright and charming, standing there with extended hands.

He said, 'Oh! Thanks. Namaste, why don't you sit down.'

'Kamal jee are you expecting some one?'

'No, not exactly', he then looked at his watch and said, 'I think I must leave now', he was about to get up, Jaya was alarmed and hastened to say, 'No, no, let us have a cup of coffee, they serve good coffee here'. Before he could say no, she rushed to the counter and brought two cups of coffee and handed one to Kamal. She saw, that Kamal held the slip of the paper, which she sent to him, he crumpled it into a ball and was about to throw it away, she asked him, 'What is that you are throwing Kamal jee?'

'Oh, it is nothing, a piece of paper.'

'Don't throw it around, let me take it and throw it in the 'USE ME'bin.'

'I am sorry, I must leave now.'

'With out meeting the friend who asked to see her?'

'How do you know?'

'Because it was me, who wrote the note', Jaya looked straight into the eyes of Kamal.

'You wrote the note! But why did you want to see me?'

'Please do not misunderstand me, I could not help overhearing you, talking to the cashier at the college office, today.'

'So?'

'If I can be of any help, I shall deem it a pleasure.'

'Thank you for your offer, but I do not take any help from others in these matters. I will manage. Now I must leave, excuse me.'

'Kamal jee, please accept this as a loan from a friend, you may return this, after you receive the scholarship amount. Take this money', she handed over the money to him. 'There was an appeal in Jaya's voice. Kamal looked into the eyes of Jaya and noticed there in, a clear pool of sympathy and earnestness. He did not want to break the heart of this girl with whose plain talk he was impressed. He took the money offered, counted and said,

'Only five hundred rupees will do and again thank you, 'he returned the rest and got up to go.

She was so over joyed, with this unexpected development, that when she came out of the library, she failed to notice the car, which had silently moved forward as she came nearer and before she could realize what was happening, she was pulled inside the car by a strong hand.

* * * * *

During the next few days, Jaya was anxious to know about Kamal's mother's health, but she was hesitant to talk to Kamal, it might give rise to gossip, she reasoned. She could not contain herself any longer.

In her next free time, she made a move towards the Science block and saw Kamal coming out of a room, she met him halfway in the corridor.

She said, 'Hi Kamal, how is your mother?'

'Oh!Thank you, She is alright now. She was discharged from the hospital yesterday. I have brought her home. She is advised complete rest. I just came to see the Professor to grant me leave for a few days. I must stay at home to attend her.'

'Is there nobody else to attend her?'

'No, I am alone with mother.'

'Oh! I am sorry.'

'It is alright.'

Jaya felt really sorry for Kamal. What hardships, he must be going through, she could'nt imagine, it only brought her unhappiness. Reaching home, she went to see Ranee, whom she could trust absolutely. She told her, how she met Kamal and under what circumstances. Could we not do something to help him? University *exams* are approaching and he cannot afford to miss his classes, since he is required to stay at home to take care of his sick mother, what a shame.

Ranee listened to her, with deep sympathy. She appreciated her concern for Kamal. She herself comes from a poor family and knows the hardship, one faces being poor. Whether her concern for Kamal was purely based on compassion or any girlish foolishness she was not sure, but such a bright boy deserves help in his difficult days, she was sure. That night, she discussed the matter with Raja. He said not to worry; he would find some solution to it. Ranee hugged her hubby and said, 'Oh! Raja, you are wonderful.'

Next day, while driving her to college, Raja spoke to her, 'Look Jaya jee', she interrupted him saying, 'Again*' Jaya jee'?*

'Okay, Jaya, I want to know about this Kamal, since when, do you know him?'

Jaya instantly knew that Ranee must have told him everything. She said, 'You remember, the day I went to the library, I met him there to assist him, because he didn't have money to meet hospital expenses of his mother. I knew him before, during a debate competition, where he participated and was judged the best.'

'So it is like that, our little sister is charmed and out to help him.'

'No, Raja *bhaiya* it is not like that, I tell you, he is really poor and is dependent entirely on his scholarship amount. Such a brilliant student and he cannot even afford to attend the classes, because he has to remain at home to attend his ailing mother. He needs some help, doesn't he?'

'It is a very sad thing, Jaya, there are so many who are needy in this world. No one can understand better than me, what poverty means. But invariably, poverty is linked with dignity which is more valuable than anything else, sometimes unsolicited help, will do more harm than good. You have already extended your helping hand, don't stretch it too far. Let him manage his own affairs. There is pleasure in it, borrowed pleasure will be demeaning. Hope you understand me.'

Jaya looked at him with renewed respect in her eyes and thought how deep Raja *bhaiya* has gone to analyze her problem.

She said, 'Thank you *bhaiya* you have taken a load off my mind. All I hope, he comes out of the difficulty unscathed.'

'He will. I have seen his type, slow and steady.'

Jaya met Kamal at the college while he was coming out of the office.

He said, 'Hi, I came here to collect my scholarship. Thank you very much for the help. Here is your money.'

'It is alright, how is your mother?'

'Well, Thank God, she is recovering fast. My neighbour is a kindly person, in my absence she remains with my mother.' He looked at his watch and said, 'I am getting late for the class. Excuse me.'

'Okay.' Jaya was glad to see that Kamal was happy.

* * * * *

On return from Poona, Ram Gopal shifted Raja to the Accounts Department as an accountant. He wanted to make amends. He felt guilty, he wasted the talent of Raja, employing him as a mere driver. In no time Raja proved his mettle and brought in professionalism to the system, enabling Ram Gopal to have a grip over his business. Day to day reporting was furnished to him and he was now in a position to divert unutilized capital, to profit earning enterprises.

He faced problems over the land which he procured at Poona where he was to build a large housing project. The land was not free of encumbrances, which became apparent when workmen were sent to the site to fence off the area. People living therein though unauthorisedly, protested. They turned violent and works had to be stopped. Raja was asked to go to Poona and look into the matter. He learnt of the ground realities, the land which was acquired by the company lay unused for several years, because of right of ownership litigation and was turned into a waste land inviting gradual encroachment. Raja found, that over the years, *bustees* were developed and eventually fifty families started living there. It would not only be inhuman to evict them by getting court orders, but may also create bad blood with local people. He wanted to follow a middle course. He called the *mukhias* and discussed the issues with them. He gave a proposal to them, it was like this; they would be allotted one room apartments per family, in the housing complex, which will be completed with in next two years, for which they have to make payments by instalments, necessary loan assistance will be provided to them through financial institutions, in return they have to vacate the land immediately. Further a compensation of rupees one thousand will be paid to each family to meet their expenses for shifting elsewhere. There was not much resistance afterwards. Papers were signed, compensation amount was disbursed and works started. Ram Gopal highly appreciated the acumen of Raja for having amicably settled such a vexing problem. He promoted him as a vice president of the company which entitled him a furnished bungalow and a car. The news gladdened Maya and Jaya. Ranee was overjoyed and at the same time sad, because they have to leave *babu jee's* house and shift to their new home.

One day, Raja sees a car in their office complex, a black Mercedes, the sight of which struck a chord in his memory. It was the same car which he repaired in the garage at Dharavi. . A shudder passed through him. Then he saw them, *babu jee* coming down the corridor, holding conversation with the man whom he knew as the *boss* or *sirjee* and more appropriately the deadly gangster in whose organization he had the misfortune to have worked and escaped in one piece. He ducked into a side room as they passed, there was also a young man accompanying them. He waited, till the party departed from the office complex and then he went to see *babujee,* in his office.

Babujee told him that one Mr. Ratan Kumar Saxena from M/s R. K. Enterprises Ltd. paid a visit to him. Referring to a business card, he said, his Firm was mostly engaged in export and import business and he also owned an automobile show room at Poona. *So this was the clean face of the don, he showed to others.*

'I saw them on their way out, what for they came ?'

When he learnt that, the *don,* his ex-*boss,* came with a business proposal of giving an advance (loan?) of rupees ten crores in hard cash to Ram Gopaljee, with out any strings attached, for investment, he had a feeling of sinking heart.

He said, '*Babu jee,* to do any business with a person, whose credentials are not known, is generally fraught with risk.'

'I have heard that this Saxena is an upcoming business man and has a good clout in political circles. He has a chain of Hotels, agency for imported cars and other business.'

'Such as?'

'What do you mean ?'

'*Babujee*, how do we know, he is not an underworld *don?*'

'Raja, you seem to be extra cautious, let us assume he is offering us black money, so what? We are not an investigating agency. Are we? We are business men and should not let go any opportunity of easy access to a capital of this amount. So don't you worry, relax.'

That was the end of the meeting. He left office with a heavy heart.

* * * * *

The final year *exams* approached nearer, it became difficult for Jaya to come across Kamal anywhere in the college. She longed to see him. Why this longing? Is it love?

There is one person with whom, she could share her thoughts. It was a Sunday and with *bhabijee's* permission she visited Ranee at her new home. Ranee was pleased to see her and welcomed her with a warm embrace. Ranee took her around to show her the new home,

Jaya was pleased and appreciated her tastes. They settled down with cups of coffee on a sofa.

'Jaya, how is Kamal's mother? I was so busy in shifting and arranging things, I could not see you earlier.'

'She is now alright, Kamal told me the other day. I was worried, you know, about Kamal, he is such a bright student and if he does not attend the classes at the end of the session it might affect his preparations for the examination'. Ranee was looking at her quizzically.

She hastened to explain, 'Oh!, Ranee, it is nothing like that......", caught off guard, Jaya kept quiet.

'So it is like that, Jayajee. Is it not? If our Jaya likes a boy, he must be a special one.'

'Oh! Ranee, you are always jumping to conclusions.' Jaya said.

'But Jaya, should I tell you something, you better stay away from this *pyar vyar ka chakkar* for some time. It is perfectly normal for a girl to love some body. It would occur in a girl's life some day. I know what it is, I pined for your Raja *bhaiya,* for one year, before I got him. Love is like that. But you are different, you are *babujee's* sister, you must take care of your career first, better concentrate on your studies, every thing in its proper time, okay?'

Jaya's eyes became tearful, she embraced Ranee and said. 'Oh! Ranee you have taken a load off my mind. Now that I opened my heart to you, I already feel light. Of course I will concentrate on my studies and rise to the expectation of my family. You are wonderful, I love you.'

Ranee said, 'Will you not invite Kamal some time, so that we may get to know him?'

Jaya said, 'Let the *exams* be over.'

* * * * *

Raja visited a hotel to attend a business lunch with a prospective wholesale distributor of their products, mostly building hardwares, which their company produced. It was Raja's idea, approved by Ram Gopal. Their company originally dealt with real estates and textiles. They have now diverted their interests to the manufacture of non-ferrous castings, forgings and hardwares for building applications. On entering the hotel, he proceeded to the vestibule adjacent to the dining hall and waited for the client to arrive. He was about to pickup a magazine, when his glance fell upon three youngsters who occupied a settee in a corner, deeply immersed in conversation. One of them he remembered to be the young fellow who accompanied his ex-*boss* during their visit to *babujee*'s office the other day. He stared at the other two, immediately it struck him, where he had seen them earlier. His blood boiled and he clenched his fists, he controlled himself with difficulty, they were those two young *thugs,* who had attempted to abduct Jaya, the other day.

He was terribly confused, and his confusion and anguish reached their summit when he visited *babujee*'s house to get some papers signed. When he reached there, he found b*abujee* and *bhabi jee* sitting in the garden having tea. Seeing him, Ram Gopal asked Raja to pull a chair and have a cup of tea with them. While Maya poured tea for Raja, he said, 'You know Raja, I have been telling your *bhabi,* that today has been a lucky day for me. Saxena came to my office, to clinch the deal I was telling you about. He gave me the hard cash. Tomorrow you will open a new account and deposit it in the Bank. I have already spoken to the Manager, he would get through the transaction and assured me about the secrecy. Secondly, this man Saxena gave me a proposal, which I was discussing with your *bhabi,* before you came.'

Raja looked at her and said, 'What is it *bhabi jee*?'

Before replying, Maya looked at her husband and said, 'Raja, I am confused, we do not know this man except that he is a business man with whom your *babu jee* has finalized a partnership, I have nothing to say about that. But where a marriage proposal for Jaya is concerned, we have to be very cautious.'

'I do not follow'

'It is like this, Raja, Saxena has given me a proposal for the marriage of his son Jackie with our Jaya', Ram Gopal jee said.

He could not believe his ears.

'Have you seen his son *babu jee?*'

'Ofcourse, you may have also seen him, that day when they both visited my office.'

'Don't say, that the young fellow who accompanied Saxena, is his son.'

'Yes he is. Is he not smart? How elegant he looked beside his father. He is being groomed to take over his business.'

"Babujee, I am too small a person to make any comments. But as *bhabi jee* expressed, we must be cautious.'

Raja left, crestfallen, after getting the papers signed.

* * * * *

He spent a sleepless night, tossing on the bed. Ranee woke up and finding him awake asked, 'What is the matter Raja? Are you not feeling well?'

'It is nothing, I felt thirsty, that is all. You better go to sleep, I will go down and get a glass of water.'

After he left, Ranee looked at the bed side table, the pitcher was full of water. At the breakfast table in the morning, Ranee observed Raja, keenly. Loss of sleep had definitely left marks on his face; he looked worried. Ranee raising his face in her hand enquired, 'What is it worrying you, my dear?'There was concern in her voice.

Raja looked into her eyes and holding her hand, told her that his ex-*boss,* about whose exploits he had already apprised her and how dangerous it would be, if this man ever sets his eyes upon him, had by some strange connivance with fate, arrived at the office of *babu jee* to strike a business deal with him. Fortunately, he was out of his way. But that was not the only reason that troubled him. Yesterday, he came to know, that Saxena, his ex-*boss* came to meet *babu jee* with the weirdest proposal, he had ever heard. The gangster was able to mould *babu jee* into believing, that he was a successful business man, and would be interested to convert their partnership into relationhip.

Ranee said, 'How ?'

'That is where he has shown his master stroke. He has proposed marriage of his son Jackie with our Jaya.'

Ranee exclaimed, 'It is preposterous.'

'But *babu jee* is inclined to agree with the proposal and he has no idea, whom he is dealing with. Even though I know his antecedents, I have to keep my mouth shut. That is what is eating me away. We must find a way out, immediately.'

'Raja, don't feel yourself guilty, on that account, we'll find out a way.'

Ranee told him that Jaya had developed a soft corner for Kamal, which is nothing short of love. She felt that Jaya must be taken into confidence, before any plan is devised to sabotage the proposed marriage.'

Now that the *exams* are over, Jaya felt like a bird on its wings, eager to fly. She decided to pay a visit to Ranee. She found her watering the plants. On seeing her, Ranee put the bucket down and came to greet her; Jaya said, 'Oh! Ranee, I feel so light and free, I want to dance and sing. She pulled up Ranee and holding her, took to the floor, dancing.

Ranee exclaimed, 'Hey! Leave me, I cannot keep pace with you, I may. fall down.'

Laughing together they fell on the sofa, breathless. Ranee was not sure, what could be the cause of such burst of joy and happiness ? Was it that, she really worked hard for the exams and now felt relaxed, or that, her brother already told her of the marriage proposal and she welcomed it.

But she had her doubt. Jaya had expressed her love for Kamal and she was serious. She could'nt brush away her feelings for him so soon.

Jaya said, 'Do you know Ranee, today I met Kamal in the college canteen and for the first time, he talked to me, with out being addressed, I felt so good.'

'She talked to you of his own accord? I thought, he was too formal.'

'Then, he offered me coffee, oh! what a change in him!'

Ranee noticed a glint in her eyes, she had no doubt now. Then they talked about the *exam* and how did she fare, at one point she asked Jaya, whether she met her *bhabi* and *bhaiya,* before she came here. 'Ofcourse, I went home straight, but as usual they were out of my reach, *bhaiya* was not at home and *bhabi* was in the kitchen. So if I were to communicate, how could I? I couldn't wait any longer.'

'Oh! Jaya, you are a darling, you did the right thing, you are welcome here, at any time. Now that you like each other, is it not time to give it a serious thought?'

'What do you mean?'

'I mean marriage, you must let *bhaiya* and *bhabi* know your feelings and let them draw their conclusion.'

'Oh! Ranee, what is the hurry, let me complete the course of architecture and set my foot in my professional career. My ambition has been to qualify myself as an interior designer.'

'It may be too late for all that dear.'

'What do you mean, too late.'

'Yes, too late, your *bhaiya* has other plans, he wants you to get married to the son of one Saxena, his business partner, atleast that is what Raja heard about.'

'But how can he, with out ever discussing it with me?'

'Forget it sister, there is no time for discussion, despair and weeping, you must bide your time and ward off the imminent danger, that is, the engagement.'

'But how?'

'You leave it to us, I will tell you what to do.'

* * * * *

Ram Gopal went ahead with the arrangements for the engagement of his sister with Jackie, inspite of the mild protest of his wife on the pretext of furtherance of Jaya's career. He said that she could complete the course even after the marriage. The responsibility of all the arrangements fell upon Raja, whose predicament was no less.

He felt that the noose around his neck is getting tightened, he cannot possibly avoid an encounter with his ex-*boss* and then it will be curtains for him. The fact that his appearance had undergone a sea change since the time he was one of his henchmen, did not give him much comfort. Shrewd and sharp as he is, it will not take much time for him to see through his disguise. He had no choice. The D-day arrived and the party of Saxena, his son Jackie and a couple of his friends reached *babujee*'s house for the function. Raja purposedly avoided coming face to face with Saxena, but for how long?

Soon, *babu jee* called, 'Raja, would you come here please?'

Getting the summons, he went inside and found *babujee* sitting with Saxena. It was the time for the acid test.

Babu jee said. 'Saxena jee, please meet Raja, he is my senior vice president. My finances are safe with him, you will not regret your investment in my business.' Saxena cast a casual glance at Raja and said, 'You seem to be lucky to have some body to rely upon.' To Raja, he said, 'Hello, I am glad to know, that I would have to deal with a competent person. In my business, there is no place for mediocrity. Hope we will be meeting often.'

Raja was searching his eyes for the slightest sign of recognition, but saw none. Saxena's attention was diverted by some thing else and he turned away.

The *pundit* reminded about the *muhurt* for the ceremony and every body proceeded towards the decorated dais where the ceremony was to be held. At this moment, Jaya wearing a beautiful saree and glittering ornaments entered accompanied by Maya and Ranee. Ram Gopal beaming with smile, prepared to go ahead with the ceremony and, asked for the ring to be brought. The bride- to- be stood at the centre of the dais and by her side, stood Jackie along with his father. The ring caskets had been opened, the rings taken out and at that moment to every body's horror and consternation Jaya collapsed and fell on the arms of her *bhabi*. This caused a great despondency among all present. The girl was shifted to the nearest sofa supported by Maya and Ranee. Ram Gopal shouted at Raja to call for the doctor, every body's attention was riveted on Jaya who was laid down on the sofa, she lay there motionless with her eyes closed. Some one said, 'She has probably swooned, make way, let her get some fresh air.'

The event for which people assembled was forgotten. Saxena and Jackie were crestfallen and stood apart from the crowd, bewildered. Ranee was applying a cold sponge on Jaya's face and by the time the doctor came, she had regained consciousness. The doctor examined her, checked the BP and said she appeared weak and must have strained herself and advised for complete rest for one week, at least. A thin smile appeared on Raja's face, which probably nobody noticed.

Supported by both Ranee and Maya, Jaya was removed to upstairs to her bed room, Ram Gopal followed them, concerned and worried. At that moment nothing was dearer to him than the well-being of his sister. He came down, a worried man. Seeing them waitng in the Hall, Ram Gopal approached Saxena and begged excuse, saying that they could not perhaps go ahead with the ceremony under the circumstances.

Saxena said, 'Of course Ram Gopal jee, let her get well, the engagement ceremony is only a formality, it can take place on any other suitable day, no harm. I only wish, she recoveres fast.' They bid farewell to Ram Gopal jee and then left.

* * * * *

Now, Jackie being the only son of Saxena, one of the rich men in the city, all the comforts and luxuries lay at his feet, whatever he wanted was his, atleast that was how, he grew from his childhood. He was given to understand that nothing was beyond his father. His mood on the day, when the engagement was called off, was that of a child, who was promised the moon and the moon did not fall in his hand. What he did, after reaching home, from Ram Gopal jee's was nothing short of a tantrum. He was not only thrown into despair, but in his anger, he began throwing things out, shouting. Costly china and crystal glassware did not escape his fury. The only witness to this harrowing scene was *kaka,* who stood silently all the while, behind a curtain. Saxena was gone to his office.

When he was completely spent and his anger subsided, Jackie lay sprawled out on the sofa, with his eyes closed and his arm covering the face. *Kaka,* quietely entered the hall and picked up the broken pieces from the floor. His eyes rested on the portrait of Jackie's mother, which was hung on the wall over the mantelpiece. He sighed.

He came to this house, almost twenty years ago, when *malik* brought mother and the baby, straight from the nursing home. With a baby in the house and a sick mother, the house looked like a nursing home. Doctors and nurses were always found in the house, attending the sick mother. Being a new recruit and just eighteen years old, he didn't understand many things, particularly the type of men, who came to see *malik,* in the late hours of the night. Gradually, he got accustomed to the strange habits of his employer and as years passed, he became the most trusted servant of Saxena. In these two decades, many upheavals occurred, that shook the 'Saxena House'and were responsible for causing the rift between the father and son.

After the birth of the baby, *malkin* did'nt regain her health and a wholetime nurse was appointed to attend her. Nobody was permitted inside the room of *malkin*, except the nurses. Jackie was put under the care of a governess and he was taken to his mother at particular hours of the day. This became a routine for the mother and son. The love between the two instead of waning, became stronger and reflected on their faces. The child grew to be a very handsome and healthy boy and became the darling of every one of us. *Malkin* used to call him *'jackie'* and the name stuck to him. At the age of seven years, the boy was sent to a *'boarding school'*, against the wishes of *malkin.* With the removal of her sole source of love and affection, her health deteriorated and her dislike for *malik* at times, took dangerous proportions. When the situation got out of control, she was sent to a Speciality hospital. The house became bare, without the *malkin* and it looked, as if it had lost its soul. The drab atmosphere was brightened, when the boy used to come during the vacations. Since, *malik,* was always busy, it fell to his lot to make the journey to the *'boarding school'* and pick up the boy. *Kaka* was very fond of the boy and their relationship was lasting. Years passed, she was brought home from the hospital, for convalescence and the boy remained with her, giving company and comforts, till the last day of her survival. He was only eighteen, when she passed away.

He had nobody to turn to. He missed his mother very much. He remembered the day his mother was brought back home from the hospital. It was so many years ago. He was eighteen and was in the boarding school. It was his last day in the school and also his birth day. He packed his box and waited in the Hall, with the faint hope, that this time atleast, his father would come to pick him up and take him to a nice restaurant on the way to treat him. But no, this time too, it was *kaka,* who came with the car to take him back to home. The usual explanation being, his father was busy. There was no communication between father and son except for a customary birth day greeting card every year, wishing him many happy returns of the day. His father had promised him to take him to see his mother at the appropriate time. He didn't forget that.

No sooner, he reached home, he asked, '*Daddy*, when shall we go to see mother?' Saxena looked at his son, he was now grown up and had the same silken hair as his mother and surprisingly the expressive blue eyes, with a rugged feature like himself. He felt proud of his son. He was a combination of both the parents, soft in the core and hard in the surface. He felt pity for the boy. Deprived of his mother's care, he was forced to lead a lonely life in the *boarding school*. But it was important to discipline the boy, after all he was the mighty Saxena's son, and would inherit his empire one day.

Aloud he said, 'Yes, Jackie, we are going there tomorrow morning, now you may take rest. I will see you at breakfast. Good Night, my son.'

Jackie went to his room, followed by *Kaka* carrying his bag. The room was sparsely furnished, a bed, a writng desk, a chest of drawers and two chairs constituted all the furniture. Walls were painted ocean blue. *Kaka* must have put freshly cut roses in the vase, his favourite flowers and his mother's too. He went to the writing desk which was at a corner near a window, facing the sea. He was not a bright student as reported by the Principal, at the end of each examination, he appeared, his grade was not satisfactrory. But in one aspect he was very regular, and that was, in writing his diary. He kept an account of his daily activities, his feelings, the persons he met, what impressed him during the day, all in a note book, meticulously maintained up todate. He brought out the note book from his bag and began leafing through its pages, he stopped at the entry dated 14th Feb 1962. He read on:—

Because I didn't do my homework, the tutor scolded me and threatened to report the matter to my father. She thought that would bring results. I never cared for my father. I knew he did'nt like me either. After the tutor left, I looked at the pages of the exercise book. It was full of mistakes, marked in red, I lost my temper, threw the note book aside and got up. I yearned for my mother's arm to get comfort, I went upstairs to her room. I reached the end of the corridor and was about to enter her room, I heard mom arguing over some thing. I stopped on my track and listened, I never heard mom talking in such a loud and angry voice.

'Don't lie to me', she was yelling, 'you murderer, you killed my daddy, you took away his life, his property and me. I will never pardon you, you will be roasted in Hell's fire. Get lost, out of my sight.'

I tip toed back to my room, I was totally confused and at a loss to know, what could have happened between my father and mother to have caused this outburst. I woke up late next day, went to my mother's room and found it empty. Mother was not there. But her bed was made up by the maid. I rushed down. Kaka informed me that mother was taken suddenly ill in the night and had to be removed to the hospital. 'Where is daddy, 'I wanted to know. Some one told me that he accompanied my mother, to the hospital. I was shocked. It was all *beyond my comprehension.'*

He shut the diary and sat there contemplating over a painting of her mother, which was hung on the wall above the writing desk.

* * * * *

During the entire drive from Bombay to Poona, they did'nt speak to each other. He was not allowed to see his mother all these years. As a child, he remembered, his happiest moments were those, which he spent with his mother. He knew that his mother was not in the best of her health. Whenever he visited her, he would find a nurse by her side, either adjusting her clothes or combing her hair or administering an injection. Inspite of her illness, her mother was always an icon of beauty and serenity to him. The picture of his mother dressed in a blue gown, her silken hair with out a trace of grey, parted in the middle and falling in cascades reaching her waist remained imprinted in his mind. As soon as he would enter, she would dismiss her nurse, take him in her arms and hold him tight. He could still smell the perfume her mother wore, some thing heavenly as the fragrance of flowers and not like the ones his girl school mates wear, pungent and irritant, mixed with their body odour. Suddenly, his thoughts got riveted on a girl, Binny, who on more than one occasion tried to get fresh with him, by unnecessarily bending too much, feigning to tie a shoe lace, when he was behind her, exposing her creamy thighs, showing her panties. He had not seen a girl's thighs before, the scene had a great effect on his adolescent mind, to be the cause of his first wet dream. Slut, he cursed. On another occasion, she had come so close to him, while coming up the stairs, that their bodies touched and his hand brushed her breast. He got a whiff of the perfume, she wore, pungent and repulsive. Everyone in the school including the staff knew that he was the son of a very rich man and specially a teen aged girl who was in the orchestra of the school had on several occasions tried to catch his attention by throwing come-hither signs with her eyes. More than anything else, he was irritated. One day, he was in a nasty mood and the girl teased him in the class room. He wanted to teach this girl a lesson. He asked the girl to see him in the auditorium after class hours. The girl could not suppress her delight and left the room casting a mischievous glance at him. He made the auditorium dark as he entered and waited for the girl. He had roped in the office peon, paying him in advance to do the rest. The girl came furtively and appeared obviously surprised at the surrounding darkness. 'Hello, is any body there?' Then the hidden loudspeakers came alive and a demonic laughter was heard reverberating through the hall. The effect was tumultous, the girl stopped on her track and looked hither and thither like a frightened hare. It was a treat to see her face, he remembered. Then the climax occurred. A skeleton came galloping towards the girl. She shrieked and made a hasty retreat. That was the end of her romance.

The car now stopped at the gate of a building which resembled a fortress, from a distance. The gate keeper talked over a phone and then opened the gate to let in the car. Freshly mowed lawn lined with trimmed green hedges met his eyes. There was no other sound than the whirr of the engine and crunching sound of the wheels over the rough surface of the road. They arrived at the porch, where a liveried servant waited to receive them, he ushered them into an office. Its mahagony furniture and lavish curtains spoke of style and grandeur. His father had a talk with an elderly person with grey hair who stood up and led them across a maroon carpeted corridor to a wide expanse of a lounge with tall doors painted white and louvred windows. They were asked to take their seats in deep cushioned sofas. Jackie glanced through some issues of 'LIFE' magazine and medical journals. He was not interested in such pomp and style, he wanted to see his mother, forthwith. What sort of a hospital is this? It looked more like a luxurious hotel to him. He looked beyond, through the windows. Lush green hills and a stream meandering its way down below, met his eyes. The serene natural splendor uplifted his depressed spirit. His father sat still. A servant with tail coat entered with a silver tray laden with tea and a jug of juice. What is all this? He was really getting bored with all these formalities. After ages it seemed, a bespectacled man wearing a long white coat and carrying a *stetho* in his hand came in, wished Good Day to father and asked them to follow him. They entered a room, painted in light blue, lavishly furnished, with a large bed in a corner, on which, he saw a thin woman, apparently sleeping. A bunch of freshly cut roses was put in a vase at the bed side table. Could she be his mother? It cannot be, the emaciated woman cannot be his mother. Where were gone her beauty and vibrant health? In place of her dark silken hair he could see only thin wisps of grey hair. He could not believe his eyes. He stopped on his track. She opened her eyes, they fell upon my father, she screamed in a thin voice and then fainted. The doctor rushed forward and ordered us, out of the room. I burst into tears and sobbed, my shoulders shaking. My father held me tight and led me out.

'I told you, you cannot stand the sight of her. I have provided her all the facilities, that are available in medical science. This is a super speciality hospital cum sanatorium exclusively meant for such patients, afflicted with rare diseases. She has been in coma for the last six years and wakes up for few hours in between. Today is one of those awakening periods. You have noticed how careful they are with the patient. It really needs very delicate handling. This hospital has all the required facilities. Only very rich persons can afford such facilities.'

'And you are one of such persons, are'nt you *daddy*', there was sarcasm in his voice. He did not forget his mother screaming at his father six years ago. Her words were still ringing in his ears. His mother was perhaps on the border line of sanity and insanity.

The doctor came out to say that they were lucky, this time she did not go back to coma, they have administered her a sedative and she was sleeping. They might see her again in few hours. He then took aside father and said, 'But, please, sir, it would be better, if you are not in her sight, when she wakes up next. Let her son see her alone. Hope you understand me.'

'Yes, doctor, it is alright.'

He said to Jackie, 'Come, let's go out and have our lunch, in the meanwhile. There is a restaurant inside the hospital. Food is excellent, they cater to every one's taste. I would recommend *tandoori* chicken, they do it really nice here.' Jackie wondered, how his father could think of food in these circumstances. He didn't say anything.

It was almost evening, when they were called to see the patient. Jackie went to see her mother alone. The room was softly lighted and he could see with great relief that her mother's face no longer seemed pallid to him. Now a mantle of peace and serenity descended on her. They had raised the upper portion of the bed so that she could recline with support of pillows. Hearing his foot steps, she shifted her eyes to look at him. Then she did some thing which he never thought possible, in her state of health. She raised her arms, her lips quivered as if she was trying to speak, he rushed to her and clasped her frail body in his arms. She was all bones and skin. But the spark glittered in her. Her touch was heavenly to him. His waiting, all these years to see her, was amply rewarded. He kissed her sunken cheeks, saw tears in her eyes flowing freely. She wanted to tell him some thing, he brought his face close to her, she whispered, 'Take me home, my son and stay with me.' Then she fell silent and closed her eyes, the effort was too much for her.

He rushed out, saw his father conferring with the doctor, he blurted out, '*Daddy*, she spoke to me, she held me in her arms.'

Both his father and the doctor were puzzled and did not believe what he said. The doctor sent for the nurse and rushed to the patient. The first thing he did, was an electroencephalography test. Jackie and his father waited anxiously, outside. The doctor emerged from the room after sometime, and said, 'Mr Saxena, I have some very good news for you, to me it is nothing short of a miracle, but I do not hesitate to say that there have been changes in the recordings. Some of the inactive cells in her brain have started functioning. Since she is at the threshold of recovery, I have given her a sedative, she needs rest for a while. If you prefer to stay here, while she is convalescing, I will make necessary arrangements.'

His father didn't make any comments and simply nodded. He seemed not to be too pleased at this development. On our way to the visitors Block, he asked me what did she talk about. Nothing in particular, I said. It had hurt me very much that day, to notice that instead of feeling buoyant at the recovery of my mother, he was sullen through out the evening and didn't speak much through the dinner. It was hard for him, to hide his feelings. We remained at the hospital for few more days till my mother was reported fit enough to undertake the journey back to home. While father signed the papers, the doctor explained that it was a rare case in medical science, a coma patient recovering all of a sudden, taking a complete U- turn. A miracle rather, he said. Then he looked at me and said, may be this young man here who came with you this time, had something to do with her recovery, one can never tell the force of love and affection. Wishing her well and complete recovery, he bid us good-bye. We left the hospital with mother.

I was scheduled to leave for U. K for studies in Business Management. It was natural for a man to wish that his son should be amply qualified to take over his business, after him. All that was pushed behind. My only concern now, was to give company to my mother and to take care of her. A live-in nurse maid was also hired.

Doctors had opined that only love and attention would do miracles and speed up her recovery more than anything else. Gradually she showed signs of improvement. I was hopeful. I summoned courage, one day, and asked father, what caused this suffering? His only reply was that it was a rare affliction and we must hope for the best. I was of course not satisfied with his reply. My mother continued with the medication and gradually started taking interest in the out side world. The nurse would regularly take her out to the garden in a wheel chair, she would stop by the garden pond and look with interest at the leaping frogs or look above at the tree branches and listen to the chirping of birds. I visited her regularly after the nurse dressed her hair and changed her clothes. She liked roses and I presented her every day a bunch of freshly cut roses which she accepted with pleasure. She would clasp my hand and a thin smile would appear across her lips.

One day, I took her frail hands in mine and asked, '*Mom*, how are you feeling today?' A weak smile crossed her lips, I looked into her eyes with deep love and asked her, 'Will you tell me, what caused this suffering?' She sighed, looked at me with lack luster eyes. After that I had not questioned her.

A year rolled by; the son and father met only occasionally at the dining table. One day he said, 'Jackie *beta,* how long you intend doing baby sitting like this, servants and nurses can take care of her. You have already lost one year, you have your own future to look to. You cannot possibly confine yourself, to a room with a sick woman.'

Jackie flared up at his father and yelled, 'She is my mother. She is my mother.' He sobbed. His father shook his head and walked away. That was so many years ago. His mother did not last long. One night after a brief breathlessnes, she passed away. He was not with her, in her last moments, the nurse came to wake him up. On reaching her bed, he saw the life less body of his mother. Her life had fled from the tormented cage of her body. He believed that she attained peace, at last.

The thin tie which existed between father and son while she lived, finally snapped, when she was no more. He lived as a rudderless boat on the heaving sea of life. He shut himself in his room, thoroughly drowned in drinks. Saxena did not bother to console the poor boy in his grief and he drifted. His diary was blank for those days, the empty space had its own story to tell.

* * * * *

The last two years, which Jackie spent in the college were indeed tumultuous. He took the liberty of being the son of a trustee of the college and made his own law. He kept to his own timings, he would enter the class room followed by his *chamchas,* at any time he chose and if the lecturer objected to it, he would graciously leave the room. He would then proceed to the college canteen with his followers and entertain them lavishly. Naturally his popularity grew amongst a section of the students and even some sportive girls in the campus, vied with each other to draw his attention. It was considered a favour to be invited to enjoy a ride in his imported red sports car. He spent lavishly in entertaining his friends and admirers and never fell short of obliging any body who sought monetary help from him. He had a deceptive appearance, always impetuous in his behaviour and ready to come to blows with, whoever challenged his authority. He used to win his ways with money power. In the core of his heart however, he was soft, a trait, which he inherited from his mother. Because of his outwardly brazen and outlandish behaviour he built a reputation around himself, which didn't do any good to him. The college authority became wary of him, but could not take any action against him, because of his father. Generally, girls avoided him and did not cross his path. Jackie suffered the consequences of his dual nature, hard in the appearance and soft in the heart. The only person who loved him was his mother, who was no more. His so called friends cared or rather feared him for his money power. Shrewd as he was, Saxena knew, that his indifference and nonchalant ardour were only a shield to protect his secret. He was worried that unless some thing was done immediately, his son might become a pshycopath and he would be lost to him forever. Though the words, *love and affection* had no meaning for him and he considered these as human weaknesses, he knew that his son was built of different mettle and could sustain his life, through *love and affection*, only. He should find a suitable match and get his son married. Once he took a decision, as in other business matters, he set out for search of a suitable bride for his son. Discrete enquiries told him that Ram Gopal's sister studied in the same college where his son studied and two years his junior. Ram Gopal had a name in the business circle and was well known in the society. He was certain, that she would be a suitable match for his son.

* * * * *

To Jackie, the entire episode proved to be a disaster. With great soul searching and brainstorming by his father, he had agreed to go through the engagement ceremony at the residence of Jaya's brother, Ram Gopal jee. At the first sight he was captivated by the beauty of Jaya. His sensitivity to love someone, surfaced and he was not able to take off his eyes from her in the brief moments he shared with her, while they were together, before she swooned. A sense of loss had captured him and he wanted to follow her while she was escorted away by her family members, but he stood there and watched helplessly till he lost sight of her. Till then, he never felt the compelling force of love. Though he had several girl friends they never attracted him, they simply gave him company, when he took them on a long drive or to a restaurant to entertain. It never occurred to him that such company would defame him in other's eyes and he was already considered as a *Casanova.* He never gave a thought to such relationships. He knew, he was invincible and nobody would win him over. But this girl Jaya, knocked him out. His glass of self confidence and arrogance had spilled over, he was mellowed down to such an extent that his father got puzzled and surprised when he almost refused to budge from that place, when the incident occurred.

Jackie was in his Final year, the *exams* were approaching, he was not concerned. His only concern was Jaya; when he opened a leaf of a book, her image leapt out of it and he would sit there for hours, gazing at it. Lest his son would be pushed to the brink of disaster, Saxena availed every opportunity to speak to Ram Gopal on the issue of marriage of his son with his sister.

Whether Ram Gopal would have considered and agreed for fixing another date for engagement of his sister with Jackie or not, an unpleasant incident which occurred and reported in the News paper, settled the matter once for all. Ram Gopal, curtly replied to Saxena that he had no intention of getting his sister married, at least for the next few years.

* * * * *

Jackie did not move out of his room for days together after he returned from Ram Gopal jee's house with a broken heart. After his return, he did some thing which he never did in his life. He held his father tight and wept on his shoulders. Saxena was touched at such an outburst of his son and he wiped his own tears. Some of Jackie's friends who attended the engagement ceremony, persuaded him to visit their favourite spots and spend some time with them to relax. Jackie was well known at the restaurant and they were led to a special table at a corner. Now what transpired between the friends, in the next few moments, could never be known. The staff and the other patrons, however, witnessed a strange scene. Jackie shouted at his friends at top of his voice calling them names and showered blows on them. People at the other tables got up, the staff had to rush in to control the situation and they were also beaten. Police had to be called in at last to restore order. Jackie was taken to the Police Station. Though charges were not levelled against him, the officer-in-charge informed Saxena, to come over to the Police Station and take charge of his son. The 'News' hounds got wind of this and the incident was reported in the morning News paper. This news item was not missed by Ram Gopal at the breakfast table, next morning.

This unfortunate incident had far reaching consequences over the relationship between Ram Gopal and Saxena. The immediate fall out, was breaking of the proposed engagement of his sister by Ram Gopal, to be followed by a retaliation by Saxena asking him for refund of the cash loan of rupees ten crores, with immediate effect. His investment schedule did not permit Ram Gopal to meet this premature demand of Saxena. He discussed the issue with Raja. He confided in him, that it was a grave mistake on his part to have had anything to do with a person like Saxena, in the first place. Raja assured him not to worry about and leave it 'to him to find a way out.

After his engagement with Jaya was broken, Jackie suffered a fit of melancholy and despair and had no inclination to pursue his studies. His erstwhile friends shied away from meeting him because of his unpredictable behaviour. He shunned company and locked himself in the room. It was only '*kaka*' who comforted him and pleaded with him not to despair. He would sit hours gazing at the portrait of his mother, as if to draw inspiration from her.

At last, he resolved to appear in the *exams*. And appear he did, bringing a great relief to his father, who was now determined to send him off to U. K for a course in Management.

* * * * *

A year later, Kamal completed B. Sc. and passed in First Class Honours topping the list. There was jubilation all around. The occasion was celebrated by a group of students, who assembled in the canteen to felicitate Kamal on his brilliant performance. No doubt, Jaya was one of them. She personally congratulated Kamal with a bouquet with a small card which she had designed herself. Kamal reciprocated her good wishes and congratulated her on her own success, she had passed B. A with honours. When they were left alone, Jaya inquired, what was his plan after graduation. Kamal promptly replied that he would apply for a scholarship in a foreign University, preferably in U. S. A.

'Oh! It would be really nice, Kamal, I am sure you deserve it', Jaya chirped.

'It is not that simple Jaya, it would require recommendations from official sources and I do not know any body, who counts.'

Jaya thought for a moment and then came out, 'Oh! Don't you worry, every thing will be alright. They parted at that.

When she arrived, the news of her passing the exams in first class had already reached home and her brother and *bhabi* stood up congratulating her. While every one was in good mood, Jaya said, '*Bhaiya*, do you know, this year, a student of our college has topped in the University in B. Sc and broken the previous records.' Ram Gopal said, 'Wonderful, really wonderful, I want to congratulate the boy in person, who has won laurals for the college. I was a trustee once, I feel proud Jaya. Why not, we invite him to our house tomorrow evening, I shall congratulate him in person. What do you say Maya?' Maya looked at Jaya and smiled, she said, 'Yes, why not?'

Then she said to Jaya, 'Is he the same boy, Jaya, you told about, who is poor and dependant on scholarship only, for his studies, right from his school days ?'

'Yes, *bhabi.*'

On the following evening, Jaya arrived home, accompanied by Kamal. The family were at the tea table. Ram Gopal and Maya were struck at the plainly attired, yet fair looking boy, with bright black eyes and a serious face. Introductions over, Ram Gopal asked Kamal, to take a chair by his side.

He said, 'Our congratulations to you Kamal, we wish you, many more successes in your career.'

'Thank you, sir.'

'What do you plan to do now?'

Before Kamal could answer, Jaya said, '*Bhaiya,* he wants to go to U. S. A for higher studies and is trying for a scholarship.'

Ram Gopal and Maya exchanged glances and smiled. Thinking, perhaps she had over stepped, Jaya kept quiet.

Ram Gopal took the cue and said, 'If you are planning to go to U. S. A, it is really a good idea, I appreciate.'

Maya intervened and said, 'Kamal, you have not taken anything, please have some. Jaya, pour some tea for Kamal.' While tea and snacks were served, Ram Gopal looked on and then said, 'I know one or two persons at Delhi, who might be of help, for sponsoring a foreign scholarship for you.'

Jaya's joy knew no bounds, she was about to clap but was prevented from doing so, by an almost imperceptible signal from her *bhabi.* Kamal gratefully said, 'Thank you very much sir, it would be very nice, if you recommend my case.' With further exchange of pleasantries, Kamal left.

Maya said, 'How is that you seem to know this boy so well, Jaya? More over you are an Arts student, while he is a science student.'

Ram Gopaljee came to the rescue of his sister and said, 'So what? Education is for learning, whether it is science or art. Our Jaya is no less, she is also a brilliant student. I am inclined to send her abroad to a good University for higher studies. What I could not achieve in my life, I would like to see my younger sister achieve it. I had a good career and wanted to become a Professor. In Western countries, Professors are held in high esteem in the society, because they impart education to the students and build their characters, which put them in good stead to face challenges in life. A country's status is known by the standards, its Universities maintain. But the state of affairs in our country leaves much to be desired. Britishers have left behind them a legacy of servitude which has engulfed the educated middle class, like moss around a tree trunk. The youngsters do not have a vision, outside their small selfish world, all that they cherish is job security and a good salary. I pity them, in the end they would not have contributed anything towards the development of the country. Education must be meaningful, that is why, I became glad when I was told that Kamal wanted to pursue higher studies.'

Both Jaya and her *bhabi* listened carefully, what Ram Gopal had to say and appreciated his views on education. Maya further understood that his husband liked the boy. Knowing him, she was certain that at the first meeting, Kamal impressed him to have earned his appreciation. Jaya never expected, that the going would be so good. Some where she read, that the first impression lasts long. She prayed God to Let Kamal, get the scholarship.

* * * * *

Ram Gopal jee kept his promise and through the recommendations of his influential friends, and his own brilliant performance in the interview, Kamal secured a post-graduate seat in the prestigious university of Connecticut, U. S. A and also a scholarship along with it. The news brought cheers from both the families. Ram Gopal asked his sister to invite Kamal for dinner before he leaves for U. S. A. Jaya was too pleased to hear of that and rushed to the college office where she expected to see Kamal. She found him with his Professor in his room. She waited outside and as soon as he came out, she greeted him and conveyed the message of his brother to him. Jaya noticed, that some thing was amiss, she asked him, what was the matter.

He did'nt reply for a moment, then said, 'Please convey my thanks to your brother, he has been too kind to me. I do not know whether I deserve the same. I find it very difficult indeed, to tell him that I have changed my plan of going abroad for studies. 'Jaya couldn't believe her ears. She was stupefied. After moments she found her speech, and said, 'What did you say?'

'I do not know really, what to say.'

'Kamal, will you tell me, what is the matter?' Kamal seemed to be in a great turmoil and preferred to keep quiet.

'Okay, whatever be the problem, please do not bother, Raja *bhaiya* will definitely be able to find a solution. Come let's go to his house.' Before he could say any thing, she took his hand and almost dragged him to her car.

On the way, Jaya observed that Kamal remained silent through out the drive, till they reached Raja's house.

Raja and Ranee were at the tea table and delighted to see Jaya and Kamal together. Ranee got up, welcomed them and asked them to have tea. Seeing both of them silent and serious, Ranee asked, 'Is anything the matter, Jaya?'

Jaya said, 'Ranee, everything is alright, Kamal seems to have a problem, which he might like to discuss with Raja *bhaiya.*'

'Yes, Kamal, may I know, what is the problem?'

Kamal said, 'I am worried about my mother, firstly, she has recently recovered from her illness and still is very weak and secondly, she will be absolutely alone in the house, once I am gone. I cannot imagine of leaving her alone and go abroad for studies. I have, therefore, decided to forego the scholarship and take up some job here.'

The silence that followed was deafening. There was utter surprise in the expressions of Ranee and Jaya. Raja didn't know what to say for few moments. Then he looked steadily at Kamal and choosing his words carefully, said, 'Well Kamal, I really appreciate your concern for your mother and it is very natural. Any body in your place would be equally concerned. But I am too sorry to note, that you have ignored to consider us, as your well wishers. Don't you consider me as your elder brother and Ranee as your *bhabi*? Your mother is as precious to me as my mother. Don't you think, we are capable of taking care of her in your absence?'

Ranee and Jaya looked at Kamal with appealing eyes, while he lowered his eyes and had no heart to look at them. Raja then took charge of the embarrassing situation and said with great tenderness and love, 'You need not brood on this issue any more, better leave it to the elders and concentrate on your preparations for your visit to U. S. A. Now let us all go and see your mother and listen to what she has to say about your visit to the States.'

Raja hugged Kamal and thumped his back affectionately. After a while they all reached Kamal's place. Jaya found Kamal very nervous, she understood his predicament, firstly he had no experience of entertaining so many guests and secondly he might not possess so many cups to serve tea. It made her laugh which others noticed and she got wilted. Kamal asked them to let him go ahead to inform his mother, Raja was about to say something but Ranee motioned him to keep quiet.

After a moment, Kamal returned with a fair looking middle aged lady wearing a light saffron colour saree and a smile of welcome on her face. With folded hands, she welcomed them into her house. At the first sight she captured their hearts, they followed her into the house which was a small two room affair, bereft of furniture except a chair and a table meant probably for Kamal. What the house lacked in external comforts was amply fulfilled by the warmth of reception meted out to them by Kamal's mother, who in the meanwhile had brought in a mat, spread it on the floor and requested them to sit, with all humility and simplicity. Kamal brought glasses of water and offered them. Kamal did the introductions.

Raja said, '*Ma jee*, please come and sit with us.' He moved and made a space by his side to let her sit. Parvati jee, Kamal's mother sat down and said, '*Beta,* after seeing you all, in my house, I feel as if *Laxmi Narayan* paid a visit to my humble abode. Look at my son, how flustered and foolish, he looks, should he have not told me earlier, that all of you are expected? I would have been prepared to receive you properly.'

Jaya was about to say something, but Ranee restrained her.

Raja said, 'It is not Kamal's fault *ma jee*, we have brought him here, almost dragged him, so to say. Jaya, here, is his college mate and we came to know through her, that he thinks of forgoing his scholarship for studies abroad and remain here, because he cannot afford to leave you alone. We appreciate his concern for you, and congratulate you, *ma jee,* for having a son like him, who is so fond of you. We are all his well wishers and are indeed glad to know, that he is all set to go to the States on a scholarship. Naturally, therefore, we are crestfallen, when we are told that he has decided not to go there at all.' He wanted to say, something further, but he was stopped by *ma jee*.

She said, 'Don't take him seriously *beta*, he is no more than a child, he does'nt know even, what is good for his mother. A mother always desires his son to strive hard, develop his personality, build up his career and one day be somebody, his mother would be proud of. If he prefers to remain a mother's baby always tied to her apron, I will be sorrier for him. I am sure, my son will never let me down and shirk his responsibility, for my sake.' She looked up at her son, who stood there quietely, absorbing her mother's words as if they were Commandments.

Raja felt very small and inadequate before such a doting parent. How nicely she has handled such a delicate situation.

'We fully agree with your views *ma jee*, and lest Kamal might harbour certain reservations regarding your security and well being, during his absence, we are not going to let you remain here all alone. You are coming with us, to stay with us.'

'*Beta*, I am used to live alone and it will not be difficult to manage. Moreover, he will be away, only for two to three years. The time will pass swiftly, I am sure. *Sankat Mochan* will be there, to give me company and with all of you around, why should I feel lonely?'

'*Ma jee,* you call me as *beta,* yet you would prefer to live alone. Am I not like your elder son ? I lost my mother in my childhood, will you deprive me of a mother's love, now? Please come with us and allow us to serve you.'

She said, 'I can never deny you anything *beta,* I don't see any difference between you and Kamal. He is fortunate to have developed so much kinship with you and Ranee *bitiya.* He is not tired of praising this lovely girl who has helped him so much.'

She hugged Jaya which caused her to blush and look down. Her reaction didn't escape the notice of Ranee, who pinched her.

CHAPTER 3

Parvati and her son Kamal, have since moved over to the house of Raja, to everybody's relief. Kamal expressed his gratitude by a simple *'thanks'* to Jaya, which was exhilarating. When Ram Gopal and Maya came to know of the developments, through Jaya, they were glad and thanked Raja from the bottom of their hearts, for his generosity. In the meanwhile, Ranee furnished, one small anteroom in the house as the *puja* room for Parvati jee, who took almost half a day to install her deities at their proper places to the best of her satisfaction and she took her food only after offering *puja* and *naibedya* to the deities. She blessed Ranee and said that it was the best *puja* room she ever had.

Ranee said, '*Ma jee*, will you let me join in your prayer everyday before I start the day's work?'

'Why not *beti*, you may join me in my daily prayer, I am sure you will experience peace and tranquility, by taking the name of the Lord, every morning. Thus: -

"*Yam Brahma Varunendra Rudra Marutah*

Stutwanti Dibyaih StabaierVedaih

Sanga Pada Kramopanishdairgayanti Yam Samagah

Dhyanabasthita Tad Gatena Manasa Pasyanti Yam Yogino

Yashyantam Na Biduh Surasuragana

Devaya Tasmai Namah"

(He who is worshipped by Brahma, Varuna, Indra Rudra, Maruta by divine prayers, Sam Vedists sing Whose prayers as ordained in Vedas and Upanishads, Yogis perceive Whom in meditation, Devas and Asuras are ignorant of Whose endless entities, to That Deva I bow.)

Ram Gopal invited them for dinner, on the following evening in his house, on the eve of departure of Kamal for the States.

It was a great occasion for Parvati to visit the house of Ram Gopal, who she heard was a big industrialist and also instrumental for the award of a foreign scholarship to his son. She was very eager to see this kind person and pay her respects to him. Ram Gopal greeted them with folded hands and welcomed them into his house. Seeing Parvati jee clad in a white cotton saree with her head covered in her '*pallu*' and a spot of vermilion on her forehead exuding a picture of purity and simplicity, Ram Gopal's regards for her grew. While the menfolk engaged themselves in talks regarding politics, business and social conditions in America, the ladies talked about cooking and house keeping, Parvati picked up a half done knitted sweater from a table and looked at it.

She asked, 'Maya jee, are you knitting this?'

'Yes, *ma jee*, this is for Jaya's brother, he is always teasing me that I cannot complete it before the golden jubilee of our marriage. What am I to do? Some work or other crops up and keeps me away from knitting the sweater.'

'May I add, few more knittings? I know this pattern, if I go wrong any where, please point out.'

Parvati jee settled with the knitting and continued confidently. Maya and Jaya looked on, with wonder in their eyes.

'Am I doing right, *beti*?'

'Of course, *ma jee*, it is perfect and you are doing it fast. Were you knitting earlier?'

'It was so many years ago when Kamal was a baby, I learnt it from an English tutor who came to teach *bibiji.*'

Ranee said, 'Ma jee, I find it very useful, will you instruct me?'

'Why not *beti,* but will you ever get time to practise it?

Ram Gopal reminded that it was getting late for dinner and invited Parvati jee, Kamal and others to accompany him to the dining hall.

Kamal's Flight was in the early morning and his send off was touching. Everybody was present including Ram Gopal jee. Parvati gave a small idol of *Hanuman jee* to his son to keep with him always, to ward off danger.

* * * * *

Through insiders, Raja kept a strict vigil over the business activities of Saxena, it was no surprise for Raja to learn that, his major income was through illegal means. He was virtually a *mafia don* and the realm of his operations extended as far as Singapore, where he had a major stake in drug trafficking. Most of his clean business in India was a façade for laundering black money and hoodwinking Tax Authorities. *Babujee* had definitely caught himself in the web, cast by Saxena, when he agreed to take him as partner, and now it is his duty to extricate his employer from this tangle. He hatched a plan, and advised *babu jee* to throw a party on the eve of Jaya's birthday, invite industrialists and businessmen including Saxena. It would send him a signal that he is relenting to his pressure and might even consider to renew talks about engagement of Jaya with his son. It might give us a lee way, to ward off his pressure, for pay back, he said.

A breathtaking party was in its full swing in the expanse of the lawn at Ram Gopal jee's house. Catering was excellent. The lawn was thronged with guests. Saxena and his son were among the guests. Jackie was recalcitrant in the beginning to listen to his father for attending the party because he felt slighted on the earlier occasion. Later his desire to see Jaya and talk to her gained ground and he changed his mind. Raja kept a safe distance from his earlier *boss.* When the cake cutting ceremony was announced to take place, the guests moved towards the table where the decorated cake with candles was kept. Jaya dressed in a dazzling salwar suit, made her appearance accompanied by her *bhabi*, Ranee and Parvati and proceeded towards the table. Suddenly Parvati's glance fell upon Saxena, standing only few feet away, she stopped on her track, blood was drained from her face. Yes, it was Ratan, her husband, no mistake about it, except that he had gained a little weight. Oh! God, what should she do? She must not let him see her. At the earliest opportunity, she slipped away from the room through a side verandah into the, safety of the lounge, which was deserted. A waiter passed by and she took a glass of water from him to sip, her mouth was dry. The room was air conditioned, she settled down on a sofa and composed herself.

She never expected to come across Ratan again in her life. It brought back to her those painful memories of her past, which she had suppressed in the innermost recesses of her mind, all these twenty years. She saw a vision of a young girl of sixteen beckoning her from a jungle path, carrying a load of firewood on her head. She seemed to be floating in the air with her nimble feet effortlessly. She felt drawn toward the girl and was about to merge with her, when someone called her, "*Ma jee, Maj ee*", she woke up and found Ranee shaking her.

Ranee said, '*Ma jee* are you not feeling well, why did you come away?'

'I am alright *beti,* my head reeled, may be due to my *upavas,* which I observed yesterday. *Beti,* I saw a tall person accompanied by a young man, among the guests, who are they?'

'They are Saxena and his son, *ma jee*. He is a business partner of *babujee*. Our Jaya was to be engaged to Jackie, his son, but it was called off for some reason'.

Ratan's son? In other words, Lolita's son. She did'nt see her. Her heart cried for her, she must find out, but how? Deep anguish suppressed for years, must have found expression, in her face.

Ranee exclaimed, '*Ma jee*, what is the matter, you don't seem to be too well. Come let's go home, you need rest.'

That night, Parvati was not able to sleep. As soon as she tried to close her eyes, the vision of a young girl appeared before her.

It was she, a village belle, hardly sixteen years old, living with her *chachi*, after she lost her parents. Her lot was to toil from morning till evening, collecting water from the stream and firewood from the jungle. She was given food, after she finished the day's work. In one of her wanderings in the jungle, collecting dry twigs for firewood, she met Ratan a young cowherd from the neighbouring village resting under a tree. She had never seen the boy before. She could have avoided and gone on her way. But no, that was the exact moment when her fate stepped in, making her to approach him and ask, 'Hey, what is your name?'

'Ratan, and yours?'

'Parvati. You do not seem to belong to this village, what are you doing here?'

'Nothing, are you not seeing? I am taking rest.'

'I can see it very well. Do you have to come this far to rest?'

'I can go wherever I like. After all God has created this earth, it belongs to me, to you and to all of us.'

'Say that to my *chachi,* she will make a pulp out of you.'

Even in her anguish, in the silence of the night, the memory of her first meeting with Ratan made her laugh. She wiped the drops of the tear which had collected in her eyes. There was no sleep in her eyes. She was wide awake. The house was silent. Everyone else had retired for the night. Memory of her younger days opened her old wounds and it was painful to bear the agony of abandonment and disdain by someone you loved. With what high hopes and expectations she had begun liking Ratan, as he befriended her, when she had nobody else to look up to. From the moment she set her eyes on Ratan, she liked his plain talks and carefree attitude. She used to see him at the same spot, under the tree, reclining against the trunk, whenever she visited the place.

She would ask him, 'How do you tend your cattle by sitting here, they may go astray and wander into the deeper jungle, if you do not have an eye on them.'

'I do not care. They will fend for themselves. They are not dunce. They are more intelligent than us. They know where danger lies. If water is deep, they will not step into it. But we have no idea about depth. Be it water, be it anything else, we will step into and drown.'

'How do you know all this, did you attend school?'

'No, I did not. I know. Do animals attend schools?'

For the first time she got terrified of him. But still she liked him. For days together, he would not come to their usual meeting place. She would miss him a lot. She would walk down to the tree, where he used to sit and try to imitate his manner of looking and speaking, reclining against the tree. On one such occasion, she must have sat there for a pretty long time, when suddenly she heard Ratan shouting at her.

'Don't move'

She looked up and saw Ratan standing in front of her. He held a stick in his hand. Before she could realize the danger she was in, he threw the stick aimed at some thing close to her. It hit with a thud. She looked in horror and saw a big snake writhing near her with its head smashed. She got up and rushed to him, clasped his body tightly, trembling all over.

Later, composing herself she said, 'Why did you have to kill the snake, it was unnecessary. It didn't hurt me, it was simply lying there, may be resting. It would have gone away, after some time.'

'Oh!I didn't know that you are so soft. For me the policy is '*offence is best defence*'. How do you know that the snake would not have bitten you? Thank God, you were sitting still, they strike at anything that moves. '

'Okay, I must thank you for saving my life.'

'Were you coming here regularly, while I was away?'

'Do you mean to say, I have no other work.'

'Then why were you sitting there for hours, idle, if you are such a busy person?'

Their conversation always ended in arguments and they would part company grumpily. Ratan always irritated her. Sometime she would leave the place abruptly, but would be back, the following day, at the same time. She remembered that those days were the happiest days of her life. She could bear all the insults and abuses, thrown at her, by her *chachi*, simply in the hope that her misery would vanish in presence of Ratan, as mist at sunrise, in the morning.

When the news of her meetings with Ratan reached *chachi's* ears, Hell broke loose. Not only she thrashed her mercilessly but she also threw her in a room, tied up and locked. Her wails and pleadings had no effect on her. When Ratan did not see her for days together, he made enquiries and decided to visit her *chachi* 's house. He saw Parvati's sad plight through an opening in the window and decided, guided more by chivalry than any thing else, to free her by any means, from the tyranny of the *chachi*. He broke open the lock and brought her out. The same night, they left the village, under cover of darkness.

In the early hours of the morning, she was overcome by sleep. That was how, Ranee found her, when she came to wake her up.

'*Ma jee* do you know, who called me this morning?'

'Who, my dear?'

"Kamal, *Ma jee*. He is coming to India on a brief visit in connection with a project. He will be arriving next week.'

Parvatijee was now wide awake. Her melancholy was dispelled at the mention of her son.

* * * * *

Since attending the party at Ram Gopal jee's house, Saxena was riding over high tides. Ram Gopal seemed to have mellowed down and expressed in no uncertain measures, that he felt obliged to him. He made Jackie, to purchase an expensive gift for Jaya, for the occasion and he watched from a distance that she accepted it with a '*thank you'* smile on her face. He felt contented and swirled the drink he held, he was about to take a sip when the phone rang. He lifted and heard.

A voice said, 'Hello *sirjee*, Namaste. *Aapan ko pehachana kya*?'

'Who is this ?', Saxena said angrily.

'I am Shekhar, the garage mechanic, you remember. I fixed your Mercedes, once. *Kya gadi hai sahib*, *thik chalta* hai *na* ?'

'*Kya bukbas kar rahe ho*, I do not know any Shekhar.' He disconnected the line.

The phone rang again, as soon as Saxena lifted it, the same voice said, 'It does not make any difference to me, listen to what I am going to say, it would be good for your health. I am in need of money, hard cash. If you want to avoid landing in jail, you will deliver rupees ten crores clean. Time and place will be intimated to you soon'. The phone went dead.

Saxena cursed, where from this bastard has sprung? He had almost forgotten and written him off. A mere hireling and *bachh*a, dares to threaten him ! He thought for a moment and then called his chief agent to trace the bastard and give him the works.

After making the calls to Saxena, Raja was not idle. He was aware that there would be a price on his head, from now on. His only safeguard were his present features and mannerisms which did not bear any resemblance to his earlier version, while he worked for *sirjee* alias Saxena. He was not so sure, after all it was a disguise and anytime it might fall apart and expose him to the bare teeth of the sharks, they will then tear him apart, without bating an eye lid. But he was an adventurer and always took risks and every time, came off with out a scratch. He checked and rechecked his plan of action, going through it microscopically to find any flaw there in. He then rang up Saxena from a public booth and told him, the place, time and date to make the delivery.

He chose a crowded place for the money transfer, it was Gate Way Of India. The time chosen was eleven in the morning and on a Sunday, when tourists will be swarming the place like bees around a bee hive. As usual, there were many vendors at the place peddling their goods ranging from picture post cards, mementoes, balloons, toys, eatables and other sundry items to cheap editions of classic and hot novels, a tourist usually buys. A group of boisterous children had suddenly appeared from a bus accompanied by teachers and a guide. The crowd was thickening. There were even hawkers, carrying their goods in person all staked in pockets specially sewn for the purpose. The clock at the Taj struck eleven. A black *'Chevrolette'* drove in, its door opened, a heavy box was pushed out on to the pavement and the car pulled out. Suddenly there was a loud pop and the place was filled with smoke. People got frightened, children gathered there, panicked and cried. There was total confusion and Police came on to the scene blowing whistles. Eventually the smoke cleared. Saxena's men posted a little far away, saw that the box had disappeared, mysteriously. On hearing the news, he could do nothing except biting his teeth. Ten crores of rupees gone like a wisp of smoke. He can never forgive Shekhar for that. He has to pay for it and it would be too dear for him, he sweared. Before the night was out, scores of Saxena's men were scouting for Raja alias Shekhar over the whole metropolis.

* * * * *

After graduation, Jaya did a course in 'interior design'and found it very gratifying. As a child she had an eye for drawings and sketches. She took part in competitions and secured acclamations. Once her brother came across her drawing copy book and found it filled with sketches of buildings painted with all imaginable colours. He even saw sketches of interiors with a variety of lay out of furniture and colourful curtains hung over the windows. For a child of seven years, her imagination was not wild but mature, he thought.

From a reputed Art School, Jaya completed her Diploma in 'interior design'. She received offers of apprenticeship from many Registered Architects. While the family was rejoicing and celebrating her success in *exam*s, news reached that Kamal had arrived from States. The news gladdened her and she wanted to see him. But how? Then the phone rang, it was from Ranee. *Bhabi* spoke to her.

'Yes, Ranee, we are glad to hear, that Kamal has arrived. Hope, he is quite well. What did you say? You want Jaya, to have dinner at your place this evening? Just a minute, hold on –', Maya, then looked at her husband, he took the phone from her and spoke into the phone,

'Hello, Ranee, —*'jeete raho'*, why not all of you come over here and have dinner with us? I am very much anxious to see Kamal, it would give me an opportunity, to have a word with him, how he is faring in the States. Convey my *Namaste* to *Ma jee.*'

Jaya was following the conversation closely and she looked forward to meet Kamal, sooner than expected.

* * * * *

Because of the change of Government after the Election, Saxena did not enjoy the same power and influence as he was used to before. He had, however, amassed considerable wealth and assets. The Income Tax sleuths were after him, so he kept a low profile. He also warned his son, not to make things difficult for him through his wasteful indulgences. His pressure on Ram Gopal to cough up the money, which was loaned out to him, had not worked. Further more, this scoundrel Shekhar outwitted and swindled him. On the home front, value of his stocks in the market, went down beyond expectation. His mood was in its lowest ebb, when the phone rang. One of his aides informed that his X-rated casino was raided by Police for illegal activities and sealed by court orders. He ground his teeth, it was nothing but, adding insult to injuries. He could no longer call his shots with the Home Minister. So much money he squandered on the fat slob and now when he needed his help, he put his tail in between his legs and hid himself in some murky corner. Out of rage, he threw the glass of wine which he held, it crashed and shattered into pieces. Calm down! Calm down! He pressed his head between his hands, this is not the time to get panicky. He must reserve his strength and compose himself. One casino closed down, should not matter. There are several casinos, bars and hotels in the chain which are churning money day in and day out. But he must be catuious. There must be a chink somewhere in the armour. Could it be again Shekhar? It was a blunder on his part, to have taken him into confidence and let him take part in some of his top secret assignments. He should have paid heed, to the objections raised by his top agents.

Oh! Shekhar!Shekhar!Shekhar! He is the root cause of all his troubles. He groaned.

* * * * *

After pulling off the trick of snatching the box, packed with money, right under the nose of Saxena, Raja rushed to a rented garage and hid the box underground. In the city, it is usual for people, to hire garages for their vehicles, off from their residences. His movements in the locality were, therefore, above suspicion. He could transfer the money in lots to several Banks using his office identity and in a short time, ten crores of rupees nestled safely in Bank accounts of Ram Gopal jee

* * * * *

It was a Sunday, when Ram Gopal invited Kamal, his mother, Raja and Ranee to have dinner in his house. When they arrived, he welcomed them personally into his house. It was a very happy occasion and all of them were anxious to hear Kamal about his experience in the States. The course for his Ph.D was almost in its last phase, he said, and everybody congratulated him when he told that he received an offer of the job of a Research Assistant under the universally acclaimed entomologist, Dr. Howard Baker.

Maya and Ram Gopal jointly, congratulated Parvati jee for his son's brilliant performance and wished his success in the career, he had chosen.

She said, 'It is God's Will *beta,* His Will only prevails.'

After dinner, when they were about to leave, Ranee extended an invitation to Jaya to come for lunch to their house on the following day and also view the wonderful pictures Kamal captured in his camera in the States.

'Hope they are not of some crawling insects', Jaya said, everyone burst into laughter.

Next morning, Jaya, in her eagerness to reach Raja's house as early as possible, forgot to have breakfast and asked the driver to bring the car around. Noticing her jubilation, Maya said. 'Well, Well, our princess seems to be really in a hurry. But my dear, are you invited for lunch or breakfast?'

'Oh! *bhabi,* of course it is for lunch.'

'Then, why do you skip breakfast, come have a cup of tea with me.' Maya hugged her affectionately and holding her hand, led her to the breakfast table.

'*Bhabi*, I am to do some shopping before I reach there. Will it be proper, to present something to Kamal on the eve of completion of his doctoral thesis?'

Maya looked at Jaya affectionately and said, 'Why not my dear, I am sure, Kamal would appreciate it.'

* * * * *

It is already a week, since Kamal has left for States. Jaya was alone in the drawing room, leafing through a journal on architecture. But her mind was else where. On reaching Raja *bhaiya's* house, that morning, she did not find Kamal any where in the house. Ranee was in the kitchen, *ma jee* in the *puja* room and Raja *bhaiya* probably gone out. While she was in a quandary as to the whereabouts of Kamal, Ranee comes out of the kitchen and finding Jaya so early, exclaims, 'My, My, you are already here. When did you come?'

Hiding her disappointment she said, 'Just now, Ranee, where is everybody?'

'I am here, who else do you mean ?' Ranee said innocently.

'Okay, I have something to give to Kamal, where is he?' Seeing a packet in her hand Ranee extends her hand and says, 'Let me see what you have brought for him.'

'It is for his eyes only.'

'In that case, I am not going to tell you where Kamal is.' Noticing exasperation in her face, Ranee said, 'Okay, Okay, don't get angry, why don't you go to the garden, he may be there.' Making a face at Ranee she went out to the garden.

Jaya sees Kamal, on a bench, in the shade of a tree, studying some papers. A cup of tea lay there, untouched. She tip toed to him unnoticed from behind and said, 'Hi!'

Kamal was startled and turned to face her. In his movement, he knocked down the tea cup and the tea was spilled over the papers and also on his clothes. Kamal was surprised to find Jaya standing before him, perplexed.

He said, 'Hi! Jaya, when did you come?'

'I am sorry, Kamal, I should not have done it, your papers got spoiled.'

'Don't you worry, I have other copies. You just wait here, let me go and change my clothes'

While Jaya was tidying the place, Ranee came carrying a tray with soft drinks, she placed it on the bench and helped Jaya in cleaning. Seeing Kamal returning, Ranee winked at Jaya and slipped away.

Seeing the drinks, he said, 'Oh! Was *bhabi* here? How thoughtful of her, I am really feeling thirsty', he picked up a glass and was about to take a sip, when Jaya, in horror, spotted a toad with bulbous eyes on her lap. The creature must have leaped on to her from the ground. Before he could realize what was the matter, she shrieked and held Kamal tightly. He noticed the frog looking balefully at him, put down the glass and brushed it off from her lap. In the process, his hand touched her breasts. A shock travelled through her body, Kamal did not realize that.

Casually, he said, 'Oh! a toad, this species is known as *duttaphrynus melanostictus,* one of the most harmless creatures on earth, yet, they are killed in thousands here and else where, for advancement of scientific research. He continued to lecture some more on tad poles etc. That he was still holding Jaya in his arms, was forgotten. Nevertheless, the scene provided *masala* to Ranee to regale her friend later. She stood behind a *neem* tree to see, what the rubber frog she dropped on Jaya's lap, achieved. Satisfyed at her handiwork, she came out from her hiding place, hearing foot steps, Kamal suddenly let go Jaya from his hold and distanced himself from her.

Ranee said, 'Kamal, what was that you were lecturing about?'

'Oh! It is nothing'. Jaya wished that Ranee could not possibly have seen her, clasping Kamal. Arranging her clothes, she stood up, embarrassment widely written, on her face.

Ranee came to their rescue and said, 'Come let's go inside, lunch is ready. '

She distinctly remembered, her heart was beating faster, when she reached the dining Hall.

She was thus reminiscing the event in its minutest details and smiled at herself rejoicing at the wondrous feling, she experienced, at the touch of Kamal. Even now she marvelled at the wave of pleasure which ran through her body at that moment. On the day before his departure, however, an incident occurred, which was far from pleasant and pained her, whenever she recalled it.

It was the day before, his departure to the States, Jaya and Kamal were strolling on the Juhu beach. People were out on the beach in large numbers, they were seen in clusters either sitting or crowding near vendors selling green coconuts or *bhel-puri*, everyone's favourite.

Jaya said, 'I am thirsty, let us have some *narial pani'*

'I will have plain water, you may have *narial pani,* let me go and get one for you.'

'It will not do, you too, will have one with me. When you come to Juhu, it is a must.'

They went together to a stall and sat on a bench holding green coconuts and sipping the fresh and cool *narial pani'*.

Then Kamal said some thing which made her heart miss a beat.

He said, 'You know Jaya, when you smile you look more attractive, but when you are angry, I am really afraid'. Jaya looked into his eyes, he might have said it in a matter-of-fact tone, for her it meant a lot. It created a ripple of pleasant sensation in her mind.

Kamal wanted to go to the Central Library for some reference, Jaya accompanied him. Inside the Library it was cool and comfortable. Suddenly Jaya found herself alone. No sign of Kamal. Where could he have gone?There was an array of lifts travelling up and down to several Floors, he might have gone into any one of those, without bothering to take her. How vexatious!. She went to the ENQUIRY and told the girl at the disk her problem, the girl paged him out, he came on the line and told her to come to the sixth floor, he would be waiting for her, he said. Though he waited for her outside the Lift, what he said made the matter still worse. He said, 'I am sorry, Jaya, I forgot that you were with me. 'Jaya was aghast and kept quiet. There was a Tea Stall on the floor, Kamal, holding Jaya's hand led her to the stall and ordered Tea. There was anger in the eyes of Jaya and she tried her best to swallow the anger, built up in her. She took the tea in silence and tried to engage her attention in observing others. She sees Jackie entering the Stall, what is he doing in the Library, she wonders. He spots them and approaches.

Ignoring Kamal, he said, 'Hi ! Jaya, I have located you at last, and who is this fellow with you?' Taken aback she said, 'Meet Kamal, he is a college mate, he is studying in U. S. A for his Ph.D, and Kamal, meet Jackie, he is an old boy of our college.'

Kamal got up and extending his hand for a handshake said, 'Hello! Pleased to meet you Jackie, have a cup of tea with us.'

Looking at him disdainfully, he said to Jaya, 'I saw you entering the Library with this chap and I followed you. Come, I will drop you at home, it is about closing time.'

Kamal was totally confused and did'nt know what to say, Jaya saw that Jackie was not in the best of his moods and might go to any extent and make a scene over here.

She said, 'Come Kamal, let's go.' Then she did something, which left both Jackie and Kamal quite nonplussed. She almost dragged Kamal by her hand and rushed for the Lift. Jackie stood there gaping at them.

* * * * *

Jackie returned home and downed his frustration with drinks. Then he went to his favourite pub to have more. He sat there, till after the closing hours. The bar tender knew him and telephoned his home. One of his father's aides came to pick him up. The morning did not improve his mood. Who is that muck, for whom Jaya spurned him. He rushed to his mother's room, the room was kept tidy and clean as was done in her time. It was cool and fragrant, he kneeled down at her bed and wept. He hid his pride. Whenever he wept, it was only at her mother's side, he put his face against his mother's pillow and shed his tears. He dreamt of his mother and heard her soft voice. On such occasions, when he was a child, she used to address him as *'baby'*.

'What troubles my *baby'*, she would say, clasping him in her arms and comforting him. She would sing a lullaby and he would go to sleep in her arms. But today is different, he does'nt have his mother to console him. Only memories linger. He touches his chin and feels a scar. That day, he was hit by a boy older than him, when he dared to take it out on him because, he threw his sketch book in the gutter. He did not bother about consequences. He returned from the school with a bleeding face and stained clothes. He had rushed to his mother, dumping his school bag in a corner. Mother was seated at the dressing mirror, braiding her waist length hair. Without caring for the expensive saree she wore, she took her son in her arms and was shocked to see blood oozing out of his cut chin. She wiped his face clean with her saree. It had taken full half an hour to calm him down. It was not the pain of injury that hurt him, it was the insult, that he was beaten. His mother, at such moments would narrate stories from '*Maha Bharat'*, how '*Bhim*'would be beaten and thrashed by '*Duryodhan*' and his brothers, but later would give them back in double measures.

He wanted to get drunk and forget his worries, inspite of *'Kaka's* stern warning, he took the racing car and drove it away, it was top less and the wind surged across his face with full force, and to add to that, it rained. He drove recklessly, some time even stepping on to the pavement, driving pedastrians helter skelter and injuring them. He stopped at a way side *dhaba* and took to drinking heavily, he behaved menacingly, rough handling the attendents. Ultimately he was taken in Police custody. News reached Saxena, who was in Singapore, at that time. He rushed back to Bombay and engaged lawyers to bail out his son. They drew blank, charges were non bailable. Jackie was charged for man slaughter, due to his wanton negligent driving, he caused grievous injuries to several persons. Saxena used his influence, his son was produced before a magistrate, who granted him bail with a surety of rupees one lakh and a condition not to leave Town.

As ill luck would have it, Kamal was out on the street when Jackie was driving past and his car fender brushed his leg, throwing him into a ditch and he sustained minor injuries. He was to catch his flight on the same night. He was taken to the hospital by Raja where the injuries were attended to. The doctor, however, suggested that he should take rest atleast for next forty eight hours, since he had sprained his ankle. That would completely upset his programme, Kamal complained. He was scheduled to present a paper, he said. On hearing of the accident, Ram Gopal jee and Jaya reached the Hospital, they were relieved to find Kamal safe. On their way to home, Kamal told his woe to Jaya, everyone was of the opinion that he should postpone his journey, as the doctor advised. Parvati was thankful to the Lord for saving Kamal's life and gave comfort to his son, saying, perhaps God Wills that way, he should rest and get well. Finding Jaya alone for a moment, Kamal confided in her that it was all his doing. He might have stepped on to the road absent-mindedly.

'What!'Jaya said incredibly.

'I must have lost control of my legs, perhaps I was thinking of something.'

'Do you know what you are talking about?'

'One moment, I was on the pavement walking and whistling and talking. Next moment I found myself on the road. This car was coming from behind and before I could step out, it shoved me off.'

'Whom you were talking to, precisely?'

'You, I was thinking of you at that time.'

Before she could say anything to this whimsical person, Raja came in to say that the hit and run driver was none other than Jackie and he was arrested by Police at a *dhaba,* this morning. Parvati was listening and when Jackie's name was mentioned she was worried and wanted to know whether they had put him in the jail.

'No, *ma jee*, he has been released on bail and they have sent him home.'

When others were not at hearing distance, she asked Jaya, *'Beti, I* saw Jackie, at your birth day party, but I did not see his mother, did she not come?'

'No *ma jee*, she is no more, I learn't from *bhabi jee*, that after suffering from a prolonged illness, she passed away, when Jackie was eighteen years old.'

'Oh! How sad it is, for a child to grow up without the care of a mother', she remarked, but later in her room, alone, she shed tears ceaselessly for the loss of her dear friend, till late in the night.

Memories of Lolita kept haunting her. She was the only daughter of *Seth jee*. Ratan was employed by him and they lived in the premises of the big house. She was of her age and eventually they became friends, inspite of the fact that she was the wife of one of the staff of the household. She addressed Lolita as *bibi jee* and could never hurt her feelings and tried to please her. She had lost her mother in childhood and became the apple's eye of her father since then. *Sheth jee* employed a host of governesses, tutors and servants for her. She was always in a playful mood and kept everyone busy to fulfil her demands and commands. She was their *choti malkin* and every one treated her as such. Once she asked them to come over to the terrace, to help her flying kites. She was fond of kites and possessed scores, of different colours and styles. She was adept in flying kites, judging speed and direction of wind, would select a paricular one for the day and assign each one of us specific jobs to handle. While she remained with *bibijee* handling the spindle, Bhola the *mali* would stand ready to disentangle the kite if it got stuck up on a tree top, the cook would be present, carrying a tray with a glass of fruit juice and fried cashew nuts, so that she will not feel thirsty, while flying the kite. Such was her domain, everybody wanted to see her happy and smiling. With the passing away of *sheth jee* in a road accident, things changed abruptly, from a bubble of joy she was transformed into a spectre of sorrow. The house no longer reverberated with her laughter and cheer. A gloom was cast over the entire household enveloping everyone, moving mechanically without a soul. She did not remain long in the house to share *bibijee's* sorrow in her turbulent days. Perhaps it was better that way, she would not have lived to see her suffer at the hands of Ratan, her husband. Well, that was another story, her eye lids became heavy and sleep overcame her.

* * * * *

Saxena didn't sleep well that night. He was worried about his son Jackie. The boy has gone after his mother, soft in heart and emotional. He never appreciated emotional people. They are all obstacles to glory, contentment, power and wealth. The world history is replete with powerful men like him, they ruled and commanded with ruthlessness, crushing all obstacles in their way. His icon is Adolf Hitler, who reached incredible heights from a humble origin. He could achieve inconceivable goals because of his strength of purpose and ruthless means. The only religion he practised was the end he wanted to achieve. He carried the nation within his fist in his self indulgence. He could draw many incidents in his life parallel to with those of Hitler. What would appear to others as cruel and inhuman was nothing but means to achieve an end, to him. In his scheme of things he found Lolita as the biggest adversary, even though he did not neglect her and provided her all comforts, as deserved by a wife. His marriage with her didn't bring her any closer to him. She remained in her room surrounded by her *ayahs* and servants. She did'nt believe him, when he told her that Parvati had left for her village with the child, to see her ailing aunt. She looked at him in utter disbelief and scorn in her eyes and thereafter, stopped talking to him. That she conceived and was going to be a mother, did'nt make any difference. Amongst the maids, there was one girl, paid by him handsomely, who reported him what transpired within her room. He came to know, from this source, that the day she knew she was pregnant, she was upset and started throwing things, whatever she could lay her hands on, at her maids. Except very few trusted ones, he dispensed with the services of others. As the time of delivery came nearer, he shifted her to a nursing home under the care of competent doctors and nursing staff. In the meanwhile, he purchased a large house at Colaba, Bombay, furnished it and kept it ready. Lolita gave birth to a son, he was present at the nursing home and had a glimpse of his son from a distance. He remembered to have felt a sense of pride and happiness at that moment. In the new surroundings and with her baby son, whom she used to address, 'Jackie, my Jackie,' she seemed to be pleased and content. Her attitude towards him, however, never changed, she remained engrossed with her baby and forgot that a world existed outside. He could get near to his son, only when she was asleep and never dared to touch the baby, lest he would wake up and let out a cry. The aloofness between him and Lolita widened; under the same roof they lived as strangers. His worry was not as much for Lolita remaining estranged from him, as for his son, who was his apple's eye, being groomed to hate him. That was, perhaps her way, to avenge. Now, Lolita is no more and Jackie has grown up to be a handsome young man, to be proud of. He satisfied all his desires and whims and so much so, that he did his best to bring around Ram Gopal an industrialist, to agree to his proposal for giving his sister in marriage to his son, for whom he developed an irrepressible desire to marry. Being thwarted in the attempt, to get his son married to Ram

Gopal's sister, it pained him and he feared, lest he might take some drastic steps to satisfy his ego. At last sleep overcame his tired limbs and mind.

* * * * *

In his saner moods, Jackie thought of several plans to win over Jaya, some *direct* and some indirect. In the end he dismissed all the plans from his mind, lest it might backfire and worsen their relationship. He rolled and tossed over the bed, till sleep overcame him. In the morning, at the breakfast table, a News item caught his eye. He began seeing rays of hope. He made few calls and left the table, pleased with himself.

* * * * *

Jaya has, in the meanwhile, completed her course in 'Internal Design' and was on the look out for a suitable job, to fill in her time. One morning, she came across an *'ad'* for an architect for renovating and modernizing an old mansion at Poona. Without thinking, she applied for the job. When she mentioned about it to her *bhaiya* and *bhabi*, they said, *no*, she cannot possibly take a job, outside Bombay.

'Anyway', she said, 'since the job called for experience, my application may be outright rejected.' The matter rested there. But not for long. She received an interview call, which was scheduled for the next day. With a little persuation, Ram Gopal jee gave his consent, but he would decide, he said, whether she would accept the job or not, if selected.

Jaya reached the place, where the interview was to be held, several other candidates had assembled, some old, some young. She had nothing to lose, this was her first interview for a job and she was certain, that being the youngest of the lot and inexperienced she would be rejected. So why not take it lightly and give a tough time to the selectors and enjoy their reaction. Suddenly, she heard, her name being called. She relished afterwards, to recollect what followed that day at the interview.

She entered the room and noticed that it was elegantly furnished and the atmosphere was tense. She took the surroundings, the wall colours, the paintings and the furniture, in a flick of her eye and then faced the interviewers sitting across a big table, all of them viewing her, as if she was a delectable dish. *'Wait, you guys, I'll make a sauce out of you, before I leave this place.'*

Aloud she said, 'Good Morning Madam, Good Morning gentlemen.'

'Won't you sit down please?', the lady interviewer said.

'Thank you, ma'm', she took her seat, at the far end of the table.

'Miss Jaya, we find from your bio-data that you are a fresh graduate and have no experience, whatsoever. Still, you have applied for the job, why?' One of the gentleman with a crooked nose asked.

'Excuse me sir, the '*ad*' did not say that persons having no experience, need not apply. I wanted to take the chance.'

'I see. You seem to depend on chances rather than on efforts.'

'I believe in the maxim, '*an early bird catches the worm.*'

'You seem to be very confident, Miss Jaya.'

'Of course, Ma'm. I have been brought up in a family which breeds confidence.

The chairman of the Board chuckled.

'A moment, Mrs. Singhal', he said to the lady member

Then he said to Jaya, 'Let me put you a question, bearing on your profession. As soon as you entered this room, what did strike you the most?'

'Well, sir, excuse my saying so, the man behind the colour scheme and placement of paintings does not seem to know his job. The combination reeks of oddity and foolhardiness.'

Silence prevailed in the room, for few moments.

The situation was being enjoyed by a person sitting before a CCTV screen, in a room adjacent to the Board room.

'What would you have done, if you were the person to have been asked to decorate the room?'

Jaya thought for a moment and then said, 'I would have given due consideration to the size and shape of the room and done away with the dungeon like atmosphere the room presents, by cutting across large windows on the eastern wall to catch the sun during the day and make it warmer in cold weather. With a pearl white ceiling and concealed lights upturned to the ceiling, I would have painted the walls with lemon yellow to bring assurance to the person entering the room that everything is going to be fine but not getting a shock with the bizarre colour of grey resembling an overcast sky.' Having said this, she looked straight into the eyes of the chairman. Another spell of silence followed.

The member, who had not spoken so far said, 'Suppose we offer you the job, how early you can join?'

'It depends whether my family would permit me to take the job.'

'What do you mean?'

'That is what I meant.'

The chairman could no longer contain himself, he said, 'Miss Jaya, you appear to be very impudent and also insolent.'

The person behind the wall spoke over the intercom, *'You fool, conclude the interview.'* It was meant only for the chairman's ears. His face reddened and after a moment he said, 'Well, that would be all. You will hear from us soon.'

* * * * *

Ram Gopal and Raja were conferring in the company Board Room, the company showed good returns on capital. The investors were happy. Ram Gopal proposed to go public and get enlisited. The Balance Sheet showed surplus, why not release few thousands of shares to the market and attract capital for expansion, he said. Raja weighed the situation. Their main business was real estates, demand for which fluctuated, Bank rates keep fluctuating, promoters may not jump into the band wagon under such circumstances, he said. Ram Gopal jee laughed and said, 'You are forgetting one thing Raja, all promoters do not depend on Bank loans, they have their own source. There is a parallel inexhaustible source of money supply in this country. People are interested to invest in *Real Estates*, because, that is where the golden egg lies. You have seen how property values are sky rocketing in Bombay and Poona these days. This is the time to make some money. Since Raja dealt only with the Bank accounts of the company and he drew a fat salary as a V. P, he kept quiet.

A small and unheard of company registered under R. G. Company, Ltd made its entry in the Stock Excange and in the first year of its operation, declared a return of flat ten percent, in the following year it was eleven percent. The share capital was about rupees five hundred crores; the Real Estate business was picking up. The investors, builders and buyers were all happy.

* * * * *

With a drink in his hand, Saxena was in a pensive mood. He reflected upon his son's doings in recent months, as reported by his staff. He rarely saw Jackie, these days. Often he was seen with friends, partying and frolicking. He was relieved that at least he did not cause any trouble. He missed him, he expected that Jackie would gradually take the reins of his business in his hands and relieve him from the strains which proved too much for him, at times. Perforce, his staff looked after his business including chains of hotels, casinos, transport companies, automobile dealerships and his core team managed the secret organizations, he wished that his son should have had a grip over the business. Suddenly, he felt old and tired. No doubt, money poured from all sectors to his coffer, it also drained through many channels. The political masters take their pounds of flesh for giving him a lee way to operate and they eye his earnings like hawks. If Jackie fails to mend his ways and indulges in spending millions in wasteful pursuits, then the day is not far enough when he will be no longer in a position to call the shots.

Suddenly his mind strayed into the past, memories of Parvati and her baby son began troubling him like a bad dream, he saw twenty years ago. What happened to them, where would they be? These questions kept coming to his mind, however much he wanted to forget that chapter of his life. The course, he has chosen for his life doesn't leave much scope for sentiments. He swirled the drink and looked at its motion, life is like that, somebody churns it, you have no control over it. He was about to take the last sip, when the phone rang. He picked up and listened. The voice at the other end simply said, "It is done."

He replaced the receiver. His facial expression changed abruptly. The gentleness and softness which he bore a while ago, gave place to the characteristic roughness and ruthlessness of a wicked and vile person. His eyes became narrow slits, his thin lips taut into a sneer. He stretched his legs, reclining, clapsed his hands behind his head and closed his eyes, his favourite position, when he wanted to visualize something. He could see Police, cordoning off the bomb blast site, people running helter skelter to save their lives and skidding of vehicles. Amidst this confusion, he could see a black sedan pulling out of the jetty and rushing toward the city transporting a fortune in gold bars to one of his many repositaries. He waited. The phone did not ring further. *No news is good news*, he thought. His tense moment passed like a dark cloud gliding across the moon's face.

* * * * *

Jaya was on her way to home, after attending the interview. She enjoyed the interview, every part of it, and specially the expression on the face of the Chairman when she fired her last salvo and how his face had undergone change of colour. It was worth seeing. She looked outside the car window, weather was cloudy, floating clouds masked the distant hills. Her mind soared, what Kamal would be doing now? Why not plunge into the luxury of dreaming? The car was racing towards the plains. She felt Kamal sitting by her side, close to her. She felt the touch and smiled to herself. Left to him, Kamal would simply stare outside and enjoy the view, ignoring her presence. She did'nt want to miss the opportunity. A lonely drive, rain water splashing against the car window, she could hear, even her palpitating heart, she was tempted to hold his hand, she was sure that the driver would not notice this. She was glad that he did not remove his hand. Emboldened she pressed his hand and felt a tremor in her body when he responded. Oh no! It is a miracle! She shifted her position and basked in the simple pleasure of his nearness and warmth, she closed her eyes. She was aroused when the driver addressed, '*Bibijee*, it is home.' She leaned on the door hand rest. Yet, the feelings lingered and brought a smile on her face.

At home, none attached much importance to the interview, except enquiring, how it went. She fell to the daily routine of visiting the library, a safe haven to enjoy few moments of solitude and contemplation. One day she was lost in her thoughts, when a hand fell on her shoulders, shaking her and saying, 'Hi! Jaya, where are you?'She looked up and saw that it was Seema, her friend, who stood in front of her and smiling. Seema pulled a chair and sat by her side.

‘Oh! Seema, what a pleasant surprise? Where were you all these days? How is everybody in the family?Hope everything is alright with you,’

‘Yes, *baba,* everything is okay with me. Now tell me, what you were immersed in? Why this pensive mood? Are you love lost?’

‘Oh! Seema, you will never change.’

‘Okay, Okay, if you do not want to share your thoughts with me, so be it, I’ll not insist.’

She pulled Jaya out of the chair and both of them went to the canteen. Over cups of coffee, they talked at length of their college days, having laughs at the expense of their professors especially about one Mr. Rubgundi who was well known for his eccentricities. His obsession of carrying an umbrella, all the time, was well known, and particularly his habit of tapping each street light pole with his umbrella, as he walked, without ever missing one, became a favourite talk among the students. One day, when Seema and Jaya went to the college canteen, they found, that a bet was on, whether Prof. Rubgundi would miss any pole, that day. Both of them bet in favour of the professor, while other girls and boys were against. They waited and followed him, at a distance. Swinging the umbrella in his hand, the professor, walked, tapping each pole, he came by, his walk was almost over and only few poles were left to be covered, students who bet against, were beaten and they were about to turn away, when suddenly, the professor turned to go to his home, missing the last and the nearest pole to his home. Seema and Jaya had lost and others cheered having won the day. But no! Seema jumped in joy, their beloved professor returned after a while and tapped the pole, which he missed earlier. Both the friends laughed aloud, at remembering the incident. Jaya suddenly fell silent.

‘What is troubling you my dear?’Jaya opened her heart to Seema and told her feelings for Kamal, who is now in the States for higher studies.

‘What is the problem then? There is nothing wrong, to love somebody. Who is this Kamal? I have not seen him; you say that he is from our college, neither I have seen you together with him anywhere. How is that our princess who always followed a principle of *Ten to Two*, without turning her head left or right, fell for this young man?’

'There is not much to tell you, Seema, It just happened. He was not in our stream, he was in B. Sc. In a college debate competition, I met him and some how got impressed with his knowledge and manner of speaking. One thing led to another and one day it struck to me that I had fallen in love with him. What am I to do Seema? I feel lost.'

"Why dear, what is wrong in falling love with somebody?"

'He is so sincere and studious, that he has no time or inclination to look at me. I do not know whether he loves me.'

Seema said, 'Well, my dear, if you love him, you will certainly win him. May be, he is shy to express his love to you. Do not lose heart. Give him time.'

The friends embraced and parted with promises to see each other again.

* * * * *

Ram Gopal's new company made good progress, in the meanwhile. Share holders were happy with their dividends. In its third year the company made good profit and the Board decided to diversify their business and enter into the field of manufacturing. Since building activities were picking up, they decided upon producing building hardwares, specially extruded aluminium and castings. The company was in search of new hands for its new project. Ram Gopal said, 'why not we rope in our Jaya to manage this new venture, after all it is her family business and she should join early.' Raja said, 'We must ask what Jaya thinks about it.'

Ram Gopal discussed the matter with his wife and they waited for the arrival of Jaya to talk over the issue. Jaya came with a thick envelope in her hand and after greeting her *bhabi* and *bhaiya,* she said, 'Look *bhabi,* you remember, I attended an interview at Poona the other day, they have offered me the job and forwarded the papers to sign. They expect me to join next week'. Maya looked at her husband and he nodded. She said, 'It is wonderful, congratulations, it proves one thing, they have judged you suitable for the job. But you are young, why waste your talent in such a job which has limited scopes. '

"What exactly do you mean *bhabi.*'

'It means simply this Jaya, you must use your talent in something bigger and satisfying.'

'I couldn't follow you, *bhaiya.*'

'I want you to join our business, which is expanding, you may perhaps go to U. K to do a course in M. B. A, which will be very useful to you.'

'That will be excellent *bhaiya*, I will welcome it, but the present job seems to be very challenging and moreover it will be completed in about a year. Why not, you let me undertake the job, it will give me confidence and self satisfaction; afterwards I may do the M. B. A course. Please *bhaiya.*'

'Okay, my dear sister, you win. I will phone Shyam *dada* to keep the house ready for you, you know I have a farm house at Poona.'

'Oh! It will be wonderful *bhaiya*, she hugged her brother and rushed to her room to fill in the papers.

Jaya wanted to give the good news to Ranee. Next morning, she went to her house and found *ma jee* in the Hall, busy in knitting a sweater which she had begun for Kamal. Greeting her, Jaya said, '*Ma jee*, do you know, *bhaiya* has agreed for my taking up the job at Poona. Oh, I am so glad *ma jee.*' Where is Ranee?'

Ranee came out of the kitchen and said, 'Who is going to Poona?' When Jaya told her about the job, she said, 'What! You will stay there alone, and *bhabi* agreed to let you go?'

'*Are meri amma,* don't you worry, I am grown up now, and I am a city girl after all, I will manage. More over, Shyam *dada* will be there to take care of me.'

* * * * *

Maya packed her things in a VIP suitcase along with a tin of home backed cakes which she liked best. Ram Gopal and Maya saw her off on an auspicious day wishing her good luck and success. Touching their feet and suppressing her tears, Jaya got into the family car for her journey to Poona. For the first time, she will be leaving them and going on her own. Looking behind, she waved at *bhabi* and *bhaiya* till they remained in her sight. She wiped her tears and settled back on the seat with a heavy heart.

She was to meet the owner of the property that evening; she rushed to the site on Khadagvasala road and was impressed at the sight of the massive white edifice from a distance. It was simply a marvellous piece in granite and white marble. She never saw such a large building before, except perhaps the Victoria Memorial in photographs. A person waited at the porch to receive her, he introduced himself as the manager of the estate and offered his employer's excuses for not being able to come. He took her around the building which had thirty seven rooms spread in two floors with an oval hall in the centre from where two magnificient marble staircases with brass handrails led to the upper storey. She was awe struck, what she witnessed was the dream of any architect. Though the building lacked lustre because of neglect, it still had some spark left, to mesmerize her.

The Manager was saying her something, which she did not hear. She looked at the massive door at the enrance, an epitome of woodwork. Her attention was then diverted to the ceiling, and her wind was taken out of her. What she was beholding was spectacular, it was something reminiscent of medieval architecture, a huge crystal chandelier supported by four brass chains hung from a rose bud shaped hook from the ceiling. The massive round ridged columns supporting the dome structure with projected balconies all around gave a feeling that one was perhaps in an age when Michele Angelo lived. Such was her mood when the Manager suggested, she would better see the room which would serve as her office. It was bare, she might furnish it according to her own choice, he said. It struck her that they wanted to test her skill in furnishing a small room, before she embarks on her project. *Okay, you guys will have it, as you desire*, she said to herself. The tour of the entire mansion took the best part of the evening. She had tea with the manager in the verandah overlooking a green expanse of a lawn freshly mown.

Back in the farm house, she kept thinking. She was clear in her mind, what to do on the following day and the days after. She went to the city's best '*furnishing shop*' and ordered simple, functional and yet elegant office furniture, curtains etc, for her office room. She asked the Manager to provide her requsite office stationeries and settled with her job.

Days passed by, she got so busy at the site, in taking photographs and measurements of the rooms, designing models of each room with computer aids, that when she returned home, she felt exhausted and tired. She used to go to bed after snatching a quick bite. In a week's day she was ready with her diagrams and graphics for a preliminary discussion with the '*boss*'. She was disappointed, when she was told that the *'boss'* was not available and she might leave her notes and diagrams etc. on his table for his comments later.

What sort of a man was the '*boss'*? She was here alredy for two weeks and yet, there was no sign of him. The assistants had no idea when he would be available. Does it not appear mysterious? Has she been taken on a ride? What she was to do? She did not bother, she liked the job and went ahead with corrections and revisions on her preliminary designs, undeterred. More surprise was stored for her on the last day of the month, before she left office, a fat envelope was delivered at her table, she found it to contain new currency notes, all of one thousand rupees denomination, numbering twenty, the accompanying note said that it was her salary for the month. Incredulous!

She is being paid twenty thousand rupees, for almost nothing. Is she being used for something else? She felt exasperated and ridiculed, she told as much to the Manager. Her burst of anger finally bore fruit. A team of architects came to discuss with her, they had a folder with them. It contained all her latest drawings and designs with corrections in red and stamped 'verifyed'. They assured her, that her designs have been appreciated by the *'boss'*, who is busy in other works, else where and has expressed complete faith in her. She may, therefore, go ahead with her works and the team will be visiting the site every month to see the progress, hold ups, if any. Soon after, a team of workers with truck loads of building materials arrived at site.

* * * * *

Parvati used to visit the Sankat Mochan temple, which was near her home, regularly for offering prayers. Monkeys were galore in the temple yard; after her '*puja*', she would go around the temple and come down the steps. No sooner the monkeys noticed her, they would come near and stretch their hands clamouring for pea nuts, she would take out the nuts from her basket and feed them with her hand, which they would accept docilely. That was her daily routine. Being a pious woman, monkeys, she considered, to be the real *bhaktas* of Sri Ram, like *Hanuman jee* and feeding them would be virtuous. Absorbed in her thoughts, she began crossing the road to go over to the other side, not mindful of the traffic, when suddenly a speeding car came by and halted within inches of her, with screeching of brakes. The car fender grazed her and she fell down on the road. People gathered around her, some one lifted her up, to her feet. Few more, rushed to the driver to thrash him. But she restrained them, saying that it was her fault. The driver, however, got down and enquired whether she was hurt and would she like to be carried to a hospital? She said, 'No *beta*, I am alright.' At that time, the car window was rolled down and Parvati had a glimpse of the man sitting in the back seat of the car. She was startled, it was Ratan, her husband. Next moment, the window was raised and the car sped away throwing a cloud of dust at her.

On arriving home, she asked for a glass of water, Ranee poured water from the jug into a glass and gave it to her. She noticed her dust ridden clothes and pallid face. Alarmed, she enquired what was the matter. She evaded and told that she slipped and fell fown and there was nothing to worry about.

'Let me get a cup of tea for you, *ma jee*, while you rest here.' Arranging a couple of pillows by her side, she rushed to the kitchen. Reclining on the sofa, Parvati reflected that this was her second chance meeting, with Ratan. Obviously, he was very much in the city, in an entirely different world, living alone with her son. Being a righteous married woman, her hand went up and touched the *mangal sutra,* which she wore and kept hidden from others' views. Holding it, she silently prayed God to bless him. He is her husband and father of her son, with whom she took seven *pheras* around the sacred fire. What if, he forsook her, that was her destiny and God's Will. He might have broken all the vows he took, it did not mean that he was no longer her husband. A *hindu* married woman remains wedded to her husband till her last breath. That was her belief.

'*Majee*, your tea', Ranee's voice woke her up. The tea refreshed her. She got up to go for a wash and change. Ranee looked at her and worried.

The phone rang, it was Jaya, from Poona. She told, that she would be coming home next day, on a short leave. *Ma jee* was delighted to hear that, the very presence of the girl always cheered her and she looked forward to meet her. Whenever she saw Jaya in company of her son, a hope almost inconceivable, stirred in her mind, which she suppressed immediately. She only hoped, that her son does not come to grief on that account. Her knowledge that Ratan has became rich in the meanwhile and even tried to get Jackie, married to Jaya brought a sense of despondency to her over the development. That Jackie and Kamal are step brothers, was known only to her and the burden of this knowledge was too heavy for her to bear. She couldn't share this with anybody. She had a disturbed sleep that night.

The dream was frightening, she woke up sweating and her throat was dry, she felt suffocated. She got up, took a sip of water, pushed aside the curtain to let in fresh air into the room. The weird vision of Ratan dragging her and Kamal and pushing them off a cliff into oblivion, remained still imprinted in her mind, she shivered inspite of the sultry weather. The fact that Kamal was thousand miles away from Ratan, brought some solace to her.

* * * * *

Day was just breaking, she tried to look into her past. It was another night. She and Ratan were now married, it appeared before her as a dream, she lay by his side in the cottage, which will be their home now. She looked at him, soundly asleep without a care in his mind. So this was her man, her husband. Oh! How sweet he was, when he held her tight in his arms, almost taking the breath out of her, and led her in the path of heavenly bliss and ecstasy. She covered her face with her hands and blushed. That was their first night, which she could never forget. Those were the happiest moments of her life. With his first salary, he bought a *saree* and a small bottle of *bindi* for her, which were still in her possession. Gradually his attitude towards her, seemed to change. He was now engaged as the driver of *seth jee* and remained most of the time at the House, busy in his works. He came home late in the evening, tired and sometimes went to bed without taking food, saying that he ate outside. She no longer looked beautiful to him, her hair seemed unkempt to him, food she cooked no longer tasted good to him. She wept into the pillow throughout the night, while Ratan slept turning his face away on the other side of the bed. Her only companions in those troubled days were two saplings of mango and lime trees which she planted with care in the backyard of her cottage, with the help of the *mali.* She used to water these plants regularly and tend them with great care, as if they were her children. Gradually the roots went deeper and the plants looked healthy and stronger. One day, a stray goat entered through the gate which was left open by Ratan and would have devoured her dear plants, but she noticed the intruder in time and drove it out throwing a *desi gali* at the goat.

It was a summer afternoon, she remembered, while she watered the plants, her head reeled and she had an urge for vomiting, the elderly cook, who visited her often, seeing her retching, enquired whether she missed her periods. What she told her afterwards, was still ringing in her ears after all these years.

'*Beti,* may God bless you, you are going to be a mother'

It brought her immense joy and exhilaration and a little fear at the same time. She waited anxiously, for sharing her joy with her husband. She was greatly disappointed and hurt, when the news did not make him any happier. That night, he did not speak to her.

She asked him, 'Ratan, are you not glad that you are going to be a father?'

'What is there to rejoice and be glad about something which will be a burden on us', he said roughly. She was shocked to hear that. To make things worse he continued, 'I earn too little to live comfortably. *Seth jee* has provided a place for us to stay, but that is not enough. He is a *kanjush*, he does not pay me enough, and now you tell me, you stupid woman, that you are with child and you expect me to be glad. Where from money will come to rear the child ? We were managing somehow, just two love birds and not a third person between us.'

She could not hear further and did not speak to him, for rest of the day.

Their relationship did not improve as the days progressed and her pregnancy advanced. Ratan used to boast, 'See, what a big car, I am driving around, it is virtually mine, though *seth jee'* rides in it occasionally. I tell you, it is going to be mine some day. I would have liked to let you ride in the car, but in your rustic get up, it would not be proper. Why don't you try to dress properly, like other women do, in this part. '

It hurt her pride very much, but could only say, 'Ratan, it is not proper to speak of *seth jee'* in such terms. He is our provider. May God bless him and make him more prosperous and benevolent.' That was the first time, she felt afraid of her husband. In the days of her confinement there was nobody to turn to, except for the old cook, who used to visit her often to enquire after her health. When the time for her delivery came near, she took her to a local maternity hospital for check up. Ratan kept himself away from home on some pretext or other. As she remembered her helplessness and despondency during those days, anger and revulsion against him, swelled in her. She remembered the day of the birth of her child, it was a dark night, lights had gone out, a thunderstorm was developing, rains poured outside and the winds howled. A kerosene lamp threw long shadows in the room. There were only two persons in the room, when the baby came, she and the kind hearted old cook, who stood by her like an anchor rock in her difficult days. She wondered, where she would be now, it was so many years ago. When the pain mounted, the old woman held her hands, mopped her forehead and softly spoke, that everything was going to be alright. She bore the pain clenching her teeth and then it happened, there was a spasm, she shrieked and then everything was quiet. She felt light and relieved, she closed her eyes. Her eyes fluttered, when she could hear wailing of the baby, as if coming from a distance, she had no strength to open her eyes. Someone whispered into her ears, '*Beti*, look at your son, hold him'. She opened her eyes and her gaze fell upon a little bundle held by the old lady. Her first impression of her child was a small head with a black crop of hair and the tip of a red nose.

'My son, my son', she spoke softly and looked at her old companion with deep gratitude in tearful eyes. The old woman nodded with understanding and softly put the baby by her side. She asked to hold the baby at her breasts. The pleasure and fulfilment she experienced, when she fed her baby was beyond description. Along with her milk, her heart flowed into the baby.

* * * * *

On seeing Jaya back home after a month, Maya rushed to greet her and embraced her, she said, 'Oh! Jaya, how thin you look. Did Shyam *dada,* not feed you well?' There was genuine concern in her voice.

Jaya said, 'Oh! *bhabi,* when will you stop treating me as a baby, I am grown up and able to take care of myself. '

'Oh! You are grown up, I did'nt notice it. But I find that your ears need a little wringing', so saying, she wrung Jaya's ears and pulled her to her bosom. Then they went inside hand in hand together.

'I don't see *bhaiya,* is he not at home?'

'He is never at home, always busy in his works. He has gone to Calcutta.'

'Oh! *bhabi*, who will tie *rakhee*, on my hand tomorrow?'

'Don't you worry my dear, he will be back by tomorrow. Moreover he has a surprise for you, this year.'

'What is it going to be this year? Anything special?'

Before Maya could reply, the bell rang. She went to open the door, saying, 'who could it be at this time?' She was taken aback, when she found Jackie, at the door.

'What a surprise, come in', she said. When Jaya saw, Jackie following *bhabi* into the Hall, she was more than surprised, it became very embarrassing for her to meet him, after her last encounter with him at the Library. But she could not escape it. She had no excuse either, to leave the Hall. Jackie was already taking a seat and *bhabi'* excusing herself, went out to the kitchen for getting tea for him. It was, therefore, left to her, to be civil to the guest.

'Hi, Jaya jee how are you', and then seeing a bag in the Hall, Jackie said, 'Hope you are not inconvenienced ? You seem to have just arrived from somewhere.'

'No, it is alright', she had no intention of letting him know that she was working on a project at Poona. Situation was saved, when *bhabi* walked in with the tea trolley. Jackie volunteered the information that his father was bent upon sending him to UK for a course in M. B. A. Without restraining herself, Maya said, 'Oh, it is good, we are also planning to send Jaya for the same course. Jaya cast an angry look at her and motioned her to keep quiet.

'It is excellent, please let me know, which college you would be joining.'

After exchange of pleasantries Jackie left, wishing good luck to Jaya. The surprise visit of Jackie, completely unnerved her and spoiled her mood for the morning, which Jaya had looked forward to enjoy.

Jaya kept tossing on the bed, sleep eluded her eyes. She picked up a novel by Mulk Raj Anand, *'Two leaves and a bud'*, which she had already read. She replaced it on the shelf. Her mind reflected on the morning's incident. The unwelcome Jackie appeared from no where and unsettled her. Why he is forcing himself on her family, she failed to understand. The chapter of her engagement with him has been closed for ever, the same has been made clear by her brother to his father in no uncertain terms, why is he trying to renew the relationship? His odd behavior at the Library and now his unexpected and uncalled for visit today, greately unnerved her. She heard quaint stories about him in her college days. When she joined college, he had already left, but stories of his escapades were wildly circulated among girls. One of the popular one was, he forcibly lifted a girl on to his bike and sped away. It turned out that the girl happened to be the daughter of a professor. The police caught them, however, at a roadside '*dhaba*', sipping *lassi* together and the girl seemed to be in an exhiliratng mood. When accosted by Police, Jackie explained that the girl wanted a ride. The girl corroborated and said,

'Yes, it was a ride worth to remember. We were almost touching one hundred kmph, the wind swept my scarf.' Such stories and others were built around him and he got the status of an icon of youth in the campus. Girls vied with each other, to talk to him and be seen with him. Not only he was frivolous, but at times he carried his fun too far. He had few *chamchas,* following him wherever he went and spent lavishly on them. The group once, were making noises in the library, the librarian asked them to keep quiet or quit. At that moment, Jackie walked in and slapped one of his friends, the librarian was appalled and did'nt know what to do.

Jackie told her, 'Are you satisfied now, madam? He will no longer be a nuisance to you.' Then he walked off the library and invited all the students who were present in the library for snacks and coffee. He was really unpredictable.

Later, she dispelled thoughts of Jackie from her mind and the void was quickly filled with the sweet memories of Kamal, till sleep overtook her and she slept. She woke up in the morning, fresh as a rose and came over to the verandah to walk up to the garden for breathing fresh air. Morning dews on the flowers, the coolness in the breeze made her spirit soar high and her thoughts went back to Kamal, she guessed that the time in that hemisphere would be about three am and he would still be in bed, probably dreaming about moths and butterflies. It made her laugh. The *mali,* who happened to be near, tending a rose bush, looked up and said, '*Bibijee*, did you say anything?'

Jaya said, 'Nothing *kaka*, I was enjoying the morning, do you know in America, it will be night at this moment?'

'Now, *bibije*', you are making a fool of me, there is only one Sun for the entire universe, how it will be day at one place and night at another?' Jaya was in a playful mood. She said, '*Kaka,* can you tell me where does the Sun go after it sets here?'

He thought for a moment and said, 'I don't know.'

'Well, it goes to America, before he says anything, Jaya rushes off.

After breakfast, Jaya says, '*Bhabi,* I am off to Raja *bhaiya*'s place, I must catch him before he leaves for office.'

Raja was getting ready for office, when Jaya arrived.

She said, 'Hi, Raja *bhaiya,* I have just come and you are already on your way out. This will not do, you have to spend a little time with me. Moreover don't you know what is today?'

He said, 'What could it be? It could'nt be your birth day, you celebrated it last month', he racked his brains to think over.

'What *bhaiya*! Can't you remember such an important festivity? It is a shame.'

'Oh! How foolish of me to forget it. Today is *rakshya bandhan'*. It is all the doing of Ranee, she should have reminded me, otherwise I would have missed you.'

'Hey! Don't put the blame on me and try to escape your commitment to your sister.' Ranee brought the *puja thali* and handed it over to Jaya, she applied *tilak* on his forehead and taking the *thali* in her hand, moved it in a circular motion around his face, doing *aarati*, seeking Blessing of God for prosperity and valour of his *bhaiya*. She then, took the *rakhee* and tied it on the wrist of Raja as a symbol of protective shield to protect him from all evils and misfortune. On this day, the brother takes a vow to protect the honour of his sister. Rituals over, Jaya offers sweets to Raja and then extends her hand before him.

Raja takes out a *thousand rupees note* and places it on her hand, at that moment Ranee says, 'Jaya, are you satisfied with that, it will not buy you even a vanity bag.' Jaya again extended her hand with a mischievous smile, Raja had to sell out more. There was laughter all around. *Ma jee* came out of the *puja* room and joined them. Jaya touched her feet and took her blessings.

Majee blessed her and said, '*Beti*, you look thin and darker, are you not eating well?'

'Oh! *ma jee*, you are all worried for nothing. I am fine. But at the moment, I am famished and would very much relish a plate of *halwa,* prepared by you.'

'Why not *beti,* certainly. You just wait, I'll get it for you in no time.'

Ma jee left for the kitchen and Raja for his office. Jaya and Ranee were left alone. Jaya pestered Ranee with enquiries regarding Kamal.

'He is fine, *baba*, so fine, that he took lots of trouble to have done some shopping, for dispatching to you a complete wardrobe.'

'Is it so Ranee, ? Let's go and see, what he has sent for me.'

'Come, he has particularly asked me to hand over the packet, when no body else is there'. She couldn't wait any longer to get hold of the packet. With trembling hands, she unwrapped the packet and took out a box, containing a white shirt, a Denim jacket, a mini skirt out of the same material, complete with under garments, a tie and a cap to go with.

While Ranee was aghast in seeing the weird dresses, Jaya was excited and said, 'Look how cute these are, I cannot wait for trying these.'

'Don't say, you are going to try these dresses. Are you gone mad?'

'No, my dear Ranee, on the other hand I am head over heels in love with–'

'Love with——?'

'With the dresses, I mean, you stupid', she stuffed the dresses back into the box.

Then, they heard *ma jee* calling them, they rushed down. Jaya's mouth watered when she saw steaming *halwa* on the plate. Taking a spoonful she said, 'Oh! Ma jee, how delicious it is!'

Then, the phone rang. it was Maya, telling her, that her *bhaiya* was back home.

Ram Gopal was glad to see her sister and said, 'Oh! How fit and smart my sister looks. Does the job suit you, Jaya?'She touched his feet and said, 'I like it, *bhaiya.*' Maya came with the *puja thali*, Jaya applied *'tilak'* to her brother and tied the *rakhee* on to his wrist. He said, hugging her, 'May God, Bless you, my child'. Jaya stood there waitng, Ram Gopal said, 'I am not going to give it, unless you ask for it, my dear'. Jaya extended her hand and he dropped a small packet in it. Opening it, she found a key.

'What is this *bhaiya?*'

He said, 'It is *khulja sim sim*, come I will show you'. He led them to the porch, and there stood a glittering bright red car, decorated with ribbons. Jaya couldn't believe her eyes, she exclaimed, 'Beautiful, is it mine *bhaiya*?'

'Of course it is, go ahead.'

She hugged her *bhaiya* and *bhabi* and said, 'I can't believe it.'

Later, in the privacy of her room, Jaya took out the dresses, Kamal had sent for her and looked at them critically. She never wore a skirt and that too a short one before, and was not certain, how it would look on her. After she left school, she did not wear any dress which would expose her legs. Though she has shapely legs, without the slightest sign of hair, somehow she was shy of it. Today she must shed off her inhibition and try it in her room. She went to the mirror and undressed. Her legs were smooth, knees were not ungainly, there was no need to apply wax on her legs. There was not an inch of extra fat anywhere on her body, she had a slender waist, the envy of a model. She put on the skirt which snugly fitted her, it came out nicely around her round hips. She then, put on the shirt which came short of her hips, the collars were, however, brazen and very low cut. She whistled, it exposed the swelling of her breasts, provocatively. Perhaps the jacket would cover the same, she hoped. She put on the jacket, oh! It was a perfect fit and marvellous, it had leather linings and a matching belt, her cleavage was expertly hidden. She looked at the image in the mirror, a beautifully dressed young woman looked back at her. Out of modesty, she tried to pull down the skirt. At that moment, there was a knock at the door. She hurriedly took off the jacket and put on a gown and then went to open the door. It was Maya, she came into the room and looking over her shoulders said, 'Well, My innocent baby, what were you up to? Did you not try the dress, which our dear Kamal took the pains to send across the seven seas for our princess?' Jaya looked bewildered at her *bhabi,* exasperated, she yelled, 'I am going to wring the neck of that *Ranee ki bachhi*. Is there nothing called privacy in this house?'

* * * * *

In her new car, she was rushing towards Poona. The scenic grandeur of Western Ghats, the cascade of water falls, the rugged cliff surfaces washed by perennial streams, cluster of tourists enjoying the view from vantage points and above all the bright sunshine and the gentle breeze coming from yonder, refreshed her. She was lost in her reverie. Kamal dragged her across a stream, the cliff surface was slippery, she slipped, Kamal gathered her in his arms. Their faces were close to each other, she was breathing hard and was intoxicated by the closeness. She closed her eyes and then it happened, in the wilderness far away from the crowd, their lips met, there was a crescendo of thousand birds singing together. She must have uttered something, because the driver asked. 'Did you say something, *bibi jee?*'

She woke up with a start, 'Nothing really, let us stop somewhere for tea'. They stopped at a motel, which was filled with the usual throng of tourists. Disgusting, where ever one goes it is crowded, endless people. It reminded her of ants' colony, nose to butt lines, struggling and striving to reach somewhere. She pined for solitude, for a chunk of blue sky above and a lump of green meadow under and she, amidst the fluttering wings of butterflies of myriad colours. With difficulty, she managed to reach a table and ordered for a cup of coffee. She looked around, her eyes fell upon a person sitting at a corner table, she could'nt believe her eyes, it was Jackie. What this creature would be doing here, she wondered. Her attention was diverted as the boy brought her coffee. When she looked back again, he was not seen, he simply disappeared, strange, she must be imagining.

She was in time for lunch. Shyam *dada* cooked well and he served her, *Basmati* rice, spicy dal, vegetable curry, green salad and sweet curd for desert. She took the food and after a little rest, went to the site for attending a meeting with the architects. Tenders were evaluated and contractors were short listed. They were required to make their presentation, before finalization. At the end of the day she felt tired.

After a refreshing bath, she settled on the sofa and was scanning the news paper, when Shyam *dada* walked in, holding something in his hand, which looked like a rag doll. But a closer look stunned her, she got up with a shriek. It was the crushed body of her pet terrier 'Rosy', covered with dust and blood.

Bewildered, she wanted to know, what happened. Shyam *dada,* meekly told, that the gardner just picked her up from the road in this condition, probably she was run over by a speeding vehicle.

'Oh!Poor Rosy, why did you have to go out?', she almost wailed. Shyam *dada* pacified her. She should not have brought her here, from Bombay; it was only at *bhabi's* insistence that Rosy would keep company with her at Poona, she agreed, at the eleventh hour. She was born and brought up at home under the care of *bhabi.* Perhaps, she missed her, and ran away to meet her death. How could she break the news to *bhabi*? It would break her heart.

Shyam *dada* and the gardner took care of the body of poor Rosy and buried it near a rose bush, a rose sapling was planted on its grave. Jaya could not take her food that evening, it was hard for her to bear the loss of the pet. Affection new no boundaries and made no distinction between a human being, an animal or even a plant. Loved ones, always live in your memory. She did not have the heart to ring up *bhabi* and tell her about the sad end of Rosy. She postponed it till the next morning. Sleep did'nt come to her, easily. The moment she closed her eyes, the vision of Rosy appeared before her, jumping for a bite of a biscuit at the tea table or pulling at her dress, to go out. Suddenly she woke up, all the lights were on, she must have dozed off in the armchair with a book on her lap, she distinctly heard a scratching sound, somebody must have been at the door. it was eerie, everybody else was asleep. She sat still, who could it be, at this hour of the night, she glanced at her wrist watch, it was three o'clock. The scratching continued with a little more urgency, a weird thought crossed her mind, could it be Rosy, the *ghost* of her, coming out of its grave? She read in stories, that ghosts of pet animals did appear before their masters to warn them of impending dangers. Dismissing such absurd thoughts, she summoned courage, got up, went to the door and listened. Silence was absolute, there was no sound, then she heard it, a distinct whining of a dog, no mistake about it. Holding her breath, she opened the door with a jerk, in the dim illumination of the corridor, she saw her dear Rosy standing there waving its tail and looking at her with its beady eyes, as if asking for permission to enter. She stood there transfixed, staring at the dog. Oh! God, what could it be, an apparition or Rosy in person? Terror stricken, she called Shyam *dada*, who came running after few moments, and seeing the dog standing there, was equally puzzled.

He said, '*Bibijee,* it is our Rosy, no doubt, see the black spot behind the ear. But how could it be, we buried it just a while ago. Could it be that it was alive and came out of its grave. I have heard stories of such resurrection before.'

'Unbelievable', was the only comment Jaya could offer, she looked at the dog minutely and did not find any scratches on its body except a little mud on its paws. . Hesitatingly, she picked up the dog and it nestled her head on her shoulders. Shyam *dada* rushed out to the garden to verify his theory. He came after few minutes, crestfallen.

'*Bibijee,* the dog we buried is still there, may be it was another dog of same size and colour which Ramu mistook for Rosy and brought it home.'

'May be, it is God's Will that Rosy is alive.'

The mystery was cleared when a neighbour informed her, that his dog was missing since last evening.

* * * * *

Due to incessant rains for the past few days, streets and suburban rail tracks in Bombay were flooded. The weather was lousy. People waded through knee deep water to reach their homes and work places. Cars were seen stranded on the road. There was no respite from the rains. *Bombayiahas,* took the rains in their stride. Human beings get acclimatized to any situation, otherwise the species could not have lasted for hundreds of thousands of years. In the distant past, there was deluge, collision, causing widespread destruction, when civilizations perished, animals and plant lives were annihilated. But now, it is different. Floods, famines and fleas are no longer nature's doings, they are man's doings. It is largely due to failure of his system. In God's design of things, the system works flawlessly. It is only due to man's interference with nature, for his so called developmental activities, there is disruption. The end results are disastrous and he suffers. If you choke a drain it spills out; things like that. There is no order in man's doings. Most of the time it is counterproductive and goes against his own interest. Look at the insects, the animal world and even at the plants. They are also part of the creation. If you study their behaviour, you will find them more civilized and disciplined than their human counterpart. When man first appeared, there was not much distinction between him and animals. He lived with them and fought with them for his survival, guided only by hunger. He mated like them but the desire was insatiable. Such desire and lust whether sensual or material became the paramount guiding factor in the future development of the species. Gradually he became the master of the Universe and even forgot the Creator. He built cities and factories and also a filthy and poisonous atmosphere around him from which there was no escape. He thought, he would excel the Creator and create for himself a world free from diseases and decay, filled with man made comforts, even fragrance, colour and sound all artificial, began enthralling him. In the process he distanced himself from the Truth, from the Creator, who has all along been a silent witness because He is enshrined in his soul.

Parvati was in the *'puja'* room, absorbed in prayer. She always prayed for the welfare of all. There was a staccato sound of rain water splashing against window panes. Outside, the lawn was already under water. The house being on raised ground, it was out of reach of water. The roads served as drains and water flowed freely as permitted by their gradients. Ranee was in the kitchen and Raja sat in the lounge glued to the TV screen, listening to the weather report, such as *flood waters receding, suburban trains running,* etc. After many unsuccessful attempts, he could contact his construction foreman over telephone, he learnt that concreting of '*A' shed columns* was stopped. The pits are flooded, they are to be dewatered after rains, it will cost extra, idle labour expenses will grow. The area where the factory is constructed used to remain dry, but now it is inundated, ground level is to be increased, it would require filling and upward revision of estimates. He was so engrossed with the problem that he didn't hear Ranee, calling him to the tea table. Hot '*pakodas*' with chilli sauce, his favourite snacks, waited for him, he took his seat by the side of *'ma jee'*, suddenly the lights went out and immediately there after, there was an ear splitting sound of thunder and emergency lights came on. The darkness outside was sinister, now and then streaks of lightning could be seen. Raja went to his writing desk, Ranee to the kitchen and Parvati was left sitting at the table.

It was another day, it rained like hell. How could she forget the horrid experience of that night. She was driven out of her home by her drunken husband, who was in no mood to listen to her pitiful requests. She was on the road with her baby in her arms, hungry and forlorn, when rains came. She ran for shelter and came on to a road side house. She stood at a corner in the verandah, with rain water splashing, the street was deserted, her only companion was a street dog, which had already taken shelter there.

It lay curled up at a corner, looked up at her and then went to sleep. She rummaged through her bag, brought out a piece of a loaf, which she had hurriedly put inside, soaked it in rain water, made a pulp of it and tried to feed her baby. The baby sucked. The dog scented the food, opened its eyes and looked at her. She threw a lump of loaf at the dog, it swallowed, wagged its tail as a mark of gratitude. Then she saw in the dim light of the street lamp, a man walking down the street with wobbling steps. He came up to the verandah, tried to open the door, when his gaze fell upon her. He seemed to be focusing his eyes on her. He opened the door, went inside and switched on the lights. The verandah was now lighted. She held the baby tight in her arms and cringed at the sight.

'Oh! A woman', he said, 'why don't you come inside, you will be comfortable, you are already drenched. 'Collecting her things, she got up to leave, braving the rains, when the man caught her and almost dragged her inside. She cried out, 'Leave me alone. Let me go.' Then the dog with a snarl pounced upon the man and bit him on the leg. The man left her, shrieked with pain, went inside out of fright. Wrapping her baby in a cloth, Parvati came out in the rains and walked on, wherever fate willed to take her. The *pariah* dog followed her. She cursed her husband, from her innermost heart, at that moment, in anguish.

What all tribulations and humiliations she didn't go through, in bringing up her child, she recollected. No doubt it is a man's world. Why don't they see the mother in a woman? Why every time a man sees a woman, carnal desire swells up in his mind? She might have been forsaken by her husband, but God is with her, faith in whom has saved her from many pitfalls. Fed up with humiliations and pains of hunger, she resolved to end the miseries, once for all. Guided by impulse, she walked on the railway track blocking her mind of an approaching train, when strong arms pulled her aside, saving her and the child. The saviour was an elderly man, who took her to his house, gave shelter and food. She told him, her woe, from the beginning. The pious man, whom other inmates addressed as *swamijee*, simply said, not to lose heart, as such tribulations serve to test God's Will. The house of the *swamijee* had been transformed into a *ashram*, where other people found shelter. They had similar horrific tales to tell.

The morning in the *ashram* began with a prayer to God, usually led by *swamijee* which was followed by the day's routine. Children were put in the care of *ayahs* while their mothers worked. Nobody remained idle, the moto of the *ashram* was '*work is worhip*'.

The *ashram* grew its own vegetables, it also had a *goshala,* the milk produced was sold in the local market.

In her seven years stay in the *ashram*, Parvati found peace and tranquility reigned supreme. Kamal grew up in the congenial atmosphere of the *ashram* under the loving care and affection of *swamijee*. Inmates were encouraged to save money out of their earnings. S*wamijee* said, this will come to their aid when they leave the *ashram*.

While at the *ashram*, Parvati got a training in dress designing, her sincerity and skill drew the attention of a garment supplier of Bombay, who used to visit the *ashram* for buying children's dresses. She was offered a job in his factory at a monthly salary of rupees one thousand. *Swamijee* said, she should leave the *ashram* and take the job at Bombay, in the interest of Kamal's future. One day, with a heavy heart, she fell at the feet of *swamijee*, took leave of him and the *ashram* and came to Bombay.

While her mother worked, Kamal studied in the local school, and outshone in all the examinations, won scholarships and finally got admission in the Government College. She remembered the day, when Kamal came for taking her blessings, before he joined the college. She was not able to provide him with shoes, he wore a pair of *chapals*, with difficulty she could suppress her tears. All these years, she had no time, to think of Ratan, her husband. One of the teachings of *swamijee* was, not to waste time and energy in thinking ill of others, as it would attract only ill will and make one a cynic. He used to say, think good, then good will flow to you from all quarters.

Rains had stopped, lights had come on, Parvati tried unsuccessfully, to hide her tears, which was noticed by Ranee.

CHAPTER 4

On the other side of the world, Kamal shut off the alarm and lay awake on the bed, thinking of the day ahead. Mrs. Smith, his land lady must be now climbing up the stairs and would be at the door at any time. There was a knock at the door. He could easily set his time by her movements. She is the first person to wish him good-morning, when she brings his daily morning cup of tea and the News Paper.

'Good Morning, Mr. Kamal. How are you this morning?' This was her daily greeting.

He said, 'Good Morning, Mrs. Smith, and how is Mr. Smith?'

'Oh! Thank you, Papa is very fine, this morning. He enquired about you. By the way, Mr. Kamal, did you turn in late last night? I found lights in your room. I am sure the time must have been *two, in the morning.* I get up everyday, at that hour, to turn over Papa on his side.'

'I am sorry for being late, I had work to do. Well, I will not have my breakfast this morning. I have to leave for the lab. early.'

Since the morning tea and breakfast are included in the room rent, if he misses any of these on any day, it would amount to a little saving for the family. He knows that, they have taken him as a paying guest to get a little extra to meet the medical expenses of Mr. Smith, who was attacked with paralysis and stopped earning. These are difficult times, costs have gone high, particularly medical treatments. They are a devoted couple, Mr and Mrs Smith. Even if their resources were meager, Mrs. Smith did her best to keep her husband comfortable and well taken care of. Their children, a son and a daughter, who were already married, lived with their families separately. They never failed to visit their parents, every Sunday, alternatively; usually they would bring food packets with them and eat lunch together. American people seem to be very pragmatic in such matters. Kamal noticed, that they never imposed themselves on others. She hired a physiotherapist, for the routine exercise of Papa. He did not come for last few days, because his Bills were not paid. When he heard of this, he was pained. Taking time off from his busy schedule, he spent hours in a Library to pour on books on physiotherapy and learnt the rudiments of the subject. He tried his skill on Papa, one evening. It worked wonders, there was magic in his touch, he said. His soft touch, repeated pressures and pulls gave great relief to the old man. Whenever he found time, he sat by his side and talked to him. He came to know that he was a war veteran and regaled him with stories of his war days. His eyes would gleam in excitement, whenever he told him some of his exploits. How on the 'D-Day', when they were dropped from the aircrafts, on the shore of Normandy, his parachute carried him afar and he landed on a buffet table on a lawn amidst gaping German soldiers. Before they could realize, what happened, he freed himself and bolted into the forest, where he found others of his unit. Surprise element in the invasion routed the German army that day. The old man used to roar in laughter. After telling him the incident, he suffered from a bout of cough. The old lady came in, shook her head, looked at him disapprovingly. She gave him a glass of water to drink. Papa, thereafter, slept, exhausted.

She said, 'He would never listen to me. He must have told that story hundred times and every time, would end like this.'

Kamal said, 'You know Mrs. Smith, except for such glorified moments of his life, he has nothing left. So, please let him have those moments.'

On the previous evening, Kamal was busy in the laboratory and it was already late. Others had left for home to avoid the evening rush. He was cataloguing a queer specimen of a butterfly received recently in the laboratory, The tag said, it was from a jungle in Indonesia. As a Research Assistant his job was to examine and catalogue. He measured its wing span, antenna, etc, and noted its shape and colour. Its wing span measured to be 30 cm, a large one. He knew some of the Indonesian species to be poisonous, he tagged it accordingly. He recorded every detail meticulously. He put back the sample in the appropriate drawer and stretched his legs. His day was coming to an end. He looked at the kettle, still some black coffee was left. He decanted it into a cup. Thank God, it was still hot. He relished hot and black coffee and began sipping. He recalled his first interview with the renowned Professor Dr Howard, on his arrival at the university. His first question was, 'Mr Kamal, what is your special interest in entomology?'

'The very fact that the world's two third of over a million of organisms are insects, made me wonder about their life cycles and what influences they may be exercising on the atmosphere and on the other species, particularly the humans.'

The Professor had smiled and said, 'Any particular insect you have in mind?'

'Yes Sir, butterflies.'

'Come to think of it, that is also my special interest.'

That was how he was admitted in the semester. Already, he has completed two semesters. As a child, he learnt about nature and its bounties from his mother, who was his first teacher. His mother used to tell him stories about her wanderings in the jungle for collecting fire wood, when she was a young girl. 'Were you not afraid of the jungle, *Ma*?', he had asked. 'Why should I be, jungle is home to so many, big animals, birds, insects, trees, plants, herbs, etc. Everyone lives in harmony and there is food for everyone. They live in peace. One day, I strayed into the deep forest and saw in a clearing, a tigress with her cubs basking in the sun.'

'Oh, *Ma*, what did you do?' 'Nothing, I kept looking at the beautiful sight. I did'nt bother them, so they did'nt bother me.'

While they stayed in the *ashram,* he loved to water the plants in the garden. He smelled the wet leaves and flower buds and marvelled at the softness. He always wondered how the tiny buds blossomed into fragrant and colourful flowers. Then he saw the butterfly, it came and settled on the bud. It had multicoloured wings, they were closing and spreading. He rushed to his mother and said, '*Ma*, come to the garden, I will show you a tiny bird, sitting on a flower bud, it has colourful wings.' He had almost dragged his mother to the spot to show his discovery. But alas! The little winged creature had gone. '*Ma*, it was here a moment ago.' His mother had affectionately ruffled his hair and said, 'No *beta,* it was not a bird, it was a butterfly, it is one of the wonderful creations of the Lord.' Then, she narrated the strange story of the life of a butterfly and how it helps the mankind. Before he could lay his hands on a book of biology in his science classes, he learnt from his mother how the (*little bird*) butterfly was born. The mystery of the nature was unfolded before him. The story of eggs, caterpillar, pupa and butterfly fascinated him. How the nature through its agents transport pollens for reproduction of seeds further mystified him. What had fired the imagination of a child brought him to the beauteous world of the butterflies and further studies relating to their scaled wings and their flight dynamics, in this distant land. With the help of his Professor, he made significant progress in his studies of these migratory insects and how they cover thousands of miles across continents, the females laying eggs for the next generation during their flight. Their flight manoeuvres made significant contribution towards development of mini aerial vehicles and how the scales covering the wings are the results of million years of natural selection to provide the necessary lift during the flight at low speed. He was glad and also thankful to the Professor that he would be completing his thesis shortly.

He came out of the laboratory, the corridor was empty. All the cabins were shut, but he found the lamp glowing in front of the Director's office. He knocked, when there was no answer, he opened the door and stepped in. Nobody was present in the outer office, his secretary probably, forgot to switch off the light. He turned to go out, but on an impulse, he opened the door of the Director's chamber and stifled a cry. He found Dr. Baker slumped on the desk, with his head resting on it's top. His pen was still in his hand, he felt his pulse and raised the alarm. The security staff rushed in, ambulance was called for and he was removed to the nearest Hospital. Kamal accompanied him. He was taken to the I. C. U and after administering oxygen, his breathing became regular. Dr. Baker's wife and daughter were informed and they arrived. He recovered, in the meanwhile, and was out of danger. The attending doctor told, that he suffered from a mild stroke of angina and passed out and had he not been brought in time, it would have caused a major problem. Mrs. Baker and her daughter Dorothy, profusely thanked Kamal and expressed their gratitude for saving the life of Dr. Baker. He was kept in the I. C. U for observation, till next morning. Kamal offered to stay behind, but Mrs. Baker said, it wouldn't be necessary, since he was out of danger and she and Dorothy would be staying with him.

On the following morning, Kamal, before going to the lab, checked at the Hospital and found, Dorothy in attendance. Dr. Baker had been removed to a ward and he found him sleeping.

'They have given him a sedative', she said, 'again I must thank you Mr. Kamal, I dread to think, what would have happened to *dad*, if you had not brought him here, in time. At least that is what, the doctor said.'

'You need not thank me, it was the least I could do for the Professor. I am glad, he has recovered.'

Kamal, then related to her, how a typical specimen of a butterfly, kept him busy till late in the evening and he found her father passed out in his chamber. Even in her sorrow, she flashed a smile and said, 'whatever, you alone are instrumental in bringing my father back to his life'

Kamal said, 'Miss. Dorothy—'

'You may call me Dorothy.'

'Okay, Dorothy, I must leave now, please take care of your father. I wish him a speedy recovery' Kamal got up to leave and wished her good-bye.

Dr. Baker was already back home and convalescing. When Kamal visited him, he was in his room, resting. On seeing Kamal, he greeted him and said, 'Oh!It is you, my wife is all praises for you, young man, for all that you did for me. We are all indebted to you. You know, that day, I felt tired and as the day progressed, I felt really bad. I got this pain coming and then I must have passed out. It was really kind of you Kamal, to have taken all the trouble. You stood like an anchor for my family. They did not face such a crisis before.'

'Really, it is nothing sir, I did, what was humanly possible at that time. Anyone else in my place would have done the same thing.'

Dorothy, who came in at that moment, heard and thought, how simple and humble this person was. Dr. Baker, seeing his daughter said, 'Now that you are hear, my dear, would you please take the trouble of opening that chest of drawers and take out a folder.' She took out the folder and gave it to him.

He took out a paper from it and said, 'Kamal, it gives me pleasure to inform you, that your thesis on '*Butterflies' Flight*', have rceived recognition by the scrutinizing committee and has been forwarded to the '*select committee*'. I am confident, that you will be qualified for the '*doctorate*', soon.'

'It calls for a celebration, Kamal', Dorothy said.

'Certainly, any time.' Kamal said.

'My congratulations', Dorothy said and extended her hand. Kamal said,

'Thank you', and took her hand. It was soft and warm, it seemed that she held his hand a little too long.

Kamal visited his Director's house, regularly to enquire after his health. No doubt, he was one of his favourite students, and after the incident he became close to the family too. On many occasions, he would stay back for dinner, at their request, and later brace himself for his land lady's icy stare. Dorothy, being the only child of Baker's, was accustomed to spend her time alone, confined to her room. She had no friends. When she grew up, she was withdrawn to herself and took to sketching and painting as a hobby. When she turned eighteen, her mother worried, she never had a date with any one. She took her to parties, held in friends' houses, in the hope that she would get acquainted with boys of her age. But no, she avoided groups and spent her time with magazines on art and drawing. Mrs. Baker, helplessly watched her child cross her teens and yet did not have any boyfriend, which was unusual for girls of her age. After a time, she did not bother too much and let her grow on her own. Her experienced eyes did not, however, fail to notice that Dorothy developed a little friendship with the young Indian student, Kamal. In his presence, she noticed a gleam amounting to pleasure, in her daughter's face. Now, that meant something. One evening, she observed, Dorothy sitting close to Kamal while sipping coffee after dinner, her body touching his, a little more intimately than necessary. It confirmed her doubts that her daughter was getting attracted toward the young man. She felt sorry for her daughter and wished that she does not come to grief on that account, in future.

Dorothy was not aware of her mother's concern. In the presence of Kamal, she seemed to be lost. Her moods depended upon Kamal, being present or not. She had no experience of love. Whether it is a feeling while looking at somebody or a touch electrifying the body, she had no idea. It was natural for her to feel happy in the presence of Kamal and sad when he was not there. His casual touch while passing a dish at the dining table or sitting close pressing his body to hers on the sofa, brought her happiness and exhilaration, which she could not describe. If that is love, then she has fallen in love with Kamal. But there is something deeper than that, he stirred in her a feeling which was far different than physical, so much so, she thought that in giving, there was more pleasure. One Sunday, she invited Kamal for lunch at home, while her parents were gone to attend the *mass* in the local church. That day, Kamal was to present a paper in his Department and with difficulty, he could manage to squeeze an hour in between to accommodate Dorothy's invitation. She had made elaborate arrangements for entertaining her guest, fresh flowers had been put in the vases, choice dishes were ordered to his liking, the table was set for two, laid with the finest crockery and cutlery, available in the house. It pained her, however, to notice, that Kamal had no eyes for her arrangements, when he arrived at her house and in a matter of fact tone, announced that he had to leave immediately for presenting his paper. This infuriated her and shocked Kamal at her outburst, which was totally unexpected.

She burst out, 'Kamal, don't you have any consideration for other's feelings and sentiments? How can you be so rude?' Then, she burst into tears.

Kamal said, 'I am sorry, Dorothy, I did'nt mean to hurt you. I am really sorry.'

'Believe me Kamal, I did'nt expect that you would be busy, on a Sunday. I thought we would be able to spend some time together. You know, I cannot talk to you freely when *dad* and *mom* are here. Don't you like my arrangements, this is the first time, I am entertaining someone.'

'Of course, Dorothy, I am honoured, your arrangements are excellent. It was foolish and thoughtless of me not to have noticed the same. You need not have gone into so much trouble. I am a man of simple habits and a plain meal would have suited me. Do you know cooking? You could have cooked something, I would have liked.'

'Really, cooking is my second hobby, let us settle for next Sunday. We will have some special dishes.'

'That is excellent, but what is your first hobby?'

'Drawing sketches.'

'Excellent. May I see some of them?'

'Why not, come, it is in upstairs'. She almost dragged him and led him to her room.

'You must excuse me, I am not good at housekeeping'. Her bed was not made, everywhere there were piles of books. She cleared a chair and asked Kamal to sit. She went to a closet and took out a roll of drawings and tried to spread them on the bed. Kamal noticed that they were all pencil sketches, mostly of trees, birds and a distant water spread. Then, he looked outside through the open window, all the subjects of her sketches were present, she had captured them all, without missing any details, even the birds' nests. Turning from the window, he said, 'Wonderful, marvellous!'

He added, 'How minute is your observation Dorothy, simply breath taking, my congratulations.' He took her hand and shook it warmly. To her, it was a sincere recognition, from Kamal. His gaze then fell at the easle and at the sketch pinned there to. Reaching there, Kamal stared, unbelievable, he was looking at a sketch of his own face, though unfinished, the drawing brought out one of his moods, superbly.

Impulsively, he said, 'Dorothy, would you present it to me, when it is done, I want to send it home.' She shook her head vigorously and said vehemently, 'No—I cannot give it away, it is mine.' Kamal was startled at such an outburst over a drawing and said, 'Ofcourse it is yours, I'll not take it away from you. I know how an artist feels for her creation, but I must tell you Dorothy, it is a masterpiece. Your sketch seems to have caught me in one of my rarest moods, that is how I must be appearing before others' eyes. It is really revealing.' Though, she was looking at him with unblinking eyes, she was far away and did not listen to what he said. She was lost in the depth of his eyes trying to listen to his heart beats.

Kamal shook her back to the present and said' Hello! Where are you? Come let's go, now I'll have to rush.'

'But not before you have your lunch', holding each other's hand and laughing, they came down. She pushed him down to a chair at the table and said, 'Now, you sit here, like a good boy while, I warm the soup.'

As she turned to go, Kamal holding her hand, said, 'Okay ma'm, at your command.'

Moments after he left, Dorothy felt the warmth and sincerity of his touch, and was so engrossed in her thoughts that she never knew, how time passed till, the key turned at the door and her parents walked in.

* * * * *

In his last letter, posted to his mother, Kamal enclosed one photograph of Bakers, narrating, how he got acquainted with the family. Ranee snatched the photograph and viewing it, said, '*Ma jee*, the young girl must be their daughter and not married.'

'Is she not a sweet girl, *beti* ? I have heard that girls in Western countries are very beautiful, and this one is so charming. Kamal has written that his Professor, under whom he is doing research, has been very kind to him and specially after the incident, the family have warmed up to him.'

'Oh! *Ma jee*, that is where our trouble lies. These *gori chamdi wallis* are very assertive and I have heard from *choti ma* that they do not have any scruples and know the art of ensnaring young handsome men. And our Kamal, who has not seen much of the world and so innocent and simple, that before he knows, he will fall under her charm.'

'Oh! *Bitiya*, you are unnecessarily worrying, do I not know my Kamal? He would not do any such thing, that would make his mother unhappy.'

Ranee was not satisfied with *Ma jee's* viewpoint. She had another look at the photograph and this time more closely. While her parents wore formal dresses, the girl, who was in prime of her youth wore tight fitting dresses, which showcased her body. It did'nt look proper and decent in her eyes. A woman's figure is only for her husband's eyes. It is not to be displayed. She considered it vulgar and disgraceful. For a moment she imagined, dressed up in such tight fitting clothes, how she would look, she shuddered to think. Her closely guarded posterior and bosoms would be offensively exposed. Something must be done to save Kamal from this irresistible *siren*. A thorn for a thorn, she decided. She rummaged through her drawer, till she came across a reasonably good snapshot of Jaya, in a gorgeous *salwar suit*, which was probably taken on the occasion of her previous birthday. She looked charming. A domestic dose of beauty might be the remedy for that fool of a Kamal, if he is infatuated with the foreign brand. She posted the photograph along with a letter from *Ma jee*, she did'nt forget to put an inscription at the bottom corner of the photograph, *'with love, Jaya'*.

* * * * *

The letter reached Kamal duly, he was pleased and kept it aside unopened, to read at his leasure at home. It was a hectic day and he reached home late in the night and went to sleep straight away. The letter remained unopened.

Next morning, he left with Dorothy for Niagara Falls. In fact, after a month of long persuation, she could convince Kamal that it is one of the rarest sights on earth and it must be seen to be believed. She told him that, he would come across swarms of butterflies of rarest varities on their way. That had clinched the issue. They decided to travel by road from Connecticut to Niagara falls, a distance of four hundred miles.

Dorothy was an excellent driver, he noted. Her poise and humour, pleased him. He admired her knowledge on varied subjects. She could talk endlessly on insects found in tropical countries. Little did he know, that being a Librarian, she had easy access to Reference Books on almost all subjects. They stopped at various places for food and drinks. Kamal was in an exhilarating mood, throughout. The cross country drive, views of trees, meadows. grazing cattle whizzing by, the curly auburn hair of Dorothy caressing his face, not only took his mind off from scientific quests but brought him nearer to nature. For the first time he saw bare nature as it is and not through prints. The creation and its splendour struck him. As the car climbed up and up from the plains, the roaring sound of the Falls reached his ears from a distance.

He was so enthralled that he wanted to share his joy with her, who concentrated at the moment in negotiating a hair pin bend. Impulsively, he hugged and kissed her. Caught unawares, she almost threw the car out of control, but regained it in a moment and steadied. She was about to shout at Kamal for his foolish outburst, but checked herself. She cast a glance at him slyly, her face reddened, adrenelin pumping into her. Kamal was his old self, pointing toward a phalanx of red and black butterflies swarming across a bed of flowers. He semed to be in ecstasy. To Dorothy, however, his enchantment for such things appeared out of place. Does he not feel her closeness, does his heart not beat in rhythm with her? His aloofness dampened her spirit, tears welled up in her eyes. She concentrated on her driving.

They arrived at the Falls at sun set and checked into a Hotel. They were allotted adjoining rooms. The first thing Kamal did was to open the windows facing the Falls. The world's greatest spectacle of nature was indeed awe inspiring and he remained mesmerized for few moments. Dorothy joined him after unpacking her bags and standing by his side, said, 'Wonderful is'nt it? I told you, unless you see it yourself, you cannot realize, what it is. I know people, who were in trance for hours, looking at the sight.' 'Perhaps I am going to enrich that list', Kamal said.

She entwined her hand with Kamal's, leaned on his shoulders and closed her eyes. She found herself and Kamal engulfed in white clouds in the blue sky, floating across the Falls, higher and higher. Suddenly they lost height and fell into oblivion. She shrieked. Kamal shook her, she gripped him tightly pointing toward the Falls.

'What happened? Did you see something terrifying over there?'

Disengaging herself she said, 'It is nothing, may be I saw an illusion. You get ready, we will go down for dinner.'

'Okay, take care', he said.

Kamal removed his jacket and while putting it on a chair, the letter, which he had put aside in the pocket, dropped. Seeing the letter, he exclaims, 'Oh! My God, it is my mother's letter.' He slits open the envelope and while taking out the letter, the enclosed photograph slips through his fingers and falls down. Dorothy, on her exit saw it and said, 'Kamal, you have dropped something.' Kamal stooped down and picked it up. He looks at it and a smile crosses his lips. Dorothy drew nearer, to have a better look and saw a picture of a beautiful young woman, wearing a marvellous dress, which accentuated her figure.

She exclaimed, 'Oh! What a beauty! Are all Indian girls as beautiful as she?'

Kamal said, 'I cannot say. I know only this girl.'

'Who is she ?'

'She is Jaya', Kamal said and he looked at the photograph with such intensity and fondness that it was hard for Dorothy not to interpret it as love. Her heart missed a beat, blood drained from her face and before she could give away herself, she rushed out of the room, Kamal stood there perplexed. She locked herslf in the room and sat on the bed, crestfallen. He has his love, back home and, therefore, has no place for her in his heart, she was certain. Her foundation of love, collapsed before her eyes. She realized, how deeply she was in love with him. He was her first love and may be the last. She could imagine how hard it would be for her, to live without him. She was lost and felt like a boat in the heaving sea, without a rudder. Oh! God!Why her heart was carried away, when her gaze fell upon him, the first time? She did not know, that love would be so much demanding and painful. In the beginning, she felt obliged to him because he was instrumental in saving the life of her father and treated him as a friend in need. Later in the days followed, she felt an odd attraction toward him, which she never experienced before, for any other being. He seemed to pervade her world. She missed every second of his absence. His absence weighed on her heavily. She was so much deeply in love with him, that she did not bother to know whether he felt as much for her. She began translating every word of his, every gesture of his, every innocent and childlike touch of his, as his response. As a matter of fact, she planned the trip to Niagara Falls to propose to him.

There was a knock at the door, she dubbed her face with a powder puff and went to open the door.

* * * * *

It was a sunny morning in Bombay, after the rains. The morning crowds rushed to catch their trains. Auto rickshas honked their way, making people to jump to sides to save themselves from a mud bath.

The city came to life. The misery of wading through knee deep water, of seeing human wastes floating along cooking vessels over the *'bustee'* areas, the abject misery of remaining without cooked food for days, were already forgotten. That is the adaptability of the populace in this country. The Government have drawn a line dividing them from others; it is BPL (below poverty line). They are poorer than poor and figure in hundreds of millions for statistical needs and PDS (public distribution system). Floods will come and then recede no doubt, not through any human endeavour, but naturally due to cessation of rains and gradual opening of river mouths. Before the next flood comes, the '*soda bottle enthusiasim*' dies down, lethargy and complacency would set in and people including the Governmeent, instead of learning any lesson from the previous flood havocks, would simply be absorbed in routine administrative matters, arrange workshops for discussing means to mitigate natural disasters and may be, set up a few task forces to draw short term and long term plans for river valley projects, strengthening embankments, improvement of drainage in urban areas etc. These reports along with the earlier ones would remain shelved in Government departmrnts, gathering dust due to want of funds or shifting of priorities. Suffering of people due to floods remain unmitigated and recur seasonally, every year.

A lone woman holding a child in her arms comes out of a *bustee* on to the road. She stands, looking furtively hither and thither before she joins a long queue of relief seekers. These people have lost their home and hearth in the floods. The woman with the child silently moves forward in the queue till she reaches the counter, where daily quota of cooked rice and *dal* were distributed through Government agencies as relief measures. Behind the counter, on the floor were arranged rows of large alluminium vessels containg steaming rice and *dal.* The queue was orderly, persons, one by one, approached, put their pans on the counter and volunteers doled out a cup of rice and a ladle of *dal* to each of them. The queue moved on.

Now it is the woman's turn. Holding the child in her left arm, she puts the pans on the counter. The woman behind protests, that she cannot be allowed to take food in two pans, while others have brought only one. The woman with the child was being virtually pushed out of the line, hearing the hue and cry, the lady in charge of the relief kitchen came out to enquire. She saw a pitiable sight, the woman's clothes were dirty and torn, her hair untidy, her eyes red and full of tears and the baby in her arm looked hungry. She motioned her to come inside through a side entrance. She learned, that the woman could not come to the relief center on the previous day, as she was laid down with fever. Both the mother and the child did not have any food since yesterday.

Tears swelled in Seema's eyes after listening to the tale of woe and misery of the poor woman. She asked the woman to sit in a corner and served them food herself, the child barely three years old looked on with his round and listless eyes innocently. Seema controlled her tears and turned away her face.

In the little child's face, Seema could see her younger brother crawling beside his mother, little knowing that she was already dead. It was another time; she had gone to visit her ailing stepmother and it was too late. The helpless woman, who had not seen nineteen springs in her life, lay there dead. Her father married this young girl and brought her home, after the death of her mother. Later she heard, that her father met with an accident and succumbed to the injuries in the Hospital. She had rushed to the village and found her step mother in a most pitiable condition. Not only she was anaemic, but she was pregnant too. Instead of grief and bereavement for the loss of her father, she was overcome by a sense of strong resentment and bitterness for the grave injustice commited by her father towards this poor girl. After completion of the last rites for her father, as demanded by traditions and customs, she put her stepmother under the care of an elderly auntee, whom she had given some money for expenses and had left the village. And now this pathetic sight unsettled her. She gathered her baby brother in her arms and left the village for good, after completion of the funeral rites of her step mother. That was three years ago. Now Gopal, her step brother is four years old and calls her '*Ma*'

In the beginning, she found it really hard to rear a child, especially while she studied. Had it not been for *moussijee*, who worked in the Ladie's Hostel and stayed in the compound, she would have been forced to leave the baby in an orphanage. *Mousijee*, became so very attached to the child, that when Seema got the job of a teachership, she left her Hostel job and came away with her. Since then, she has been with her and has taken full responsibility of the child.

* * * * *

Raja and Ranee decided to celebrate their second marriage anniversary, some where outside, at a Hill Station. It was at the insistence of Ram Gopal jee, that Raja ultimately agreed to plan for the visit. Progress of the construction of the new factory was satisfactory and *babujee* said, he had been toiling hard for the Project and it is time that he should take few days' leave and go on a holiday, he saw a twinkle in his eyes, he blushed. When he broke the news to Ranee, she was over joyed. She has never been out of Bombay, after shifting from Calcutta. Further, when she learnt that they are to take a flight from Bombay to Delhi, she became apprehensive, what if something happens in the mid air and the plane falls down lika a *kati patang*. This would be her maiden air journey, she did'nt want to share her apprehension with others lest they may stamp her as a *dehati.* Raja knew, as they walked down the tarmac, to board the plane, that she must be chanting *Hanuman Slokas'* for their safety, he took her hand in his and pressed. She looked up and there was concern in her eyes, he gave her a smile of assuarance. Once aboard, Ranee was thrilled. The *apsara* like airhostesses guiding them to their seats with charming smiles, offering them, a little while later, chocolates, and above all, the cool fragrant atmosphere of the cabin, made her feel as if she was in a different world. When she saw Raja, fastening the belt, she asked, what was that for?

Raja said, 'These are safety belts for passengers' safety to avoid possible injury during take off and landing of the aircraft'. He showed her how to fasten the belt. When the aircraft speeded up and took off, Ranee got frightened and held on to her husband. The land slipping away and the plane suddenly rising above the ground made her head swirl. But after some time the plane levelled and everything became quiet. She could not hear anything, Raja asked her to take off the cotton from her ears.

'Is this thing not moving?', she asked.

'Yes, it is travelling at a tremendous speed, may be three to four hundred kilometers per hour. It is not like a motor car or a train travelling past trees and fields, to get the feel of speed. The plane moves in the sky.'

'How wonderful', she squeezes Raja's hand and looks at him with deep love and affection in her eyes. She leaned on his soulders and closed her eyes.

They landed at Delhi Airport. It was warmer. The Hotel where they were to stay, while at Delhi, was very luxurious and it was her first experience of staying in a Hotel. Being a *bustee* belle, born and brought up in an atmosphere far from comforts and luxury, the air conditioned hotel appeared to her as heaven. The bellboy led them to their suite and depositihg their bags, closed the door behind them. They were now left alone. Ranee never felt before, the surge of passion, so much as of now. Out of her own volition, which she never experienced before, she hugged her husband with all intensity. Caught suddenly in her embrace, Raja fell down on the bed, with his wife on top. She did not give time to Raja to collect and react. She kissed him fiercely and then tenderly, all over his face and buried her face on his chest, her arms holding him tight. He took her in his strong arms and said, 'Oh! My darling, how sweet you are! What is in your mind?' She must have felt the urge of passion in her husband and wanted to extricate herself from his arms. But, no, his grip over her, tightened.

Ranee said at, last, 'Listen, there is a knock at the door', Raja's grip loosens and Ranee wriggles out and gets up.

'See what you have done, you have spoiled my clothes.'

'What of that, we have to change our clothes, before we go down for dinner.'

Raja opens the bag and takes out a saree for his wife, 'You wear this one, tonight. You would look marvellous in this.'

'Oh! What a beautiful saree, it looks expensive. It was not there, when I packed the bag.'

She went to the mirror and began to take off her clothes.

'Not here my lady, there is a dressing room over there and the wash room behind the curtain. Or do you prefer, that I should assist you in changing your clothes?'

'You naughty fellow, wait for the night. I will see you then, I am going to teach you a lesson or two,' she said mischievously and picking her new saree, she left for the wash room. Raja shook his head and blew a kiss to her.

While she dressed, he sat on the bed contemplating. He was very fond of his wife. She stood by him, in his difficult days as an anchor rock. When he was a desperado, chased by Police, it was she who came to his assistance and provided shelter in her *jhumpdi*. How could he ever forget that night when the bullet missed him by a fraction of an inch, which otherwise would have finished off his hand for good. She nursed his wound, gave him food and shelter.

He was deeply lost in his thoughts, when Ranee came out of the dressing room, fresh and looking gorgeous in her new saree. Raja looked at her in wonder. She looked like a fairy without wings and yet appeared to be floating across the room erffortlessly. He rushed to catch her, Ranee rushes to the door and opened it.

* * * * *

Later in the night, when they were in bed lying in close embrace with no barrier in between, their bodies warm and sweaty, with fulfilment and contentment written all over their faces, they snuggled to each other and tried to get few winks of sleep in the wee hours of the morning.

* * * * *

Jaya's rapport with the team of experts of her esteemed client was so well, that none of her recommendations or suggestions were ever rejected or even modified. It worked both ways. She, however, respectfully paid attention to the boss's comments. The work progressed well, with such mutual faith and admiration. The boss wanted nothing less than best. She, therefore, gave personal attention to every bit of work, however minor it was. She had to stay at site till late in the evenings.

One evening, Raja arrived at the farm house of Ram Gopal and learnt from Shyam *dada*, that *bibijee* had not yet returned. While he was having tea in the lounge, Jaya's car entered the driveway. She parked the car under the porch and came out. Her hair was dishevelled and her face was ashen, as if she had seen a ghost.

Seeing Raja, she exclaimed, 'Oh! Raja *bhaya*. when did you come? I am a bit late today'. Raja noted, that her voice was not steady. He said, 'It is alright Jaya, but is anything wrong, you look so pale?'

'No it is nothing except that I am bit tired, the day was strenuous.' She slumped onto a chair and gulped some water.

Raja and Shyam *dada* exchanged glances, with concern showing in their faces. They were certain, that she was hiding something.

Jaya debated in the meanwhile, whether she should tell them or not about her experience in the evening. Was it an illusion? The illusion or whatever it is, occurred while she was packing her things in her bag and getting ready to leave at the end of the day, as usual. Others had already left, and she was practically alone in the mansion. She had this feeling, which she never had before. At first, she wanted to brush away the thought as nonsense. What if, this big house, which was closed for almost two decades, was a haunted one. She is a brave girl and belongs to modern school of thoughts and the common belief that ghosts and spirits prefer to stay in old and uninhabited premises did not make any sense to her. One moment, her mind struggled against two extremes, the next moment, she heard the eeri voice coming from the space, piercing the graveyard silence of the house, '*Get out of my house, you intruders*.' Then she heard sound of foot steps dying out. She felt lifeless for a moment and stood still, completely unnerved. She rushed out and fetched the guards. She enquired, whether they saw anyone entering the Hall a little while ago.

'No, Ma'm', they said.

Raja had been observing Jaya, all the while. Her silence and puckered face disturbed him deeply.

'What is the matter Jaya, did you hear or see something srange?'

Composing herself, she related the entire events without omitting any details.

'Now, tell me, *bhaya*, could it be my imagination or something else?'

"Well, it could be an imagination of an over stressed mind. You don't know what the mind is capable of. I would suggest, you better take it easy and give your mind a rest, every thing will be fine. Now, Jaya, let me take leave, I have to reach home early.'

After he leaves, she sits with a cup of coffee and contemplates. She could not help her mind wandering over the idea that the house might be a haunted one. In that case the voice, which she heard, must belong to the original owner, who is dead long since and forgotten by others. Now, she lets her imagination run amok. The Hall is bustling with guests celebrating someone's birthday may be the rich man's daughter's. Waiters moving around with trays of food and drinks, and every one enjoying the occasion, suddenly the lights went out and a gun shot was heard, some one screamed. Lights come on accompanied with more screamings. To everybody's horror, the host's body was seen lying on the floor in a pool of blood, riddled with bullets. Then a young girl comes running, claspes the lifeless body of her father and wails. It is so pathetic. Suddenly there is a ripple in her mental plane and the vision disappears.

Shyam '*dada'* was telling her something, '*Bibijee* your coffee is getting cold. You have not touched it.'

'Oh! I did'nt notice it. Let it be, please serve dinner *kaka*, I will be ready in a minute.'

She could not sleep well that night. The weird voice and sound of the retreating foot steps, still haunted her.

In the morning she got up tired and exhausted. Her reflection in the mirror showed dark rings around her eyes. She splashed cold water on her face and went out to the garden for a walk. She noticed a fluttering butterfly over the flowers. How care free it was. Image of Kamal, suddenly crossed her mind. He would have chased the butterfly in gay abandon. It brought laughter to her. Yes, that is her Kamal, always running after bees and insects. Then a funny idea came to her mind, should he be running after girls? No, no, he is better off as he is. Girls did'nt interest him. Ma jee, once told her a funny incident of his childhood. Kamal, who was ten years old then, came running home weeping, from the school, one day. Komal, a sweet little girl with a round face and braided hair, was his friend. She always sat by his side, in the class room. Whenever the teacher asked her any question, Kamal would write the answer boldely in her note book and she would repeat the same. The girl was shrewd and brought presents such as chocolates, colour pencils etc, for Kamal, in return. One day, however, the girl was not so lucky. The teacher asked her, 'How many colours are there in a rainbow?' By force of habit, Komal looked down at her copy book, she found written, 'seven of course, you fool.' The girl repeated the same to the chagrin of the teacher and the entire class roared with laughter. For her affront, Komal was asked to squat outside the class room for an hour, as punishment. The girl did not take this kindly and remained in search for an opportunity to pay back Kamal, who did not suspect of her intention. One day, she got the opportunity. While playing outside, Kamal showed her a prize toad, which he picked up from a drain and concealed it in a round tin box. It was really ugly and frightening to look at. Komal had a plan. After the play hour, they walked back to the class room and took their seats. As the teacher ma'm entered, Komal kicked the tin box containing the frog, and it rolled down towards the teacher. Kamal rushed to pick it up, seeing that Kamal was running after something, she shouted at him, 'Kamal what is that you are running after?'

'It is nothing ma'm', he said innocently and was about to return to his seat, the teacher got angry and said, 'Come on, give it to me.'

Kamal had no choice but to give it to her. In exasperation, she opens it and a big frog leapes out of it and lands on the shoulders of the teacher, who shriecked in terror and brushed it off. The frog then took another leap and landed on the desk in front of a student, who shrieked and stood up on the chair. There was pandemonium in the class room for a while. The teacher, in a fit of anger, slapped Kamal and asked him to leave the class. Remembering the younger days of Kamal made her heart lighter. She felt the urge for hearing about him and also to see Ranee.

On the following morning, she left for Bombay and arrived at Raja *bhaiya's* place. They were all pleased to see her, in particular Ranee, who had a lot to tell about her holiday trip. *Ma jee* took Jaya in her arms and blessed her. Then she left for her *puja* leaving the young women together. Both of them sped to upstairs to talk to their heart's content.

Ranee lost no time to show her, the family photo of the American professor, which Kamal had posted.

"Beautiful is'nt she?"

'Yes', Jaya said and pouted her lips.

'But you need not worry my dear, I have taken care of that. Lest our hero feels lonely and inclined to pay attention to the American beauty, I dispatched to him, one of your best photographs in a striking pose."

'Don't you worry Ranee, I have full confidence in my Kamal, he would be a cold blooded creature to anybody else. With one or two tries they would give up.'

'You can never tell with these *gori chamdi wallis'*, she grimaced.

'Now, you tell me, Raneejee, how was your honeymoon trip. I am dying to hear from you.'

Like a new bride, she blushed and said coyly, 'Oh! Jaya, I am not that young any more.'

'Ranee, may I ask you something, when you are alone with Raja *bhaiya,* what do you talk about?

'I thought you college girls are more educated in such matters. You read novels, romances and what not, to teach you everything about love. What more do you want to know ?'

'How do you know all these, Raja *bhaiya* is your tutor and he is feeding you with a lot of romantic talks, I am sure. Or else how can you talk about novels and romances. Now the cat is out of the bag. You must tell me, what you have learnt in this trip?' She tickled Ranee till she laughed.

Suppressing her laughter she said, 'Really Jaya you are getting naughtier and naughtier and I took you to be the studious type, always immersed in books with no interest in the outside world, the innocent baby of *bhabi jee* and *babu jee.* You want to learn something? Come, I will tell you.' She pulled Jaya nearer and whispered something in her ears. Jaya 's face coloured and she covered her face with her hands. Ranee tickled her till she doubled up in bouts of laughter.

'You want to know something more ?'

'No, no, please let me go.'

'Okay, but not before I give you something.'

She brought out from her bag a beautiful photo frame with wood carvings and said, 'This is for you.' To make the gift meaningful, Ranee had inserted a recent photo of Kamal sent by him from America.

Ranee said, 'Does he not look cute in that sweater?'

'Thank you, for your wonderful gift.' She hugged Ranee.

* * * * *

The property where Jaya worked not only had a formidable fence all around, but it also had a thick growth of ivy, all along the fence, which with its thick leaves completely shut off the inside view of the property from public view. Boards were put up with letters in bold, *'Keep Off, Private Property'*, at regular intervals, all along the fence. With such forceful preventive measures, Jaya thought, it would be almost impossible for any outsider to trespass. She also toyed with the idea, for some time, that it might be an inside job, if no credence is given to the ghost theory. She had in front of her, on his desk, the plan of the house and also of the basement, spread out. It was in three sheets, one for the basement, one for the ground floor and one for the first floor. She concentrated on the basement plan. There were two gradients, one at each end leading to the ground floor, one for the entry and the other for the exit. Referring to the sections, she found that it was an interesting combination of arches and columns, as in old bridges. That was reasonable, at that time reinforced cement concrete structures were not designed. The architects had to contend with brick columns and arches. That fixed the year of construction to 1930 or there about. Besides the parking space for vehicles, some space was marked for storage; in a corner, however, she noticed steps were shown leading further down. A cellar? She marked it with red and decided to inspect the same at the earliest opportunity, unobtrusively, of course.

The works progressd satisfactorily and were nearing completion. Her plan was to progress in all floors and prepare modules to be fitted in such a manner as to conform to the ultimate design and shape. A separate team was assigned to monitor and report slacks, if any. Till now she had not met the employer. Well, she thought, how does it matter? It may be a partnership or a company, payment to staff and suppliers were regular and nobody complained. The employees were a disciplined lot and normally did not cause any trouble.

Salvador, a Goan, was, however, different from others. He could never stay away for more than an hour, from his dear *bottli,* which he carried with him always. Consequently, he remained drunk most of the time. Twice he was warned. His favourite recess, where he would lie drunk unnoticed, was in a corner in the basement, from where steps led down to the cellar, which was always closed. That was the place which exactly fascinated Jaya. It was mere coincidence that when Jaya visited the basement, assuming the place to be deserted at that hour, she found to her surprise, the place to have been occupied by a person, who lay there drunk. She stepped back hastily and left the place.

On the following day, while she was in the office, a person came to see her introducing himself as Salvador, one of her workers. He had a strange story to tell.

He said, 'Madam, I may be excused for telling this, which may appear to be absurd to you. I am now in my perfect senses. Last evening, I beg your excuse, I got drunk and slept off in a corner in the basement. When I woke up, it was absolutely dark and then I remembered, that I must have slept in the basement. I was trying to sit up, when I heard a weird sound coming out of the cellar nearby, which was always locked. Before I could collect my thoughts, I heard distinct sound of footsteps approaching me and suddenly I felt a chill wind blowing over me. The sound of footsteps died down. I got up shivering and sweating. I didn't move out till day break. At the first day light, I rushed to the garden fountain and took a plunge in the pond. The cold water brought life to my nerves. I tell you ma'm, I was never more terrified in my life. I am not sure whether it was a dream or something else.'

Jaya listened to this account with alacrity. So this was the man, she encountered at the entrance of the cellar, last evening.

'Did you tell this to anybody?'

'No, ma, m.'

'Well, then, forget it and do not spread this story among others, if you want to keep your job.'

'Thank you, ma'm; , he said and left the office.

Jaya sat still for some time, after he left She was now certain, that two different persons, at different times, could not have had frightful dreams of similar nature. The cellar seemed to be shrouded in mystery. There may be two possibilities, she reasoned. One, there are people who do not want the work to go on and are bent upon to drive them out by frightening them out of their wits. Two, the place is haunted and there is a ghost, who is freely moving about. She must unravel the secret of the cellar. But how? It is definitely not a girl's job. Who knows, what dangers may be lurking behind. She must tell this to Raja and take him into confidence. She called him over telephone and apprised him of the recent developments regarding the cellar. After hearng her story, he told her, not to worry and that he would be reaching Poona on the following day, which is a Sunday, when they would discuss the matter, in all details.

Now that, she unburdened her mind, she felt relieved and busied herself in the works. She did not go home for lunch. She ordered soup and sandwiches from the site canteen and sat through the afternoon, in her office, gazing at the *Plan* of the house. The more she contemplated, the more the mystery got deepened. Ghosts exist in stories, she couldn't come to terms in believing that there might be a ghost in this house and that too trampling people in their sleep. Alternatively, it might be hallucination, which can't be ruled out. Human mind is capable of conjuring things out of nothing. She has read about *yogis,* who could conjure up fragrance in the air belonging to any flower, one wishes. Satya Sai Baba of recent times is said to produce hot metal out of air by twist of his fingers. But, they are all *yogis*. Such thoughts served, only to cloud her mind.

Raja arrived in the afternoon and in the privacy of her room they discussed at length about the probable cause of such weird occurrences. The cellar held the key to the mystery of foot steps; it was clear to them. A visit to the cellar alone, would solve the mystery, they concluded. After dinner, therefore, they arrived at the basement for their secret operation. In the dim light and enveloping darkness and silence, the basement looked eerie. They were equipped with a torch and Jaya had collected a bunch of old keys from the care taker, a day before.

The door to the cellar was heavy and it took some time for Raja to open it. Inside, it was pitch dark, Raja focused the torch and they saw a flight of steps leading down to the cellar from the basement. Why this was not depicted in the sketch of the Plan, Jaya had no clue. Probably this was an afterthought of the owner, after the drawings were finalised. They located a switch board on the wall by the side of the door, but the switch, when put on, did not light up any things inside. They had no alrenative but to depend on the flash light they carried, for their mission. Little did they know, that all of their movements were watched by a third person who hid himself, behind a column in the basement.

They entered the cellar, the air was foul, probably there was no ventilation. Raja, holding the torch moved ahead, asking Jaya to follow.

The smell was typical of a ware house lying closed for long. Raja focused the torch down and saw a big rat near a box staring at them. Rats will be there of course, they feed on insects and cockroaches. Lots of rags and damp clothes were there, for them to multiply, he said. One rat even dared to nibble the foot of Jaya, who screamed. A row of steel trunks and wooden chests were found lined up on the floor, leaving space in between, through which they now moved forward. The boxes were not locked. Jaya held the torch, while Raja opened the lid of a large wooden chest, inside they found all sorts of household materials, such as brass ware, kitchenware, miscellaneous hardwares, etc. In one box they found rolls of carpets, rugs, curtains, etc. Expensive looking furnitures (period) were dumped in a corner, all draped in white sheets. After crossing the array of chests, they reached the other end of the cellar, where a large cloth covered object, which looked like a framed photograph or painting rested on the floor. Raja was about to remove the shroud, when Jaya stopped him and drew his attention to the floor where the object rested, with horror written on her face. What they found, chilled their hearts. Clear foot prints were marked on the dust ridden surface, as if some one stood there, a while ago. They looked at each other, Raja focused the torch a little further up along the way they traversed. The dust carried only two pairs of foot prints. Silence fell heavily upon them. More horror was in store for them when Raja pulled down the cloth cover from the framed object. A shrieck escaped from Jaya and Raja gaped at the portrait from which blood seemed to be dripping. Under the glare of the torch the portrait looked awesome. It was an oil painting of an elderly man, fifty years of age probably, done in a standing posture. The subject wore a three piece suit, perfectly tailored, holding a walking stick in his hand. The immaculate suit was blood stained, his head smashed, oozing blood. The eyes were bloodshot and lifeless. The picture was ghastly. Who could have painted such a monstrosity?

Unbelievable! Jaya spotted at the rightside bottom corner, something written. It *was 'Seth Mohan Lal/ 19th August 1945'*. Then suddenly, there was a chill wind blowing over them and a distinct sound of foot steps were heard approaching them, *thuk thuk, thuck*, the torch slipped from the hand of Raja and the light went out. The place was plunged in thick darkness, Jaya groped for Raja's hand and held it tight. No more sound of foot steps. Raja groped and got the torch, it worked, there was light. In the light, what they saw, completely baffled them. The painting, now they saw, was of a middle aged person of noble bearing, beaming with smile. The ghastly looking person with blood stained clothes had vanished. What sort of tricks they were subject to? The silence and the enveloping darkness were too much to bear. They made a hasty retreat and reached the door. They came out and locked the door. Without any further exchange of words, Raja and Jaya returned home. A pair of eyes was following Jaya's movements, till her car went out of the gate.

Reaching home, they discussed. May be they fell victims to some sort of hallucination. But, other causes, however absurd they may look, were not ruled out. They weaved a story around the mysterious portrait, which seemed to be the focal point of the strange occurrences. Obviously it belonged to the owner of the building, Seth Mohan Lal, whose name was inscribed in the painting itself. The building, from the style of architecture and furniture found in the cellar, appeared to be fifty years old. It was reasonable, for them to assume that, Seth Mohan Lal was no more and the property must have passed on to his successors. Here, their reasoning stopped, The building was left, unoccupied for long and stripped of all furnishings, furniture and other household materials to be stacked in a cellar, all these years, why?There was no plausible answer to that question.

Jaya talked, Raja kept quiet and listened. After a while, Raja said, 'However incredible it may seem, Jaya, there is some supernatural force, involved in this, which we cannot ignore. If you combine all the occurrences, to which three persons are witnesses, it is pointing to one conclusion, that is, someone is trying to tell us something. Take the portrait, for example. Suddenly, it appears to wear a death mask, blood oozing out from the face, which means the person might have died in an accident out of head injuries. Then it is transformed into a normal portrait of a noble man with a benign smile. The foot prints end near the portrait. Whether we believe it or not, the spirit or whatever it is, resides in the portrait. It steps down from its regal throne and wanders, hither and thither in the night.'

Jaya said, 'We may safely guess, Raja *bhaiya* that Seth Mohan Lal was a rich and a popular person of his time. The painting was done in 1945, almost thirty years before, and I guess, from the condition of the house that it has been left unoccupied for the last twenty years or so. In which case we may limit our searches to the period 1945 to 1955.'

'Wonderful, my dear Miss Sherlock Holmes. I can guess what would be your next port of calling.'

'Thank you my dear Watson. I am going to visit the office of' *Decan Herald'*, first thing tomorrow morning. Don't you feel that, we must get down to the root of the mystery of the haunted house, as early as possible.'

'Of course, Jaya, I am one with you, you go ahead and let me know, what you find.'

CHAPTER 5

After her return from Niagara Falls, thoroughly shaken, Dorothy tries to immerse herself in works to forget the painful realization that Kamal's heart throb is someone else back in India. Try she might, it was hard to suppress her love for Kamal. It had taken deep roots in her and kept surfacing up, time and again. She could not concentrate on her works, she composed love letters to Kamal, which she never posted. To mention one: -

My dearest,

Kamal, my love, this is someone who loves you from the moment she met you. At the first glance you captivated my heart. I never experienced what love was, till I met you. It is not some thing abstract, but a material thing, which sits upon my heart making it throb. I just cannot get out of it. It is a feeling of oneness, a binding force between two beings, the ultimate chemistry of bringing two together. It defies all laws of gravity and makes me fly in the space with a care free mind to a land far away from the bustle of the world, where you and I lie together on a bed of flowers, lost in their fragrance and softness, our lips melting in each other……

Being a very pragmatic girl, she did not do anything foolish. She did not see Kamal and let her feelings run amok. She suffered her loss, in isolation. Her nature was to give and not to take. Whether he loved her or not, did not change her disposition towards him. The little flower always adores the sun, till it drops dead. These were her thoughts in the last days of Kamal's stay in USA. She arranged a farewell party in honour of Kamal, at her home, to which she invited some of her friends. Kamal wanted to bring one of his dear friends to the party and Dorothy said, yes, he might.

Mrs. Baker noticed her daughter, withdrawing to herself and maintaining a disturbing calmness, after her return from Niagara Falls. She knew, her daughter being a strong willed person would be brave enough to meet any situation. Being a doting mother, she could realize what happened, during their trip to Niagara Falls.

Kamal arrived accompanied by his friend Martin, who appeared to be a mere boy by his dress and hair style. Kamal introduced him as his assistant and euologised his assistance in his research work. Dr. Baker shook hands and received them warmly. Introductions over, they settled in the lounge. Mrs. Baker excused herself and left for the kitchen. Dorothy took care of her guests and brought drinks for them. She found Martin a pleasant person to talk to. Though he looked somewhat younger, he must be around forty, she guessed. He seemed to be a chain smoker and she had to empty the ash tray a number of times.

He was talking about some thing, suddenly turning to Dorothy, said, 'What do you say about that Miss. Baker?' Caught unawares, she blurted out excuses and left to assist her mother in the kitchen. In fact, she was not listening, in Kamal's presence, her thoughts centred around him only.

To keep the conversation going, Dr. Baker intervened and said in a lighter vein, 'Dorothy must have been miles away, thinking of something else. She has been like that, since she learnt thinking.' There was laughter all around.

* * * * *

Saxena finds it hard to keep his organization intact, without active participation of his son. After all it is his family business and it is growing by leaps and bounds, with foreign investments. His foreign partners are only interested in quick returns and to satisfy them, he always did the dirty part of the business in India, he had to struggle and spend a lot in appropriate quarters to buy safe passages for his clandestine transactions. He had no time to keep watch over his son. So long as Jackie did not cause any trouble and bothered him, he was happy. He had a guilty conscience, however, concerning Jackie. Did he really care about him, except providing him with unlimited credit cards? One thing, however, he could not give him; his son wanted to marry Jaya, the beautiful sister of Ram Gopal, he made the arrangemnts but fate intervened and the engagement was called off. He knew his son, he was not used to accept defeat easily. It must be eating him away. In many ways, he is like his mother, some what soft in the heart. The moment he thought of Lolita, his mother, his memory took him twenty years ago.

That night, he was heavily drunk, as he entered the room of Lolita, daughter of *Sethjee*. Finding him entering her room, unannounced, at such an odd hour and that too in such an inebriated condition, must have annoyed her and she told him to get out. It was too much for her to bear such an affront by a mere servant. She called him names and was on the verge of pushing him out, when he lost whatever little sense and propriety he had at that time and pounced upon the poor helpless girl, pushing her inside. For the next few minutes, he forgot that he was dealing with the bereaved daughter of the Late *Sethjee*, who died only few days ago, in a road accident, which was engineered by him. From Ratan, the docile and obedient driver, he was transformed into Ratan the maniac, the rapist, who violated her in her bed. When he realized what he had done, his fate and the girl's fate were already sealed.

He ran away from the scene of the incident, but not from its aftermath. On the following morning, he saw Lolita weeping over the shoulders of his wife, in her room. The look of his wife, told him everything. He was no longer a simple and brave rustic, who came to Bombay, in search of his fortune, few years ago and found shelter in *Sethjee's* house. Who stood there, that day before the two women, was a scheming and ungrateful creature. There was no remorse in his behaviour, for his dastardly act. He planned his next course of action, keeping the plan to himself. Before the end of the day, as the weather took a turn for the worse, he did not waver to ask his wife to leave the house with his child. She must have seen venom in his eyes, when he uttered those words. Her appeal went unheeded. She packed her things in a bundle, picked up her baby son and left the cottage, which was her home, for the last two years. With his wife gone, he carried out the rest of the plan without any remorse. After all these years, he had no regrets. To win the ultimate battle, in the game of chess, pawns are to be sacrificed. Parvati was one such. He had married Parvati, because it suited his purpose at that time.

They were young, when they married. They had run away from an obscure village, near Cawnpore and arrived at VT, Bombay, finally, after having spent several hours at way side Railway Platforms, thrown out from the compartments for travelling ticketless. It did not deter them to complete the journey. They were two love birds and found solace in each other's arms. They went without food and shelter till Goddess Laxmi shone on them, one day. Ratan, hungry and haggard, sat on the sea beach, looking at the vast ocean with a vacant look in his eyes. It was early in the morning. The Sun had just risen in the distant horizon throwing an orange glow over the waters, slowly spreading. There were few early risers out, for strolling and jogging. The sea was calm and a cool breeze blew. Parvati still slept on rags placed inside a huge RCC pipe, lying at the beach, which provided them shelter, during the night. Many people like wise, lived inside the pipes. '*Sarkari*' guest house, they called those. Ratan came to Bombay with great hopes and dreams. He had heard that, Bombay was a city, which is the abode of Goddess Laxmi, where riches and pleanty, abound. He further heard, that '*goras*' have left the country, leaving all the wealth in the hands of the natives and one has to be at the spot to pluck the spoils. But things turned out to be different, he went door to door, asking for jobs and was turned down mercilessely. Even some, let loose their dogs on them. Now, the oppressors were dark skinned and not '*goras.*' The question was not of race, foreigner or '*dessi*'. The question was of rich and poor. Those who possessed money and status did not care to come down from their citadels to exend their hands of cooperation to the down trodden. Years ago, before Independence, as a young boy, he attended a meeting addressed by Mahatma Gandhi. He must have walked miles, to hear the Mahatma, who addressed the masses, '*karo ya maro*', '*swaraj is within your reach*'. He had asked someone in the gathering, '*chacha*', what is this '*swaraj*'?' He said, '*arey beta,* now our country is ruled by foreigners, from the other side of the ocean, they plunder our wealth, our gold and carry them to their own land, we have become poor. Once we get *swaraj*, we will be master of our land, the rich harvest will be ours and there will be enough for everyone.' He had returned home happily.

He was the son of a farmer and helped his father in tilling his land. He ran small errands for his mother, whom he remembered as, always sick and sitting near a smoking *chullah*, coughing all the time. She would yell at him, 'Ratan *beta,* where are you? Go and get some dry wood, this is all damp, how will I light the *chullah* and cook?'

Dropping his *gilli-danda,* he would say, 'Yes *ma*, I am going to fetch the wood' That was almost his daily routine. As soon as *'ma's* cooking was over, he would carry lunch for his father, which consisted of few handfuls of rice, a piece of onion, *mirchi* and a pinch of salt. On seeing his son arriving with his meal, his father would free the bullocks from the yoke and let them loose. They would move to a field, near by, to graze. He would remove his *pagdi*, wash and wipe his face clean from dust and sweat, with water from a pitcher, kept under a tree, which though not thick with foliage, could just provide a little shade to father and son, shielding them from the schorching mid day Sun. Ratan had no schooling in his childhood. His father could not even afford '*that eight annas'* to pay the monthly fees of the teacher for teaching him alphabets and numbers. He remained, therefore, an illiterate for many years. But he was very intelligent and possessed a sharp memory. The local *bania*, owner of a grocery shop engaged him, at a monthly wage of two rupees. When he handed over his first earnings to his mother, she huggd him and wept. It was of great help to the family resources. In those days hard cash was very scarce to come by. Only, *sarkari naukiri* could fetch a salary in cash, for which one must be educated. Ratan was now nineteen years old and well built. He brought home regularly, five rupees every month, with which they could purchase essential commodities such as, cooking oil, *mitti ka tel*, and a little vegetable at times. After year long hard toil in summer and rains, whatever the land yielded, half of that would go to the land lord as his share, from the other half, the *bania* would claim a substantial portion, towards provisions etc. What was left then? Almost nothing. That was precisely the economic condition of a farmer, those days.

Ratan knew the pangs of hunger and poverty, at a very early age. He also knew the value of money. Circumstances made him acrimonious and bitter against the system, which made the poor, poorer and the rich, richer. Why he was born poor? Is he destined to suffer poverty, all his life? He must run away from the claws of poverty, he decided. He must build his future elsewhere.

He remembered the day, his mother died. Since morning, rains poured in torrents, the roof leaked. His mother, who was sick, lay in the corner which was dry. The son and father, both sat by her side, while his father stroked her head, he massaged her feet. Suddenly he felt that her feet became cold and lifeless. Father stopped stroking and looked at her face with so much sorrow in his eyes that, he knew, his mother was no more. His first feeling was anger and frustration against the world. He wept, holding the limp body, in his arms.

The day dawned and with help of others, they performed the last rites of the poor woman. Ratan could no longer bear the sight of his father, sitting motionless for hours, in the house, staring at the place, where his mother breathed her last. He did'nt stir out nor he took any food. Being already old and frail, he did'nt last long and ultimately died in his sleep. His last tie with his home and village was sheared that day.

Sun had risen over the horizon, in the meanwhile, the beach became a little crowded. He sat there, looking particularly at nothing. Suddenly, his gaze fell upon a middle aged person, who sat at a little distance. He seemed to be enjoying the sun rise. From his bearing and attire, he appeared to be a rich person. He abhorred rich prople and looked away. He saw the sun rising above the waters and he guessed that it was going to be another hot day. He heard someone shouting, he turned and saw that the elderly person was chasing a young man, shouting, '*Chor, chor,* he has snatched my purse. 'He was no match for the thief, Ratan saw, that unless caught, he might escape. He got up and gave a chase. In no time, he caught up with the thief and grappled him. A crowd gathered and gave a good thrashing to the poor fellow. The purse was recovered and handed over to the elderly man, who had arrived there, in the meanwhile, panting.

'May God bless you, young man. I had almost, lost hopes. Thank God, the money is safe.' Then, the man offered Ratan, some money as reward for his good deed, which he delined politely, stating that he was merely doing the duty of a good citizen and it would not be proper to accept money for the same. The *Seth* appreciated the good manners of the young man and asked him, what was he doing for a living?

Hopes stirred in Ratan's heart and he said, 'I am unemployed, sir. I am a poor farmer and have just arrived from my native village, near Cawnpore. If you would provide me with a job, I will remain indebted to you.'

'I see' the *Sethjee* said, "but, I stay at Poona, that is where my business is. If you are prepared to come to Poona, I will see what can be done. 'Thousands of rays of hope burst in Ratan's mind, his joy and gratitude knew on bounds.

He said, 'I do not know sir, in what words, I should thank you. Kindly permit me to break this good news to Parvati, who will be glad to know of my good fortune.'

'Who is she?'

'We are together, sir, she came with me.'

'You mean, she is your wife?'

'No, sir, we are not married, there was no time for that.' Then, he related to *Sethjee*, their love story and how they escaped from the clutches of her wicked aunt.

Sethjee said, 'I see, you go and fetch her. As soon as, we reach Poona, I will get both of you married, in a temple.'

Then, he asked, 'What is your name, young man?'

"It is, Ratan Kumar Saxena, sir, you may please call me 'Ratan'. 'He rushed to wake Parvati up.

* * * * *

He remembered their first night, in a cottage, attached to the manson of Seth Mohan Lal. They were not accustomed to electric lighting and therefore, when the Chowkidar came to switch on the light and a lamp glowed on a bracket fixed to the wall, he was wonder struck. So much has happened since then, it brought a smile to his hard lined face. What a simple folk they were! Left alone, they had turned to each other and had a good laughter. Being together, as husband and wife, in an isolated cottage, both of them wearing garlands with blessings of *Debi Ma*, Ratan turned to Parbati and tried to take her in his arms. He distinctly remembers, what she said.

'Hey, what are you doing? *Koi dekh lega*.'

'Go, put out the lamp, I do not care, you are my wife.'

'You are shameless.' With the light off, the room was plunged in darkness and then a fox from a near by field howled. In fright, Parvati came running into the extended arms of Ratan. They forgot, that they were two selves, they became one, melting in the warmth of their bodies with unlimited passion and ecstasy.

Was it love or pure passion? He could never tell. He was not made for love, he was sure. Love and affection are signs of weakness in a person's character, according to him. The last time, he saw his wife, was on that dreary night, rains splashing and winds howling, when she left the cottage, gathering her baby, casting a scornful glance at him. When he came out of his drunkenness, it was already morning and he lay there sprawled on the floor all alone.

* * * * *

Jaya laboured hard in the office of Decan Herald in scanning through bundles of old News Papers in search of some clue regarding death of Seth Mohan Lal. While going through Papers of 1955, she came across a News item dated Twntieth August 1955, as under: -

20. 8. 1955/ Poona

BUSINESS TYCOON SETH MOHAN LAL

DIES IN A ROAD ACCIDENT

Renowned businessman and philanthropist Seth Mohan Lal met with a serious accident today, on the Poona-Bombay Highway when the car, he was travelling in, skidded down a slope and hit a tree. There was no other passenger in the car except for his driver Ratan, who sustained minor injuries. It is reported that the door in the rear opened during the crash and Sethjee was thrown out and sustained head injuries. Both of them were removed to the Poona Medical College Hospital, where Sethjee died without regaining consciousness.

(A photograph of Sethjee was inserted with the News item)

Armed with this information, Jaya got herself busy in the archives of the News Paper to get more information about the *Sethjee.* She was amply rewarded. From the obituaries published, she learnt that, from a humble origin, Seth Mohn Lal rose to the pinnacle of success, in his time. He was truly a philanthropist, several charitable Trusts were founded by him managing temples, hospitals, orphanages and schools. His death was condoled in a public meeting where rich tributes were paid to him. He was survived by his only daughter Lolita, the sole inheritor of his estates. The palatial building, which he built in Poona was named after his daughter. She pursued her research but failed to get any further information about Lolita. She disappeared from the public memory. Where could she have gone? Is she alive ? How the present owner came into possession of this building?

All these questions troubled Jaya. She did not find any answer. She drew a blank from all quarters. At times, she toyed with the idea, to handover the issue to a private investigator. The next moment, she brushed away the idea, as far fetching. First thing, what right she had, to trespass into somebody's privacy and secondly, incase there is something sinister about the portrait of a person, who died years ago, what would she achieve?

Inquisitive, as she was, she came to one conclusion, however sordid it was, that something was the matter with the portrait. There is no doubt, that it belonged to Seth Mohan Lal, who died an unnatural death. The painting tallied with the photo published in the News Paper. Was it an accident or something else? Her mind traversed in fathomless depths. Is the portrait possessed? She shuddered to think about it. The echoing foot steps, foot prints left on the dust covered floor, could not be easily ignored.

Taking time off, from her busy schedule, she visited libraries and studied books on spirits, spiritualism, '*tantra*', journey of soul after death, etc. Some of the books even narrated events with names of persons and places, where communication with spirits was narrated. They were reported to have appeared before mediums as apparitions. Instances of mediums calling spirits for leaving messages through them were also cited. She studied experiments carried out with planchettes. She read with interest the hair-rising experience of one Mr. Robert, who visited an old castle in Scotland, at the behest of one of his friends and contacted the caretaker, a pretty old lady of indeterminable age, known to be a spirit caller. She took him to one of the attics through cold and damp corridors, carrying only candles and made him sit on the stone floor. She spread out a cloth on which triangles of all sizes were stitched, making odd designs resembling a jigsaw puzzle. She gave him a blank paper and a pencil, asked him to hold the pencil over the paper, placed on the cloth. They sat quietly, putting out the candles. The room was plunged into darkness. Robert could not even see his hand. He lost count of time. Then he heard, the sound of a galloping horse approaching and some one dismounting from the steed. Heavy foot steps were heard coming nearer and then sound of someone, removing armour from the body and hanging them on the wall was heard. He felt someone behind him and even his hot breath over his shoulders. He was on the verge of fainting, when miraculously he, rather his hand, began writing on the paper. The writing went on for several minutes, and then it stopped. All this happened in absolute silence and darkness. The lady struck a match stick and lighted the candles. His eyes fell upon the sheet of paper, on which something was written in strange letters. The calligraphy, though, century old, was Anglo-Sexon, the lady explained. As the story goes, the lady said, a nobleman rode from the castle to a battle field promising his newly wed wife to return soon. When he didn't return, the noble lady, heart broken, jumped over the rampart and killed herself. They say that the spirit of the young wife is still roaming around the castle, waiting for the return of her lover. Mr. Robert was touched with the pathetic tale and when he turned to express her gratitude to the old lady for the 'spirit calling', to his utter surprise and bewilderment, he did'nt find any body, the old lady had vanished. Only the cold and silent castle stood there.

The story itself, frightened Jaya. Would she go ahead with the experiment of spirit calling? What if, the spirit of the *Sethjee* appears and takes hold of her? What would she do? A simple experiment would end in a catastrophe. Alone, she would not try. She decided to take the help of Raja *bhaiya.*

She chose a Sunday, when others would not be present and they would be left free to pursue the '*spirit calling*', without interruption. Raja arrived in the afternoon and they discussed about the plan, she had thought of. It was agreed that he would take a passive part and mostly keep Jaya under close watch. She would act as the medium and through her the spirit would communicate, if at all it appears. She was confident, that the spirit would be a benign one and may not cause any harm to them.

They carried a bag containing candles, a match box, a coloured cloth with triangles drawn at random, sheets of paper and a pencil. Before stepping into the cellar, they prayed for the departed soul. The time was five in the evening, when they reached the portrait. Candles were lit, which threw long shadows over the walls. Jaya swept the floor clean in front of the portrait, spread the cloth with the motif and placed a sheet of paper on the cloth, holding a pencil in her hand. Thus far, everything was in order and in accordance with the plan.

Jaya sat, reflecting on the noble spirit of the departed soul, riveting her attention on the portrait with closed eyes. Raja sat, a little far by her side, so that, he could keep Jaya, under observation, all the time. Time ticked away. The atmosphere was eeri, the silence was too much to bear. Nothing could be heard, except for their heart beats. Then, a strange feeling came over Jaya, she became unstable and swayed. Raja observed to his horror and amazement, that a blue tinge of light appeared around Jaya, which was not earthly. There was a gust of wind and the candle was put out. The place was plunged into darkness. The blue light seemed to be dancing around Jaya. Raja's heart was in his mouth, praying God with all sincerity not to let any harm befall Jaya. She seemed to be possessed by the spirit or whatever it was. The upper portion of her body swayed and she emitted a peculiar sound which was almost guttural. Then, everything became quiet, she became steady and the blue luminous halo disappeared. In the enveloping darkness, he did not see anything further. But he heard a peculiar sound in the stillness, that of a pencil scratching over paper. He perspired and became breathless. After a shortwhile, something happened for which he was not prepared. Jaya shrieked and then there was silence. He could not contain himself any more, he groped for the match box and lighted a candle. In its illumination, he saw Jaya sitting still, her head resting on her chest and holding a pencil poised over a sheet of paper.

He shook her vigorously, she woke up, as if from a trance. After gulping a glass of water, which he offered, she uttered, 'Where am I *bhaiya*?'

'It is okay. Are you alright?'

'Yes, but I feel weak. What happened? One moment, I sat in meditation, my thoughts concentrated on the portrait of the deceased, then suddenly, I seemed to become weightless, as a dry leaf and was drifting in strong currents, till you woke me up. Raja gave her a detailed account of what he witnessed and again enquired if she felt alright.

'Of course, *bhaiya*, I am fine. I cannot believe that I was really possessed by a spirit and it controlled my actions and thoughts, I do not remember anything that happened in that period.'

'Now, let us look at the sheet of paper, on which, you seemed to be writing something.'

Whatever doubts they entertained in their minds, about the existence of ghosts and spirits, were completely washed way, when they saw a message on the sheet of paper, written clearly in some one's hand writing. The message was as follows: -

I am Seth Mohan Lal. I never met you in my life.

But the moment, you sat in front of my portrait and started thinking about me, the thought waves, crossing the space of twenty two years, touched me and awakened my spirit. You are the one, I am sure, who will release me from this bond. After my painful death caused by that scoundrel Ratan, I now reside in this portrait, which was gifted to me by my wife. My only child, Lolita is no more. Her son, who is my heir, does not know me. He has not even set his eyes upon this portrait. How could he?

Ratan, stripped the house of all that wore my touch, my signature, my memories and dumped them here, in this dark space. It is suffocating, I move out some time to get some fresh air. My mortal remains are buried under the lemon tree behind the cottage in south of the garden. I ask you, to recover the remains and handover to my grandson for immersion in Holy Ganges for my deliverance. Secondly, whatever jewellery, my dear wife possessed and wore, are all stored in a secret chest inside the heavy frame of this portrait, which you will find by pressing the white knob in the bottom right hand corner and sliding the cover, you may remove the jewellery, keep it in your custody and hand it over to my grandson.

God's Will will prevail and my blessings are with you, my dear child.

Please do not try to call me again. These are my last words. Good Bye.

They read it over and over again in that candle light. Raja said, 'Jaya, the message of the well meaning Spirit looks to me to be an order, which we must obey. Let us fulfil both the instructions, tonight itself. You show me the torch, I am going to try the portrait first.'

Jaya focused the light on the portrait, they found the white button, after wiping the dust clean from the frame. After several trials of push and slide, the cover slided to reveal the hidden chest and inside they located a beautifully decorated wooden casket. With shaking hands, Raja picked up the casket, which was heavy. When the lid was opened they found glittering jewellery studded with diamond, ruby, emerald and saffire, of the like, they had never seen before. After closing the hidden chest, they left the cellar. It was midnight, when they came out. Though the yard was well lighted, the silence was frightening and a distant hooting of an owl added to the mystery of their mission. Their path to the cottage lay across a patch of woodland, with low branches of trees above the path shutting out, whatever little light the sky had to offer. They covered the distance, focusing the torch at the ground lest they may tread upon a crawling snake. They reached the cottage, at one point Jaya stopped on her track and whispered, 'Did you hear some sound as if some one is following us?' Raja listened and said, 'No, it is highly improbable at this hour, unless our late lamented *Shethjee* has decided to follow us.' Jaya shivered. They found the cottage well maintained, opening a small gate, they entered the yard, Jaya swerved the beam of the torch and located the lemon tree at a corner. There was a nice aroma in the atmosphere. Throwing the beam of light above, they saw the tree laden with ripe lemons, hanging from the branches. Jaya even plucked one or two and pocketed them. With her touch, the tree seemed to come alive and dropped a big sized lemon at a place near the trunk. By intuition they dug at the spot and hit a pot buried there. It was a small copper vessel with its lid sealed. They covered the spot with loose earth and left. A shadow separated itself from a nearby tree, after they left and melted into the gathering darkness.

* * * * *

Raja knew, he was skating over thin ice. It would not be many days, before Saxena catches him. Their paths might cross at any moment and then it would be farewell for him. How could he disclose the identity of Saxena to *babujee,* that a gangster and virtually a *don* was masquerading as a businessman before him, without exposing himself? He was at a cross road, torn between loyality and security. He was tortured for days, with this mental agony which he couldn't share even with his wife, till he took a decision to lay bare the entire story before his employer. He wrote a note to Ram Gopal jee, about his earlier association with the gangster and his guilty feelings about it. In these circumstances, he said it would not be moral and ethical to continue in his present employment under him and he cautioned him against Saxena, to keep away from him. He begged for his pardon, for keeping him in dark about the true identity of Saxena and he was prepared to face the consequences for it. He had a sense of foreboding that his end was near and beseeched him to provide shelter to Ranee when he would be no more. He ended the note, stating that he was resigning from his post with deep regrets. He left the note at his office. This done, he became free from the guilty conscience, which troubled him, all these days.

He drove towards the sea coast, to a secluded place and walked over to a rocky bed, where waves were regularly breaking, causing water sprays to rise above. He sat there looking afar, seeing the graceful flying of a sea gull. He was lost in his thoughts, taking him years in the past, when he was a young boy racing across the field, holding the string of a kite, hoping it to take off above the ground and up into the sky. Suddenly there was a gust of wind and the kite was jerked away from his hand. He had wept that day in anguish.

The same gust of wind, today, made the marksman to cry out, 'Oh! Shit.', when the gun jerked in his hand a little and the target was hit, not in the head but in the shoulders way below. Joshi never used to miss, cursed, pocketed the gun in his breast pocket and left the site.

Raja fell down into the shallow water below, which turned crimson with his blood. Two birds, perched on nearby rocks, flew away with cries, as if under protest. He lay there unconscious, amidst silence and vastness, bleeding, till he was discovered by a young couple, who had come down to steal few kisses. They raised an alarm, Police came and finding the body warm, shifted it to the hospital.

Ram Gopal received a phone call from the Police, late in the night. He reached, breathless and learnt from the Sister-in-charge at the Emergency OT, that the patient was still unconscious and there was loss of blood. He was asked to arrange two units of blood of Type B+, immediately. His vision was blurred, he took few faltering steps and slumped into the nearest chair, to give rest to his thumping heart.

Suddenly it struck him, how helpless he was without Raja. His heart flew toward him. He composed himself to brave the situation. He contacted his office to collect the blood from the Blood Bank and rushing to the Doctor's office, learned that they were preparing the patient for surgery, to remove the bullet. After completing the formalities, he rushed back to the OT, where he found a police constable on duty. Introducing himself, he learned from him, that when police arrived at the spot, the person lay in a shallow pool of 'water with a gun shot wound on his left shoulder, profusely bleeding but alive. He was shot at. They brought him to the hospital an hour ago.

He telephoned his wife, explained the grievous situation and asked her to bring Ranee to the Hospoital, as quickly as possible. When, Ranee arrived at the Hospital, her condition was pathetic. Hair dishevelled, tears rolling down her face, clothes in disarray, she resembled a figure, which passed through a hurricane. Ram Gopal comforted her; doctors were attending him, he said. She was inconsolable and wept on the shoulders of Maya. The situation was tense, everyone's attention was on the *OT*, where a red lamp kept glowing. After an hour a nurse came out of the *OT*, to break the good news, that the operation was successful. Doctors were able to remove the bullet from the body and the patient was out of danger. Ranee wanted to see her husband immediately, the nurse intimated that the patient was still under the effect of anaesthesia and she could see him after he was shifted to the cabin. Maya comforted Ranee, that by God's Grace, Raja was safe and she would be seeing him soon.

Ram Gopal was in utter confusion, what was Raja doing in that desolate place? Did he go there to keep an appointment? Why would any body want to kill him? Only Raja would clear the suspense. He must wait, till Raja regains consciousness. But Ranee could not wait any further, she pleaded with the Doctor to let her see Raja. 'Okay', the doctor said, 'please come with me'. He took her to a room with glass panels and asked her to peep into. Ranee saw, Raja lying on a bed, his chest and shoulders bandaged, tubes running from his spine, chest, stomach and wrist, connected to a cluster of instruments near the bed. Finding Maya beside, she buried her face on Maya's chest, sobbing. She consoled her and led her to a bench, where Ram Gopal waited suppressing his emotions.

* * * * *

The sniper, having done his job, coolly left the place, rode his byke and went to a phone booth to make a call. A courteous voice asked, 'yes ?', 'It is done'. Make yourelf scarce and leave the city', the voice, said.

But the man had other plans. He was a professional killer, he wanted to make sure that the victim was really done for. He stopped on his track, there was a police man at the spot. He saw, that they lifted the body out of the water and shifted it to the waiting ambulence. By their handling the body, he guessed that the person was alive. He made a hasty retreat.

* * * * *

It was a bad day for Saxena. He suffered a huge loss at the Stock Market, further, one of his contraband consignments was seized by Customs. There must be a mole in his organization, to have squeaked before the police, he believed. 'Dam'n it', he said, aloud, while he was heading home. When the traffic lights turned Red and the traffic came to halt, to his great consternation and disbelief, he had a glimpse of Shekhar, the rascal who cheated him, in another car, held up, alongside. It was no doubt Shekhar. Though wearing a cap and a suit with a tie, without his sideburns and long hair, his features, looked from the side, gave him away. No doubt about it. Here is the man, who outwitted them and gave the slip. Instead of leaving the city, for good, to save his skin, look at his temerity, he is driving around in the city, dressed in expensive clothes, as if he owns it!He ground his teeth. Next moment, as the lights turned Green, when he wanted to have another '*dekho*' at him, he was gone. He cursed.

He reailized the danger, he was in, the rascal was not only very much in the city, but did'nt leave any chance to intimidate him; he is a fly in the ointment. He must be taken out and squeezed, like this. Saxena made a gesture of squeezing a fly with his fingers. He missed him in the stream of cars, rushing by, with their tail lights, blinking. But he had his car number. Next day, he put a tail on him. One of his men spotted his car and followed him to Ram Gopal's office. He waited outside, after a while, he saw both of them coming out together. The shadow reported the matter to his *boss.* It did'nt take much time for Saxena to put the things together. There was no doubt, that Shekhar and Raja were one and the same. Still he wanted to verify. In his business, he could not afford to take chances. He asked one of his agents, who acted as a contact for Shekhar while he was in his organization, to find out about the person, whom he believed to be Shekhar. It was. therefore, Raja's turn, to get the shock of his life when he spotted the person, whom he knew as *'chota bhai'* in the gang of his Ex- boss, in the crowded restaurant, he frequently visited. Could it be a mere coincidence or they have finally caught up with him? That was when, he saw '*chota bhai,* who waved at him and came towards his table. His heart missed a beat and he bolted like a hare, from the place. He was successful in giving him the slip, but he was now certain that *sirjee* would get him whenever he wanted and his days are numbered. He decided to put all his cards before *babujee* and caution him against Saxena. He wrote a long letter adressed to him, and putting it in a thick envelope, left it in his office drawer. It was unfortunate, that Ram Gopal did not open the drawer in time.

* * * * *

Few hours after the surgery, to everybody's relief and delight, the doctor intimated that the patient regained consciousness and they could see him but cautioned them not to agitate him. Ram Gopal, Maya and Ranee were too eager to see him and they marched in silently.

Raja's eyes were still closed, as soon as he felt the touch of his wife, he opened his eyes and looked at her, which seemed to say, not to worry and everything was going to be fine. Parvati joined them in the meanwhile. Their eyes dampened, when they got Raja's feeble smile in response.

The Police, in the meanwhile, registered a case of culpable homicide against a person or persons unknown and began investigation after recording a statement from Raja.

With proper care and medical treatment, Raja recovered fast and on a fine sunny day, he was discharged from the Hospital with advice to take rest atleast for a fortnight before joning duty. Jaya, on hearing of the incident, had rushed from Poona and stayed with Ranee till Raja gained consciousness. Parvati jee sat in the *pooja'*room doing *jap* all the time. Raja slowly gained strength with the loving care of Ranee.

CHAPTER 6

Ram Gopal used his contacts in the Police Department, for expediting the investigation and apprehend the gunman. He attended office, on the next day, and while searching for a File in the drawer, came across a thick envelope lying there, unopened, he did not remember having put it there himself. Sender's name was neither written. Who could it be ? He opened the envelope and took out few sheets of a closely written note. Immediately he recognized the handwriting of Raja and with great trepidation went through it at one breath. He was almost in tears. My God! the scoundrel, must have been after him, surely. But he was in a fix, if he goes to Police with this letter, it would implicate Raja badly and Police would begin seeing the case as a feud between gangsters. What should he do? He was in a predicament. He contacted immediately, the Inspector in charge of the investigation, to know its progress. Twenty four hours have passed, yet there was no arrest. Police had no clue. He felt guilty, to have suppressed the information provided by Raja. It could have provided the motive behind the crime to the Police. The Inspector paid several visits to Raja, but he was not of much help.

Inspector Pradhan was one of those sleuths, who did not give up easily. The most important factor in investigation of any crime, is the motive behind it. This, he knew, but in this case, Police failed to establish any motive. Raja steadily denied of having any enemy, known to him or any one who would be benifited by his death. Meticulously, he recorded all the statements given by Raja.

One evening, Pradhan was in his office, going over these records. Raja was honest enough to spill out, what was his occupation at Calcutta, before he shifted to Bombay. Police had double checked this, with Ranee's statements. He, therefore, knew that Raja was a small time operator in a smuggling racket, and definitely not a key person to invite any vengeful action against him. His running away from Calcutta might not have caused any serious upheaval in the organization. More over he was being paid for and he had no shares in the spoils. He had no Police records, as such.

All the while he was looking at the sealed packet, lying before him. It contained the bullet recovered from Raja's shoulder blade. Death pill like metal shell, which when fired was meant to pierce his skull. It was a miracle that he was safe. It was a close call. The man behind the gun must have been crack shot, judging the distance and the crops of rocks jutting out.

He sat brooding over it. Suddenly his brows knitted. He got up, went to the File cabinet and picked up a File marked 'UNSOLVED CASE'. He leafed through the pages and came across a case diary, read it carefully. That was about a wanton killing, which took place years ago. Motive could not be established and killer was not found. Shooting had taken place in a crowded Railway Station, the victim was not fortunate, the bullet smashed the skull and was found lodged in it. With a thumping heart, the Inspector went to another cabinet and got hold of the sealed envelope, he was looking for. He examined the spent bullet, inside the envelope. A cursory glance told him, that both the bullets looked similar. A theory was building up in his brain. To be certain, he marked the envelopes containing the bullets and forwarded them through a special messenger to the Forensic Laboratory for conducting ballistic tests on them. On the following day, he received the test reports and he was one step ahead in his inverstigation. He saw a ray of hope and it alleviated his despondency. The reports said, that the bullets were fired from the same gun. The indelible marks were there. While the objects, places and the times were different, the gun and most probably the gunman were same. From his experience, Pradhan knew, that killers almost get attached to a particular weapon, the attraction was rather an obsession. Both the cases bear one similarity, ie; no motive could be established for the crimes. The killers did not leave any clue. On both the occasions, they vanished into thin air. But he was not lucky this time, the victim lived and quite likely, he might give it another try. He knew, how a killer's mind works. A job unfinished does not add laurels to his sadistic perception. He usually returns to the scene of crime, to go over the sequence to find the cause, however subtle, which made him miss the target. It was like a tiger's prouncing upon the prey and catching thin air.

Pradhan's perseverance in searching the locality, which provided an unmarred view of the spot, where Raja sat at the time of being hit, paid dividends. He found a butt of a cigarette, at a secluded corner, behind a crop of rocks, from where one could have a clear view of the spot down below. He fished out a binocular from his pocket and looked. There it was, the rock where Raja sat, even the names of lovers with a sign of cupid's arrow, were clearly visible. Putting himself in the killer's shoes, Pradhan could imagine, how the man would have stood there with a cigarette between his lips and having kept the victim in his view, whisked out his gun, weighed it up in his hand, tossed it up once or twice in the air, pulled out the trigger, aimed and then fired.

The silence was broken by a sound caused by a peeble being dislodged. His years of experience and ever alert mind told him that he stood few feet from death. Then, a voice spoke, 'Don't move or you may be dead.' It came from behind. It flashed in his mind, that the killer, as expected, paid a second visit to the spot and must have been equally surprised to find him there. He knew the psychology of these dangerous killers, they are trigger happy, the slightest wrong step and they would let fly a bullet, no remorse. Killers never repent. The person moved and stood face to face, before him. He saw him, his search was over. He was looking at the most cruel face, he had ever seen. There was a perpetual grin in his face, a cigarette jutting out his lips and with the gun hanging loose in his hand, he was the coolest man on the earth. The most dangerous part in his face, were his eyes. They were steel grey, like that of a cobra, unblinking, ever ready to strike. Pradhan weighed the situation and waited. The person spoke, 'Pradhan, are'nt you? I have heard about you. It is a pleasure to meet you. I would have shaken your hands, but for the gun. Don't you entertain any foolish idea in that brain of yours, a flicker in your hand would make this tool in my hand jump and blow it to bits.'

Pradhan was thinking fast, so far so good, let him go on boasting, terrorizing the victim in the process. They take pleasure in such rhetorics. It gives them a feeling of superiority. The man had nothing to fear, the place was deserted, a cool breeze blew from the sea, except the sound of ripples lapping over the rocks, nothing could be heard. The set up could not have been more suitable for a quiet murder. He could even imagine, the morning News Paper, carrying the News in bold and black, '*murder at the rock, Inspector Pradhan assassinated. Police Department Shocked'*. Sound of the trigger being pulled out, brought him to his senses. Steady, steady, his inner voice told him. Then, Pradhan acted. Summoning all calmness, he could muster and putting acid in his voice, he said, 'You are a fool, Mr. Killer to have walked into the trap. The poor fly enters the spider's parlour. You are surrounded from all sides. Before you send a bullet into me, hundreds of bullets will be fired rapidly and turn your body to smithereens. Look.'

A slight shift of his eyes was enough for Prdhan to pounce upon the man and knock out the gun from his hand. Both of them tumbled over the rough surface, the man was trying to get hold of the gun. Pradhan had a firm grip on his wrist and with his other hand he grappled his body. But the man proved too good for him and instantly overpowering him, came on top of him and showered blows on him. Pradhan felt out of breath, hit by such heavy blows. The moment, Pradhan's grip loosened, he freed himself and got hold of his gun. Before he could take aim and fire, a gun appeard in Pradhan's hand and roared. A cry escaped from the man, the gun holding hand was pierced and hung loose, dripping blood. The man was whimpering in pain, he sat there clutching his injured hand. Escaping from sure death, Pradhan took few deep breaths.

Later, when the assailant-was safely locked in the lock up and his hand attended by a doctor, Pradhan sat at his desk looking at the dreadful gun lying before him. The killer weapon looked frightening. Few lucky persons might have escaped, after being at the wrong end of the weapon. He shuddered to think, that an hour ago, he was one of them. He made a detailed entry in the Police diary, of the day's incident and dispatched the gun to the labotatory for test, which would clinch the case against the man as the '*wanted person'*.

A small note book was recovered from the person's pocket, besides a wallet containing five thousand rupees in cash. In its fold, it had a photograph of a little girl. The note book listed certain numbers and to crown it all, he was surprised to find that the little diary also carried a detailed account of his earnings and expenses till the day, he was caught, This showed how meticulous he was. The last entry was a bus ride. Leafing through the pages, he did not come across a single entry for purchases of drinks or any expenses on account of girl friends. He seemed to lead an austre life. But as a hunter kills animals for earning a livelihood, he kills, men instead. The up-to-date balance as noted in the book was rupees five thousand, which tallied with the cash found in his person. Pradhan mused, that these traits normally point to a man of exactitude and ruthlessness. In his profession, there is nothing called mercy or compassion. When a victim falls down at the pull of his finger, he is neither sad nor pleased, it is a job accomplished. He would then wait for the next assignment.

He clammed his mouth shut, when questioned. Pradhan did not worry, the silent witnesses were the bullets and the gun. The laboratory tests confirmed that both the bullets were fired from the same gun, killing one man and injuring another. Still, he wanted to follow the trail of the only clue found in his Note Book-the telephone numbers. He saw a faint ray of hope, that the trail might lead him to the man behind the killing.

The numbers were traced down to a Railway Enquiry, to a grocery store, still another was traced to a convent school at Calcutta. That the man called from PCO's, was apparent from relevant entries in his Note Book. Did he not have any address?

To begin with, Pradhan paid a visit to the St. Joseph Convent School, Amherst Street, Calcutta, carrying with him a photograph of the man. When he introduced himself and presented the photograph to the Head of the school, he got all the information, he needed. The man's name was Virendra Joshi, father of Miss Loila, a little girl of eight years, studying and staying as a *'boarder'*. Pradhan concocted a story and told the Head that Joshi met with an accident and lying unconscious at a Hospital in Bombay. He requested her, not to tell the girl, anything about this, as it would upset the little one. He wanted to see the girl and asked her if there were any dues to be paid on her account. He learnt that Mr. Joshi paid every thing in advance. A little girl, bright and smiling walked in, after a while and greeted the Head with *'Good Morning M'am*. Pradhan wondered, what a contrast between the father and the daughter! While one was a hardened criminal, the other was as innocent and pure as a morning *lily*. The Head made the introductions and said, 'Loyla dear, your *daddy* was not able to come and hence asked this gentleman to come and see you. Please take him to the visitors room and be nice to him.' The little one said, 'Good Morning uncle'. Pradhan said, 'Hello, baby, how are you?' Pradhan noticed that the little girl was trying to hide her tears. He nodded at the Head, said his thanks and led the girl out of the office.

Instead of going to the visitors room, he led the girl out to the garden and made her sit near him on a bench, in the cool shade under a tree. As soon as they settled, the girl asked Pradhan, what kept his father from coming to see her. More over, she had not seen him since long. Pradhan looked at her and thought, here was a girl pining for the company of her father, obviously the only living parent, completely oblivious that he was arrested and faced serious charges of murder. How sad!

He never raised a family. He is a bachelor. He found it difficult to deal with a child. He remembered, how once, he put himself in jeopardy, while trying to please the little son of his *'boss'*, during his visit to his residence on official matters. While he waited for the '*bos*s', he spotted a large *'doberman'* at a corner in the verandah, safely chained to its post. The brute ignored him, but kept him under observation, lying still. So far so good, now he did'nt like dogs, he never encouraged them, by whistling at them or by throwing biscuits at them. This dog seemed to dislike him. While engrossed in such mutual dislikes, he noticed the door opening and expecting the '*boss*', he got up and kept himself in readiness to salute, but he saw a lad of about five years entered, wearing an uniform of a cowboy, complete with wide brim hat, a belt and a toy gun. Seeing the boy, the dog stood up and whined. He noticed that the dog was really huge, nothing less than two and a half feet, almost the height of the boy. The boy noticed me and said, 'Hello uncle, are you waiting for daddy?' "Yes, *beta*, and you look good as a cowboy.' The little fellow said in a sweet voice, 'He is dressing, it will take time. Why not we play *'chor and police'*, in the meanwhile. But you will be the *chor* and I the police. You pick up this paper weight from the table and run. I will chase you and send a bullet into you, okay?'He committed the blunder of telling, 'Okay *beta'*. Casting a deprecatory look at the brat, he picked up the paper weight and started running. Firstly, the dog did not like the man, secondly it saw the man snatching a thing belonging to the house and running away with it. It was too much, it's intuition dictated to catch the thief. In a twinkle of an eye, it broke loose from the chain and rushed at the supposed to be thief. Pradhan stepped down the verandah and ran towards the garden, the little fellow chasing and shouting, *'chor, chor'*, raising the toy gun to shoot. Pradhan, quite unaware, that a *doberman* was rushing at him, sprinted from bush to bush, playing the game to the hilt. When a twenty kg something of a dog, with its momentum, jumped on to the back of a man, however sturdy he may be, that the result would be catastrophic, there was no doubt. Pradhan felt as if he was hit by a bolt from the sky and let out a deep throated resounding cry, which reverberated around the place. It drew everybody to the spot, including the DCP, his '*boss*'. He found the Inspector, sprawled on the ground and the dog pinning him down firmly with it's fore paws. The little boy quietly withdrew from the scene. An *orderly* came running to take the dog away and Pradhan got up, his starched uniform, muddy. Seeing the DCP, in front of him, he saluted in '*attention*' position. The DCP took in the situation, smiled and simply asked, whether Rocky was there. Pradhan looked foolishly, debating in his mind, whether Rocky was the name of that brat or that brute.

While he was reminiscing his earlier experience with a child, Loyla tugged at his coat sleeve and said, 'Uncle! Uncle! What did my *daddy* tell you?'

Pradhan looked at the child and bringing a smile to his face said, 'He asked me to see you and handover these gifts, with lots and lots of love from him.' He brought out a beautiful bunch of roses and a box of chocolates from a bag and gave to her. The little one immediately put the roses to her face and said, 'How sweet these flowers are! Do you know, uncle, my *'mom'* liked roses, ——*(-Pradhan smelled danger)* the nurse brought roses every morning and put them in the vase, by the side of the bed in the Hospital. Daddy took me there and cautioned me not to disturb her. She was sick, he said. She looked very pale to me. The nurse gave me an apple, when I visited her. One morning, when I visited her, I found her lying still with her eyes closed, she was covered with a white sheet and rose petals were strewn on it. People had gathered around her and all of them were praying. I held on to my *dady's* hand. He led me out. That was the last time, I saw my *'mom'*. They told me that she had left for God's Abode. She died that day, didn't she uncle? Now, I know what death means. Pradhan noticed complete serenity on the girl's face. He almost broke down and hugging the girl, said, 'Death might have removed her, from you, my dear, but her love and affection shall always be with you. Be sure to light a candle before Mother Mary, every day in the church and pray for her. '

'Sure, I will do that, uncle.' The girl's mood changed, she took out one chocolate from the box and gave him and took one herself. He took her by his hand and led her back to the visitor's room. He shuddered to think, what would happen to the poor motherless child after Joshi was convicted and sent to jail. He remained with the girl for some time, engaging her with talks regarding her studies, friends and what gifts she would like on her birth day. Parting from the child was painful. Promising to see her soon, he left the convent. He gained, however, a little knowledge, that Joshi used to take her daughter, during holidays, to Bangalore. With a little prodding, the girl told him, that she liked the place in Bangalore, where he took her. There was a zoo near it and they visited the lion safari. There was a twinkle in her eyes, when she related how the little cub followed its mother and once she saw the lioness, feeding its baby.

On his return to Head Quarters, he contacted Police Head Quarters at Bangalore to assist him to locate Holiday Homes or Guest Houses near the zoo. He got an address, it was 'Parijat Residency'.

* * * * *

Saxena was a worried man, not only because Raja lived, but his agent with license to kill, was also missing. There was no news about him, after his last telephone call. What could have happened? He had no clue. He turned his attention to a more urgent matter, possibility of Raja spilling the beans before Police, about his earlier association with Saxena and the enemity developed between them. Probably not, otherwise Police would have questioned him, by now.

Under the loving care of his wife and prayer of *ma jee*, Raja's recovery was fast and satisfactory. Whenever *babu jee* visited, he could not look at him in the eye. Ram Gopal talked to him normally, without letting him know that he had read his letter. Raja, however, did not feel comfortable, in his presence. On one occasion, Ram Gopal found him alone, Ranee and *ma jee,* having gone to the temple for performing *puja*.

He looked affectionately at Raja and said, 'Why did you take such a desperate step and put yourself in the death's claws? Did you not realize for a moment, what would have happened to Ranee, had you been hit in the head?'

Raja held his hands and said, *'Babu jee*, I was in total perplexity, when I knew, that they found out my identity, of being Shekher, who betrayed them. I was certain that they would kill me. Before that, I wanted to caution you about the real identity of Saxena and make you abreast of everything. Neither I had the courage nor the morality to tell you that I betrayed you and kept you in dark about my hideous activities. I wanted to get away from the whole thing. It did'nt even strike me, that I was putting myself in grave danger, when I went to that place. I wanted to get away from the crowd and find solace in solitude.'

'Why did you ever think, that I would have taken it amiss, if you had come to me with your story, in the first place? It is not only your battle, Raja, it is our battle from now on. We must fight out against him, without letting police know.'

'I have a plan *babu jee*.' He told of his plan to Ram Gopal jee, who gave his consent with great reluctance, since it was fraught with great danger. He asked Raja, that he may join office only after, he feels fit. He hugged him and left. Raja wiped the tears, collected in his eyes.

One day, a person walks into the office of Saxena, unannounced. The man guarding the front office saw him and stood bolt upright, and stared. *Chota bhai* least expected to see Shekhar, in the office. He couldn't be mistaken, the same angular face with side burns, long hair and wearing a suit, ties and dark glasses. What the Hell, he was doing here? Some time, he masquerades as Raja and at other time as Shekhar. He had ticked off this man, after hearing from Joshi. Scarcely, he misses, but this time the man lived. He was shot at, as Raja and now he is standing before him, in the version of Shekhar.

Taking off his make up, Raja said, '*Chota bhai,* you better go and inform the *boss,* that I am here to see him, with an important proposal, instead of standing there and gaping at me.' He rushed to the inner room and came out after a short while. He said, 'Yes, he will see you. You may go in. Before that, let me——you know, in case——.' He searched him and let him enter the room. Raja found Saxena, some what relaxed and yet ever vigilant, looking at him with his X-Ray eyes. 'will you not ask me to sit, *sirjee*?'

'Yes, you may take a chair, do I know you?'

'Otherwise, you would not have called me inside.'

'May be I know you, but you have changed a lot since then.'

'What is there in appearance, *sirjee*? Your man did'nt make any mistake to find me from thousands and hit me. But your old Shekhar is still alive and kicking and stands before you.'

'Or may be Raja, for a change.'

'So you knew then."

'Not at the first meeting, but later I spotted you, driving a posh car. My suspicion was confirmed by my man, later.'

'I know and then you decided to take a pot shot at me.'

'In my business, I cannot take chances.'

'I am not going to give you any more chances, *sirjee*. Before I came here, I left a note, giving details of your activities, in an envelope, with instructions to open it, if anything happens to me. So, don't get any funny ideas, in that rotten brain of yours.'

Raja enjoyed the situation, he smiled at his adversary, who was reeling under his scathing attack. He has hit him in his gut, sure enough. 'What do you want exactly Raja, if I may call you so.'

'Yes, why not. I would like to bury Shekhar. He does not exist any more. I am Raja for everyone, including you. I, for one, would not consider your position enviable, *sirjee*. You are sitting on a volcano, any time I want, a visit of Inspector Pradhan could be arranged for you. He would be interested to ask you a question or two about pumping of bullets in my body. He has had several talks with me and would be very much interested to know whether I suspect anybody.'

'I repeat, what exactly do you want from me?'

'If you want to save your skin, keep off from me. I am a peace loving man, I have a family to take care of. Let us call a truce. We shall not dirturb each other. Now, how you conduct yourself is entirely your business.'

'If you have finished, you may take your blasted self out of this place and consider yourself lucky.' Raja knew that the interview was over, he got up and left his office. Raja knew, he tricked him. When he turned his back and walked out of the office, he had a tingle of fear, expecting at any moment, a volley of bullets piercing his body. The feeling lasted till, he cleared out of the building and came out to the open.

Saxena smashed his fist on the desk out of exasperation and cursed Joshi, to have left the job, unfinished. Where could be this s. o. b? Has the earth gobbled him up? What guarantee is there that Raja was not double crossing him? He dialled a number and spoke to somebody over the phone. From that moment, Raja was kept under twenty four hours surveillance. He must be cautious and in the present juncture, he did not want to be on the wrong side of the law. He cautioned all his men to keep the jackpots run dry for some time and strengthen the security, at all the game centers. He has a reputation as a law abiding citizen and none of his actions should jeopardize it.

* * * * *

Having come away unscathed from Saxena's lair, Raja headed straight for his house and rested for a while. His encounter with his ex-*boss*, in his lair, was too much to digest. He wondered why, police was not yet on to this gangster and he was free to run his business without a hitch. It was high time, to drop a pebble in his pool of quietude.

The inertia of the department made the police to move slowly. One of the places which was in the list of the Inspector, to be looked into, was 'Hotel Ranjit'. Being midway between Victoria Terminus and Flora Fountain, most of its clientele were sales representatives and businessmen. The tarrif was reasonable and the rooms, comfortable. One evening, a middle aged person walked to the Reception Desk and booked a room in the name of Mr. Ramesh Dalal from M/s United Brewary of Calcutta. He was shown to his room in the first floor, facing the Lift. After a while, Dalal came down to the lounge dressed in casuals and sat on a sofa at a corner, where others were seated. He saw a bill board, displaying that a cabaret show was scheduled for seven pm, in the dining hall. He looked at his watch, the time was six thirty. Still there was time for the rendezvous with the person. Why not? He moved over to the dining hall on the ground floor and sat at a corner table. The stage was dimly lighted and a crooner was at the mike, swinging her hips. Gradually the tables were filled up. Waitresses were moving with trays of drinks and cigarettes. The clock struck seven.

The stage went dark. Then the light beam focussed at the centre and into the beam came a woman gripping a cloak around her body. The orchestra struck a crescendo which reverberated around the Hall. The dancer had shed her cloak and stood dressed only in essentials, a pair of scanty underthings, and a panty hose of skin colour; she appeared nude. The crowd went wild and clapped. Then she moved her slender limbs nimbly, shaking her lithe body in suggestive manners to the delight of the audience. There was silence except for the soft voice of the crooner, accompanied by a lilting music. The cabaret dancer moved across the stage, with the light beam following her. She seemed to be floating in the air, with arms held high above her head, she swirled like a mechanical top, almost on the tips of her shoes. The tight garment, she wore strained at the seams and looked as if they would burst. The audience held their breath. After few more such erotic displays, the show ended and the audience applauded. When the lights came on, Dalal was not found at his table.

He found himself, in a long corridor, with rooms on either side, and proceeded towards the Lift. The place was dimly lit and thickly carpeted. Suddenly, a door opens and a hand pulls him inside. The room was dark. He could see only a dark shape, holding on to his hand. He had an urge to punch the person and free himself, but at that instant, lights came on and he was staring at the beautiful face of the cabaret dancer.

The woman spoke, 'Inspector Pradhan, I believe'. Pradhan nodded. She showed him a chair and continued, 'I have already risked my life, in inviting you to this place. Cabaret dancers do not have any name, but you may call me Pushpa, that is my real name. I am almost a prisoner in this set up. I do not have much time, the next show is scheduled after one hour. I must tell you my story, in brief.'

Pradhan listened to Pushpa's strange story. She was an accomplished *kathak* dancer from Banaras, who came to Bombay, to try her fortune, in the film city. Being a divorcee, she wanted to earn a living as a dancer and lead a respectable life with her daughter, who was only six years old. She came to the city with her baby daughter and reached Bombay. Since she had no address to go to, a taxi driver brought her to this hotel and finding the place suitable, she took a room and moved in. How was she to know that a fly had walked into the spider's boudoir. Her first mistake was to confide in the receptionist who appeared to be a decent and cultured lady. She expressed her sympathy and told, that she knew few persons, who had contacts with film producers and it might not be difficult for her to get a contract. She agreed to meet the person who would introduce her to the producer. A meeting was arranged and I accompanied the agent, let me call him Manthan, to the Producer's office at Chembur. I waited in the hall, where several others had gathered. There were even few girls, who looked like college students, all in their teens. Soft drinks were served to us. After a while, Manthan came and whispered in my ears, that the *boss* would see me and I must show him all of my references, certificates, photographs of my stage performances at Banaras and generally be nice to him. I did'nt follow, what he meant. Entering, I saw a fat man, sitting on a, generousely cushioned chair, of the like, one would usually find, used for brides and bridegrooms during marriage receptions. He chewed *pan* continuously, stuffing in his mouth, one after another, replenished from a silver case on the glass top of the table. His dome was covered with a cap. Probably, he was bald. When he smiled, his pan stained teeth showed. I waited to hear from him, with a thumping heart.

When he spoke, it was like a thunder.

'So, this is our lovely Pushpa, the danseuse from Banaras. You know Manthan, Birju Maharaj is a very good friend of mine. I tell you, these days, to have a skill in *kathak* style of dancing, is a great asset. Moreover, Pushpajee, with your figure, you will scale heights. There is no doubt.' Then, he favoured me with a lecherous look, probably he was mentally undressing me. I lowered my face. He was telling Manthan. '*Aap, inke liye ek date le lo, phir audition ke liye, le aao.*' The meeting ended and I returned to the Hotel.

Few days later, the audition took place and it went well. I hoped to get the contract, the same day and also some advance, as my Hotel Bill was mounting high. My hopes were shattered, when the *bhadiya* showed his teeth, I rushed out from the bastard's office. That was the end of my film career. Pradhan was listening to the story and waited for Pushpa to continue. She almost wept, when she told him, how they transformed her from a dancer to a bar maid and then to a cabaret dancer by sending her daughter to a remote boarding school and meeting all of her expenses from her earnings. She has not seen her child since last three years. She cannot run away from this slavery without endangering the life of her child. She told him, that they are also running a casino behind the Hotel, secretly.

It was time for Pushpa's next show. Pradhan slipped out of the room and went to his suite.

* * * * *

The next target for screening and elimination was a place called 'Elegant Bar' which served drinks to elite customers off the counter. Entry could be gained through membership cards. The bar was licenced and there was no reason for the police to conduct raids. Serving drinks was fairly lawful. There should be some other way to gain entry, other than the front door. The building was in a corner block, at the intersection of two roads, at right angles. On one side, there was the neon sign of '*Elegant Bar*' and on the other there was a space measuring twenty by ten, housing an indoor electrical sub station with a steel collapsible door marked with a sign of a skull and cross bones with the inscription of 'DANGER 11000 VOLTS', followed by other shopping centers. While reconnoitring the area, Inspector Borde applied his ear close to the collapsible door, he did'nt hear the usual humming noise of an energisd Electrical Transformer. It meant that the sub station was dead. Strange, it semed to the Inspector. Where from the premises is getting power? A telephone call to the City Distribution Engineer clarified the matter. Power was fed from another source and the indoor sub station was now defunct.

In the evening, a truck bearing the sign of the Electricity Supply Company, was seen parked beside the building. Workmen wearing uniforms and helmets, carrying tools and implements got down. A welding machine was unloaded and a trailing cable was connected to a piller box, nearby. A foreman was seen instructing the workmen, who was none other than Inspector Borde. A hole large enough for a man to enter, was made in the brick wall, behind the electrical transformer. While the other workers were busy in dismantling the connections. Borde in plain clothes entered inside the building, through the hole. He found himself inside a dark room. Flashing the torch he carried, he found that the room was filled with discarded furniture, disused control panels, coils of cables and other sundry items. There was a steel door on the other side, he moved towards this cautiously and found it locked. He listened. There was no sound, suddenly he heard a whirring sound of machinery. The sound abruptly stopped, again it started. It dawned upon him that he was next to a Lift shaft, where lift cables were running. He retraced his path and instructed the workmen to rig up immediately a gas cutter to open the door. The door opened to the buffer chamber of the Lift. A flight of steps led to the ground floor, through a steel trap door which held tight. He heaved the trap door up, it opened out, on its hinges. Borde came up and found himself in a deserted corridor, dimly lighted, At last, he was inside the building.

He did not risk the Lift, it seemed to be too frequently used. He took the stairs and reached the first floor. Finding no activities there, he climbed another flight of stairs and reached the second floor. He was about to come to the corridor, when three persons came out of the Lift and headed straight to a room ahead. They entered without knocking. He came out of his hiding place and entered, as others did. The door opened to a vestibule, thickly carpeted and dimly lighted. There was silence, he was in a very vulnerable position and if found by some body, he might be challenged, he did not find any place to hide. Suddenly his eyes fell upon a door, with a 'MEN' sign. It was a wash room, thank God, he went inside and keeping the door slightly ajar, kept watch on the lounge. Two persons came out of a room farther down and came towards his hiding place. He waited with bated breath, but they moved along. He rushed to the room and entered, there was nobody to challenge his entry. All persons, entering this area were supposed to have been cleared by security, he thought. He found himself, in a big game room, buzzing with activity. People sat around Tables, concentrating on whatever game that was being played. He found, people standing around, watching others play and sliding into seats, whenever they got vacated. He did'nt want to attract attention to himself and mingled with the crowd, where it was thicker. It was a roulette table. None noticed him. Everyone's eyes were focussed on the game. The magic of the swirling ball on the wheel and its dropping into a hole, each time the wheel stopped rotating, drew a cry of exhilaration or despair, depending on whether the players gained or lost. Betting was pretty high, he noticed that the players were loosing more often than not. Lakhs of rupees were swept away, into the casino's coffer, each time the wheel stopped. Borde, then moved on to one of the cards table where '*teen patti*'(poker) was played. There were about seven players around the oval table, the shuffler sat at one end, shuffling cards expertly. He distributed the cards so skillfully, that each card landed at the intended player, not an inch this way or that way. He observed the players, each one had his own style. After all the three cards were dealt, there was lull at the table, one by one they picked up their cards and furtively had a glance at the cards, deliberately in slow motion, taking their own time without betraying any emotion on their faces. There were a couple, who did not even pick up their cards and simply let them lie there, but took part in betting when it started. The stakes increased from rupees one hundred to one thousand, gradually. Notes piled up at the center. Now the persons, who were calling blind, picked up their cards. Borde observed them, they were impassive, one of them lighted a cigarette and inhaled deeply, filling his lungs with the tobacco smoke, before he let it out through his nostrils. He coolly increased the stake to rupees ten thousand. By this time, there were only four players left including the shuffler, others had quit. Now the remaining players had two alternatives, they may continue with staking rupees ten thousand indicating that they have an equally strong hand or quit. Out of four, two players quit, leaving in the field only two. The shuffler picks up the cards and views one of the three, it was an ace. He looked at his opponent, who stayed cool, and seemed satisfied with his lot, otherwise he would not have raised the stake. The atmosphere was electric, Borde looked on, the spirit of the game caught him, for a moment, he forgot why he was there. The shuffler didn't want to quit without a fight. He saw the other two cards, they were a king and a miserable seven. The opponent must be having a minimum of two aces, he reasoned, if he quits he would be saving ten thousand, no doubt. If he is bluffing with lesser cards, then he may look to be a fool to have lost several thousands. He put rupees ten thousand and asked for a show. Now, whoever had a stronger combination, would sweep the stake. The opponent put down one card, it was an ace, this was matched with the ace of the shuffler, then the opponent came out with a king, this was also matched with a king of the shuffler. The atmosphere was tense, it was the turn of the opponent to show the last card, it would win or loose about thirty thousand rupees. Borde looked at the shuffler closely, these are tough guys, he thought. He would have played far bigger stakes, won lakhs for the owners with deft shuffling, he waited for the moment, which would decide the game one way or the other. Then he turned his attention to the opponent, he held the card closely guarding it, he looked at the shuffler, he matched his eyes with him, gambling is a fight of wills, so what, ten is a decisive card, take it bastard, win it if you can, he spoke silently and let go the card from his hand, it was a ten of spades, there the three cards lay exposed, ace, king and ten, a deadly combination no doubt. Everybody's attention was on the shuffler, with a thin smile on his lips, he threw his card, a mere seven and said, 'You win buddy.' The opponent picked up the spoils, quite a sum, may be for the last time at this joint, Borde thought and left the table on his way out.

Police lost no time to raid the places and seized cash, dope and arrested the operators. Many escaped from the police net through secret exits. The places were sealed and licenses withdrawn. The News papers howled and added *masala* to their stories about the raids and bravery of the police. Phones at the Commissioner's office continuously rang, complaints regarding excesses by police during raids, were lodged. The Police Commissioner held a meeting in his office and congratulated the officers who took part in the raids, especially he praised Pradhan and Borde for their exemplary services.

* * * * *

At the breakfast table, Raja read the news of police raids on several hotels, bars and their findings about gambling and drug trafficking carried out at these places, clandestinely. A thin smile appeared across his lips and thought it is about time that police tightens its net to catch the mastermind behind all this. He has joined office in the meanwhile, to the utter delight of Ram Gopaljee, who said that he must take it lightly and not overstress himself. Ranee joined him at the table and exclaimed, 'Why Raja, you have not touched your tea, it is already cold. What are you thinking about?' He said, 'Nothing dear, except that, my shoulder is still painful and I am not able to hold you in my arms and plant a kiss on those lovely lips of yours.' Ranee said, 'Oh! Raja, will you ever be serious? I will never know what you feel, really. Does it really pain or you are joking?'

Jaya walked in and said, 'Hello, everybody.' Raja and Ranee were glad to see her. Ranee said, 'Look Jaya, your *bhaiya* is still complaining of pain in his shoulders and yet he joined office. Should he not have continued his leave?'

'Of course, he should have. I have a proposal for his relaxation and also change of climate. Why not all of you come over to spend few days with me at Poona. The place is peaceful and the climate at this time of the year is excellent. I'll telephone Shyam *dada*, to prepare the rooms. We will travel tomorrow by a Flight.'

'Excellent idea, my dear, what do you say, Raja?' Ranee asked. *Ma jee* joined them in the meanwhile and said, 'I heard Jaya *bitiya's* voice and finished my *pooja* sooner. How are you, my dear?' Paying her respects, Jaya said, 'I am fine *Ma jee*, I was proposing, that all of you visit Poona and spend few days with me, it will also offer me an opportunity of showing you the place where I worked. I am sure you will like the place, *Ma jee.'*

That was the last place Parvati wanted to visit. Once it was a heaven for her, but now what it has to offer ? With Lolita no more, the place has no attraction for her, rather it will bring back memories of her past which she has been striving to forget. But she did not want to disappoint Jaya and suppressing her emotions, she forced a smile in her face and said, 'It will really be a pleasure *beti,* to visit the place and see your handiwork which I am sure will be worth praising.'

'Oh, Ma jee, you are an angel.' Jaya hugged her.

They left for Poona on the following day. Shyam *dada*, received them at the farm house. Ranee and *Ma jee* were overjoyed with the serenity of the place. The house was located in the outskirts and away from the traffic with a thick cover of trees. To *Ma jee*, it was a revisit. Little did these people know, that she spent her younger years at Poona. She walked behind others, as they entered, but she was years behind, in her thoughts. She was again the young Parvati, the village belle, who came away with Ratan, leaving behind her village. Her chain of thoughts was broken when Jaya called her. They were all waiting for her at the tea table.

Jaya told them, that her works at the site were coming to a close and she would take them on a visit to the place in a day or two. She left for site, reminding Shyam *dada* that *ma jee* takes boiled vegetables along with rice and *dal* and nothing else. Ranee observed, 'How mature our Jaya has become these days. So young and so responsible. *Ma jee*, shall we not get them married, as soon as Kamal returns?'

Ma jee said, '*Beta* everything is in His Hands. I want to see them only happy.'

The sky was overcast and it had started drizzling. The weather was chill. After many days, Raja could sleep soundly, with out a care in his mind. Seeing him asleep, with a child's freshness in his face, Ranee did not disturb him. It was already *eight* in the morning, when he got up. He got ready and came down to the breakfast table, where others waited for him. He sat by the side of Jaya and remarked, 'Jaya, you look so happy this morning, any good news?'

'Yes, do you know, I have, almost, completed the job, for which I was hired. Probably, I may leave Poona, after few days. I never relaxed in these two years. Oh! how quickly the time has passed, really.'

Everyone welcomed the news. Ranee asked, 'When are you taking us there Jaya, to see your showcase?'

'I thought of taking you down there, today. But see, how the weather has changed abruptly. It may not suit Raja *bhaiya.*'

'Oh! no, please do not postpone on my account. No problem at all. I am fine', Raja said.

'Then it is settled, we will leave after breakfast', Ranee said.

* * * * *

The Supervisor of the *'eloctronics surveillance firm'*, received orders from the owner to dismantle all the hook ups of cameras, monitors and other equipment from the rooms, just before the false ceiling works were taken up. A truck, loaded with the materials, passed through the main gate, as Jaya and others arrived.

The clouds had lifted and there was bright sun shine when their car approached the house. Driving on a washed tarmac was a pleasure. Road side trees glistened in the sun rays, water dropping from their foliage. Car window glasses were rolled down to offer them views of distant mountains, looking grey in the morning sun light, blue sky in the background and patches of white clouds hovering above them. Traffic was thin at that time of the day, except for few long body buses, on the highway. Suddenly, the house, radiantly white, appeared at a little distance to the left. The sight was a grandeur. Freshly painted, the house caught the sun rays in its glazed surfaces, throwing reflections, which dazzled the eyes. The car followed a winding gravel path lined with exotic potted palms and finally came to a halt under the portico.

Wide steps led to the verandah. They got down, Ranee marvelled at the sight and followed Jaya and Raja, up the steps.

Parvati remained behind, gaping at the house, mesmerized. She could not put a step forward. Was she dreaming? Her mind raced back twentytwo years, across the time and her eyes searched for some one, who would emerge from the Hall and come rushing towards her with extended hands, as she used to do, when Parbati lived behind the big house, in her small cottage. Nobody came. Suddenly she came to her senses. Gone are the days, when the loved ones lived here, *Sethjee*, Lolita and her husband. This is the house, where she spent some of the happiest days of her life. She ran behind and there it was, her small cottage still intact, but wild bushes had encroached upon the little garden path, which led to the cottage. She ran inside and was thrilled to see the mango and lemon trees, which he nourished with water drawn from the well. Yes, the well. But where is it? It must be some where here, she found excavated soil and heaps of rubbles at the site. Seeing an elderly lady roaming alone, the gardener working on the lawn at a distance, came over and asked, *'Ma jee*, are you searching for some thing?'

'Yes, *bhaiya*, there used to be a well over here, where is it?' The gardener, a middle aged man with a dhoti tied tightly, around the waist and a a turban tied around his head, stared at her for a long time, before he spoke. A broad smile broke on his face and he exclaimed, 'Parvati jee, is it you? I am Bhola, don't you remember me?' The name struck a chord in her memories and her eyes registered recognition and joy. She was overwhelmed. Tears flowed down from her eyes. When she spoke, her voice was choked. 'Yes, you must be Bhola, the young boy who brought me flowers for my *puja*. How are you Bhola? You look already old with greying hair.'

'It has been a long time, Parvatijee. Where have you been all these years? And how is *babua?* Suddenly, you disappeared from the house with the child. We were told, that you left for your village. Things changed rapidly after you left.'

'What happened?'

He swallowed and then said, 'Don't you know? Ratan married *bibijee.* The marriage was a simple affair. No body attended, there was no celebration. We were told that the marriage was solemnized in a court. After the marriage, *bibijee* was not seen outside. Only the old cook was left to give her company. Many of the household staff left, but I continued for my love of the garden, which I tended in my hands. The plants are like children to me.'

Parvati listened, suppressing all emotions within her. The ruthless and cruel actions of Ratan changed the world of the people who lived in the house. She could imagine, the house which flourished in the time of *Sethjee* with laughter and gaiety, mostly contributed by Lolita an emblem of purity, love and beauty would have fallen to pieces, once they were gone. After all Ratan married *bibijee.* What a cruel justice meted out to her. She suppressed tears with great efforts and asked, 'But, Bhola what happened, why the house was abandoned?'

'It is a long and sad story, Parvatijee. After you left, Ratan dispensed with the services of *bibijee's* personal maids, one after another, she was virtually left alone in the big house. The old faithful cook was her only attendant. After some time, *bibijee* took to bed. One day, I saw her taken to the hospital. She appeared very thin. Afterwards, we heard that she gave birth to a son. It was good news. We were under the impression, that the lost glory of the house would return, with the birth of a heir. But no, our hopes were shattered, *bibijee* did not return to the house with her new born. Ratan had other ideas, he got her settled in Bombay. We never saw *bibijee* again. 'He continued.' Strange things occurred in the meanwhile. Rumours were afloat, that the house was for sale. Several promoters visited the site, for inspection, But one incident, turned everything upside down. You would remember, that a large portrait of *Sethjee* was hung over the mantelpiece in the Hall. One evening, Ratan stood under the portrait, discussing with a prospective buyer, suddenly there was a heavy gust of wind, which dislodged the huge portrait from its wall anchors. The portrait fell down and crashed on the floor. Ratan was saved by hair's breadth. That was really a bad omen. Perhaps, he read through it. He decided, not to dispose of the property. Do you know, what he did afterwards? He removed all the furniture and other articles, the portrait and other photographs, paintings, vases, fixtures, carpets and everything that was removable, including kitchen wares and dumped them in the underground cellar. For twenty years, the house has remained bare, nobody has visited since then. Watch and ward and general upkeep have been vested with a private agency, who pay my wages as well. Do you like to see your old cottage, Parvatijee, I have the keys.'

She said, 'Not now, I have people with me. But, you have not told me, where is the well.'

'Well, that is another story. Before I tell that, I must tell you one thing, Parvatijee, this house is haunted. Nobody knows, especially the people who are engaged in the renovation works, which you see in progress. These modern people, however, do not believe in ghosts and spirits. But, the fact is, I have seen the ghost of *'Sethjee'*, roaming around here. I have seen a shadow, emerging from the cellar and then roaming around the house and finally disappearing near the lemon tree, behind your cottage. This occurs, every '*purnamasi*' night. The apparition appears to me regularly, over all these years. I have not divulged this matter to any one else, lest I may be suspected of imagining things to bring disrepute to this house. Many strange things are happening here. The holy remains of *Sethjee* were buried under the lemon tree. It was I, who dug the soil and put the copper vessel containing the ashes in the soil, under the lemon tree. Now, coming back to the story of the well, Ratan had a plan to build a bungalow over this place. Excavation for foundation was taken up. No sooner the foundation pits were excavated, the land caved into the well, completely filling it up. The project was abondoned. The incident of the portrait and then of the well, must have completely unnerved Ratan and I have not seen him, since then.' Parvati would have liked to talk to Bhola on many matters, but she saw Jaya coming towards her and kept quiet. She came nearer and finding *ma jee* conversing with the gardner, said, '*Ma jee*, what are you dong here, we have been looking for you all over. I see that you have found Bhola, the gardner. He is a very sincere worker and the beautiful garden you see around, is entirely to his credit. I am told, that Bhola has been living here since long and knows many things connected with this house. I have been wanting to talk to him, but could not find the time, specially about this small and beautiful cottage and the persons who lived here. The atmosphere is so peaceful, *ma jee*, look at those mango and lemon trees standing there as silent sentinels, they must have their own story, to tell. What has he been telling you, *ma jee?*'

Parvati and Bhola exchanged glances. She said, 'Nothing *beta*, I was just congratulating him for maintaining such a beautiful garden and wanted to know the varieties of rose plants, he has grown here.'

'Let us go, *ma jee*, others are waitng for you. Bhola, one of these days, you must tell me, about this place. '

'Yes, *bibijee*', he said. They left. Bhola stared after them. Tears dropped from his eyes, he addressed somebody *bibijee,* after so many years, the word brought back to him the old memories. He remembered the day when *bada malik's* body was brought and laid down in the Hall, in front of the mantelpiece, above which, *Sethjee's* portrait was hung. The news spread like wild fire and all the staff gathered there. Everyone was weeping and staring at the body. They didn't believe their eyes. An earthen lamp was lit near the body, which kept burning without a flicker, Bhola steadily looked at the lamp and then rushed out, when he returned there was a bunch of freshly cut roses in his hands. With folded hands, he proceeded towards the body and placed the flowers on the chest of his beloved master. That was his last and humble tribute to *sethjee*, at that moment, he took a vow, looking steadily at the lamp, that he would never leave the house, as long as he lived and tend the garden as his own child and grow roses for offering daily to his master, wherever he would lie. Since then, he has been offering a fresh rose bud at the lemon tree, where the master's ashes lie. Tears flowing, he remembered the day, when for the last time he waited under the porch, as usual, with a freshly cut red rose bud in his hand to give *to bada malik* as he came down the steps, wearing a long coat and a silk *dhoti,* with a white cap on his head. Ratan held the car door open, the master accepted the flower from his hand, patted him and put it in the button hole, got into the car and drove off. He had stood there with folded hands till the car was out of his sight.

As soon as Parvati entered the Hall, accompanied by Jaya, her glance fell upon the bare wall above the mantelpiece. Bhola told her about the portrait, she kept her thoughts to herself. She joined, Raja and Ranee, admiring the beautiful interior decorations, which were the handiworks of their Jaya. She took them around the house, showing the rooms till she reached a large room in the first floor, which was beautifully done. That must be the room, *bibi jee* occupied, Parvati simply stared and crossing the time barrier, she found herself back in the room with Lolita. She had no eyes or ears for anything else.

Jaya was saying, 'This room is not only the largest but its layout, I found superb, it is an architect's dream. Throughout the morning, it catches the sunlight and also the southern wind through these large windows. I, therefore, decided to do the walls with a mixture of colours, so that the sun rays would diffuse and the light would be soothing. The shades of the curtain, bed covers and sofa covers are chosen accordingly————', she went on.

* * * **

She was assisting Lolita in dressing her hair in front of the mirror. The room was cool and fresh with fragrance of flowers put in vases, placed on tall mahagony stools at each corner. *Sethjee* used to order the flowers from reputed nurseries of Poona, to be delivered each morning at the house. He took all the measures to keep his mother less child, happy. Parvati would come to the room, every morning to help *bibi jee* with her hair, after letting Kamal sleep, soon after his feeding. That had become a routine for her. Lolita would be expecting her, and if she was late on any day, it would upset her and she would not speak to her for few moments. Then she would burst into laughing, embrace her warmly and forget her anger. One day, she led her to her wardrobe, which was full of dresses of all colours and designs, and asked her to pick up any one and wear it. She would hesitate, but *bibi jee* would insist. Once, she made her wear, one of her expensive dresses and bade her to sit quietly at her study table. At that moment, there was a knock at the door and before she could get up and answer, it opened and Ratan walked in. Seeing him there, her heart beat faster, *bibijee* was in the bathroom. She lowerd her head and remained silent. Ratan approached from behind and placed his hand on her shoulders in an impromptu manner. She turned abruptly and faced him.

Ratan exclaimed, 'You!What are you doing here? Where is Lolita?'

'I am here', said a voice from behind. Ratan was nonplussed and to cover up his misdeed, said that *Sethjee* sent him to fetch his cane.'

'In that case, you should have gone to *daddy*'s room', Lolita said in an angry voice. He withdrew and walked away.*'Bibi jee* said, 'Take care of your husband, before he goes astray.' Her face had become red in shame and she did'nt talk to Ratan for few days, after that incident.

* * * * *

She came to the present and surveyed the scene. The room was richly and artistically furnished, but lacked the vivacity and sprightliness, which Lolita could only provide. This was no time to lament her loss, which was irreparable. She composed herself and directed her attention towards the lush green lawn, down below, through the window. She heard Jaya, speaking, '*Ma jee*, you appear sad, what is the matter?' Parvati said, hastily, 'Nothing, *beta,* it just crossed my mind, who were the people owning this house and where are they gone?' What Jaya said, in clarifying this quandary, completely unnerved her. Jaya knew that Seth Mohan Lal owned the house, he had a daughter, Lolita and that he died in a road accident. What more she knew, Parbati did not venture to ask.

Parvati bit her lips and kept quiet, smitten by anguish and guilt. How long, she would be able to conceal the horrible truth from others, that it was her husband, who was responsible for the misfortune, this house suffered.

Even after her return to Bombay, the past which she had almost forgotten, the painful memories associated with the house, which lay buried in the deep recesses of her mind, surfaced to torment her. In the solitude of her room, she could not restrain her tears to roll down.

After working for few months as a handyman in the house, Ratan endeared himself to *Sethjee* and inched his way to his offices, carrying Files and things for him. In the meanwhile he learnt driving and replaced *Sethjee's* old driver Sambhu. He drove Sethjee, wherever he went and remained absent from home for long hours. She did not venture out of her cottage, which was her little world and kept herself busy with the child. What pained her most was, Ratan never looked at her son nor ever held the baby in his arms. That was too much to bear and she never forgave him, for that. Their love life had almost ended and gradually they became strangers to each other.

One day, she saw, a young girl, who came down the steps of the manson and went to the car under the portico, whose door was held open for her by Ratan, wearing a chauffeur's uniform complete with a cap. Then he drove away. She had no idea, who was the girl. Could she be the daughter of *Sethjee?* The cook aunty told her that, *malkin* was no more, she died leaving only a daughter. How lovely and elegant, she looked in that beautiful dress, she wore. She began imagining, that it was she, who was in the car, driven by Ratan. He stopped the car at a jeweller's shop and took her by hand, inside. She was dazed by the glitter of ornaments, all around. He asked her to chose one and she pointed to a necklace studded with bright stones. The sales girl took out the necklace from its case and handed it to her. Touch of the gold necklace enthralled her and she looked up at Ratan with love and gratitude. He put it around her neck and clasping it, asked to look at the mirror. In the mirror she saw her reflection, multiplied by numerous mirrors placed all round. She closed her eyes in ecstacy, when she touched her neck to feel the necklace, her hand touched the thin and cheap *mangal sutra*, she opened her eyes and found her standing at the gate of the cottage.

Next day, she learnt more about *bibijee,* from the cook. Mostly, she remained indoor, under the strict eye of her governess, whom *Sethjee* engaged after the death of her mother. Lolita lost her mother when she was hardly five years old. She was never sent out to school for her education, instead she had her instructions at home. She never goes outside except for a little drive in the car. She lives as a princess in a palace, she said. Parbati felt very sorry for Lolita, she must be feeling very lonely, in that big house, at least she has the baby to play with. She suddenly longed to make friends with Lolita, but being the driver's wife, she could'nt summon courage to approach her. More over, Ratan may not approve of it. All these thoughts troubled her.

But, to her surprise and delight, one day she saw, Lolita coming towards her, while she stood at the door step of the cottage, holding her baby. Now, she knew why the cook aunty called her a princess. She was a princess, no doubt. As she approached nearer, her charm and gait captivated her, she simply stared, words failed her.

Lolita asked, 'Aren't you the wife of Ratan?'

'Yes, *bibijee'*, she said, meekly.

'What a lovely baby, is it a boy or a girl?' The question brought a smile in the face of Parvati.

'Of course it is a boy *bibijee'*, and she lifted the baby up above and said, 'Look for yourself', that brought a burst of laughter from both of them. From that moment, they became friends.

She said, 'I am Lolita and what is yours?'

'Parvati', she said.

'Well. Parvati, will you not call me inside?'

'Oh! *Bibi jee*, please step in, this is your house'. Lolita swept in, her *dupatta* trailing behind. Parvati remembered that moment, she felt as if she carried a fragrance with her. Lolita was impressed with the tidiness of the little cottage. The sweet aroma of the incense sticks burning before the framed pictures of Gods and Goddesses placed at a corner, filled her nostrils.

'Oh! How nice, Parvati do you pray before the Gods ?'

'Yes, *bibijee.*'

'What do you ask for, in your prayers?'

'I ask for peace and happiness for everybody.'

'Really, me included ?' Then she laughed and said, 'I do not have pictures of Gods in my room, but I love flowers and have pleanty of them in my room. I like their softness and freshness.' She touched the face of the baby and said, 'As soft as your baby.'

'*Bibi jee,* flowers are the best creation of God. When the plants blossom, they bring joy and happiness to so many. More than anything else, God loves flowers. That is why we offer flowers to God. To love flowers is to love God.'

'Oh! Parvati, how cleverly you speak, where from you learnt all this?'

'I am a poor village girl *bibi jee.* Lost my parents in my childhood and then grew under a tyrannical *chachi*, who sought pleasure in giving pain to others. She used to send me to collect fire wood from the jungle. I suffered blisters from thorn bites on my tender feet. Gradually I became stronger and got used to the jungle, its plants and beasts. I have seen tigers at a distance restIng under a tree with their cubs, they did'nt bother me. In those days I came closer to God and His creation, I felt one with the nature. After all, God exists in everybody, whether it is material, plant. animal or human being. I accompanied once *chachi* and attended a holy gathering in the temple, where a discourse on '*Bhagavat*'was given by a '*pundit*'. He spoke about the ten *'avatars'*, forms that God assumed for the benefit of his '*bhaktas*' in different aeons, such as, *satya, tretaya, dwapar and kali.* These were, *machya* (fish), '*kachapa'* (tortoise), '*sukara* (boar),' *nrusingha*'(half man and half lion), *vamana* (a dimunitive ascetic), '*parsuram*'(wielder of a sharp weapon), *'Rama'*, '*Balarama,' Buddha',* and '*kalki'* (destroyer of evil). Beyond these, *bibijee*, I do not know any thing.

Lolita listened with rapture and said, 'Oh! Parvati, I want to spend more time with you, to learn things. You know so much and I, so little. You must come to the house, when my *daddy* and Ratan are away. We'll spend the day together, I have pleanty of toys of my childhood days, your baby will be happy to play with. Now I must go, it is time for my English lesson and my English tutor, Miss Rose Mary is expected at any time. She is an English lady and very punctual. In England there used to be a Queen Mary, who was detested by her subjects for her cruel deeds and they named her 'Bloody Mary'. I wrote on a copy book once, the name 'Bloody Mary' and she took me to task. She reported the matter to '*daddy'*. In her broken Hindi, she said, *'Sethjee, tumara beti Lolita galat rasta me ja raha hai, hamko gali deta hai.'*

She mimicked the voice of her English teacher and they laughed together, then she kissed good bye to the baby and almost ran towards the house. That was in short, Lolita so lively and charming.

* * * * *

Then the catastrophe struck. One day, it was time for Ratan to have returned, but he did not. Since he never kept to any time, she did not take it amiss. Having put the baby to bed, she waited. She must have slept. She was aroused by some one, calling her name. She woke up and found cook aunty, by her bed side, and she appeared to be in shock. She implored her to get up and come outside. Not fully awake, she managed to come outside, the lights were on and she found an ambulance parked under the porch, people had gathered and even few police men were seen. She was now fully awake and in a shaky voice asked aunty, what had happened. The old woman, almost dragged her and said, 'Come', she followed her, as if under a spell and reached the Hall. It was full of people and everyone was sobbing. She did not comprehend, what could have happened. Then she spotted, the young Bhola, who told her weeping that *Sethjee* was no more, he died in a road accident and they brought his body, which was lying in the Hall. Then the calamity struck her in full intensity, the first words that escaped her were, 'Ratan, where is he, is he——', she started wailing. The cook aunty consoled her, saying, 'Hush, nothing is the matter with your husband, he is alright, he has minor injuries and is in the hospital.'

She had then rushed to see Lolita, who had shut herself inside the room, aunty following her. They knocked, she did'nt open. Her maids, standing outside in a group said that after seeing *Sethjee* being brought in, shrouded in a white sheet stained with blood, she fainted and they brought her here, she regained consciousness after a while, asked them to leave her alone and, shut herself inside. Grief stricken, Parvati shouted, 'Lolita, it is me, Parvati. Please open the door for God's sake.' Finally she opened the door and seeing Parvati, held her tight and sobbed on her shoulders, her body shook uncontrollably. Between themselves, they led her inside and made her sit on the bed. They did not have any word to console her. Parvati stayed that night with Lolita, aunty returned to the cottage to take care of the child.

Things, thereafter, started happening abruptly, akin to a river leaving its course on plains and falling across a precipice in cascades down below, losing its identity for ever. After discharged from the hospital, Ratan, curiously enough became a changed person. He assumed full charge of the Late *Sethjee's* affairs. Lolita was in no position to take any interest in her father's business or assets. She didn't come out of her room and with great difficulties and efforts, Parvati was able to make her eat a little, aided by the cook. She seemed to have no zest for life. She would sit hours at the window, looking at the garden fountain, as if expecting some spectacular show to take place.

While her father was alive, she rarely went to his room; on the twelfth day of his demise, after the consecrated water was sprinkled all over, she picked up courage to visit his room through an interconnecting door. All the articles used by her father were there, lying on the desk, at the bed side, at the dressing table, proclaiming that his father had gone out and would return soon. Even a pair of freshly laundered *kurta, pyjama* set was kept ready at the bed side, by his personal servant, for his change, after return from office. This brought fresh tears in her eyes and Lolita sat down on the bed and broke down.

Lolita told her, 'Do you know Parvati, two days before his death, *daddy* had a discussion with me and asked my opinion regarding my marriage?'

'Your marriage! What did you say?'

'I opposed, I said, nothing doing *daddy,* I am not going any where, leaving you. Do you know what he said? He hugged me and said, *who talks of letting you go any where, even when married, my dear, you will continue to live here in this house with your husband. I cannot let you go any where leaving me.*'

In her bereavement, one day, she showed her a photograph of a handsome young man. She asked her, 'Lolita, who is he?'

'He is the one, *daddy* wanted me to marry. I do not know even his name. He wanted to discuss with me later, that evening, on his return.' Then she broke down and said, 'Oh! *daddy,* why did you leave me?' She could not speak further and sobbed. She had no words to console her.

* * * * *

It was a bright sunny day in Bangalore, when Lalan, the gardener at the Parijat Holiday Home decided to take some time off from lawn mowing and rest for a while in the tool shed. He took a little *chun*(lime) and tobacco from a pouch and was about to mix the two on his palm by his thumb to prepare a dose of *khaini* when a large shadow fell upon him. He looked up and saw a young man in *dehati* clothes, standing at the entrance.

'*Kaun hai bhai?*'

The stranger touched his feet and said, 'Lalan *chacha*, I am from Samastipur, son of Kishen, your *chachera bhai.*'

Lalan holding the *khaini* in his hand, looked at him and said, '*Kishen ka ladka ho, eishan kaho, tab to hamra bhatija thahre na? Ka nam hai tora bitwa?*'

'Mata Prasad', the young man said.

'*Baitho, baitho*'. he welcomed the young man inside. He put the *khaini* in his mouth, wiped the palms and said, 'You are tall and strong, not short and lean as your father used to be. *Chalo achha hai, kheti me hath batatte ho na?* I told your *bapu,* at the time of leaving home for *pardesh,* to eat well and be strong. He chose to remain at home to do farming. When I left the village, you were a young boy of fifteen years then, and my daughter Sashi was already married. You may not be knowing *beta,* I had to mortgage my land and bullocks to the Zamindar for a loan to meet her marriage expenses. No other alternative was left, but to earn a livelihood outside. These people pay me well and I have been sending every month money to your *chachi,* to pay the interest to the Zamindar and set aside a sum to pay the loan amount. It is a tough time for farmers, *beta.'*

'Yes, *chacha,* it must be really hard for you, to be away from the family.'

'How is everybody at home. It has been ages since I saw them. How is Kishen?'

'He is fine and always remembers you. He gave me your *thikana*, so I came to see you. I have come with others, mostly farmers along with the *sarpanch* of our village, under a scheme to visit South, for studying different farming techniques. We are leaving tomorrow morning.'

'I am glad, you came to see me. *Beta, hamare sath do roti khake jana.*'

'*Thik hai chacha*. But, I don't see anybody else here.'

'*Hai na beta*, the *chowkidar,* he has gone to arrange the marriage of his daughter. It is no problem, I am able to manage alone. Any way, at this time of the year, very few come to stay in the guest house. Since the last visitor came, a fortnight ago, nobody has turned up.'

'*Chacha*, may I help you a little in doing the rooms, while I am here, I will feel good. Please say no. It will be my pleasure.'

'*Thik hai, tab aao hamare sath,'* He took him on a tour of the bungalow. There were only six rooms in all and a lounge. Lalan said, '*Ek kam tum kar sakte ho, kamarwa kholke, chaddar bagairah badal dalo.'*

'*Jaisa tum kaho, chacha.*'

Lalan opened a cupboard and brought out freshly laundered bed sheets etc and gave those to him.

'Kam khatam karke, aa jana beta, tab tak hum roti banai lete hain.' Then he left.

Left alone, Mata Prasad, who was none other than Inspector Pradhan, went to the reception desk immediately and scanned the Register where records of arrival and departure of guests were maintained. He found an entry in the name of Joshi, who stayed in the Holiday Home, few days after the incident. Perhaps that is the way of relaxation for the hired killers after they shoot some one. Nice hide out, coming away to a distant place to hibernate is a clever way to escape the hot breath of police on their trails! He brought out his Toyoflex, Japanese camera and took a snap of the page, where the entries were made, complete with signature of Joshi. Well…Here is some thing at last. He opened the room occupied by Joshi, he was greeted by a pungent smell of tobacco. He went to the bed side table, where an ash tray was lying. It was full of cigarette butts, he picked up one and found it to be of the same brand as of the one, found at the site of shooting. He made a thorough search of the room and also the bathroom and did not find any thing of worth. The last item he went through was the waste paper basket, he found torn pieces of cinema tickets and shop vouchers. He was about to discard these, when suddenly some thing scribbled on the reverse of a voucher caught his eye, it was a number written in a hurry. He folded the voucher and pocketed it. He finished the job of changing the bed sheets, pillow covers, towels, etc in the rooms, but not before looking outside the window, to find if some thing was dropped, only a perfectly mowed lawn met his eye. While doing one of the rooms, Pradhan found a pack of condoms under the pillow, well, he chuckled, some one probably was cheating on his wife. But, nothing like that in Joshi's room, his entertainment lay some where else. He came out and joined his supposed to be *chacha,* in his cottage. Lalan said, '*Kam kar liye beta? Ab hath, muh dhole. Roti kha jaye.*' Before sitting for lunch, Mata Prasad gave a packet to Lalan and said, '*Chachajee, bapu* has sent some sweets and *achar* and also *debi ma's prasad,* for you.' After eating his lunch, he took leave from Lalan with his blessings with the thought, that when the old man returns home and the real Mata Prasad presents himself before him, he(Pradhan) would not be there atleast, to mark the surprise on Lalan's face.

Pradhan went to a pay phone in a local Post Office and contacted his office at Bombay. He asked them to find out whether the number he gave them belonged to a telephone, a bank account or a locker. He was not very happy with his findings so far. It was like chasing a wild goose.

CHAPTER 7

On his return to Head Quarters, Pradhan was informed, that the number, he gave them, was indeed a telephone number of Bombay Telephone Exchange and it belonged to a pharmaceutical store at Dadar, some thing at least to go on, he thought. He asked his men to keep the Store under vigil round the clock, listening to any one, asking for messages, if any. The police vigil was rewarded, one day. A man came into the store and asked the sales girl, at the counter, whether there was any message for him. The girl scanned a note book and replied in the negative. The man was tailed, when he left the stores. Tails were changed, every now and then, so that he would not suspect. The policemen, in plain clothes, tailing the subject, were continually in touch with a wire less control van parked in the vicinity and passed on messages, which were relayed to Pradhan.

The subject, Mathew was a small cog in the big wheel of the set up. His job was to collect messages from operators and pass on to a person addressed as 'Saheb'. He went to the Stores, every two days to collect messages. Amongst other things, he was instructed not to keep company with women. But that was really hard on him, they were his weaknesses, he could not resist a beautiful woman, when he sees one. Now the sales girl at the drug store was a stunning beauty; visits to the stores were, therefore welcome. His employers, however, paid him handsomely and he did not want to lose either his job or his head for any transgression. He knew that the people he worked with must be very dangerous and might not hesitate to do away with his life, just as throwing a banana peel. On one occasion, however he could not resist the temptation. The girl gave him the *come hither* look and he followed her to a cubicle size room, used for storing medicines. In the cramped space, the girl made a space on a table and lay down, her skirt pulled up baring her round thighs. When Mahews was about to mount her, the girl stopped him and pointed to a box of condoms, lying on a shelf. 'Okay baby, all the way then', he said.

His next stop was a coffee shop, which he frequently visited. He liked the coffee and more than the coffee, the waitress with her tight uniform and a mini skirt always attracted him. Once to his good luck, she had to bend down to pick up some thing from the floor and he got a breath taking vision of the red coloured panty she was wearing. With the hope of getting some such sight, he entered the coffee house. The sleuth tailing him followed and went to a corner table to keep an eye on him. He had a small microphone fixed to his shirt collar, through which he could speak to and be in touch with the wireless van. In the meanwhile, Mathew called the waitress to take his order and to the horror of the girl, he cupped her buttocks when she turned. He was rewarded with an angry stare from the girl and he grinned at her. The policeman knew such lecherous goons and did not bother. Mathew came out of the coffee bar and headed straight to the pay phone booth, at the street corner. All such phone booths, in and around the Block under police surveillance, were wired. The policeman following Mathew, reported the booth number to the man inside the wireless van. By the flick of a switch, the operator could see on a screen, Mathew lifting the receiver and inserting a coin and dialing a number. Then he spoke to some body. All the images and the voice were filmed and available for review at the Head Quarters by Inspector Pradhan, within minutes.

* * * * *

Saxena was worried stiff, these days. He learnt from his office, that his son withdrew huge sums of money, for reasons unknown. Did he dump it on racing and gambling? He wondered. His hands were already full in dealing with Tax authorities and also with the Syndicate, for his secret dealings, which brought him huge money. Jackie has been his problem child. Taking after his mother, he is obstinate and stubborn. Seeing so much wealth around him, he never felt the necessity of knowing, how it was earned. His pleasure lay in spending it. He tried to rein in his son but failed miserably. He didn't have the heart to cut short his money supply. Some how, he had a soft corner for him. Was it because of love and affection? But these are not the traits, natural to him. He did not care for Parvati and her child for that matter. He had no remorse for having let her go. She was tough and would take care of herself and the baby, as a tigress would, for its cub. Lolita was different, brought up in riches and comforts since her childhood, she was not exposed to the real world, selfish and cruel. Whatever he is now, it is because of his selfish nature. He has never gone begging for money and comforts. He has snatched them, as an eagle would do, diving at its prey. Others may be jealous of his wealth and inclined to believe, that he is fortunate enough to possess so much. Careful schemings were behind all of his actions. Sometimes he had to wait for years, to spring for his kill. On one occasion in his life, he committed the gravest blunder, which was not in his scheme of things. Being in a tempestuous mood, he was drunk, he forced himself into the privacy of Lolita and assaulted the poor girl, who had just lost her father. That was one occasion for which he did not excuse himself and will bear the guilt, as long as he lived. Besides acquiring wealth, the other thing that was dear to him was, Jackie.

He picked up the phone and spoke, 'I want to know, how the money was spent.' The wheels in the organization moved and a report was prepared for his digest. Obviously, Saxena guessed that his son was up to something and as he went through the report, his face broke into a smile. If few millions could make his son happy and would draw him out of his melancholy, then nothing is lost.

* * * * *

Jackie was in a jubilant mood, his toil over last one year has begun bearing fruit. The old house, where his mother lived and played is now completely renovated and looks so grand and colourful from a distance that, it gives an illusion of a medieval castle with its arches and domes. He was in his office, going over the beginning phases of the project, in his mind, which he took up as a ruse to recruit the services of Jaya, as an architect, with the sole purpose of being near her, see her and hear her voice through the CCTV. He never took the project, as such, seriously, but as the works progressed, he was not only impressed but also touched with her sincerity and confidence with which, Jaya got herself involved in the job. The experts appreciated her ingenuity and he decided to give a free hand to her and opened the strings of his purse. The entire perspective of his original scheme, changed thereafter and he began seeing Jaya not as an object for viewing but a subject for admiring. And this admiration turned into adoration, when he followed her into the dark cellar and witnessed the entire scenes of her sitting with poise and serenity, before the portrait of his *nana jee* with Raja, who accompanied her, and their removing something from the portrait, which he could not see. He later followed them to the lemon tree in the backyard, where they recovered an urn which was buried there. He had absolutely no doubt that this girl for whom, he developed an obsession and treated her as an object to be possessed, was really an angel sent by God, from heaven, to let him know the family secrets, which hitherto, lay hidden from him and bring a little sunshine in his gloomy life. He suppressed his desire, to come out from his hiding place and lay before her every thing, from day one and apologize. Silently, he retreated. He had no qualms about what he did. Even if his intention of taking up the project was not pious, his reward at the end was bounteous. He could never forget the moment of his witnessing the hair raising event of spirit calling of Jaya and the sequences that followed. No doubt, he would remain indebted to her for what she did for him, that night, throwing her very life into the grave risk of being possessed by a spirit. He would ask her, some time, what prompted her to do that.

His position was that of a shipwrecked person in deep seas without a life jacket. He didn't see any hope of coming to terms with Jaya. He had projected his image in the worst possible manner, before Jaya. His last encounter with Jaya was the climax. He must see her immediately, to judge her mood, he decided. He planned a visit to Raja's house, who was very close to Ram Gopal jee's family and therefore to Jaya jee, also. Moreover, a visit was due to Raja jee to enquire about his health after the serious mishap.

When Jackie arrived at Raja's house and rang the door bell, he was not prepared to find Jaya, opening the door. He was taken unawares and standing face to face, did not find any word to greet her. It was Jaya's turn to register shock and surprise.

'Oh! It is you', she said.

Holding a bouquet in one hand, with the other hand at the bell push, Jackie felt akward and blurted out, 'Yes, it is me. How are you Jaya?'

'Fine', she said and stood there aghast, perplexed, not knowing what to do next. A voice said 'Who is it Jaya?', Ranee came out and seeing Jackie at the door, stared at him.

She said, 'Won't you come in, Jackie?'

Jaya stepped aside and Jackie walked in. He enquired, "How is Raja *bhaiya*, Ranee jee? I hope he is well. I was away. As soon as I came to know about the incident, I came rushing. I have brought flowers for him and wish him a speedy recovery. ' He handed over the bouquet to Ranee. At that moment Raja came down, and suppressing his surprise at seeing the unexpected guest, smiled at him and invited him to the lounge. Jackie returned the greetings and enquired about his health. The conversation picked up. Jaya sat there without taking any interest in their talks. Jackie tried to catch her attention, but she purposely avoided. Ranee came with a tray laden with tea and snacks. Jaya prepared tea for all.

Ranee said, 'Jackie, do you know, Jaya is currently engaged in a project, doing interior designs of a palatial building in Poona. We have been there, the other day, and I tell you, she has done a creditable job, we are all proud of her.'

Jackie said, 'I know——' He abruptly checked himself and said, "I mean, she passed with Honours, that is what I heard. You know, I passed from the same college, earlier. But I didn't do well. My mother expired, I was terribly upset and kept myself aloof from every thing. I was on the brink of a disaster. Some how, I survived, may be my mother wished that I should continue my studies. Hope, I am not disturbing you, by forcing myself upon you, unexpectedly.'

'Not at all Jackie, you are always welcome. We are sorry to know that, you have lost your mother and you have been missing her so much. Please accept our condolences. I know, you are a brave young man, you have braved the loss with fortitude.'

There was one person in the house to have shed tears that day after hearing Jackie, she was Parvatijee. She was entering the lounge and seeing Jackie inside, stopped on her track. Her heart missed a beat. She was looking at *bibijee's* son. He was little younger than Kamal, may be by a year or two. Had *bibijee's* complexion and Ratan's features. She could'nt contain herself, when she heard the boy lamenting the death of his mother, her *bibijee.* She wanted to rush and take the boy in her arms to console him. She checked herself, she did'nt want to expose herself, yet. Jaya, who was putting sugar in a cup, stopped halfway, to listen to Jackie's tale of woe, she was surprised to find him in such a mood. For the first time, she noticed a different Jackie, pouring out his owes, before somebody. Parvati came in and Raja introduced, Jackie as son of Saxena. Jackie got up and paid his respects to her, by touching her feet. She looked at his tall figure, touched him affectionately and said, *'Jite raho beta.'* For a moment she felt, as if she touched *bibijee.* Raja said, "Jackie, *majee* is Kamal's mother.' Jackie simply said, 'The world is so small. I have already met Kamal *bhaiya, majee.'* This utterance sent a wave of current through the body of Parvati and for a moment, she got panicky that probably, Jackie knew, she was his step mother. The silence was broken when Jaya said, '*Majee*, he graduated from the same college, as I have.' Jackie wished her not to elaborate further. To divert the issue, he changed the topic and asked Raja, how the incident occurred.

Parvati now had the opportunity of looking at Jackie more closely. Both he and Kamal had a triangular face like Ratan and thick hair. While Jackie appeared flamboyant, may be due to his upbringing, Kamal was rather unassuming, and fairer. While she was immersed in her thoughts, he got up to say good bye and to everybody's consternation, she told him softly, '*Beta,* please visit us again.' After his departure, she turned her face away and wiped her tears, without anybody's notice.

On her way to Poona, Jaya was engrossed with the thought of Jackie's unexpected visit to Raja *bhaiya.* It was hard to believe on her part, that he came to see Raja and enquire about his health. She didn't expect a social visit from him, after her engagement with her was called off. What could it be due to, then ?

She was so engrossed in her thoughts that she did not realize to have reached the site so quickly. Workmen were seen engaged installing a polished black granite name plate at the gate post with engraved letters, which read LOLITA. She had no information of this earlier, perhaps that was an eleventh hour decision of her nutty employer, she smiled to herself. But more surprises awaited her at the Hall, she saw the huge portrait of the *Sethje*e being hoisted and fixed to the anchors on the wall above the mantelpiece. That was beyond her wildest imagination. The portrait, perhaps was given a brush up and looked fresh and somehow it appeared to her, as if it had a life of its own and looked happy to come home. Her chain of thoughts was interrupted, when a foreman came to discuss with her about, some finishing touches, needed in a room. She cast one more glance at the portrait and left the Hall.

After Jaya left, Jackie came out from a side room and stood before the portrait of his *nanajee,* in silence, for few moments. The Hall was deserted. He had a vision. His mother appeared before him, she looked sad and melancholic. Why she was so unhappy, he never knew. He kneeled down before the portrait and wept.

'Oh! Mom, I could not do anything for you, to make you happy. What was, that you suffered from?'

He felt wretched, he looked around the house. For a moment he was lost in a reverie. He could hear her mother running about in playful moods, in this Hall, as a child, her ringing laughter reverberating around the Hall, reached his ears. Many questions raised their ugly heads before him? Why his father abandoned this house and stripped it from all furnishings and dumped them in the cellar, out of bounds of everybody? Why his father did'nt ever bring him over here?

He heard a sound and looked behind. He saw a man standing at the door silently, with folded hands. He got up and went to the door. The man bent down and touched his feet. Taken aback, he asked, 'Who are you? What are you doing here?' He said, 'I am Bhola, your gardener, Sahib. You may not know me, but I have noticed you coming to the *haveli,* and you look so much like *bibi jee*, I could guess that you must be her son. All of us heard that, she was blessed with a son and *the haveli,* would have its heir to bring back its glory, which it enjoyed in your *nanajee*'s time. But no, she did not return. We have not seen her since then, nor her baby son. It is exactly, twenty two years, since your mother left this place, that you have stepped into this place. Alas! all others have left this place at one time or other, it is I alone, who continued, to stay along.'

Their talks would have continued, but for the sudden appearance of a black Mercedes, which entered the porch and stopped. The door opened and then a person wearing expensive clothes and shoes lowered his leg. Jackie, knew who it was, but not the poor Bhola. By the time, he could recognize him, he was already climbing the steps and coming up. He was none other than Ratan, the last person, he wanted to see on earth. A little aged, but there was no mistake about the angular face with cruelity stamped on it and one more chacteristic added to it, that is, a perpetual grin. To his great relief, he ignored him and passed on to meet his son. Bhola, calmly slipped away.

Jackie knew what was coming and he prepared himself for a bout. On the contrary, Saxena did not have any parlance with his son. He merely smiled and patted his shoulders. Jackie took him around the house showing the modification and beautification carried out. He did not comment, till he was shown the largest room upstairs. He saw this room, which was occupied by Lolita, twenty two years ago, an age since. What Jackie explained about the designs, which rendered the room so beautiful, did not register. He was far away in the past. The ghastly scene of Lolita lying on the bed shattered in body and spirit when he left her, danced before his eyes. That single incident had changed the course of his life. There after, events took place in quick succession, his marriage to Lolita, birth of his son, abandoning *Sethjee's* house, settling down in Bombay in a new house etc.

Jackie's birth was a big event in his life, his responsibility grew. This tempted him to acquire more wealth for securing a bright future for his son. His lust for wealth took him to the dark alleies of criminal activities and gradually he was drawn into the criminal world and he became a *don* of the underworld. He looked around the room, so much has happened in these twenty two years, Lolita is no more, Jackie his son, is now a handsome young man and is definitely capable of taking the reins from his hand. His forehead was furrowed when he looked at his son and wondered what made him to spend a fortune to refurbish this old house? The name plate on the gate post, hanging of the old man's portrait in the Hall told him a part of the story. The rich and fabulous decoration of Lolita's room and freshly cut roses in the flower vases told him the rest. His love for his mother was sincere and profound. What his millions could'nt provide him, a room where his mother lived years ago and saturated with her memories like the fragrance of the fresh roses, gave him in ample measures; that is happiness. He could see it in his face. It brought tears in his eyes, he turned his face away.

He hugged Jackie and said, 'You have done a good job, my dear boy. Really, the house looks like *amarabati*, a show piece. Do you like to live here? I would like to see you settled in life, married to some one, who will bring you peace and happiness.'

He knew, he made a mess of his life in pursuit of wealth. Love and affection had no place In his life. When he roamed the forests and rough terrains, as a cow herd, he would let loose the cows and lie down under a tree, always dreaming of green pastures, where there would be enough food and water for them. He found that cows were more clever than him, always leading him to pleanty. He would play on his flute, a long one, which also served him as a stick to brandish at errant cows. The animals would heed to his note and return before sun set. His search for pleanty, once carried him to the precincts of the village, where Parvati lived. He met her and was attracted to her. He was not aware of such attraction before. He did not know the meaning of love between man and woman. But before long, forgetting his dear animals, forests and his dreams, he ran away with Parvati from the village, one day, and reached Bombay. His meeting with *Sethjee* was a turning point in his life, which brought him to his earlier track, leading him to green pastures of his dreams. Within months of his working with the Sethjee, like a water diviner, he could sense, there was a possibility of tapping the immeasurable wealth lying with *Sethjee*.

Leaving his father brooding, Jackie came out of the room to the corridor and standing there, viewed the Hall down below. There was no sign of Bhola *chacha,* he had vanished, just as mist, at the sun rise. He made a mental note, he should learn more from him about his parents. Saxena came from behind, put his hand on his shoulders and said, 'Well, Jackie, you did not answer me.'

'I have other plans about this house, *daddy.*'

'What plans?', he sounded irritated.

'I want to convert it into a house for destitutes and leave aside a considerable sum of money for its maintainence. I have a person in my mind, who will take care of that.'

Saxena was flabbergasted at this weird proposal of his son. He said, 'What has come over you? Are you in your senses?'

'I am perfectly in my senses *daddy.*'

'If you want really to help the poor, we may build orphanages, else where. But why this house, which is your ancestral property. Your mother lived here. Don't you have any attachment for this house?'

Jackie laughed and said, 'Were it so, why didn't you treat it as such, instead of dumping every thing in the cellar, blotting all the signs of people who lived here? My mother was born here, grew up here, when I close my eyes, I can imagine her running in her small feet, all over this place and *nanajee,* running after her. Why did you have to do it *daddy*? I have accidentally come across, the furniture and other house hold articles dumped in the cellar and above all, the portrait of my *nanajee*, gathering dust there. Do you know, who led me there?'

'Who?'

'It is Jaya, Ram Gopal's sister.' Saxena's surprise was complete. He asked, 'Where does she come in?'

'I hired her for the interior decorations, she is an architect.'

'Oh ! I see. *Tum to chupe rustam nikle, hum jahan hare, tum baji mare.* Where I could not succeed to make her your bride, you could hire her as your paid employee. Well, I like it. This is good indeed.'

Jackie kept quiet for few moments and then said, 'It is not as you think. She does not even know that I am her employer. Neither she has seen me in the premises, till today. A recruiting agency selected her for the job, that is all. Now, let me tell you some thing, which is stranger than fiction.' Jackie related to his father, his experience of the evening, when he followed Jaya and Raja into the cellar and then to the backyard of the cottage, behind the house.

To Saxena, Jackie's account was, as if his past was being unfolded before him. He did not want that his son would ever come to know of his secret. With the death of Lolita and removal of Parvati from the scene, he was certain that his secrets were well guarded, and now to his utter dismay and discomfort, he finds that his son was exposed to the grave danger of learning the secrets of his father's dubious past. His resilient nature, however, did'nt permit him to brood over the issue, longer. His concern was to attend to the present, otherwise it will be lost for ever and you can never realize your dreams. Life is like a foot ball field, there is no time to think and brood. Every player is chasing the ball, to take it to the goal post. If you think too much of the shot missed, you may also miss the next shot.

A moment before, he was elated about his son winning the heart of Jaya and prospects of her settling down with him in the house, looked brighter. But, now the situation looked grave and hazardous. The girl whom, his son was to marry, posed a grievous threat to his schemes. He did not know, how much this stupid girl knew of his past, He would not endanger his future by the idiotic action of an inquisitive girl. He had to settle his score against Raja, who has assumed the role of a quintessential rogue. He should not be let loose. Brushing away all turmoils and disturbing thoughts from his mind, he regained his composure, he addressed his son, 'I do not know Jackie, what that girl and that character Raja are up to. Take it from me, that she is bad medicine for you, stay away from her. You know, how she ridiculed you, that evening at your engagement ceremony. Her falling unconscious was all melodramatic, I knew it. The girl wanted to avoid the engagement. Shun her. If she has completed the job, let her go and forget her.'

His apparently well meaning words fell flat on Jackie's ears, whose mind was, at that time, churning thoughts like a speed boat throwing sprays of water. The agonizing words of his mother, '*you murderer, you killed my daddy, you took away his life, his property and me*' were still ringing in his ears. He knew for certain, that there was some mystery lurking behind the marriage between his mother and his *dad*. One day, he must find out and nothing can stop him.

He said calmly, 'I cannot forget her, *daddy,* after what she has done to this house, which you did your best to destroy. You must be thankful to her. She has put life in the brick and mortar.'

Then, pointing to the room he said, 'Is this the room, my mother used? From its size and design, I would guess so.' Pointing to the bed, he asked, 'Is this not the bed, where my mother slept?' Pointing to the dressing mirror, he asked, 'Is this not the place where she sat and did her hair? Does it not strike any chord of your memory, that my mother lived in this room, walked on its floor and breathed the air coming through the windows, carrying with it the fragrance of the flowers, still in bloom over there in the garden?'

The relation between the son and father was never cordial and now after such exchange of words, it became worse.

On the following day, Jackie sent for Bhola *chacha* and was surprised to learn that the cottage, where he lived was locked and nobody knew his whereabouts. He wondered, whether his father had anything to do with his disappearance.

* * * * *

Pursuing his line of investigation, Inspector Pradhan found out that, advocate Rathod was the contact who passed on messages to Joshi. In a gear train, when a small wheel does not rotate, the movement of the gear train stops. With the arrest of Joshi, the link of communication between Rathod, Mathew and Joshi was broken. Rathod was a member of an exclusive club in the city and one would always find him at the Oriental Club every Sunday evening. He enjoyed a game of chess with his friend Mistry, a senior advocate of the High Court and also the chess champion of the club. One evening, after having a satisfactory contest with Mistry *sahib*, where he could checkmate the opponent's *king*, he was returning home from the Club and on the way he came across a road block. He stopped the car and came out, he looked up and down, the road was deserted, he smelled a rat and turned to go back. Suddenly a bike rider comes from the opposite side, takes out his gun and pumps few bullets into his body and vanishes.

By the time Pradhan knew of the incident, day was breaking. He saw the body of the advocate, lying at the site riddled with bullets. The *post mortem* confirmed that death was due to loss of blood, caused by multiple bullet injuries, sustained at about 11pm in the night. So that's it! They are really fast. Before he could reach him, they got him. The only link, through which he could get closer to the enemy, was lost to him forever. His adversary was always one step ahead of him. He rushed to his office and there too he was beaten. Somebody had already made a good job of it. The office chamber was ransacked as if a bulldozer went through it. The intruder did not leave anything untouched. All drawers, shelves, cupboards, bookshelves were broken open, their contents spilled on the floor, sofa cushions ripped open, a complete mess, so to say. Even the wall papers were not spared. The chap or the chaps were thorough in their job. Without losing time, Pradhan rushed to the Bar association chamber, where Rathod practised and located the locker used by him. He beat his adversary this time and found the locker intact. Breaking open the locker, he recovered all objects there in, including a lawyer's gown and shifted them to his office.

The objects lay stacked, on his table, in neat piles. There were case records, some law books with markers and a box of cigars. He noticed the brand, they came expensive. He smelled, though he was not a connoisseur of tobacco, he could guess, it was of high quality, may be Golden Virginia. He was familiar with this scent. He tried to recollect, where he smelled this. Yes, it was at a party, thrown by the D. C. P, on the occasion of the birthday celebration of his daughter. There was a gentleman amongst the guests, who smoked this brand. Would he remember the man? Why not try ? It is a wild guess though. Most likely it will be Rathod. But it was not so. He rang up and learnt that the man who smoked the brand was R. K. Saxena, an industrialist of repute. Now what does it mean ? Can two persons not smoke the same brand? Can two persons not have the same taste ? Very likely, but it is also likely that they may be known to each other. Probably yes and probably no. He noted his observations in his note book. Then, he had a hunch, which he wanted to verify. He visited the cell, where Joshi was locked. He asked him, whether he knew one Saxena, Pradhan waited for the answer with bated breath. The answer was no. He looked at the face of Joshi. It was very hard to guess, what was going on in the person's mind. The same expressionless face, when he was shackled and brought in to the cell. He was then, given an injection of *truth serum.*

Pradhan asked him, 'Joshi, do you know Saxena, one R. K. Sxena?'

'No.'

'Joshi, I have visited your daughter Loila, at the Convent.'

His face softened and he said, 'How is she?'

* * * * *

Thousand miles away, in United States, Kamal was busy in packing his things, for his homeward journey. He said his farewell to Dorothy, who in the meanwhile helped his ailing father in the management of his Research Laboratory. They parted as good friends. Having said '*Good Bye*' to him, Dorothy rushed to her room upstairs, from where she could see Kamal's car. She stood at the window to have the last glimpse of the man, who became so close to her heart. Tears rolled down her face and she let them fall.

Kamal got his *doctorate* and though he was offered lucrative assignments in the University, he had declined. He had no doubt, that his future lay in India. Whenever, his mind wandered across the seas, reaching the shores of his country, besides his mother's, image of one person always featured in it, and it was Jaya. Now that he was free from his studies and research, the prospects of seeing Jaya and be in her company, gladdened him. Being a man of science, he hobnobbed with concrete issues and not with dreams. Dreaming was a luxury, he thought, which he could not afford. He termed it as an idle mind's exploration. But now, he reailized its worth, since it took him nearer to Jaya. The picture of walking with her, chasing butterflies or engagimg in idle talks, gladdened his heart. What is this feeling ? Could he term it as love ? Was it in any way different from liking a person? Liking Dorothy, for that matter. He knew, he liked her. She was good company and gave him indeed, pleasure and happiness. She lifted his spirit from the mire of mundane grossness to heavenly bliss. With Jaya it was something else. Being with her was a perpetual joy, which he felt in the innermost recess of his heart. The very thought of her, made the space between them seem smaller. Yes, he was truly in love with her and she would be his soul mate. He looked for her a proper epithet and found one in a sonnet of Shakespeare:—

'In faith I do not love thee with mine eyes,
For they in thee a thousand errors note;
But 'tis my heart that loves what they despise,
Who in despite of view is pleased to dote.
Nor are mine ears with thy tongue's tune delighted;
Nor tender feeling, to base touches prone,
Nor taste nor smell, desire to be invited
To any sensual feast with thee alone:
But my five wits, nor my five senses can
Dissuade one foolish heart from serving thee
Who leaves unswaye'd the likeness of a man,
Thy proud heart's slave and vassal wretch to be:
Only my plague thus far I count my gain
That she that makes me sin, awards me pain.'

He was in one such pensive mood, when the phone rang. It was Ranee *bhabi jee.* She wanted to know, on what date, he was expected. Before he could say any thing, she said, whether he would like to speak to Jaya. The prospect of hearing her voice, so unexpectedly, brought an effulgence in his face and he gripped the receiver tight. A sweet voice came floating over the wires.

"'Hello, Kamal, how are you ?'

He took few moments to answer her and he could hear distinctly the vibrations in his ear, caused by audio transmission of her breathings, over the wires. He felt her near him and would have continued to remain in trance, when again her voice came to him.

'Kamal are you listening ?'

'Yes, Yes, I am listening. How are you, Jaya?' Then, there was heavy static, followed by disconnection. So much he wanted to talk, but the blasted line sabotaged. He cursed his fate and slammed the receiver down on the cradle.

* * * * *

Frequent Bank robberies in suburban areas, posed a big problem for Bombay Police. Because of the nature of transactions in these Banks, cash balance at the closure was, normally, never more than ten to fifteen lakhs of rupees, unless heavy deposits were received at the end. It was, therefore, not felt necessary for the Banks to transfer the cash to their Head Offices. Police advanced the theory that the miscreants took this opportunity to break open the cash chests and decamp with the cash easily, as the Banks, mostly, functioned in rented buildings. The Bank authorities held that, robberies to have occurred all of a sudden, when there was no such incidents in the last ten years, was by itself peculiar and Police should look at this angle and investigate. The media then, took up the issue and began publishing interviews with public, who were outspoken in their views against the Police. The same public and Press, who were vociferous in their praises of Police, for checking and stopping drug trafficking and gambling in the city successfully in recent times, were now belligerent. As a fall out, the Police eyes were alerted, small time thieves and criminals with police records were rounded up at various Poice Stations and roughed up for extracting information. Police drew a blank. The public outcry died down, like soda bottle enthusiasim. The worst sufferer was the Central Bank, which operated maximum number of Branches in the affected zone. It has its Head Office at Kurla. It is a large Bank serving to a large number of customers. Rohit Sharma, the Chief General manager was in his air conditioned office on the top floor and his visitor at the moment was Pradhan, Inspector of Police. It was a customary visit by Police for overseeing the security arrangements of the Bank.

Pradhan finished discussions, with the Chief General Manager; he got up to leave. On his way out, he stopped at the windows and drew open the curtains and looked out. On one side, he saw carriages drawn in and boxes and other materials being unloaded, while on the other side, an abandoned construction site met his eyes. Both the areas were quite close to the Bank.

He asked, 'Mr. Sharma, the field behind you is the Municipal Ground, I believe. Some activities seem to be going on in that place, what is it, do you know?

"Don't you know, there is going to be a cirus show in the ground, after one week.'

'It has not come to my notice, permission must have been granted by the Municipality with the knowledge of the local Police Station. I'll check it up on my way. What about the construction site, how long has it been lying like this, any idea?'

Sharma said, 'I am seeing it like this, since I joined, that is since two years. I have heard that the site belongs to some political bigwig and the construction plan has since been cancelled by the authorities. Our Bank has been trying to acquire it, because we need it for our expansion, but the party is not willing to part with it.'

'However, better acquire it quickly, it is too close to the Bank,' Pradhan said and bid good bye, to the Chief General Manager.

* * * * *

When posters were displayed all over the locality with pictures of lions, elephants and acrobats, a crowd mostly consisting of youngsters started gathering at the Municipal ground to witness the erection of the tent, unloading of equipment and accessories from carriages, animal cages on wheels being drawn to site and other sundry activities. It was a tough job to keep the children away from the animal cages, specially those housing the lions and tigers. When the elephants marched inside the ground, they were worshiped by womenfolk as Lord Ganesha. Such were the fervour and encouragement shown by the people of the locality in welcoming the circus. In few days the entire circus arena was ready for the opening show. People waited for the event with glee and expectation. Finally, the day for inauguration arrived and with great fan fare, a local big wig cut the ribbon to declare the show open and public rushed in to see and enjoy the show.

A powerful search light was installed on the mast of the circus tent, to throw long reaching beam of light all around, to proclaim that show had begun. The entire atmosphere was one of fun and gaiety. Vendors of nuts, chocolates and balloons had a busy day. Children of all ages, in colourful dresses, accompanied by elders thronged the gate every day. Their main attractions were the clowns, who with their baggy pants, painted face and peach shaped nose kept them roaring in laughter from beginning to the end. The show went on day to day gathering momentum. '*Diwali*' was approaching, preparations were afoot to hold special shows on the occasion. A mammoth crowd was expected and the circus management took every care and precaution so that the ticket holders may not be inconvenienced, they sought the assistance of Police to maintain law and order in the area, on *diwali.*

The tent was packed with spectators. The ring side seats and the gallery were almost filled up, all tickets were sold out. Everyone was waiting eagerly for the show to begin. There was great expectation in the air. Above the din of the voices of the crowd, the loudspeakers blared to announce that the show was to commence. Silence fell on the crowd. Everybody's attention was fixed on the circus arena, which glittered with silken banners and colourful festoons. A large sized earthen lamp filled with oil was placed on a polished brass stand at the centre, as a symbol of celebration of *diwali*. The circus band with its drums and trumpets played and two clowns holding a banner with the message' Happy Diwali'. written on it, walked into the arena. The crowd rejoiced with a thunderous applaud. With the accompaniment of the band, the clowns circled the arena. Then the chief guest was led to the centre of the arena by the Manager to light the lamp. Amidst clapping and shouting the lamp was lighted. This was followed by a group of young girls dressed in gauddy clothes, who entered and stood in a wide circle around the lamp. They raised their hands, joined in

Namaste sign, welcoming the spectators with blowing of conch shells. Then they retreated single file, waving at the spectators. The much awaited gong was sounded and the show began.

A juggler entered the arena dressed in a black tail coat, wearing a tall hat and holding his magic wand. He took out his cap, bowed before the spectators and went around the arena, showing that the cap was empty. Then he moved his wand over the cap, suddenly two white piegeons flew out of the cap. Next, he picked up a garland, which he presented to the chief guest. The crowd cheered. The show continued with a group of girls in boxers and shirts, entering the arena on one-wheel cycles, holding each others hands, going around, some time forward and some time backward. While on wheel, one girl balanced another girl on her shoulders and the crowd cheered. Then was shown an item, which was specially meant for the children, a monkey dressed in a shirt and a pant and wearing a cap, entered the arena, pulling a mini rickhaw with a parrot as the passenger. Unconcerned about the attention and laughter it was drawing from the audience, the monkey went on pulling the rickshaw, even ringing its bell, to the joy of the children, around the arena. Then came the galloping horses with a monkey rider leading, followed by the item *'human canon ball'*. A canon was drawn inside and placed at the centre. Two persons were seen dragging a man in chain, who turned out to be one of the clowns, who was seen weeping. But his tears came out like jets, which sent the crowd roaring in laughter. The clown was pushed into the canon and its door shut. To everybody's horror, the canon was ignited, there was a loud explosion and out came the clown, projected like a missile and caught by a net. The crowd cheered.

There was an announcement, it said that they were going to present some shows fraught with danger and risks. All were requested to pray God that nothing untoward should happen and to maintain silence, during the show, because it called for concentration and breath control by the artists. The circus band stopped playing and the crowd fell silent. An archer entered the arena with bow and arrow and took position. Workers brought in a board with a target fixed on it and placed it about fifteen yards from the archer. The crowd looked on. The archer took aim and shot an arrow, on it went and hit the bullseye. Then a man was brought in with his head covered in a black cloth. They let him stand at the same spot where the board was placed. An apple was balanced on his head and the archer pointed the arrow upward and prayed for a moment, before he took aim. The crowd gasped, some of them even closed their eyes. There was absolute silence. The archer took aim and shot the arrow, in a twinkle of an eye it had pierced the apple and carried it away. The crowd burst into applause.

Then, an elephant with gorgeous headgear and its *mahout* sitting on it, entered and at the command of the *mahout,* trumpeted and stood still at a corner, waiting for further commands. Workers brought a mattress and a thick wooden board and placed the mattress on the ground, a *pahelwan* bare to the waist walked in with beating of drums and bowing before the spectators, lay down on the mattress on his back. The crowd waited holding their breath. The wooden board was then placed on him. He motioned to the *mahout* and inhaled, the elephant came and crossed him over the plank. The five thousand strong human mass kept quiet. The board was then removed and the *pahelwan* got up and flexed his muscles. The crowd heaved a sigh to see him safe and sound. The last in the series was *'a jump in a jeep'*. Pre-fav ramps were erected on both sides leaving a gap of about twenty feet, over which the jeep would jump. Sound of accelerating of an engine was heard from a distance, it was terrific, then from a corner a jeep was seen coming with a tremendous speed towards the ramp and before the spectators could realize what was happening, the jeep was over the ramp, cleared the gap, flying in air and landed on the opposite ramp with a thud and disappeared from view. It was unbelievable. Later, the racing driver, wearing a crash helmet and racing suit presented himself and bowed down before the spectators. There was a thundering applause.

Then, the animals were brought in. The elephants led the show. Four of them were there. Four heavy iron stools were brought in. The ring master, ordered them to go to their respective stools and sit. Obedientely, the giant animals sat on the stools on their haunches with forelegs raised. They looked so funny, that the spectators roared in fits of laughter. The ring master, then, led them out. The time was eight pm. and the last two items, but the major ones were left. These were, the wild animal shows and acrobatics by trapeze artists. An iron cage was erected inside the arena, jointing folded iron grills, into which animal cages were drawn. Tigers were drawn in first and let loose inside the iron cage, a trainer wearing coat and breeches, holding the electric stick entered. As soon as the tigers saw the trainer, they went meekly and jumped to the stools arranged inside. The trainer, then shouted some words and the animals changed their places and growled. He went to a corner where three stools were kept and sat on the middle stool. Then he did something at which the crowd gasped. He brandished the stick at the tigers and to the horror of the spectators, two Royal Bengal ones jumped and occupied the side stools on either side of the trainer, keeping their fore paws on his padded shoulders. The scene was picture perfect and many cameras, from the ring side flashed. That was the end of the show and at the shout of the trainer the animals entered their cages, like obedient children. The trainer bowed to the public and got ready for the next show.

Now, the cage of the king of the jungle was brought in and let loose inside the iron cage. It was a huge one with a magnificient mane and looked majestic. His eyes were slits when he looked at his trainer. The trainer raised his stick and shouted some words at the lion, and it circled the cage and went and jumped on to stool, kept at a corner. Now the trainer was to perform the most dangerous and blood curdling act of the show. A hush fell on the spectators. The big cat opened its mouth, showing its five inches long fangs and yawning mouth, the trainer positioned himself nearer and put his head almost inside its mouth, almost all present in the crowd shut their eyes; on opening, they saw the trainer had taken out his head, the animal had shut its mouth and he was patting its head. Was it purring like a cat, who could guess? But the crowd went wild and showered coins and money in the arena.

The last show on the agenda was the trapeze act. The trapeze artists climbed up to their respective platforms high above the ground and started performing on the trapeze, swinging and reaching the other side. They switched over from one trapeze to the other in mid air in perfect timing and grace. Their act of holding the other by hands, hanging down by knees supported by the trapeje bar and swinging together in mid air, captivated the imagination of the spectators. The atmosphere was charged with joy and exhilaration and everyone's attention was glued on the performers. Then, there was a roar of laughter when the crowd saw two clowns getting up and held on to the trapeze at either end. They began swinging in the mid air and instead of switching over from one trapeze to the other as the acrobats did, they lost hold and fell down together on to the net stretched below, they got down and added to the mirth of the crowd by slapping each other.

Just as the gong was struck to announce the end of the show and all the artists assembled in the arena along with the Manager of the circus, to bid farewell to the public, that being the last day of the circus, there was a heavy explosion some where and the tent caught fire. To make the matter worse, the lights went out. What was once, an atmosphere of joy and laughter, turned into a picture of chaos filled with cries and shrieks. There was a mad rush for the exits, to get out of the inferno. The fire was spreading and the heat was intense, luckily, there were three exits and people surged through, to safety. The entire compound was thrown in darkness, except for the light of the blazing fire. The tent in the centre, seemed to be a bonfire, and ironically what a tribute on the day of the '*diwali'!* Then the sirens of the fire brigade were heard and moments after, jets of water directed at the burning tent, which anyway was reduced to a pile of smoking canvas, burning wooden stands and furniture, shorn of its glamour and glory. Only, the tall masts still fighting the fury of the fire, remained to tell the tale.

Fortunately, however, there were no casualities, except for few, who suffered minor injuries, due to the stampede. Providentially, all the animals were safe, in their cages and enclosures, mainly due to a forest wall and a pond in between, protecting them from the fire and heat wave. The last cages to be withdrawn from the circus arena were the cages of the lion and a lioness. The lion, a specially favoured animal, was known as the King and to spare him from lonliness, his cage was always placed beside the cage of the lioness. The jeep which pulled the cages from the arena back to their enclosure, was half way when the fire broke out and the driver leaving them inside the forest, ran toward the campus to join others in fire fighting. By the common effort of the fire brigade and the circuss staff, the fire was brought under control and the day was almost breaking, when the last crackle had stopped.

The extent of damages was to be seen to be believed, in the day light. There were no signs that a circus performed there twelve hours ago, everything was reduced to ashes, only the charred remains of the masts stood as silent witnesses. The management was thorougnly shaken at the losses suffered, and were thankful to God for saving theirs and the animals' lives.

* * * * *

It was a normal day at the Central Bank, as any other day. The Bank opened at 10.00 am and all the staff were at their respective places getting ready to receive the customers. The Chief Cashier accompanied by the Deputy Manager went to the Bank vault in the basement for opening the double safety steel doors. On opening the doors, they stood there thunder struck, with gaping mouth, they looked at the opened steel chests, all the shelves were empty. They could not believe their eyes, they were speechless, all the chests were burgled, lockers opened and everything removed. The cashier was the first to find speech. He said, 'The Bank has been robbed, sir.' The Dy. Manager did'nt respond, he stared. The cashier pressed the alarm. The armed guard posted at the door, entered and a little after, the Manager rushed in. The Manager took the situation in, he was mystified, he could'nt make out anything out of it. How?How? and How?, those were the questions that rattled his mind. He checked his watch, it was ten minutes past Ten, precious time was being lost, he steadied himself and informed Head Office and the Chief Security Officer about the robbery, then asked the Security to put down the shutter of the Bank and hang the 'CLOSED' sign. He made an announcement that '*there has been a crisis and an emergent situation has arisen, the staff and visitors are requested to stay inside for the time being and maintain calm.*'

The Chief General Manager arrived, accompanied by the Chief Security Officr and few others in about ten minutes and immediately proceeded to the strong room. There was a buzz in the Bank, people were discussing in groups, something was amiss in the strong room, but nobody knew, for certain, what could have happened.

Inside the strong room, the atmosphere was tense, the CGM took stock of the situation, discussed with the chief cashier and the chief security officer, verified the cash book, balance sheet, ceased further transactions and called in the Police. The time was half past Ten. The Police arrived and took charge of the investigation. The Bank authorities were relieved to know that the adjacent vault, which housed the lockers for use of the customers was not ransacked, it saved the Bank from pleanty of troubles and litigation, even the jewellery, bonds, shares etc, hypothecated to the Bank against loans were not touched. A brief statement on behalf of the Bank was issued for the notice of public and media *that a robbery in the Bank was committed, investigations are in progress and there has been no estimate of losses, yet.*

Police began their investigations by taking photographs of the Bank vaults from all angles and taking statements from all officials and security staff, concerned. Inspector Pradhan of Bombay Police arrived in the meanwhile and took charge of the investigations. The fire incident that occurred in the adjacent Municipal Grounds, the evening before, ravaging the circus tent, further clouded the mystery surrounding the Bank robbery. It gave food for thought to the Inspector. He asked others to clear out of the vault and spent the next hour in a microscopic examination of the room. He was told that the walls and the floor were made of twelve inches thick reinforced concrete. The vault was almost impregnable. The floor was covered by a thick asbestos cement matting, which was fire proof. The safes and the chests were placed over the mat, arranged in a row, with the exception of one single chest measuring '*two and a half by two and a half*', placed at a corner. The door of this chest was still locked, he tried to push, it did'nt budge, it was heavy. He asked the Manager to open the chest, it was seen to contain thick Ledgers and Records stacked on the shelves on their edges. There were four shelves and three of them were packed tight with Ledgers, while the bottom one was empty, it had nothing. But what caught the attention of the Inspector was that the steel plate of the bottom shelf seemed to have a fresh coat of paint. Pradhan was thinking fast, a shudder went through his body. He did'nt want to see, what he believed to be lying underneath. Out of impulse he tapped the plate, it sounded hollow. He told the CGM, 'We must be now prepared to see the worst, let us remove this plate.'

The plate was cut by a gas cutter, they stared with utter consternation at the gaping hole, underneath. It was a dark hole of two feet in size, extending nobody knew where. A hole had been cut through the concrerte, rods and all, incredible it seemed, but it was done. The Manager and the Inspector exchanged glances, silently. How it was done, was beyond anybody's comprehension. But, it was obvious, that the intruders entered through the hole from outside and decamped with the cash and valuables. How? and How? was the big question, that intrigued the Inspector. In his twenty years of experience in crime detection, he had not come across such an ingenuous method of committing a theft. His immediate concern was to find out, where the tunnel, if any, opened. He conferred with his staff and the operations began. He telephoned the DCP and half an hour later, a van carrying equipment and staff arrived at the Bank. The DCP ordered immediate road blocks and check of all vehicles, going out of the city, on the major roads.

A measuring rod was lowered down the pit and it was found that it sruck ground at six feet from the floor level. A search light was plugged to the power outlet and focussed down the pit, it showed that the vertical shaft took off at right angles to the right. *Was it a man made tunnel or an existing burrow dug by some mysterious animal ?* Would it be safe to lower a man to investigate. Better leave it to experts, he decided. On second thought, he did'nt think it to be prudent to leave the issue in others' hands, who might take their own time to solve the mystery of the tunnel and give an opportunity to the criminals, to escape with the loot. He discussed the matter with the DCP, who agreed with the action plan of the Inspector.

* * * * *

There were road blocks and police barricades, throughout the city, putting the commuters to great inconvenience. Traffic on the highways almost stalled, at many places police faced public wrath. But the checks continued. Two large container vans rolled down the road, seemingly oblivious of the police check posts ahead. At a bend, the vans slowed down and moved steadily and slowly towards the check posts, till they collided against the posts and stopped a little further away, blocking the road. There was a commotion and the armed guards rushed toward the vans and asked the drivers to get down, at the points of their guns. Getting no response, they boarded the cabins and were surprised to find the cabins empty. The ignition key was in the dashboard. In the meanwhile, a chain of vehicles was building up in the rear, hooting their horns. Everybody's patience was on its wane. To make the matter worse, the animal cages of the circus, which were on their way to their next destination, joined the line of the stranded vehicles, which was already pretty long and unmanageable. As if the din of the stranded commuters, hooting of the horns, was not enough, the roaring of the lions and the growl of the tigers, made it tumultuous and attracted the attention of people, far and near, who thronged there to have a view of the wild cats from close quarters. The crowd became unmanageable. The police forces were reinforced, and the crowd pushed back to safe distance, as the animals were getting restless. Police drivers were engaged to shift the offending vans, to the road side, to let the traffic move. The cages on wheels moved slowly, towed by jeeps, and let the other vehicles overtake them.

The animals were to be fed and sheltered from the scorching sun, the carriages were therefore, parked off the road in the reserved forest area, far from the traffic and habitation. The place chosen was a mountain side, a stream flowed nearby and ruins of a century old temple were seen at a distance. Loads of fresh tree branches were brought on the back of the elephants, for feeding them. After taking care of the animals, in their charge, the men retired to a shady place to have their lunch and enjoy a little siesta, to rest their tired limbs, after the hectic activities, in the last night, at the circus ground, due to breakout of the fire. Some of them, were also injured, in stumbling over things, in the darkness.

The elephant keeper was relating his tale, 'You know, *bhai,* after the show, I was expecting a quiet rest in my tent, then I heard this explosion, which was quite out of place and I came out and saw the circus tent in fire. I rushed and rang the fire alarm. All others came out, the fire being at the top, we helplessely watched from the ground. The fire was spreading rapidly, engulfing the entire tent and to make the matter worse, the lights went out and surprisingly enough the emergency lights did'nt come.'

Gulam, one of the attendents in the last act of trapeze artists, said, 'They were at the last act of swinging and swaping trapezes at the middle, when the explosion occurred and fire broke out. There was no time for them to conclude the show, I shouted *'Jump! Jump*!' and they let go of the trapeze and hurtled themselves down to the safety net. I rushed and helped them down. The fire was blazing and at that time the lights went out. I saw people from the ring side and the gallery rushing toward the *'Exit'*, the thick canvas of the tent was still holding, as we ran out to safety. I learnt later, that the stands were emptied before the tent crashed down, blazing.'

The loins' cages were parked a little away from the others, the keeper Mustaq had seen to that. He chose a secluded place to contemplate. He cursed the moment when he was accosted by a stranger wearing an overcoat and a bowler hat, he could'nt make out his face clearly since he had upturned the collers of the coat and put on a pair of dark glasses. He couldn't know how he came to his tent and picked him up. He asked him to follow him to his van parked ouside the compound. He had no choice, because of another man who accompanied him, a veritable monster, almost pushed him ahead. He saw a van parked outside under a tree, quite away from the road. The man turned to him and spoke, 'Look Mustaq, here is a proposal. If you follow my instructions you will be a richer person. I know you are poor and with difficulty you have been supporting your family consisting of your *bibi* and child.' He found his voice to speak, 'How do you know all this?'

'Forget it, you listen to me, I do no have much time.' Then he laid down his proposal before him, which was totally unacceptable to him and he said that he could not possibly do it.

'Okay, in that case you will lose your darling Muni.' He said.

'What do you mean, what that has to do with my daughter?'

'Simply this.' Then he motioned his man, who went to the van and opening the door brought out a little girl whose mouth was taped. Seeing her, Mustaq cried in despair, 'What have you done to her, leave her alone.' He rushed to her, but the muscleman stopped him with one of his hands while holding the girl with the other. The stranger said, 'Don't do any such thing, my man is quite capable of strangling you by tightening his hand a litle around your neck.' Mustaq gasped, the man loosened his grip and let him go. The girl kicked the man with her little legs, it was like hitting a rock. Mustaq cringed before the stranger with folded hands and said, 'I will do whatever you wish but leave my child. I assure you, we will not breath a word to anybody.'

'That will not be necessary, your daughter will be safe wih us. No harm will come to her and once the job is done, she will reach your home safely. And keep this, you will not be sorry. More when the job is completed.' The man gave him a wad of Notes and then drove off with his daughter. He had no options, he did whatever the stranger wanted. Then it had occurred, the date of payoff arrived. On the day when the circus tent caught fire and he was resting after the fire fighting beside the lion cages, lamenting over his fate and worrying about his wife and child, a shadow loomed large before him and in the dim moonlight, he saw the stranger standing before him. Then he saw the men behind him. They appeared like ghosts in the moonlight. He stood up and faced him. The man said, 'Come on, hurry up man, now is the time, the bags are to be dumped in the hidden boxes. Show us the way,' There were one hundred bags in all, to be shifted from the van to the hidden compartments built into the cages. It had taken them the best of two hours and the operation was carried out in the darkness, away from the centre of smoke and water jets in the circus area. He didn't dare to ask what the bags contained.

He looked at the cages of the lion and the lioness. The huge animals rested in their cages after a hefty meal. He knew, his ordeal was not yet over. So much has happened, yet the stranger did'nt come to collect the bags, which were concealed in the under carriage of the cages. What an ingenuous idea of the man!He had not much difficulty in convincing the Manager that the old cages were not safe since the iron rods were aleady loose and the wheel axle bearings need replacement. He had finally agreed to build new carriages with suitable reinforcements. Provision of concealed chambers in the under carriage was however a secret only known to Mustaq and the contractor, who was the stranger's man. The new cages were built, to the specification of the stranger, the animals were shifted to the new cages, the transfer was smooth except for a little resentment shown by King, the prize animal of the circus. He did'nt want to leave his old abode, but with a little prodding from his keeper, he walked into the new cage.

King, surveyed the scene, through the iron bars, casting a longing look at the surrounding forest, which was once his realm, where he roamed and ruled. Now his limbs were tired, out of inactivity and he was getting old. Years ago, when he was brought in and under training, he crazed for liberty and out of disgust and discomfiture, refused to take any food. They brought his mate inside his cage, to give him company and comfort, but, it did not work, he clawed her, out of rage, they had to remove the lioness. The keeper was perseverant and kept on trying to make him shed his gloom and resume to take food. He spent most of his time, in front of his cage, pushed choice meat inside, but all his efforts failed. The lion became lean and lay down most of the time with closed eyes. While all these were taking place, the keeper's little daughter, a mere nine years old, stood a little away and watched the big animal with awe and wonder with her round eyes. She did not fear him; one day, when there was no body else near the cage, the little girl approached and stood with her face, close to the cage bars. King sensed her and opening his slanting eyes looked at the fearless girl. A signal seemed to pass between the beast and the girl, communication was established, the girl asked, 'King, why have you forsaken food and drink, you have grown so thin.' She outstretched her hand and stroked the lion's rugged face. Though the huge beast looked dimunitive inside the cage, it measured not less than nine feet from head to tail. It smelled the girl's hand and knew intuitively that it was a friendly and affectionate gesture and deserved a response. He licked the girl's hand, the bond between them grew. The girl said softly, 'King, come on, stand up, let me see, how tall you are.' The lion looked at her lovingly and stood up majestically to its full height of four feet. The girl found a large bowl filled with water, lying inside, and pushed it near the lion with her hand and said, *'Now drink.'* Obediently, it brought down its face to the water and lapped it up. Its parched throat of so many days felt satiated and he growled to let others know that he was hungry and willing to eat. The keeper came out of his tent and reached his cage and saw the wonderful sight of the animal standing on its legs and his little girl at the cage, stroking its foreleg. He was stunned and didn't move. Later, emboldened, the keeper went to the cage with a piece of meat and motioned his daughter to offer it to the animal, the girl took the meat and put it near him. The hungry lion guzzled it and thus broke his fast. That was years ago, the old keeper had already left and along with him, his little one. He yearned for sometime, the company of the little girl, but she didn't come. He felt bored and just pulled on, following the monotonous routine of eating, drinking, sleeping and at times going for the performance. He didn't bother, what happened outside the cage. When his keeper wanted him to shift into the new cage, he resisted but later gave in.

Today he had a good lunch, soft and bloody meat, followed by pleanty of water, which he relished, the day being very hot. He was not as active as the lioness in the other cage, he felt lazy and slept. While the other workers rested here and there after their lunch, in the shade of trees, a little far away.

Mustaq felt drowsy and tired after a strenuous day, his eyes closed and he slept, dismissing all the worries from his mind. Suddenly he felt the touch of somebody's hand upon his shoulder, which made him start. It was the stranger with the bowler hat and dark glasses. He had come so noiselessly, that he could not notice his approach. In his presence, Mustaq felt like a lump of clay to be moulded, which ever way, he liked.

The stranger said, 'I kept an eye, you people took your own time.'

'Yes, there was a hold-up on the way. You know, we are travelling with animals, our movements will be naturally, slow.'

'Of course, let us be on our job. Are you ready?'

'Yes, come.'

Together, they proceeded towards the lion's cage. Mustaq kneeled down near the cage and sliding a panel, opened a hidden chest, which was filled with canvas bags. He pulled out the bags one by one and passed on to the man, who carried them to a van, which lay hidden behind a rock near the cages. The bags appeared heavy and it took them nearly an hour to shift the entire lot from the lion's cage. Mustaq slided back the panel and shut the secret chamber. A similar chest was inbuilt into the cage of the female lion, which was opened by Mustaq and bags stacked therein, were removed and carried over to the van. There were one hundred bags in all and by the time the work was over it was 2.00 pm in the afternoon. The man was heavily sweating, but not tired, rugged as he was. He locked the van and came over to Mustaq, who waited for him with pleading eyes. The stranger said, 'Thank you *man,* I appreciate your help. Don't you worry, your daughter is safe and will be reaching home this evening. You forget, that you ever met me. You take this money and enoy life.' He handed a thick packet to Mustaq and left. He tried to forget the incident, it was difficult for him to do so. Suffered he did, but he was richer by few thousands, just for accommodating few bags under the cage. He never bothered to know what the bags contained, the stranger told him that they were printed matters, which were banned in the country. He had let it go at that.

The stranger drove the vehicle down a jungle path and arrived at his destination. Ruins of an old fortress, home to wild creepers, bats hanging at dingy corners, heaps of rubbles from caved in roofs, met his eyes. He thought of everything in advance, that is why his plans never failed. Stealing is an art, he argued, but what follows is, more important and vital to the purpose. The loot must be hidden from the searching eyes. In his wide travels across this wild terrain, he spotted these ruins of an earstwhile fort, which was believed to have been once used by *Chatrapati Shivaji*, during his campaigns in Decaan, fighting against the Moguls. The surrounding forest being impenetrable and infested with poisonous herbs and snakes, no one ventured to come near the fort. This place fitted perfectly into his plan. The sun was about to set, when he reached the temple precincts. The path was ridden with wild bushes and rubbles, through which he negotiated the vehicle. It moved slowly with its precious cargo. The compound walls were still existing except for breaches, here and there, due to ravages of time and weather. Earlier, during his scouting of the area, he had located a breach, through which he passed now and reached a huge statue of bull, built in an open space adjacent to the temple. Stopping the vehicle in front of the '*bull*', the man got down and with confidence walked behind the statue and removed few stones from the heap of rubbles lying there; a door way came into view and behind it there was a room. He flashed a torch and found it reasonably clean except for few rats scurrying away to nearest holes. He had come across this room accidentally, while admiring the sculpture of the statue, when a loose stone from the heap tumbled down and fell, a little short from his feet, during his earlier visit. He took the bags, one by one, from the van and put them inside the room. He rearranged the stones, one over the other, and left the site, satisfied that the door was perfectly concealed and the heap looked natural enough. He was about to move, after changing the gear, when he saw a strange sight. A cobra slided down, from the '*bull*' and disappeared into a crevice. For Ratan, it was a good omen.

* * * * *

Searching through the iron chests inside the container vans, yielded nothing. Police came to know, that it was a red herring, thrown at them to divert their attention. Twelve hours passed since the robbery was detected and still, Police had no clue. Where could such a huge amount of money, approximately one hundred crores of rupees and the gold, be hidden, and in such a short time; Inspector Pradhan, who had been put on the job, wondered. All the vehicles passing through the check posts were searched, the money seemed to have vanished, or else hiden some where very close, to be removed conveniently, later, he reasoned.

CHAPTER 8

After his altercation with his father at Poona and finding that Bhola was missing on the following day, Jackey felt very low and dejected. He tried to hold conversation with Jaya, soon after he returned to Bombay, but failed. His own disrepute had distanced her from him. How could he communicate that, he no longer desired to marry her against her wishes and he felt sorry if he ever caused any fear or misgivings in her, on that account. Neither he was in a position to disclose, that he knew of her spiritual communication with his grandfather, in the cellar at the house, in which case, he would have to explain her so many things, which might upset his applecart, to be on good terms with her. He could not take the risk. His earlier visit to Raja's house to win back the confidence of the family, was of no help, either. It was rather embarrassing for everybody. He was not prepared for a '*how do you do*' chit chat. Jaya's cursory remarks and greetings confirmed, that in her eyes he was still bad medicine. He had no place to turn to, for solace and comfort. When Saxena returned home that night, he found his son in that mood, sitting in front of the fire place, with a drink in his hand and a forlorn look in his eyes.

Saxena needed rest very badly, his back ached and limbs were tired. He poured a drink for himself, gulped it down neat and looked at his son. He loved this motherless child. He held himself responsible for his son's worry and despondency, he took another drink and tried to push away his melancholy. He loved his son in his own way, may be as a recompense for the treatment he meted out to his mother. At times he felt guilty; when she lived, he wanted to make amends and really tried to care for her, if not for love, at least for the poor woman, whom he used as a dice of the game and went on using her to achieve his target. He was not made for love, he knew. Greed for amassing wealth had taken possession of him and he had no use of women in his life, except in so far as they fitted into his designs. There were only two women in his life, Parvati and Lolita.

When he roamed the forest lonely, as a cloud in the sky, while he was a young cow herd, Parvati came to his life to fill his lonliness. In her company, he felt chivalrous and saved her from the clutches of her wicked aunt. But he was not prepared for the end bargain. He had to marry her at the insistence of the *sethjee,* who was kind enough to provide both of them with food and shelter. Being an intelligent young man and seeing far into the future, he spared no means to put *sethjee* under his obligation. From a mere domestic help, he rose to be the most trusted servant of his employer and within a year he was driving his car, as his chauffeur, and accompanied him, wherever he went, to the office, to the stock market, to the Bank, to his club and to his friends. After the so called accidental death of *sethjee,* which was not so, he possessed Lolita, his daughter, though not out of design, but certainly to his advantage, and married her. He had no compunction, whatsoever, to throw away Parvati and her child, just like a speck of dust from his shirt sleeve, to get rid of them from his life, forever. The thought never entered his mind, that he had broken Lolita in body and spirit, by taking her forcibly, when she was defenceless and was mourning the death of her father. Thereafter he did not find any smile on the face of Lolita. Her soul was tortured within the cage of her body and she never forgave him for his misdeed and monstrous behavior, till she died. She never took interest in what he did. The only silver lining of the cloud of her miserable life was her son, who came to her to bring a little happiness; that was all she possessed dear to her heart, till the last moment.

As he approached his son, he called in a soft voice. 'When did you come here, my dear boy?' Jackie looked up and did not reply. He sat there, in silence. Saxena took a chair and sat by the side of his son.

'Have you had your dinner, yet?' Still, no answer. He summoned the servant and asked him to serve dinner for both of them.

* * * * *

Inspector Pradhan was a worried man, he didn't lose any time in taking steps to find out, where the vertical shaft from the Bank vault led to. Before nightfall, he found out that a three feet wide and twenty feet long tunnel was bored from a deep foundation pit, earlier excavated and abandoned at the construction site, up to the Bank vault. Lowering himself down the shaft, dug under the steel cabinet, fortified with a flash light and wearing a gas mask, he almost crawled on his hand and knees to reach the mouth of the tunnel. It was a difficult task, as the tunnel sloped upward. He struck the opening, after toiling for half an hour. The mouth was covered with rubbish, to camouflage the opening. The pit was seven feet deep. That was the end of it, from there, where to?

Next morning, Pradhan was at the construction site with a police dog. He didn't want to waste time to find how the job was done, his immediate concern was to know where the money was transported to. To solve any problem, one makes assumptions. He assumed, that the money was siphoned out from the Bank to the tunnel mouth, though it seemed incredible considering the time at the disposal of the robbers. He let loose the dog, after letting it sniff the surroundings. The animal circled around for some time, before it rushed in one direction and it pointed towards the Municipal Grounds. Next moment, it had cleared the compound wall and jumped over to the other side. He followed, by scaling the wall. The ground was covered with litter and leftovers of circus animals and was stinking. Yonder, there was a pond and beyond, the ground stretched, where the circus tent was pitched. Now, nothing remained except for the charred remains of the tent poles. The scent of the animals was so strong in the area that it was natural for the dog to miss the particular feeble human scent, which it picked up from the construction site. But, it was obvious from the dog's movement, that the persons crossed over to the Municipal Grounds; a closer scrutiny of the ground, confirmed that. Several footprints, overlapping, were noticed. The track stopped at a place, where faint marks of carriage wheel tyres were seen. Evidently, several trips were made by some persons between the wall and the carriages, which were there on the night, when the robbery took place. Tyre marks of an automobile were also seen near the wall. Pradhan stood there and thought for a while. A thin smile crossed his lips, as the picture became clear to him. He hurried to his office and made a call.

* * * * *

Jackie made elaborate arrangements for holding a special function for dedicating the superbly styled house in commemoration of the fortieth birth anniversary of his mother. All the rooms, especially the bed room of his mother, were lavishly furnished and decorated with flowers. The polished marbles and the brass, glittered under the bright chandeliers hung from the roof, replete with nicely carved figurines on ornamental brackets. The central hall looked majestic, adorned on one side with the huge life size portrait of the *sethjee,* which seemed to stare benevolently at the gathering, assembled on the occasion. The invitations were sent out under the name of Jackie. The crowd was swelling, and everyone was full of praises for the splendid interior decorations and the combination of colours which brought out the depths of the magnificient architecture of the building.

It proved too difficult for Jackie, to plan the whole thing. Firstly, though he was the producer of the show, he never came to the forefront. Nobody except a very few trusted assistants, knew how he toiled day and night in organizing the constructional activities, holed all the while, in a small obscure room, glued to a screen, monitoring the progress on all fronts. Secondly, he had no idea, what would be Jaya's reactions, once she came to know, that he was her *boss* and she gave her best to please him and earned a fat salary. The very purpose, which literally drove him in a frenzied manner, in going ahead with the project, calling all the shots himself, was totally defeated, when accidentally, he discovered the hidden truth about the house. From that moment onwards, his sole purpose was to restore the past glory of the house in which the memories of his mother and *nanajee* were enshrined. He left no stones unturned to make the function a great success and to that end, he invited political bigwigs and media persons too. He fortifyed himself with a strong drink to face Jaya and bear the brunt of her tirade, accusing him for the deception.

On the contrary, Jaya was the person, to have been most surprised and puzzled to know that her mysterious employer was none other than the cantankerous Jackie, whom she despised all along. It seemed unbelievable, that the magnificient edifice really belonged to him and he was the heir of the deceased *Sethjee*, to trace whom she spent several days in making enquiries and had given up ultimately, as something uncanny. The realization that the room for which she did the internal decorations, giving her best, was really the room, once occupied by his mother Lolita and the mystery behind the sudden appearance of the portrait of *sethjee'* in the Central Hall, together with so many other unexplained events, brought her face to face with a truth, that was shocking and astounding. Still, she was not able to find the missing pieces of the zig-saw puzzle. It was hard to believe, that Jackie, who was such a hard nut, could foster so much love and affection for his mother, that he almost built a memorial for her, spending a fortune. Her eyes searched for him in the crowd and finding him conversing with a senior architect, moved towards him.

Jackie saw her coming and averted her eyes. Jaya addressed him, 'Hello, Jackie', there was admiration in her eyes, 'So, you are behind all this. Hope, you will not mind, my addressing you by your name, you are still my *boss* and I owe my pleasure of achieving something, to you. Under no stretch of imagination, I could think that you were the kingpin, around which everyone of us revolved. I have no words to thank you, Jackie. 'Her voice was choked. Jackie looked up, there was sincere gratitude and admiration in her eyes.'

He said, 'It is the other way Jaya, I should thank you, for all you did in aid of my dear mother's memory and also to bring a sense of purpose in my life.' Jaya looked at him, his eyes were intent and searching. She instantly followed, what Jackie was referring to. She had no doubts in her mind that, Jackie must have followed her into the cellar and witnessed their experience of spirit calling, that evening.

Gradually, they had company of others, who thronged around them. It was Maya, who spoke, 'Jackie, you are a *chuppa Rustam*. Had I known that it was you, for whom our jaya toiled, I would not have allowed her. But you proved too clever for us. Did you achieve, what you wanted?'

'Yes, *bhabi*, much more than that. Jaya helped me not only to get my lost property revive its past glory, but also provided me with a soul stirring experience of coming face to face with the past. I must thank you, that you let her take the job.'

Parvati came and joined the group. She blessed Jackie, for doing so much for his mother. She could not hold back her tears. It was hard for her to stand there in front of Lolita's son and yet behave as a stranger. Then one thought, completely unnerved her, what if, Ratan walks in and confronts her? She became unsteady and lost her colour. Seeing her disconcerted, Jackie hastened to say, 'Ma jee, is any thing the matter? Come, please sit here and relax'. He led her to the nearest sofa. He gave her a glass of water to drink.

'It is her fasting day', Jaya explained.

'I am alright *beta*, you better go and take care of other guests.'

Jackie said to Jaya, 'I hope she is alright. Please call me, if you need.' He saw a group of media people entering and rushed to receive them.

Suddenly there was a hush, everybody stopped talking. A contingent of policemen entered, headed by Inspector Pradhan. The appearance of Police was quite unexpected. Everybody looked askance. The police semed to be chasing someone and they were armed.

The Inspector said, 'Excuse me, ladies and gentlemen, for the intrusion. We are after a criminal, who came this way and entered the precincts through the main gate, he disappeared there after. He was in a van, there is no trace of the van either.'

Exasperated, Jackie thought that it was too much and moving forward drew his full stature before the Inspector and said, 'Look, Mr. Inspector, I am Jackie Saxena, the owner of this property, celebrating here an important and solemn function, the birth anniversary of my deceased mother. Your intrusion is definitely unexpected and I am truly shocked. More over, what you speak, does not make any sense to me. How a person with a van could vanish, is beyond my comprehension. Are you casting any aspersion on my guests present here? Definitely, you owe me an explanation.'

The Inspector said, 'I have no intention of hurting any body's sentiment, gentleman. I am merely doing my duty. I have checked the parking lot and the missing van is not there. I am afraid, I must ask you to cooperate and allow me to verify the identities of all persons present here and the particulars of the vehicles they came in.' Instinctively, Jackie glanced at Jaya, she nodded.

Jackie said, 'Okay, Inspector. I will not stand in your way, you may go ahead, but better be quick.'

Inspector Pradhan asked his men to close the main door and requested the guests to come forward, one by one, to the adjoining room and furnish their identity and particulars of their vehicles. Police did not find anything incriminating during their investigation. The

Inspector was in a quandary; the fugitive was seen following the straight road ahead and it led only to this house. Where could he have gone ? After profusely thanking Jackie for his cooperation and the guests, for their forbearance, he left the premises with his men.

But he was not a man to accept defeat so easily, after asking his men to leave the premesis, he turned around and approached the house, this time by scaling the boundary wall with the help of a tree branch. It started drizzling, he cursed and dropped silently to the soft ground on the other side. Saving himself from the rains, he kept close to the trees and reached the backyard. He hid himself behind a column under the porch, which was dimly lit. He stood there like a statue, motionless. His vigil paid dividends, after a while. He heard a distinct sound other than the music floating to his ears from the Hall. It was that of an automobile approaching, may be a guest arriving late. But what the Hell! This one was headed straight to the back porch, where he was hidden. Luckily the head lights of the vehicle were switched off. Holding his breath he melted into the darkness. A man, wearing a dark suit got down from the vehicle, he was alone. He was now climbing the steps and about to enter through the back door. Well! Was he the wanted one? He could not see his face.

The party was in full swing. It was Parvati, who noticed him first, a gasp escaped her mouth. It was Ratan, her husband! He had entered through the back door, hidden behind a heavy curtain. His entrance was dramatic and its effects were varied. Her worst apprehension came true. She hid herself behind others. Jackie's first reaction was one of awe and surprise, he had not expected his father. Suppressing all his indignation and anger, he welcomed his father, with a genial smile. To many of his guests, his father was a stranger and others who knew him were surprised to find the person, the legendary Saxena, the tycoon, always dressed in Savile Row suits, to have appeared amongst them in dirty clothes and dusty shoes, as if he walked miles to reach the place. Not withstanding the sneer and shock registered in the faces of many, at the obnoxious appearance of his father, Jackie said, 'Come, *daddy*, I will introduce you to my friends and well wishers', and began the introductions.

Jackie approached a group of persons, behind whom Parvati was hiding and before Ratan's eyes fell upon her, a voice was heard from the door. It was the Inspector, who was saying, 'Will you not introduce your father to me, Mr, Jackie?' Everybody's attention was drawn towards the Inspector, who had left the Hall, a little while ago. The last person, Saxena wanted to see at the moment was the Inspector, whom he thought, he had successfully warded off. Naturally, therefore, he was perturbed. He was at a dead end from which there was no escape. But he was not afraid of him yet. His mind raced through like an Express train, analyzing in his fertile brain, whether he possessed any incriminating evidence on his person. Suddenly his eyes caught sight of Parvati, amongst the persons standing close to him. He stared at her, dumb founded. What the Hell! What she was doing here?Their eyes met, a cold shiver ran through him. No doubt, it was Parvati, his wife. Even at that grave moment, he hit upon a plan to use her as an escape channel. She stood almost next to him and in a twinkling of an eye, he fished out something from his pocket, pressed it on to her hand, hissing between his treeth, *'Hide it and keep your mouth shut.'* If anybody noticed her face at that momemt, it was ashen and she was sweating all over. But everybody's attention was on the Inspector, who approached Jackie and his father.

Jackie said sullenly, 'What brings you back, Inspector? I thought, you had finished your business and left for good.'

The Inspector said, 'I had, but for this gentleman.' He smiled at Saxena and waited.

'He is my father, Mr. Ratan Kumar Saxena. You must have heard his name.'

The Inspetor raised his eye brows, looked more closely at Saxena and said, 'I have heard, but I did not know, till this moment, that he is your father. He has every right to be here.' He extended his hand towards Saxena and said, 'I am glad to meet you sir, I am Pradhan from Crime Departmnt, Bombay Police.'

There was a lull in the atmosphere, music had stopped, everyone looked at Saxena, who was all smiles for the Inspector and said nonchalantly, 'Yes?'

'I am sorry, sir, if I have offended you in any way, but we are keeping track of everyone who came here this evening, this is merely a formality. May I put you a question?'

"Of course, but please be quick, I have had a long drive and feel tired. Nothing is more desirable to me, at the moment, than a good hour's sleep between cold sheets'. This was delivered in the manner af a king addressing to one of his subjects. Pradhan thought, '*why an hour, you will have a life time to sleep in the gaol*' and said, 'Did you see a Desoto van overtaking you, while you were coming this way, Mr. Saxena?'

'Well, Inspector, I cannot say for certain whether I noticed, however, there was traffic bothways. Now, if you excuse me,' he then addressed Jackie, 'Will you send somebody to fetch my valise from the car?', he left the Hall, murmuring excuses to the guests.

Jackie said. 'Yes, *daddy.*' A servant was dispatched to get the bag, Inspector Pradhan followed the servant, muttering an excuse to Jackie. Jackie shook his head in disgust and requested the guests to assemble at the buffet table, since dinner was already served. While the guests were being led to the dining hall, Raja saw her; a young lady in jeans, with a camera hung from her shoulders in the group of media persons. He rushed ahead, brushing against several, to catch her up. She was in the midst of a conversation with another reporter, when some one addressed her, 'Excuse me.'

She turned and faced a gentleman in a formal suit with a winning smile.

'Yes ?' Raja faced her, the same handsome face with a couple of dark spots on the skin like pockmarks. She looked smart and professional in her jeans, but with no sign of recognition. He could'nt be wrong. She was definitely Rohini. Then his glance fell on the photo ID. It said Smitha, Nav Bharat.

Raja was astonished. Could they be twins. He mumbled an excuse and said, 'Are you not Rohini ?' Raja distinctly saw a line of fear crossing her eyes.

'How do you know Rohini?'

Raja caught her elbow and led her to a corner out of hearing distance. He related her the incident of rescuing the girls in Bombay. He saw a flash of recognition in her eyes.

She exclaimed, 'Oh, my God, are you Shekhar *bhaiya*?'

'Yes. You are Rohini then. But this Smitha, who is she ?

'Smitha and Rohini are one and same. But, Shakher *bhaiya,* you have changed now, you were different then.'

'You are right, I was Shekhar then, now I am Raja, which is my real name.'

'And Smitha is my real name.'

'May I ask, how did you fare after you reached Poona?' Her eyes became misty and she said, 'It was not easy going at first, then I met Rakesh accidentally. He owned a News Paper and was struggling with it to get it off the ground. I was in search of a job and one day came to a park to rest for a while in the scorching heat. I found a discarded News Paper on the bench, where I sat and came across an ad for the post of a News Reporter. I wanted to give it a try. The interview was on the very day. I rushed to the office and found a middle aged bespectacled man in the Editor's chair. The interview was short and the kind person offered me the job. It carried a meager salary of two thousand rupees per month and I accepted it. The Editor was Rakesh and he owned the Paper too. That was two years ago and I am married to him now.'

'My congratulations, Smitha.'

'Thank you. Come, I will introduce you to him, he is here somewhere.'

Seizing his wrist, she took him to a tall man in *khadi,* in conversation with a group of persons and said, 'Rakesh, meet Raja, he is the same Shekhar *bhaiya,* I told you about.'

He turned and faced Raja and said, 'It is my good fortune to meet you here, Raja babu. I was looking forward to meet you some day. Smitha, my wife never misses a day without remembering you. She narrated the entire story of her escape, which would not have been possible without your assistance and bravery.'

Raja said, 'My bravery was nothing compared to hers. Probably, she was too modest to tell you her part in that rescue mission. It was really her plan and she executed it at a grave risk to her life. It is me, who should be indebted to her.'

It was a very happy occasion of meeting of old friends and Smitha and Rakesh invited Raja to their humble abode for a celebration before he left for Bombay.

The Inspector went round the car, it was a black sedan, Chevrolet, coated with a thin film of dust, showing that it did a long distance.

Lifting the bonnet, he peeped inside and touched the engine, it was hot. The situation was getting murky. His theory, that his man had hidden himself somewhere inside the premises and would reappear after sometime was simply blasted.

After a cold and refreshing bath and dressed in proper clothes, Saxena entered the Hall reassured, that everything was in control. When he found that, most of the guests were gone including Parvati, he felt relieved; her sudden appearance in the crowd, was a shock, from which it was hard to recover. But he was resilient enough not only to have bounced back in time, but also to turn the event to his advantage. When he was almost at the threshold of striking gold and make his fortune, he would not permit the old woman to topple the apple cart. He must find out from his son, how Parvati was invited to this function, later ofcourse. That Inspector chap was proving to be a pain in his neck. It was always a game of cat and mouse in his profession. He was certain that he was a step or two ahead of police, but it was prudent to be cautious of him.

He found Jackie with a drink in his hand and in contemplation before the portrait of *sethjee.* As soon as he saw his father, shaved and looking fresh and trim and with a glint in his eyes, he was sure that he was no longer the man in a crumpled suit and an object of ridicule, a little while ago, but who stood before him now, appeared to him no less than a buccaneer, out for a fresh assault.

He asked, 'Why this sudden *avtar, daddy*? You told me, you were going out and might not find time to attend the function and you materialized like a man returning from a bull fight.'

'I changed my plans and decided I would rather be with you, on this solemn occasion.'

Sarcastically, Jackie said, 'How considerate of you, *daddy,* thanks.'

'What that Inspector was doing here, Jackie?'

'You heard him, he said, he came in search of a criminal. As a matter of fact, that was his second visit, earlier this evening he was here with his men. They interrogated all the guests enquiring, how they came. It was very embarrassing. He even asked you, regarding a Desoto van. What is all this about *daddy,* is it anything to do with you?'

'Nonsense, these *Policewallahs* are usually a mischievous lot, always barking at the wrong tree. You need not worry about that. I may have to speak to the Commissioner. By the way Jackie, who was that lady in a plain blue saree with a vermillion spot on her forehead?'

'Oh! That was Parvatijee, staying with Raja *bhaiya.* You know, he works with Ram Gopaljee.'

'Yes, ofcourse, I have seen him, in his office. After all that insult, how can you bear those people, Jackie?'

'*Daddy,* have we not talked about it at length?'Saxena let the matter rest there.

* * * * *

Later in the seclusion of his room, Saxena laughed out, that he had beat the Inspector in this game of hide and seek. Let him boil and rage over his failure. What troubled him at the moment, was the sudden appearance of Parvati. It took the wind out of him. Life is a chess board for him. All the pieces lie before him including the adversary's, he knows the moves and prepares for the kill. But if he finds a piece, even if it is a pawn, hitherto unnoticed, suddenly blocks his path, it might cost him his game. He must not let it happen.

* * * * *

Parvati and others returned to the Farm House, quite late in the night, after the dinner, saying thanks to Jackie. The events of the evening had shaken each of them.

Sleep completely eluded her. Parvati had not yet recovered from the shock, which she experienced, on suddenly confronting Ratan, after all these years. What hurt her most was, she did not find any sign of remorse or repentance or even recognition in him; but just a stony and cool stare. He was the same domineering and insolent person, as he was, twenty two years ago when he mercilessly expelled her with the baby, on that stormy night from her home. Tears swelled up in her eyes, he was the same selfish brute, who cared for himelf and his wealth and nothing else.

Jaya observed a great metamorphosis in the character of Jackie, which she found hard to believe. He exhibited all the syndrome of dual personality. She wondered, whether he had followed them into the cellar and witnessed their act of spirit calling. Should she show him the writing on the blank paper. He being the rightful heir and grandson of the late *sethjee,* is solely entitled to execute the wishes of the departed soul. She decided to hand over the holy remains of his grandfather and the jewellery of his grandmother, to him at the earliest opportunity. The only thing then, remains to be solved is the matter relating to a person named Ratan who was accused by *sethjee*, in his communication, to be the cause of his death and ruin of his home. The name Ratan struck a chord in her memory. Was he the stranger of the evening introduced as *Ratan Kumar Saxena* by Jackie, today? And he had addressed him as his *daddy* too!The unfolded secret struck her like a ton of bricks. The cobweb of mystery surrounding the *sethjee* was getting thicker and thicker. She got up with a jerk and sat on the bed: Ratan was then *sethjee's* son- in- law and must have married Lolita, his only child!Her throat felt dry, she switched on the lamp, the time was two o'clock, Parvatijee was asleep by her side, she got down from the bed slowly and tiptoed to the fridge for a bottle of water. After a sip of cold water, she felt composed, but churning of several possibilities in her mind kept her awake for rest of the night.

After his plain talk with Saxena in his office, Raja was no longer afraid of him. Nevertheless, he was wary of him. This person is capable of going to any extent to achieve what he desired. The unexpected appearance of Police at the scene, while chasing a culprit and the dramatic appearance of Saxena in a crumpled suit, later. to be followed by a visit of the Inspector, led him to keep guessing. His accidental meeting with Rohini, another victim of the *mafia* Saxena, whom he had helped to escape from his henchmen, brought him great pleasure and he deemed it a God's Blessing to see the unfortunate girl settled in life.

* * * * *

He might boast of a heart of steel, yet Ratan felt his heart sinking at the sight of Parvati at Jackie's reception in the evening. He had almost written her off from the moment, she left the house. That she joined forces with Raja, his arch enemy, in the meanwhile, and stayed with him, was alarming, no doubt. The situation was deadly explosive. After successfully pulling all the strings when he hit the gold pot and was about to reap the benefits, her appearance was really disconcerting. It called for a meeting with the old lady. He put a man to follow her and keep watch over her movements. He knows now, that she visits the '*Sankat Mochan*' temple, every Tuesday afternoon, by herself. He made a plan to accost her on a Tuesday, after ascertaining, that Police didn't follow him. His security people reported him, that there was a tail behind him everytime he left home for office or for Air Port. Being conversant with methods employed by police, he found out soon that policemen in plain clothes were detailed twentyfour hours near his residence. He was not dealing with any Scotland Yard detectives, they were easily spotted. The fat slobs, either loitered aimlessely on the footpath or stood with their face hidden behind a newspaper at the news stand or sat in the cafetaria, opposite his residence. He pitied their plight, their shift was changed every few hours. What a colossal waste of Public money, he grimaced. They could instead spend it, on the welfare of the employees' families.

On a Tuesday afternoon, having conveniently shaken them off, he was able to park his car near the '*Sankat Mochan*' temple. He waited for the arrival of Parvati. It had started drizzling, so far so good. The crowd assembled near the temple, dispersed quickly, leaving only few persons, who took shelter under the vendors' shops. Then he saw Parvati, coming out of the temple, carrying a *puja thali* in her hand. He smiled looking at her, even at this age she was still beautiful, but not as fresh as she was, when he first met her. Her natural colour, freshness and haughty temper had attracted him and forced by circumstances, he had to marry her. Even today, she wore the sign of a Hindu married woman, a spot of vermillion on her forehead. She walked to the taxi stand and waited, there was no taxi. The rains thickened, she pulled her saree to cover her head. He drove the car near her, opened the front door and almost pulled her inside. This went unnoticed.

When she saw, it was Ratan behind the wheel, she pulled her saree tight against her body and shrank back against the door, away from him. She was so much terrified, that she could not utter anyword. She trembled all over and her heart bet faster. Ratan offered her a towel and said, 'You better dry yourself, or else you may catch cold.'

She had no strength to reply, she took the towel and wiped her face, which was hot, even with rain drops trickling down. After a moment she regained strength and said, 'Will you please let me get down, immediately.'

She held the *puja thali*, firmly in her hand, as if it would protect her, she prayed silently to '*Lord Sankat Mochan*' to rescue her from this demon.

'Of course, I will let you go, I have no desire to take you anywhere with me. But, I find that you still wear, a married woman's symbol on your forehead. You are an epitome of Indian womenhood, I must say. However much, they are humiliated and tortured by their husbands, Indian women would never untie the knot that was tied in the marriage and continue to live in the hope that sometime they might regain love and respect from their errant husbands. This is the reason, why in our country, women suffer and lament that they are not given their right place in the society. Nobody gives anything for asking.'

Parvati had no other alternative but listen to this tirade, she repeated, 'Will you please, let me go ?'

'Ofcourse, I will, but I have to tell you something before I let you go. What happened to that son of yours? Do you require any help fom me for his education? I am running several charitable institutions in the city which were earlier owned by our beoved *sethjee*.'

Parvati was boiling in rage, her voice was choked when she spoke, 'Thanks Ratan, for your kind offer. I do not require any help from you for Kamal's education It is better that he grows without the aid of your tainted money. Now, you tell me, what you have to say.'

'I hear that you are living in Raja's house, whom I dislike most, make sure and behave that we are complete strangers to each other, before others. He looked sternly at Parvati and said, 'I hope, you have with you the packet, which I passed on to you, that evening, at my son's party. You may give it back to me now.'

'Whatever it is, I carried it with scorn and hatred, you better take it and begone. You have not changed with time, you are the same vile person you were twenty two years ago, selfish and conceited to the core. Why don't you ever think of, that at the end you will be answerable to God and try to mend your ways. Wealth is not all in life, it only brings unhappiness and misery at the end. See, what you have achieved, you will always carry with you the burden of the hideous crime you committed, which caused the accident, killing *sethjee*, who provided you with food and shelter, when you were starving and homeless. What an ungrateful creature you are!You dishonoured Lolita and married her, you might have got access, thereby, to her wealth, but only earned her hatred and curses as long as she lived. And now her son despises you. You are a big zero and nothing else.' With tears rolling down her cheeks, she looked the other way.

'Okay, Okay, I am in no mood to hear religious discourses from you, give me the packet and begone', he stopped the car, Parvati took out a small packet from her bag, gave it to him and got down. Slamming the door shut, Ratan drove off.

* * * * *

Pradhan knew, that conclusion on the basis of certain assumptions and analysis, will not stand to scrutiny by the the law of the land, if challenged. It must be supported by reasonable evidence. He sat still for a moment in his office and then took out a Note book from the drawer, containing day to day records of the Police investigation of the Bank robbery. He took out another fat File, which contained News clippings, published in leading Dailies regarding the robbery. He went through the records of the investigation, maintained chronologically.

However incredible it might appear, the findings pointed to one thing, the loot was definitely brought to the circus ground on the night, the tent caught fire, and surprisingly enough, near the cages where the lions were kept!The entire process of thinking stopped there. Unless ofcourse, the money was transferred to the lions'cage and then transported outside, under the very eyes of Police through the check posts. That was the only logical lead he could follow, which he could not discuss with any body else. On the fifth day of the Bank robbery, a report was received in his office, which confirmed his wild imagination and he set out on a journey, which would take him very much near to the solution of the mystery of the robbery. It was time to clinch the case, as the pressure was mounting on the Department to apprehend the culprits and recover the money.

* * * * *

Mustaq was rushing to his village, by a bus, to make sure, that his daughter was safely conducted to home, by her kidnappers. There was a bulge in his inner pocket, which was a lot of money, he knew, and which must be put somewhere safely, as soon as he reaches home. It was early in the morning, when the bus dropped him at the crossing, which was almost two kilometer away from his home. He had walked across paddy fields, to cut short the distance. A couple of stray dogs barked and waved their tails at him, as he approached the village. That was the only sign of welcome to him. He saw people, indistinct, squatting, behind trees and bushes to release themselves. He was back home, almost after one year. A chill wind was blowing over the fields, heralding that winter was already in the corner. Then, the cries of the muezzin, *Allah O Akbar*, was heard from the local *masjid*, calling people for their morning *namaj*. Mustaq hurried towards his home. He knocked at the entrance, which opened to the courtyard. A little while later, there was a sound of a bolt of being drawn and the door opened by his *bibi*, Fatima. Seeing him standing at the door, her joy knew no bounds and she exclaimed, 'Oh! By Grace of Allah, you are safe. Oh! *Gulab ki Abba, meri to jan nikal gayee thee*, they brought the child day before yesterday and threatened me not to spell a word to anybody, they have not harmed the child and she is happy, they have given her toys and sweets.'

'Let me go inside, if you have finished the talking. I hope, you have not breathed any word to others', then added slowly, 'They may be generous but very dangerous.' Mustaq put his bag down on the verandah and stretched his legs. His wife said. 'The child is sleeping, shall I wake her up.'

'What for? Let her sleep, I will see her, afterwards. I hope she is not suffering from any shock. Such things are not easily forgotten. We are lucky, to have got her back, unhurt.'

She was about to say something, but Mustaq stopped her and said, 'Not now, later I will explain everything, better you go and make some tea for me.'

After his wife left, he thought over the matter and decided not to disclose his encounter with the gang, who were most probably responsible for the Bank robbery. Since he had been paid handsomely, why should he bother? Moreover, he did'nt know anything about the stranger, nor about the bags and what they contained. It was only, his conjecture, after he came to know about the robbery, on the next day from the News papers, that the bags might have contained the loot. But he couldn't do anything, because his lips were sealed. Even before his wife could bring his cup of tea, he heard a vehicle stop in front of his door and some one knocking. On opening the door, he found a man, standing there with a smile on his face. The man was showing an identity card and said, 'Mustaq, I believe. I am Inspector Pradhan from Bombay Police, Crime Branch.' Meanwhile, Fatima *bibi* joined them, holding a cup of tea in her hand.

Pradhan said, '*Namaste bhabijee*, it is very cold outside, a cup of tea for me also will be welcome.'

Mustaq was stunned, hearing the name of police and became speechless. Fatima, seeing a stranger at the door and also a car outside got bewildered, but had the presence of mind to step ahead of her husband and speak to the person, thus, '*Aap kaun ho babujee.*' Pushing aside his wife, he said, '*Tu chup kar*', and then to the Inspector, 'We may be excused *sahib,* please come in', and then to his wife, *'Tu ja, charpai le aa, aur chai garam kar, ye Pulish ka bada sahib hai.*' Fatima, tightening the *dupatta* around her head, left, to put a charpai in the courtyard and receded to the inner quarters. Pradhan followed Mustaq inside and sat upon the charpai, Mustaq remained standing at a distance. He then, went inside and returned with a cup of steaming cup of tea and handed it to Pradhan. 'What about yours?' '*Mai bad me lelunga na sir.*'

'*Nahin, hamare sath pio.*'

As Pradhan sipped the tea, Mustaq looked on with great apprehension, for the outcome of this unexpected visit of Police to his humble place. His wife stood behind a door, staring at them with palpitating heart. Now, she realized, that her husband must have committed a serious crime, for which Police is after him and the child suffered as a consequence. She stifled a sob by stuffing a croner of the *dupatta* into her mouth.

Pradhan said, 'Mustaq, I know that you have helped the people, who robbed the Bank, to transfer the money by using the cages of the lions, ingeniously. I want to see the spot, where actually, the money was transferred from the cages. I am sure that, they must have put some pressure on you to help them. I am not interested to know the details, atleast now. We must recover the money, before it is too late. You must cooperate with us, in this case and be a Public witness, when the time comes. No charge will be framed against you. There is no time to be lost, we must start now.' Mustaq said, 'I will do, whatever you tell, *sahib*. Let me have a word with my wife.' He went to his wife and told her, not to divulge before anybody, of this visit, he would be going with the Inspector on some urgent business and would be back soon.

The car sped on the highway and then took a branch road and reached a spot, after three hours, as led by Mustaq. They stopped by a stream flowing near by over which there was a bridge. They got down from the vehicle, Mustaq led the Inspector, a little away from the road and stopped near a grove of mango trees. He said, 'It is here, we stopped for feeding the animals and their afternoon rest. I had to purposely bring the lion cages to this place, under the pretext that the beasts require a cool place to rest for a while after a strenuous journey in the hot sun. But the actual reason, as you would see, was to keep the transfer of the bags, secret.' Pradhan surveyed the scene and found it was so.

Then, Mustaq related, how the bags were transferred from under the carriages to the van, one by one. 'Did you not know then, that the bags contained cash and gold?'

'Truly speaking *Sahib*, I had no idea. The man told me that they contained important *sarkari* papers. I did not question, I wanted to complete the job, so that the *bastards* would release my daughter.'

'I see, you have told me enough, we will question you later for details, now you show me which way the man drove his vehicle' Mustaq showed him a path in the jungle leading away from the road towards the stream. From the description of the vehicle given by him, Pradhan guessed it to be a Desoto Station Wagon. He went back to his car and sent a wireless message to the control room. After some time, a Police team arrived at the spot and reported to Pradhan for further instructions. An officer was asked to accompany Mustaq and drop him at his residence; Mustaq was advised not to breath any word regarding the matter, to others and remain at his residence, till he was called for. No sooner the keeper of the lions left for his home, Pradhan began discussing with his colleagues regarding his plan of action. it was the fifth day of the robbery and the criminals had enough time and respite to hide the money at a safer place after transferring the same from the most incredible place on earth. He did'nt disclose his findings, to his subordinates. He could'nt believe, what he heard from the keeper of the lions. It was more important to trace and recover the treasure, before it became absolutely impossible.

He could'nt but praise the ingenuity of the person who masterminded the job, as they struggled to follow the track of the van in the dense jungle, running alongside the stream, in their four wheel driven jeep. The jungle was so thick that, even at noon hours the sun rays couldn't reach the ground. The only sound that reached their ears was that of the gurgling stream. The stream was almost hugging a branch of the Western Ghats, the track, they were following, led them up the hill. Up they rode, till the ruins of a fort was visible at a distance. Pradhan, a Maratha himself, felt proud to remember Chatrapati Shivaji who conqured and built numerous forts, during his reign in seventeenth century, in such difficult terrains in the Western Ghats. The one they approached, must have been one of those, he believed.

Was the person again fooling them, to lead them to a three hundred years old fortress in search of the loot? Maybe or maybe not. But this was the only possible path, he could have taken. They pushed on, suddenly the driver saw some thing on the gravel and stopped. He got down and picked up a gravel from the road and smelled. 'Definitely, it is engine oil, sir.' He passed it on to the inspector. He touched it and smelled. 'Yes, it is', he said, 'fact is always stranger than fiction. How he managed to drive a van in this hilly track, which was built for use for troops on horse back or on foot, is beyond my comprehension.'

They reached the summit and came across the ruins of the fort. They found, jungle bushes had completely invaded the ruins and what remained of the walls were covered by wild creepers. The track, they were following suddenly ended and heaps of stones obstructed their path. They were on a slope and the stones seemed to have rolled down from the ruins above. Strange, Pradhan thought, how then, the man with all that loot, could have entered inside to hide it. Some thing caught his eye, he knew then, a recent land slide caused the stones to roll down The stones carried with them green twigs and mud along with them. There must have been heavy rains recently, in this mountainous region, he thought. *Could it be, that the man hid the loot some where inside the ruins and thought to return later to recover, and the land slide occurred, in the meanwhile. In which case there is a thin possibility of the treasure being still there.*

He prodded his men to climb the hill for a distance of a hundred feet or so, to reach the top. The view from the top was spectacular, for miles around, ranges of Western Ghats were visible; below, the stream appeared like a streak of silver ribbon meandering in its course to empty into River Tapti. They entered the ruins of the fort through an opening and were struck at the carvings on some stone pillars, which must have once carried a roof above them. They approached a courtyard, where these pillars stood. The main temple was in ruins, but a gigantic bull carved out of stone, in a sitting posture with the fore legs bent forward, told that the temple was a Shiva temple. Then, one of the team officers shouted and said, he found some thing, others rushed to the spot, where he stood, and looked at the place, he was pointing. It was a burnt match stick, a simple thing, but carried with it a ton of message. Evidently, the man with the loot was at this place, on the second day of the robbery. In other words, he was here, exactly three days before. A shiver ran through Pradhan's body. He came this way with the bags, that was certain. Where could he have hidden the bags. The bags were heavy, as told by the keeper of the lions. He looked around, his eyes met only wildernss and desolation, the aftermath of cruelity of destiny of a country.

'Oh! God, where should I look for?' God answered his prayer. A snake wriggled out from the heap of rubbles, close to the statue of the bull. Men standing near by, stepped back. 'Yes, why not', Pradhan was thinking fast. He asked his men to dislodge the rubbles, and what did they find there?A black hole. More stones were removed, a small door way was found, opening to a small room. Battery lights were brought, when focused, he found the stone floor was littered with dry leaves, blown by the wind, something else caught his attention. The floor appeared to have been swept and the dry leaves pushed to one corner. On closer scrutiny, he even detected scratches on the slabs, they appeared fresh. There was no doubt in his mind now, that the bags were dumped here and then shifted elsewhere. Most probably, he was a day behind the criminal. He had no time to lose, he must get back to the wireless van and find out from the control room, if there was any trace of the van, following the description given to them earlier.

No sooner he raised the radio, message was heard over the ear phone, that a van answering the description, was seen heading towards Poona and a patrol van was following it. *'Got you this time, you cannot escape now, your game is over'*, he hissed and clenched his fist. The police vehicles rushed to Poona. They were on the Highway and caught up with the van, which was moving faster and faster, beating them at every bend, it was throwing so much dust, that at times it was invisible to the police, in hot pursuit. They were steadily losing distance till the van was completely lost from sight. They came upon an estate with posters marked' KEEP AWAY PRIVATE PROPERTY. They had left the High Way one Km behind. No doubt, the van came this way. They saw several treads of tyres on the road surface, road signs indicated that they were entering 'Saxena Estates'. They saw at a distance an imposing building, a little later they came across massive gate posts, with a guards cabin. The name 'LOLITA' was inscribed on a name plate in polished black granite, on one of the posts. The gates were open and the police party drove through.

CHAPTER 9

Saxena was in his office, drumming his fingers on the table top. He was worried; it was a close shave, that evening at Poona. Luckily, he was able to shake off the police, following him. The dense roadside green hedge, through which he swerved suddenly and entered an abandoned ranch, hid him sufficiently, to escape from the notice of the police. He saw the police party rushing by. That Pradhan chap, was an enemy to be reckoned with, how quickly he could lay his hands on that keeper of the lions! No doubt, by sheer fright, the timid fellow must have spilled the beans and sent the Police after him. He could already feel the hot breath of the Inspector upon his neck. In his plan of things, this blessed Inspector was not in the list to be ticked off. Unless, he takes some quick damage control steps, his hard acquired treasure is as good as gone. He knew, there was a reservoir inside the ranch, which once upon a time served as a source of water supply, for the animals and their trainers and was deep enough. Existence of the ranch, at this place, was not known to many. In pre independence days, it was owned by one of the earstwhile Maharajas. Later, after merger of the states, due to lack of maintainance and disuse, the ranch which was once a reputed breeding centre of race horses, in the country, became a barren land and lay there unnoticed and forgotten. In his younger days, when he served in the household of the *sethjee,* his adventurous spirit led him to this place often and he used to play his flute in the wilderness and be once again with the nature reminding him of the days, when he roamed the forests, as a cowherd. He discovered the reservoir fed by the rains and many other places and structures, not visible from the roadside. He used to spend hours at this place and breathe the fresh air. He remembered to have seen among others, sumps to store water for the animals at various places and selected one now, for his immediate purpose. He was desperate and wanted somehow to dump the hot substance to avoid detection, which was imminent. The sump was empty and dry, but covered with wild creepers, which would do well to conceal the loot. He strived and strained to shift the bags from the van into the sump, rearranging the creepers to look natural enough. Once, that was done, he drove the vehicle toward the reservoir, which was now covered with water lily. He kept the engine running, put it into gear and got down, letting the van roll down into the water. There was a splash and the van was sunk in deep water, few bubbles rose to the surface and there after there was no sign of it. There it must lie, till the reservoir was dewatered, which was unlikely, in the coming few months.

He walked the distance to the High Way and taking a bus, reached the city. It was almost evening, as he stepped into the automobile show room, which he owned, taking the staff by surprise, at his unexpected visit. He had a personal garage, behind the show room, with a fleet of cars for his own use. He picked up a black 'Chevro' and drove down to the house, where his son was holding the party, for which he was already late.

* * * * *

Parvati was thoroughly shaken, when she arrived home that evening from her visit to the temple. After her unexpected and painful encounter with Ratan, she was exhausted in body and spirit. She retired to the seclusion of her room, sipped a glass of water and reclined on the bed. She sweated and the cool air thrown out by the a/c was comforting. Gradually, she composed herself and dismissed the entire episode as a bad dream. She did not come down for dinner, that evening. Raja and Ranee, however, noticed that *majee* looked upset after her visit to Poona. May be, she was missing her son, the mail which was sent by Kamal, yesterday, might have something to do for her melancholy, they thought.

On the following morning, when Parvatijee came for breakfast, Ranee wanted to know about the letter of Kamal. She said, 'It is as usual *beta*, half of it, filled up with advice to me that I should be regular in taking food and also medicine for my BP and above all I should cut short on my fastings.'

Ranee said, 'See, *majee*, how concerned he is about your health. It is but natural.'

'You youngsters are all same, you should give some credit to the elders' wisdom and listen to what they say, instead of telling them what to do. He never tells me, whether he takes a full breakfast before he leaves for his work, whether he says his morning and evening prayers. Now, you may see as well, for yourself, what your dear husband has eaten. He did'nt touch his breakfast, which you have so painstakingly prepared and probably rushed off, after sipping a little juice. 'Ranee avoided to answer and asked, what else Kamal *bhaiya* wrote.

Majee said, 'Do you know *beta*, he is expected here by end of January, after submission of his thesis, so he wrote.'

Ranee burst into clapping and said, 'Oh! *Majee*, that is really good news, worth celebrating.' She was about to speak further, but restrained herself, after seeing a shadow of gloom covering the face of *majee.* Abruptly, Parvati left the table, went to the *puja* room and sat in meditation with a string of *rudrakshya*, in her hand.

Ranee was puzzled, she was certain that something troubled *majee*, which she was not able to disclose. She busied herself in the kitchen and decided to speak to Raja about this, later. He returned home, in the evening, skipping his lunch. He had a busy day, he explained.

Parvati decided not to disclose the secret of her relationship with Ratan, as she knew how much Kamal loved her and what foolish steps he might resort to, once he comes to know that Ratan was his father. With great effort, therefore, she managed a relaxed and smiling face, when she met them in the evening, in the lounge. Seeing her happy, Ranee beamed at her and said to Raja, 'You know, Kamal is expected home, this January. We will throw a grand party to celebrate his homecoming.'

Raja said, 'Certainly! It is such a good news, my congratulations *majee*, see how quickly time has passed, it is only the other day, we gathered at the airport to see him off. Ranee, does Jaya know of this?'

Ranee said, 'Why not we call her for lunch tomorrow, which is Sunday, and give her the surprise.'

'That would be excellent. '

* * * *

The mystery of the missing van was accidentally unearthed and brought to light by a group of children playing by the roadside, when they broke into the abandoned ranch, one day, in search of the cricket ball, which was driven straight into a bush inside. The search led them to the reservoir and one of the boys noticed some glittering object in the middle of the reservoir, reflecting the sun rays. It looked like a dome. Out of curiosity, one boy picked up a stone and threw, it struck and there was a metallic sound. The news spread and finally reached Police, who visited the site to see and report. The news reached Inspector Pradhan, who came to the site to investigate. A crane was brought, the van was lifted and brought out. The doors were jammed, they were cut and opened. The inside was filled with mud, the ignition key was 'ON' and it was the 'De soto'van, Police was after. Police combed the premises, nothing was recovered. Again he was bet by the scoundrel, Pradhan grimaced.

Saxena did not sit idle. He paid off huge sums of money to his creditors, who knew how to launder the money. Still, large chunks of money and the entire bulk of gold were left over in the makeshift vault hidden in a discarded water sump. Since he had no other partners in the venture, he had nothing to guard against. One evening, however, while he was inside the ranch. he noticed that water level in the reservoir was low and the top portion of the body of the van was visible, even from a distance. The situation was alarming and it called for immediate transfer of the booty, elsewhere. What better place could there be than the underground bomb shelter, which *sethjee* had built, for shelter in the event of air raids, during the second World War. Besides *sethjee*, it was only he, who was aware of its existence. It has been almost twenty years, since he paid a visit to the chamber. This chamber was accessible through a wall in the kitchen. By a rare feat of architecture, *sethjee* was able to erect a sliding door into the wall, which could be operated by inserting a key in a hole suitably camouflaged. *Sethjee* showed him once, how one could enter the bomb shelter from inside the kitchen. He had to make several trips between the ranch and the house, to shift the entire loot.

That, Saxena was a business icon, Pradhan had no doubt. A chain of hotels, bars, restaurants, real estate etc, proclaimed the extent of his wealth and business. He learnt from the Income Tax Dpartment, however, that many of his firms were not recording profit and he was supposed to be losing heavily on his investments. Moreover, his son spent lavishly in modernization and modification of his huge estate at Poona, of which he was aware, when he chanced to arrive there in his wild pursuit of the hot van. Notwithstanding all this background, he cannot possibly pin Saxena down, for the Bank robbery. At the most, he was a potential suspect, that was all. The man was wily and ruthless. However minutely he went through his case history, he could not detect any kink in his armour. The man was adept in covering up his path, as a dog would cover up the hole, where it buries its bones. He was damn sure, that the van which was recovered from the depths of the reservoir was the same one, he utilized to transport the treasure from the ruins of the fort, while Police searched for the same at the house. Then suddenly, something dawned upon him, it was only a flash of brainwave, as a lightning across the sky. He said to himself, 'Yes, why not.'

* * * * *

While others were gone to receive Kamal at the airport, Parvati meditated in the *puja* room, her thoughts reposed in the Lord. But she was not successful in her meditation. Time and again, the scene of her recent encounter with Ratan flashed across her mind, disturbing her. His threats were ringing in her ears. Oh God! How long she was destined to be under such perpetual stress of hiding the facts from the world. Her heart cried for her child, come what may, she would not disclose the secret and make his life miserable. Voices were heard outside, perhaps they arrived. She wiped her face and came out.

Kamal came rushing to her, others following. She took her son in the folds of her arms. What pleasure and peace it gave to her tormented soul!For a moment, she forgot that Ratan existed. Her world consisted only of Kamal and she held him tight. Raja, Ranee and Jaya witnessed the scene of spontaneous love and affection between the mother and the son and their eyes became moist.

Ranee said. 'Kamal *bhaiya*, now, are you satisfied that we have taken good care of *majee*?' He turned to face them, smiled and nodded. Raja placed Kamal's baggage in a corner, assisted by Jaya. He said, 'Ranee jee, Kamal must have forgotten the taste of Indian tea, why don't you go and prepare some?'Jaya volunteered, "No, no, you may all sit and talk, let me go and make the tea.' Ranee was prompt to remark, 'Yes, yes, why not, you only know, how to sugar Kamal's tea.' Jaya left for the kitchen hiding her coy smile.

After the tea ceremony was over, Ranee, seeing furtive glances being exchanged between the two love birds, said, 'Jaya, would you not care to take Kamal to the garden, I have noticed rare kinds of butterflies, fluttering their wings, over there.'

At this time of the season, the garden appeared as a bride decked with jewellery, all the seasonal flowers being in bloom. The beds of Dahlia, Chrysenthemum. Petunias, Dianthus, Phlox, Cosmos and dwarf Marigolds, to mention a few, were the show of the garden and attracted Kamal so much, that he felt drawn to the soil, amidst the fragrance of the flowers, the matchless creation of God. He breathed the fresh air and basked in the cool atmosphere. He closed his eyes and reailized the sublime difference between his motherland and foreign land. He opened his eyes and looked up at Jaya, who stood beside her exuding warmth and love, completely pervading his mind and obliterating the image of Dorothy, forever. He took her hand in his and squeezed, electrifying Jaya, who responded. With no words spoken, they spoke to each other in volumes in mute acceptance. Their reverie was broken, when Ranee appeard in the balcony, calling them inside.

* * * * *

Jackie was no fool, he was in Bombay, thinking over the incidents, that occurred at LOLITA, day before. The Inspector's visit to the house, was by no means, an accident. His father's sudden appearance in a rumpled suit was neither a coincidence. He decided to pay a visit to the house.

* * * * *

A day after, Saxena arrives at LOLITA,. He possessed a latch key and had no difficulty to enter. It was dark inside, save the flickering electric bulb glowing permanently, under the portrait of *sethjee,* in the Hall. The atmosphere was eerie. He moved towards the kitchen, situated behind the Hall, he opened the door, entered and then closed it behind him. Locating the switch board and unscrewing the cover plate, he inserted the special key in a hole hidden behind the jumble of wires. He put on a switch, there was a click sound and then a part of the wall slided silently, behind a cupboard. He swung the cupboard on its hinges, exposing a small opening on the wall. There were steps behind, leading to the underground chamber. It was dark inside. Again, he flipped a switch, a, light came on. Thanks, for the electricity, it has not failed. He stepped inside. The bags were exactly in the place, where he had put them. Though the bomb shelter was never used for the purpose it was built, it served him now, when needed. He remembered the day, *sethjee* took him to the underground chamber and told him that he spent a considerable sum of money in it, but there was no occasion to use it. But, in life, he said, one has to plan for everything, so that one is not caught unawares. *Sethjee* was right.

The bags were quite heavy and he dragged them on their wheels, through the small sliding partition into the kitchen. He closed the door, by turning the key and swung the cupboard back to its position. In few minutes, he would be out of the house and racing on the road to the rendezvous, where people would be waitng to take delivery of the money and the gold, discounted at ninety percent for credit to his account against bogus Bills raised in their favour. He was very happy with the arrangement and was about to open the door, when he heard someone opening the latch of the main door. A heavy curtain covered the kitchen door, he could see the door opening and his heart missed a beat, when he saw Jackie entering.

Jackie looked elegant in a black suit with a open color white shirt. For a moment he forgot the fortuitous situation, he was in and felt proud of his son, who in the recent times matured enough, before his eyes. He had half a mind, to tell everything to his son, but as usual he didn't allow his heart to take the reins. He waited with bated breath, for the next movement of his son. Jackie switched on the lights of the Hall, stood still for a while and then came near the portrait of his grandfather, almost three steps ahead of the kitchen. What if, he decides to take a glass of water? Instead, he said, *'Hello! Grand pa, how are you?'* Then, he went upstairs to his mother's room. Saxena waited for a few moments, and then dragging the bags painstakingly, he proceeded toward the side entrance.

Jackie went to his mother's room and switched on the lights. He was greeted by a sweet fragrance, which he experienced in the presence of his mother. Then he heard the gurgle of water inside the bathroom. His heart nearly stopped. He exclaimed, 'Oh! No. It can't be'. The water was still running in the bathroom, as if, someone was under shower. His heart was beating faster, he tiptoed to the bath room and called. 'Is anybody there?' No answer, he knocked, still no answer. He turned the knob and opened the door, the shower was running, but there was no body under it. He went to the writing desk at the corner, where he had placed a framed picture of his mother and sat there, looking at the photograph. Taking out his diary, from inside a drawer, he began writing.

Saxena looked up and knew, that his son would remain in his mother's room for a while and would provide him sufficient opportunity to clear out. But Goddess Luck was no longer on his side. No sooner, he began shifting a bag from his hiding place, he heard the door bell ringing. He stopped midway. Who could be this late caller?

Jackie got up from writing, switched off the CCTV and came down to answer the callng bell. There was a smile on his face as he climbed down. A lot of visitors, this evening, he thought. But his smile turned into consternation, when he opened the door and found Inspector Pradhan standing there. He was the last person, he wanted to see, that evening. *It was a very strange coincidence again, that the Inspector was right at the heels of his father*. It upset his plan, nodoubt, but he was not perturbed. The Inspector grinned and said, 'Hello, good evening', Jackie stood barring his path.

'Are you not asking me to come in.'

'Yes, of course. Come in.' There was silence for some time. Then the Inspector spoke, 'You must be wondering, why, I called on you, so unexpectedly.'

'I am waiting.'

'I came for Mr. Saxena, your father. I know, he is here. I want to question him, regarding the bank robbery.'

'How are you sure, he is here? He does'nt stay here. You should call, at his Bombay residence, intead of disturbing peace in my house, every time.' There was annoyance in his voice. Saxen a who heard their conversation, thought that this would satisfy the devil and he would go away. But no, Pradhan proved stubborn and he wanted to search the premises. He, even produced a search warrant from his blasted oversized pocket. He failed to understand, why police Inspectors, always have bulging pockets and produce everything they require from it, just as a magician from his hat. Jackie had no option but to take the Inspector on a round of the house. No sooner the Inspector followed Jackie, to the upstairs, Saxena slipped out of his hole and bolted to the guest room, by the side of the kitchen. Hearing the sound of a door being opened, Jackie came down and feigned surprise at seeing his father, who appeared to have just come in. He said, 'Hello, *dad,* when did you come?'

'I just came by the side door, you know, I have a latch key for that.'

'Yes, ofcourse, I came an hour ago. 'Then the Inspector came into the scene and seeing Saxena, was puzzled as ever. Saxena on the other hand, was unruffled and showed no embarrassment whatsoever, in seeing the Inspector. This man, he realized, was no doubt a fly in the ointment, he was proving too bothersome. With the hot stuff in his possession, he could not possibly escape the inivitable and prepared himself to face the Inspector.

'Well, well, it is Mr. Saxena again. Nice meeting you. You really make it very hard for me, to find you for a chat, Saxena.' Jackie noticed that for the first time, the Inspector had dropped the 'Mr' from his *Daddy*'s name. He was enjoying the scene between two stalwarts, in the arena.

'Look Inspector, I am a responsible citizen, who pays his taxes regularly and runs his business strictly as per rules. I have to move sometime on business. If anybody wants to see me, he can easily do so, by appointment. There is no need to chase me all over the countryside, to have a chat, Inspector'. Jackie marvelled at the nonchalance of his father and waited with his tongue in cheek, for the policeman's reaction.

'Well, Saxena, don't play being the smart guy with me, if you are up to date with your information, you would be knowing, how close the police have come to apprehend the man behind the bank robbery.'

Daddy's rejoinder was something like this, 'You make me laugh at your imbecility, Inspector. Recovery of an old van from a pond, cannot construe that its owner was involved in the crime. You have to bring three factors together, namely, the vehicle, the driver and the stolen goods, before you come any closer to clinch the case.'

'Well, my dear Saxena, you need not be so confident, we have the vehicle, we have you, we have now only to find the cash and the gold robbed from the Bank. I am sure that the money is hidden somewhere in this house and I have a search warrant for the same. It is now, only a matter of time, before I get hold of the same.' He spoke into his wireless telephone, asking for men, to conduct the search.

'I see that, this is going to be a long drawn affair, Inspector, and we may be required to stay here for hours without any food or drinks. I have no facility for the same here, gentlemen. Let me go and order some snacks and drinks.' Jackie said. Suddenly, he looked at his father, to fathom his thinking about the situation, he was in. On the screen of the CCTV, he had seen his father, dragging the heavy bags from the secret chamber to the kitchen floor, for shifting them, God alone knows where. The sudden appearance of the Inspector must have jeopardized, his plan. He cannot escape from being caught redhanded. But, what surprised him, was, he did not notice any sign of fright or apprehension in his face. On the other hand, he appeared to be jovial and carefree and engaged in repartees with the Inspector. He has never been able to judge his father.

The men came and the search commenced, in the ground floor and upstairs. Most of the *almirrahs* and cupboards were not locked. Pradhan remained with Saxena and Jackie in the Hall. Jackie almost gasped, when the heavy curtains in front of the kitchen door were pulled aside and the door thrown open. Nothing, no sign of the bags, he was sure, *daddy* put the bags behind the curtains, when the Inspector called. What the Hell! He looked at *daddy*, he was impassive as ever. The search was over, the Inspector drew a blank and appeared disappointed.

Pradhan said, 'Well then, I am calling off the search, to be continued later. However, I must ask you, Mr. Saxena, to accompany me to the Police Station, for questioning in this regard.'

'Okay, I will come, but you have to be quick.'

'You are not going anywhere, *daddy*. If any body ought to go, it should be me. You have been wrong, Inspector, through out. You are after the wrong person and suspecting *daddy,* all along for a crime, which he has not committed. What a fool, you have been; because he has a criminal record, you took it for granted that he has also committed the bank robbery. You must have been glad, that you found your man, when you lifted the van from the pond, no? Because the van belonged to my father, you jumped to the conclusion, that he must be the culprit. You relied more on indirect evidence than on direct evidence. Man, where is the money, that has been robbed? It must be with the man, who has robbed, is it not?' Both, Saxena and Pradhan stood still, watching Jackie.

The Inspector broke silence and spoke, 'Well done, you will be a good defence lawyer, unfortunately this is not a court. You are wasting your time and mine.'

'If I would say, that the money is with me, what would you do?' Pradhan looked bored and said, 'I would arrest you for robbing the Bank.'

'Then, arrest me, I have the money.' Saxena jumped, what is the boy up to?. Has he gone mad?

'Jackie, this is no time for playing games, you are grown up and be quiet. Let the Inspector do his duty.'

'*Daddy*, I am not joking, I am serious, I have the money with me and want to surrender the same to the Police.'

Saxena shrieked, 'No, you can't.' He checked himself and looked shockingly at his son.

While this high drama was going on in front of him, Pradhan was switching his attention from son to father, in quick succession, to grasp, what was being said, which was really difficult. It was hard to believe that Jackie had anything to do with the robbery, and here he is proclaiming that the money is with him. What they are trying to do? Is it a conspiracy, well planned, to gain time, for shifting the treasure somewhere, in the meanwhile. He must take these two wise guys in custody for further questioning and detain them to be produced before a Magisrate.

'Very well, both of you will accompany me to the Police Station and face charges for the Central Bank robbery.'

While, Saxena accompanied the Police Inspector, Jackie followed them in his van, with grim determination written all over his face.

What followed at the Police Station, not only floored the veteran police man but also put the mighty and invincible Saxena in a most disaggreable position. What to speak of a Jail sentence pronounced by a Judge, what his son was going to give him, was worse than that!

They all heard Jackie, and were stunned. Saxena pressing his head in his hands, sat specchless and the Inspector kept staring at Jackie. He made a statement to the effect, that he committed the robbery at the Bank. Whatever is left of the spoils after spending, is now stacked in his van, parked outside and he is surrendering himself along with the loot.

Pradhan rushed out and seized the van. Its darkened window glasses were raised. After satisfying himself, that huge number of packets of Bank Notes and boxes of gold biscuits were staked in rows inside the van, he called the CGM of the Central Bank to come and testify. Secrecy was maintained by the authorities, while the grave situation was being handled at the Police Station. Jackie was taken into custody.

Saxena said to the Inspector that his son was trying to save him, it was he, who planned and committed the burglary and he was prepared to give a written statement explaining everything, which could be verified. Pradhan said, 'I knew all along that it was you alone, who could do the job, but I am still perplexed about the methods you chose to dig the tunnel and whisk away so much money and gold from the Bank vaults in such a short time and how your son is now in possession of it unless he is an accessory.'

Saxena began the story. 'I had an eye to rob a bank, because my finances were in shambles. I had an account with the Central Bank and while visiting the locker room, I observed, there was not any partition between the locker room and the bank safe vaults. I could see the vaults and their construction. One armed guard was, however, posted at the door during banking hours. The bank was located at a central place in the city and its clientele consisted of shop keepers, hoteliers, industrialists and others, all rich people. This bank had also its branches in the suburbs. To cut the story short, I made a guess that its deposits must be running to crores. The bank also dealt with 24ct gold biscuits. Now, let me come to its site plan and how it helped me to decide, that it would not be impossible to get into the vault and lay hands on the cash and gold deposits. I reconnoitered the area and found that there was an abandoned construction site beside the building of the Bank, to which there was access through a blind alley, not frequently used, on the opposite side of the alley, there was the Municipal ground with a good expanse of green cover, mostly trees and bushes and even there was a pond. That was the lay out.'

'So, you decided to dig a tunnel from the construction site right up to the Bank vault.'

'It was not easy though. As a builder, I have the license for importing tunnel excavating machines and during my travels abroad, in connection with my business, I came across some of these machines; using advanced technology; their operation was almost soundless. I witnessed one operation for digging a tunnel under the road for laying High Tension cables and water supply mains. I had this in mind, while I planned the Project 'Speed'. I handled this Project through one of my subsidiary companies. Components of all the required equipment including PTT were imported and delivered in the last month.'

'What is PTT,' Pradhan asked.

'That is, *'pneumatic tube transport'*. Packages weighing up to 2 kg can be put inside capsules which move inside the tube fast, negotiating bends and elevations under force of compressed air.'

'I see, so that was how you could transport hundreds of packets of currency Notes and gold, out of the vaults to outside, in such a short time, hats off to you, Saxena. It was humanly impossible, and you took help of machines! But, the method, you employed to transport the treasure across the city through police check posts, was unbelievable, had I not myself verified it.'

'I know, you followed me closely and in your chase to Poona from the hills, I was almost done for. I almost took a plunge into the ranch through a gap in the hedge, which you did'nt see and rushed past. That was the closest you came in catching me.'

'But, how come, Jackie had the money and you had no knowledge. Where did you hide the money in the house, after you shifted it from the ranch. Is there a secret repository in the house? We could'nt locate the money.'

'Does it concern you, Inspector? You have the money with you or most of it and the thief, who is admitting that he has committed the theft. You may arrest me and frame charges against me and let go my son, who has retrieved the money and surrendered it. He has not committed any felony. May I, request you to grant me a favour? I want to be left alone with my son for some time, before I am formally put behind bars.'

Jackie was a silent listener to all that transpired in the room, so far. As soon as Pradhan left the room, leaving them together, Saxena turned to his son and said in bitterness, 'Why did you have to do it, my boy, you could have let me handle it. I know, you met Parvati, your step mother, a fact which I hid from you, all these years. She was the best friend of Lolita, your mother. I cautioned Parvati not to breathe a word to anybody about my early life. But, when you met her to know about the packet, I passed on to her stealthily at your party, she could not perhaps control herself and must have told you everything, taking you in her arms. Did'nt she?'

"Yes, she did. I felt, as if, my mother was holding me. How could you be so cruel to your wife and to your son, *daddy*? How could you be so indifferent to lead a luxurious life, leaving them in the lurch? I hate myself to think, that I led a protected life in luxury and abundance, while my *badi ma* and my elder brother Kamal lived in dire poverty in a *bustee*. I monitored your movements through CCTV and saw you entering the secret chamber by inserting the key and depositing the bags. Then, I decided to expose you and hand you over to the police. But excuse me saying so, that would not have been the appropriate punishment for the vilest person that ever lived, I thought. An idea took shape in my mind. Why not, I take the blame upon myself and admit that I committed the theft and serve the sentence, which will be nothing less than seven years. I had prepared a duplicate key, in the meanwhile, and picked a day, when you were out of the city, for my operation. I got similar travelling bags, as the ones you used, got them filled with old news paper and junk of the same weight and left them there. I took out the bags with money and gold and hid them in the large van, I use for transport. I can't but admire the stamina and strength, you possess *daddy*, at this age, to have been able to handle the heavy bags, single handed. I sincerely hoped, that the police would find the money, during their search. But, what is obvious, never appeals them. You never wanted to get caught with the money, you carried all the bags, back to the secret chamber, which contained only trash. But, how you were to know? I beat you *daddy*, finally. You live for wealth and never care for anything else. Why don't you let me go to the prison and lead your usual life, outside, shorn of care, love and affection? I don't think, there is any punishment more stringent than that. To live with the knowledge, that the son dear to your heart languishes in gaol for a crime he has not committed, the woman who gave birth to your son and relinquished all her properties, which you enjoy, never loved you, while she lived, the woman who loved you once and married you, when you were penniless, roaming Bombay in search of jobs, whom you forsook, for sake of fortune, lived her life in dire poverty in bringing up her son, a step brother to me, who does not know you even, is more horrendous than any other punishment, that can be thought of.'

Saxena's head was hung in shame, before his son, the only being, he loved in this world. When he looked up, it was a void. Oh! God, he has made a mess of his life. No doubt, it has been a story of rags to riches. But to what end! Parvati hates him, Kamal does not know him, Lolita is no more, he tortured her soul and lastly his own son despises him. For the first time in his life, he prayed God, to show him a path, to give him deliverance. He wants to make all amendments necessary, even at the cost of his life, to bring happiness to his family. He wants to change himself, he wants to convert himself. He wants to give them all that were denied to them. He had a vision. All around him were his victims shrieking at him. *Sethjee*, looking at him sternly and shouting, why did he do it, he could have given whatever he wanted, Lolita asking to return her life, Parvati with a baby in her arms cursing him that he would not be pardoned by God for his sin and lastly Jackie sitting before him with a smile on his face and telling him, *'Daddy, where will you go from here? You have destroyed us and in the process destroyed yourself.'*

'No, my dear son. I will not let that happen. I will admit publicly, that Parvati is my wife and Kamal is my son. He will share my estates along with you. You go and get my lawyers, I have lot of works to do'

Inspector Pradhan walked into the room, looked at them and said, '*Kya khichidi paka rahe ho, aap dono*?'

Saxena said calmly, 'Nothing Inspector, I have called for my lawyers and will give you a written statement, admitting how I committed the crime. My son was in no way involved in this. I sincerely request you, not to frame any charges against him. I cannot but admire you, in giving me a good chase and seizing the booty. I have lost the race, I cannot tell you, what I have gained.'

Pradhan smiled and said, 'Of course, Mr. Saxena, once we have the big fish in the net, we do not need the small fish. Do we? He is free to go. '

The News hounds made a bee line to the Police Station, to get the reports and their teleprinters remained busy throughout the night, transmitting the startling news to all the News Agencies.

The morning news papers carried the News in their first pages. Nobody believed, that R. K. Saxena, the industrial tycoon, was behind the Central Bank robbery and how Inspector Pradhan apprehended him with the loot, while he was trying to escape. The high drama played at the Police Station in the night before, never came to light.

Soon after, telephones in all his offices, factories, show rooms and other concerns, kept buzzing. Financial institutions, banks, other creditors, Insurance companies, share brokers and everyone concerned with Saxena's business empire, were mad to get the news in details. Nobody answered. The chief executives were not available for comments. Police seized all his Bank accounts, but could not get a writ mandamus for seizing his offices and premises.

Saxena held a meeting, in the morning, with his lawyers and his Accounts Officers. He directed them to make good the differences between the Bank's cash balance as on the closing of accounts on the date of theft and amount surrendered at the Police Station, by liquidating his assets, without encumbrances, as necessary. He didn't touch the gold, lifted, he said. The total demand putforth by the Bank was of the order of one thousand million rupees. Half of his estates had to be mortgaged, bulk of his shares in blue-chip companies had to be transferred, to raise the capital. Once these transactions were completed, duly approved by the I. T authorities and Registrar Of Companies, Saxena felt relieved. It made big news. It was unprecedented, in the crime history, that a criminal was chastened by circumstances not only to surrender and confess to the crime, he committed, but also made good all the money, he robbed from the Bank. This was unparalleled indeed. For days, it puzzled the crime reporters and criminologists and even a section of the public tried to make a hero of Saxena, who blasted a hole in the security system of the Bank and made the Police a laughing stock.

Saxena made another news, when the case was listed for hearing; he did not engage any lawyer for his defense. He pleaded guilty to all the charges. It made big news, indeed. The media played it to the hilt. The judge reserved his judgement and adjourned the court proceedings for a week. The accused was remanded to judicial custody.

Saxena surprised everyone with one of his statements. It raised eyebrows in many circles. It read, that Kamal Saxena, son of Ratan Kumar Saxena and Parvati Saxena was appointed as a vice president of the company registered as 'Saxena and Company Pvt. Limited' with immediate effect. He called Jackie to the prison and had a long discussion with him. He urged him, to go and see his *badi ma* and beg her to forgive him, if she could, as he did not have the moral courage to face her and her son. He wrote a long letter to his wife, beseeching her to forgive him and agree to live with his son in the house at Bombay, which he bequeathed to her.

When the news was made public, that Parvati Debi was Saxena's wife and Kamal was their son, it was received in awe and wonder by everyone concerned and no less by Raja's and Ram Gopal's family. The most shocked receipient of the news, however, was Kamal. He didn't believe his ears. He remembered, when his play mates and class mates would tease him that he had no father, he would return home crying, and ply his mother with questions, concerning his father. Every time, she would calm him down and say that when he was a baby in her arms, she was forced to leave his father and come away to live alone. She never turned back from that day. Then she would relate him, that it is the mother, who takes care of the baby, right from its birth and fulfills all its needs. All beings, be they, birds or animals or humans are created by the God who sustains His creation through love and this is provided by the mother, she used to say. He was a little one and didn't undersand much of what, she said. But he became sad, when he used to see his mother weeping afterwards and wiping her tears, silently. When he came of age, he understood and loved his mother all the more. When he won a cup for standing first in the Entrance examinations, he had come running to show the cup to his mother. He remembers the occasion vividly. He said, 'Look *ma*, what I have won! Are you happy now *ma*'? Please don't weep. I can't see you weeping, it makes me miserable.' She has not wept, since that day. From very early days, his mother's sacrifices, hardships, privations she suffered, due to no fault of her, made him resolve, that if ever, he comes to face his father, he would disown him.

A person, who is in the news, for several weeks and has been a hot subject for discussion, at all places, accused of grievous charges and facing a sentence, in short a criminal, now discloses, that he is his son. The situation was most untenable and humiliating. Kamal took it as an affront to her mother and to him. He rushed to his mother and looking straight at her eyes, asked her to deny straightaway such defamatory statements. Parvati didn't say anything, she lowered her eyes and nodded. Bewildered and shocked, Kamal left the place abruptly.

Raja and Ranee were silent and discrete witnesses to the scene of Kamal, accosting his mother to learn the truth, which was stranger than fiction. After Kamal left, they went to *ma jee's* room and found her sitting, with her hands cupping her face and sobbing. They were crestfallen and did not know how to comfort this mother, who was just passing through, the most difficult and critical time of her life. Ranee put her hand softly on her shoulders, Parvati looked up with tearful eyes. She held tight Ranee and said, '*Beti*, I knew, one day, I would have to face this situation. Truth cannot remain hidden for long. At the moment, he is completely broken. I am afraid, Raja *beta*, for him. He went out, despair written all over his face. Lest he may do something horrible, please go and fetch him.'

At that moment, Jackie and Kamal arrived together. Seeing the brothers together, Raja's joy and relief knew no bounds. He exclaimed,' Look, *ma jee*, who are here in your presence! They look like Krishna and Balaram. Parvati and Ranee looked up.

Jackie said, '*Badi ma*, Kamal failed to recognize me, but I could see him from a distance. He was alone in a park, looking at wild flowers growing over the hedge, unconcerned that it was drizzling. See his clothes, they are wet. I almost dragged him over here.' Parvati looked at both of them; tears held up so long, rolled down her face freely.

Jackie said, '*Daddy* knew, that I met you and you told me everything. You were my mother's best friend, weren't you? May I call you my *badi ma* and Kamal, my younger brother?'His voice was chocked.

'Ofcourse *beta*, I am your *badi ma* and Lolita, your *choti ma.*' She extended her arms and took both of her sons in her folds. She felt, as if she held her lost world in her arms. Raja and Ranee were silent onlookers of this rare scene of reunion after a twenty two years long separation.

Jackie sat at the feet of Parvati and said, entreatingly, '*Badi ma*, now that, *daddy* has atoned for the sins he committed and made a public confession for the same and awaits his retribution in his cell, will you not forgive him?'

A heavy silence fell. The atmosphere was charged with emotions, everybody looked at her. Her face was calm and composed. Underneath, waves after waves of her traumatic experiences broke upon the shore of the evening of her life. She has suffered all the ignominy of a woman, shunned by her husband and spent the best part of her life, in bringing up her son in dire poverty. He is all, that she possesses in this world. Her happiness lies in his happiness. To forgive Ratan or not is not the question. It is not for her to forgive him. If he truly repents for his sin and stands before God, praying for His forgiveness, He alone may forgive him.

Aloud she said. '*Beta*, I am his wife and wearing *sindoor* in his name, till today. It is he who broke all the vows made before God, during *sat phere* in our marriage. God, alone can forgive him for his guilt.'

Jackie handed over the letter, addressed to her, by his *daddy*. It was the first letter, ever written by Ratan. She took it with great misgivings. She began reading it. It was full of confessions and repentance. He wrote, that he did not deserve her forgiveness for his abominable acts and bahaviour. Apart from the punishment, the court will award for his crimes, he was prepared to suffer the anger and hatred at the hands of his son Kamal, whom he had not seen yet. Whether he would outlive his sentence or not, he was not sure, but he would like to see his son for once, before he is sent to jail to serve the sentence and hoped that she would fulfil his last desire. The letter ended with a remark, *'I loved you once, forgive me, if you can'*

Parvati, silently handed the letter to Kamal. He took the letter with great trepidation. In the last twentyfour hours, from the moment, he came to know, that the star criminal of the time, was none other than his father, who was virtually non existent, as far as he was concerned, his hitherto peaceful life became tumultuous. He was more worried for his mother. It would have been better, if the man would not have surfaced at all. He looked up at his mother, he tried to gauge, what was going on, in her mind? What did she expect from him? Her mother has given him, everything in life, what has he given her in return? Does she want that, he should meet the man, who has given her all the pains in life, should it give a little pleasure to her, if she did not stand between father and son. He looked at his mother, she looked calm and composed, bereft of any emotion. He came to a decision. He said, 'Yes, *ma*, I would go and see him.' Kamal didn't fail to notice, a thin smile crossing her face.

The tense atmosphere of a moment before, disappeared and everyone beamed with pleasure. Ranee went to *ma jee* and hugged her. She said, '*Ma jee*, you need not worry, everything will be alright.'

Jackie said, '*Badi ma*, our house at Bombay, has been transferred in your favour by *dad,* in the meanwhile. The lawyer will be bringing the papers to you, today. *Dad* has requested you to live in the house, along with Kamal.'

Parvati said, 'No, *beta*, we are quite comfortable here, moreover, I do not want to leave Raja and Ranee.'

Jackie pleaded, 'Would you let me leave alone in that big house, having seven suites of rooms?'

Raja stepped in and said, 'It is alright *ma jee*, we will be pleased to let you go and live with your sons, there. You have suffered enough; you deserve a little peace and pleasure in living with your sons. Moreover, we will be visiting and seeing you often, how can we leave you ?'

Ranee said, 'I will go with you and help arranging things, so that you may settle there, comfortably.'

Jackie said, 'You need not worry *bhabi jee*, the old faithful *kaka*, will take care of everything, there are also other servants.' But Ranee was insistent, she said, '*Ma jee* can't do without me, I have to go there, to furnish her *puja* room.'

Parbati said, '*Thik hai beti, chale ana*.'

* * * * *

While surprises after surprises were unfolded with the detention of Saxena and later his arrest by Police, in connection with the Bank robbery, served with usual *mirch masala* in the News papers, the news took Ram Gopal's family, in particular, Jaya, by storms. That Saxena was the mastermind behind so many crimes including the murderous attempt on the life of Raja, and he was a don, was unbelievable. The public announcement made by Saxena, that Parvati was his wife and Kamal was their son, completely unsettled them. Jaya brokedown and sobbed uncontrollably. Maya had no words to console her. It was now for certain, that her brother would never accept Kamal as an acceptable match for her. A criminal's son! A jail bird's son!For your husband? No, never, he would say. All her hopes and aspirations were shattered.

She was to visit Raja *bhaiya*'s house, next day, to see Kamal. After his return from the States, she had no opportunity to talk to him. But now, the bizarre situation altered everything. She was more worried for Kamal and knowing him, she would very well judge the state of his mind in the present circumstances. She wanted to be near him, to share his distress. Ram Gopal was equally distressed, to find her dear sister upset over the issue. He was not able to find a solution to this knotty problem. True, he wanted to see her married to Kamal, whom she loved, and as a matter of fact, he decided that the marriage should take place, soon after his return from the States. But, could he proceed with this now, in the face of his acquiring a stigma of being a publicly disgraced criminal's son? He did'nt find a way out from this situation. He must talk to Raja, in this matter. What he learnt from him, removed his dilemma.

Parvati did not wish to see Ratan in the jail and said so, to Jackie. He understood and did not insist. Kamal and Jackie were on their way to visit their father. The visiting hours being in the morning, they had started early. What a strange way of visiting one's father after twenty two years, he thought. His mother, once showed him the photo of his father, it was years back, in the photograph, his father looked youngish and was in a wedding dress, turban and all that. It was their wedding photograph. How young and shy, her mother looked. Kamal became pensive, she had no inkling, what fate had stored for her. His eyes became moist. Jackie understood the feelings of Kamal and said, to cheer up and not to worry. They reached the visitors'room in the jail and after signing in the Register, waited. The grey bare walls and the murky atmosphere, saddened Kamal. The thought, that this room must have witnessed, many such interviews between the hardened criminals and their families, further lowered his spirit. After some time, which appeared to him unending, a door on the opposite wall opened and a person sporting a trimmed beard entered and sat in the opposite chair, facing them. He was looking at one of the most handsome persons, suave and with a sad welcoming smile on his face. Kamal was speechless for a moment, Saxena was extending his hand towards Kamal, Jackie watched the situation with a lump in his throat. Both the father and the son were weighing each other. So this young man was his son, Parvati's son, he had forsaken twenty two years ago in a fit of anger and drunkenness, he is fair, he noticed, has an angular face like him, soft expressive eyes like his mother and above all a pleasing personality. Kamal was torn between his erstwhile hatred for this man who had forsaken and forgotten them all these years and his affection now seen through his eyes and the extension of his hand. His mother's appeal in her eyes came to his mind; his father was addressing him, 'Hello, Kamal, my dear boy, you are so grown up and handsome, how are you?'

Startled, Kamal took his hand and felt his soft hand engulfed by the massive hand of his father. He said, 'Hello, *dad.*' Saxena looked at Kamal and was pleased to see, that he had gone entirely after his mother, soft in voice, colour and manner. He gripped the hand of his son, in both of his hands warmly and said with a tremor in his voice, 'You tell your mother, Kamal, that I want to see her, I want to say her something in person.' The time of interview was over, the guards came to take him in.

Kamal was silent on their way back. The touch of his father had galvanized him. Did he speak earnestly, when he said, that he wanted to see his mother? Did he notice a spot of repentance in his eyes, when he was speaking to him?

Jackie asked Kamal, 'How did father impress you?'

'I really feel sorry for him and pray God to forgive him. Do you know Jackie, from the days of my childhood, I was hoping that father would come back to us, one day, and we would live happily, thereafter. Look at the twist of destiny, how things have turned out to be. We have to live all our lives with a guilty feeling that our father was a sinner.'

Jackie said, 'Kamal, no doubt, father sinned, but now that he has confessed to his crimes and prepared to face the conviction and the sentence, and recompensed everybody concerned, should we not forgive him and look forward for better days?'

'Honestly Jackie, I do not know, what mother thinks about all this. But one thing, I am sure about and that is, she would like to see all of us happy.' Jackie pressed the hand of his brother and smiled.

When they reached, Raja *bhaiya*'s house, they found everyone present. Kamal was particularly glad to see Jaya. Presence of Jaya's family was significant; in the circumstances Kamal would have liked to have a word with Jaya, but not now, may be later. Parvati looked at her son, with a question in her eyes. He understood and nodded. The crisis had passed, she thought.

CHAPTER 10

Two years later. Parvati was alone, in the garden, sitting under a tree and looking at the dry leaves scattered all over the lawn. Spring was in the air. Now and then, the wind would blow and the dry leaves would be swept away afar. Afterall, they are dry leaves, withered and having no utility. Once they shone on the limbs of the trees, in the morning glare of the sun, like ornaments. Discarded by force of nature, they make way to give berth to soft, tender and fresh ones. Human life is likewise, she thought. She has lived her life, and may be the time has come for her to be scattered away like a dry leaf.

The scene in the court room, came to her mind. They had all assembled, that day, when judgement was delivered in the case of State vs. Ratan Kumar Saxena. She sat there among others, on a wooden bench, facing the Judge. Ratan stood to her right, in the box meant for the accused, holding the railing, with both of his hands, as if to steady himself. He appeared relaxed. Suddenly she felt his glance on her. She looked up, their eyes met. This time, she didn't shrivel before him. She searched his eyes and noticed nothing but deep compassion and love tinged with sorrow. What was happening to her? She felt herself amongst cattle and birds, sitting close to Ratan. When she opened her eyes, she found herself in the court room. Silence reigned everywhere, the Judge was deliverying the judgement. He read out the charges, found him guilty of all the charges and sentenced him to seven years RI. She had no heart to raise her eyes to look at him. As the Judge rose from his chair to leave, everyone kept standing. The prisoner was led out, by the police.

Parvati accompanied others, to see Ratan and have a word with him, before he stepped into the black prison van. Bringing Jaya forward, she said, 'Ratan, see your daughter-in-law, wife of Kamal, bless her.

Tears rolled down his face, he said, 'God, Bless you, my child. Forgive me for the wrong, I was going to commit.' Jaya stooped down, to touch the feet of her father-in-law. The scene was touching, there were tears in everybody's eyes. Before the door of the van was shut, Parvati looked straight at Ratan and said, 'I will wait for you. Have faith in God.' The van drove off.

* * * * *

Kamal and Jaya are now married and live in Poona at LOLITA, which was gifted to Jaya by Jackie as her wedding present. He said on the occasion, that the house rightly belonged to Jaya, who brought life to the concrete and masonary by infusing into them, a character of their own. It was she, he said, who revived the spirit of his *nanajee*, which lay buried in the ruins and made him realize, that true happiness was in giving and not in taking.

Jackie got completely immersed in his father's business and tried to revive it. Most of the assets, which he and Kamal inherited, were liquidated, to pay off the creditors. It was Ram Gopal, who came to his rescue and reimbursed the amount of rupees twenty crores, which he considered as given on loan to him by Saxena.

Parvati broached the subject of his getting married, several times to Jackie, which he tried to avoid. He would say, 'I am busy, *badi ma*, would you like to have your daughter-in-law, spending her time alone in this house? No *–na?*' She had an answer to this. She would say, '*Beta*, I am getting old, I want to see you married and settled, before I die.' He would clap a hand over her mouth, hug her and say, 'No, you are not. You will live, hundred years. 'Then he would leave, throwing the words at her,' I have works to attend, I will not come for lunch. 'She would watch his receding figure, helplessly. This pattern of exchange of words continued for several months, till Parvati gave up. But fate willed otherwise.'

One day, while returning home, Jackie had an impulse to visit the Central Library, which brought back to him, memories of his student days. He would enter the library, with friends, without the slightest intention of reading, but entirely for viewing beautiful girls and their gaits. How spoiled he was, he could reminisce! The memories concerning Jaya pained him. Those were his cloudy days and he shuddered to think how close he was in destroying her and Kamal. He thanked Jaya from the bottom of his heart for showing him the light and purpose of his life. Truly he had no interest in any other girl. However, he remembered one, a serious one with spectacles for a peculiar reason. They had named her as '*chasmis*'. She, a junior in the college, avoided company. She became their object of observation and bet. She would visit the library every Sataurday and arrive sharply at '*ten*' o'clock in the morning, when the library opened. One of his *chamchas* would be detailed to watch her movements. It was observed, that she would come by Bus, get down at the Royal Cinema junction and walk down the distance to the library. Her timing was perfect, as she would step into the library, the clock would strike '*ten*' and she never failed. This was reported to Jackie. So a bet was on, amongst the friends. Every one, who bet against the odd, lost. The next bet, was to make her speak and they failed. Not only, she rebuffed their attempts, but returned them, an icy stare. Now it was Jackie's turn to make her speak. Jackie had an idea, which he did not disclose. Insead of greeting her, when she arrived, he feigned a fall and slipped on the floor, in front of her. She exclaimed, 'Oh, my god! Are you hurt?'

He said, 'It's nothing, I'm alright.' She even helped him to get up. She adjusted her *specs* and without even looking at him, walked off. He had won the bet that day and the memory lingered. Amongst other things, the image of that girl came to his mind, as he climbed up the steps. That being a Friday evening, there were only a few visitors. Pushing the big glass door, he entered the Hall. The same set up, he remembered; News and Magazine stands, coffee and snack bar, few benches and the receptionist's desk. He felt light, away from the hustle bustle of the office, the stress of demands of staff for more and more facilities, with no concern for the plummeting of profit and acceleration in overhead expenses. *Dad* must have been a superman to handle all these so efficiently without a care in his mind, he thought. Kamal did'nt care to take any interest in business and left everything in the hands of his brother. He whistled, as he entered the library till a sign, 'SILENCE PLEASE', glared at him. He shut his mouth and observed silence. He forgot, why he came to the library at all. He never liked books and thought of reading as a waste of time and an idler's pastime in his childhood. With great difficulty, he went through the text books, when he was a child, at the chiding of his mother. However, he possessed a sharp memory, which helped him to scrape through *exams*. One subject, however, interested him. That was mathematics. How numbers grew by addition, multiplication and indices, fascinated him. In the solitary confinement of his room in the Boarding school, his favourite playmate was an *abacus*. He spent hours with it. A book on mathematics, always refreshed his mind, as a novel would, to others. He read somewhere that many of the great philosophers were mathematicians. As characters unfold in a novel, the numbers unfold in mathematics, he said. Naturally, therefore, later, he was at home with stock investments, dealing with shares. dividends, returns, etc. His legs carried him to the shelves of books on mathematics and he stood there, when somebody spoke to him from behind. It was a woman's voice.

'Are you looking for some titles, sir?'

Jackie turned, he was looking at a face, which took him ten years behind, in the memory lane. He stared. The same angular face, the same pair of *specs*, the same expression. It was '*chasmis*', no doubt. Inaudlbly, he said, *'chasmis'*.

She said, 'Did you say something, sir?' He kept staring at her. In that brief moment, thoughts spanning a gap of ten years amalgamated to form a beautiful compound.

'Did you say some thing sir?'She repeated

Jackie started and said, 'Nothing, but, is it not strange to meet someone, whom you were thinking about, a little while ago?'

'Do you know me ?'

'Tell me one thing, were you not at the Hindu College in 1970?'

'Yes, I was'

'Then you must have heard of Jackie, a young fellow, who was also a student, at the same college?'

'Are you by any chance, referring to a student, who had such a reputation, that girls avoided him?'

'Oh! You know then. Will you be surprised to know that I am that student?'

'No, I am not. You have not changed, you still run after girls.'

'What do you mean, can a gentleman not come to the library, Miss—'

'I am Seema, but what are you doing in the library? You had other interests.'

Jackie avoided the question and said, 'I remember you, we used to call you '*chasmis*'.' He reailised the slip of his tongue, but before he could say anything else, she said, 'Oh!'and turning abruptly, she left the place. He followed her to a room, on the door of which there was a sign which read '*SEEMA AGARWAL, ASST. LIBRARIAN*'. The swing door had already closed on his face.

Seema entered her cubicle, sat down and took a glass of water. She was boiling in rage. '*Chasmis*, my foot', she hissed. Now, everything came clear to her mind, she was a young girl and a shy one. She did'nt have any friends, except few, who filled her ears with gossip and counselled her to keep distance from a boy named Jackie, who was worst of the lot. She raked up her brain and remembered to have seen a group of boys sitting and loitering under the portico of the library, looking at their watches, every time, when she arrived. She would walk past them, with her head lowered. Now it was certain, that it was she, they targeted for and must have named her as *chasmis*. Her chain of thoughts was disturbed, when there was a knock at the door. She said, 'come in.' Jackie entered. Seeing him, she said, 'Oh! It is you.'

'Will you not ask me to sit down?'

'Yes, you may.'

'Look Seema, I am really sorry, I have no intention to insult you. But to be frank, when I saw you there after so many years, the image of a young girl with *specs* sprang up before me——'

'And you called me *chasmis.*' Then to the utmost delight of Jackie, she smiled. To him it was most captivating and warm.

'Why not you join me for a cup of coffee, for old days sake?'

Now is the time to give a jolt to this haughty person, she thought.

She was silent for few moments and then said, 'Thank you, for your offer, but I cannot give you company. Someone will be waiting for me, at home. I have promised him to be early.'

'Who is he?'

'He is, Gopal, my son.'

Jackie's spirit took a dive. He said, 'Oh! I didn't know.'

'Yes, he is my responsibility. You know how it is with little children. If you promise something and do not keep it, they would raise hell.'

He wanted to say, 'You are telling me!', but kept quiet. Seema waited.

He said, 'Well then, carry on with your motherly duties. May be, some other time.' He got up to go, hesitated and then said, 'May I drop you at your home, so that you may attend your baby quickly?'Seema noticed that there was an edge in his voice.

'He is not a baby, but a boy of six years.' Seema saw him fidgeting with the car keys, she collected her bag, got up and said, 'Okay. Thanks, let's go.'

Jackie dropped her at her place and was about to drive away, when she said, 'Are you not coming inside to say Hello, to Gopal?'

'Let it be another time Seema jee', and then added, 'I have more important works to attend to.' He changed gears and drove off. Seema looked at the receding car for some time, shrugged her shoulders and walked into the apartment.

* * * * *

It was Tuesday and Parvati was getting ready for her routine visit to the *Sankat mochan* temple to offer *puja*. The temple was a little away and she preferred to walk the distance. She carried a *puja thali* and walked up to the *zebra* crossing and waited for the green light to turn red. A sizeable crowd had gathered, to cross over. When the red light came on, there was a sudden rush and the crowd behind, surged forward. She could not bear the onslaught and fell down. But before she touched the ground, strong arms pulled her up and supporting her, carried her to a safer place. During the fall, Parvati had sprained her left ankle and could not stand up properly, as she tried to look up at her saviour. It was a young woman, lovely and vivacious. She said, '*Jug jug jio beti, Sankat mochan teri bhala kare.*' She held on to her and appeared to be in pains. The young woman said, '*Ma jee*, you seem to be hurt, where do you stay? Let me leave you at your home.' She called an auto rickshaw and with the help of the driver gently lifted her to the seat. As soon as the rickshaw reached the porch, *kaka* came rushing, they took her inside and lowered her on to a *divan*. He gave a glass of water to *ma jee* to drink. Parvati felt a little better and said, *'Aao beti mere pas baitho.'* But the young woman, bending down lifted the saree and inspected her left ankle and saw a little swelling over the ankle, she seemed to have sprained it. She addressed *kaka*, who stood near, perplexed, *'Ma jee* was at the crossing, the crowd behind pushed her and she was about to fall, I happened to be near and somehow pulled her out. If you have a pain balm, please get it.' Kaka rushed to get it.

Parvati whose attention was riveted on the young woman asked, 'What is your name *beti* and where do you live?'

'My name is Seema, *ma jee*. I live near by and come to have a *darshan* of *Sankat mochan,* every Tuesday.' Kaka came with a bottle of Iodex. She took it and applied a little over the ankle, rubbing it with a circular motion several times, softly.

She said, 'Take rest *ma jee*, you will feel little better.' She got up to go. Parvati looked past her and saw Jackie coming in, from his morning jogging. He could'nt see Seema's face and seeing *badi ma*, lying down and someone at her side, exclaimed, 'What happened, why is she lying down?'

Then Seema turned and faced him, seeing it was Jackie, she was surprised. Now it was the turn of Jackie to be taken aback. What the Hell! What is she doing here?

Aloud, he sald, 'Oh! It is you Seema, what's the matter?'

Seema said, 'Jackie, how is that, you are here?'

'What do you mean, I am here?This is my house.'

Circumspectly, she said, 'This is your house! And *ma jee?'*

'She is my *badi ma*.'

Parvati was listening and said, 'Do you know each other?'

'Yes, *badi ma*, I know her, she was in the same college, where I studied.'

'It is all His doing then.'

'What do you mean?'

'Nothing, you may not understand it. Beta, I was about to be trampled by the crowd, during the rush hour, at the crossing, while I was on my way for the morning *darshan* of *Sankat mochan*, suddenly this girl came and helped.'

Ha, a girl, may be a sweet sixteen, in her eyes! She seems to have won the heart of badi ma. Once, she comes to know that she is the mother of a six year old boy, her dreams about her may end.

Aloud, he said, 'Oh, my Goodness! Hope, you are not hurt.'

Seema told him, 'She appears to have sprained an ankle, there is a little swelling and I have applied an ointment over the area for immediate relief, but it would be preferable to have an X-Ray taken out. ' Jackie expressed, his thanks and Seema said, '*Ma jee,* I have to leave now, I have to attend office.'

'*Beti,* you have done so much for me today, how can I let you go, just like that, don't you worry about getting late for the office, Jackie here, will drop you at your place. Please stop for a while and have breakfast with us. After a long time, I am having someone to talk to.'

Why badi ma is pampering this haughty person, I don't understand; Jackie's anger was mounting.

Before, he could say something, Parvati said, 'Jackie *beta*, you better hurry and come down for breakfast.'

After he left, Parvati asked Seema, to come and sit by her side. She had a close look at her and was struck by her features. Though not very fair, her complexion was pleasing, a pair of black rimmed glasses resting on her sharp nose added to her beauty, she looked mature enough and appeared to be a no-nonsense girl. She was pleased and asked, '*Beti,* who else are there in your house?'

'Nobody else, *ma jee*, only my son.' Her interest seemed to ebb; suppressing her feelings, Parvati exclaimed, 'Oh! My dear, at such a young age!'

Seema, abruptly realized that *ma jee* took her to be a widow and to clear her misunderstanding, she said, 'No, no, *ma jee*, it is nothing like that, the child is my stepbrother and he calls me *mama*.' Then, she related her story, behind her adopting the child. Parvati was very much touched with the soul stirring experience of this girl and her hopes soared high. May be, her long search to find a life partner for Jackie, has come to an end. Her searching eyes, made Seema blush and she lowered her face.

Parvati raised her face fondly and said, '*Beti*, I see that you have suffered enough, further it is difficult to live alone and bring up a child and give him all the care it deserves. Have you ever thought of getting married?'

Before she could reply, Jackie came in, dressed in white, even his shoes were white. He saw, both of them, in intimate conversation and wondered, what they were talking about. He could not bear the sight of Seema getting so chummy with his *badi ma* and wanted to get rid of her quickly.

He said, 'How do you feel now, *badi ma*?'

'I am already feeling better, *beta*. Seema's touch, has worked miracles. I am observing *brat* today, ask *kaka* to serve breakfast for both of you. Go *beti*, I will lie down here, for a while. Please come again and see us, I shall be looking forward to it.'

Oh! What she is doing? Why this effusiveness for this woman, whom she does not know? I have to talk to 'badi ma', soon enough, to dispel from her mind, any kind thoughts, she might be entertaining about Seema.

While driving, to drop Seema at her place, Jackie thought of this girl during his college days, when Seema was just a plain girl, who was called *chasmis* by his friends and dismissed as dumb and drab. He never expected to see her again. But what a transformation! Seeing her after so many years in the library, it struck him that he was looking at the most beautiful girl on earth and for a moment, he felt that his heart missed a beat. The same pair of glasses, which earned her the name *chasmis* now seemed to enhance her beauty. He had followed her to the office enclosure, as if drawn by a magnet and would have certainly acted foolishly, had his spirit not been dampened, by the remark thrown by her, that she had a son, six years old. A moment before, he felt like a bird on its wing, soaring high and then the sting of the remark, brought him down mercilessly to the ground of stark reality. Suddenly, he felt the pressure of her hand on his shoulder, Seema was telling him something. He realized, that he had reached her place. 'Oh!', he said. Opening the door, Seema got down and said, 'Thanks'.

Mechanically, he banged the door shut and drove off. She stood there, looking at the receding car.

Seema found the child still asleep and the *maid* busy in the kitchen. Only, half an hour was left, for her to get ready for office. The school bus would be coming, in fifteen minutes. She shouted at the *maid,* to pack the tiffin box for the boy and hurried to wake him up, brush his teeth, dress him up, put his shoes on, hoist the school bag on to his shoulder and rush him to the bus stop, the bus was just arriving. She almost lifted the boy on to the bus and heaved a sigh of relief, when it drove off with its load. She walked back to her apartment, exhausted, gulped the cup of tea offered by the *maid*, placed the sandwitch in her bag to eat it later and almost ran to the bus stop.

It was a busy day at the library, her time was spent in listing and cataloguing the new arrivals and putting them at the proper places, in the shelves. By the time, she arrived home, the *maid* had finished cooking the evening meal, Gopal had already changed into his night dress and was seen playing with the building blocks. What an obedient and disciplined child, he was!

The *maid*'s voice was heard from the kitchen, '*Bibi jee*, may I place your dinner on the table, before I leave? Gopal *baba* has already eaten and I have warmed the milk and poured it into the glass.'

After the *maid* left, she put Gopal to bed, came to the drawing room and stretched her legs on the sofa. What a day it was!The scenes unfolded in her mind like a photo seqence. First, *majee,* she supporting her, in her arms, as she was about to fall at the road crossing and then taking her, to *Saxena House*, her home. Second, Jackie, the son of '*ma jee'*, entering the scene coincidentally and registering shock and distress in seeing her. The events had brought them together, for a second time, in the last few days. Her mind flew to the distant past, when she faced Jackie, for the first time. She was a shy girl and had no friends. She lived in a girls' hostel, managed by one Mrs. Bregenja, a Goan. She was a strict disciplinarian and wanted all her charges to be in their rooms, strictly by seven in the evening. While, girls of her age freely moved with boys, in the canteen and in the library, she never dared to talk to any boy. In the college, scraps of gossip about Jackie fell into her ears, that he was a bully, a girl hunter and would run after anything in a skirt——all these talks frightened her to the core. In her mind, she imagined this person to be a monster, always on the look out of young girls. She shuddered to think, what she would do, if she ever comes across this monster. She was so much engrossed in her thoughts, that she didn't look ahead and bumped into somebody. Her load of books, which she carried slipped from her hands and lay scattered, all around her. Before she could bend down to gather her books, a long arm reached ahead to pick up the books. She looked up and stared at the brightest blue eyes, she had ever seen, set on a handsome face with a winning smile. For a moment she was stunned. Breaking her stupor, the handsome man spoke, 'Here, take your books, they are really heavy.' He gave her the books and went on his way. He had'nt looked at her.

Some senior girls who were approaching, remarked, 'Hey, you stupid girl, take care, whom you are bumping into, while you walk. Do you know that hero, who was talking to you, a while ago?' She was about to explain, but the girls walked away, throwing at her a lewd remark, 'Trying to be fresh with Jackie Saxena, *hun*?'

The word *Jackie,* jolted her. In hurried steps, she went to the library, deposited the books at the counter and retreated to a corner, away from the door. She was breathing heavily, the library was almost empty at that hour. She was all alone, her hands were damp with sweat. She wiped her hands dry, and sat still for some time, till she regained her composure. That was her first encounter with Jackie; she carried with her that impression of Jackie, a set of blue eyes on a suave face. He remained an enigma to her. Many stories were woven around him, while he was in the college. Those were not very complimentary. Most of the stories related to his escapades with girl friends. She didn't believe in these stories and dismissed them as baseless and originated out of jealousy and malice. While she was still in the college, Jackie left and she didn't see him, thereafter. Seeing him after so many years at the Central Library, she was taken aback, no doubt, but somewhere in her heart's recess an absurd feeling, which lay suppressed, all these years, bubbled up to the surface and exploded, bringing her face to face with the stark reality, that she loved this man, from the moment she had set her eyes upon him. All that happened afterwards, were merely prompted by destiny. She knew, that again she lost him, when she thwarted his attempts to come closer, by simply dropping a hint, that she had a son. The turn of the events, provided her the opportunity of learning something, which was very dear to her heart. She saw, the shadow of disappointment and utter loss, engulfing his blue eyes. Did he care for her, then? Oh, God! What did she do?

Nothing was lost, she realized, when fate brought her again face to face, with the man of her dream. *Ma jee's* discreet enquiries and her concern for Gopal, no doubt, kindled the flame of hope in her mind. She had no idea that, she spent the entire night, lying down on the sofa, in the drawing room. Her legs were cramped and her back ached, when she tried to get up. It was morning, the first rays of the sun, filtered through the glass window, fell on her face, rejuvenating her and bringing her the sweet memory of her last thought, before sleep had overcome her. Her dinner was still lying on the table, covered and untouched.

She heard the door bell ringing. Oh! It must be the milkman, but why so early? She adjusted her hair and clothes and went to open the door. She stared, at the door, she saw someone, making her heart do a somersault. Jackie stood at the door, still his hand at the bell push. Both looked at each other, with soul searching glances. He must have taken the stairs insead the lift, he was panting.

'Jackie, you?'

'Who else, you dumb and stupid girl, you '*chasmis*', ——'

'What the——', Jackie did'nt allow her to speak, he stormed into the house and took her in his arms. The years' waiting was over, she melted in his arms, closing her eyes, savouring his closeness. Then, she realized, that her feet were not touching the gound. He had lifted her up and was showering kisses on her. No, no, she didn't want it to happen this way, however much she would have liked it. She got the chance to whisper in his ears, 'Hey, what are you doing, the door is still open, somebody may see. Put me down.' There was urgency in her voice. Planting a soft kiss on her lips, he put her down and pushed the door shut, at the same time. Both were breathing heavily.

'Have you gone mad, what happened?', Seema asked.

'*Badi ma*, told me everything, I wanted to come last night itself, but it was late.'

'So, you came early in the morning and charged like a bull. You took the wind out of me. Is this how you behave with your girls?'

'How do I know? You are my first girl. What could have come over me, Seema? I couldn't sleep, I tossed in the bed thinking of you only. You know, after dropping you here, I went to office, I was in a turmoil, couldn't concentrate on works. Your image jumped from the papers, I looked at. I could'nt reconcile with the fact, that you were lost to me forever, I realized what it meant to lose someone, whom you found after years. I reached home late in the night and saw *badi ma*, waiting for me, anxiously. When I started to go up, she called me back and holding my face in her hands, ever so fondly, looked at me with deep intensity and asked, 'What is it that troubles you, my dear son?' She must have seen something in my eyes and said, 'Is it Seema? Do you love her, my boy? Then, why are you torturing yourself? I have talked to her, she is a girl after my heart and you would be lucky to have her as your wife.'

I hastened to say, 'But, she is married, and has a son. Didn't she tell you?'

She said, 'Of course, she told me her story, how she lost both of her parents and brought back her step brother, who was only six months old, at that time. She has been bringing up that child since then, as her son. The child, now a boy of six years, calls her *mama* and he has nobody except her.'

'Do you know Seema, how I felt, when *badi ma* told me that you are all alone in this world?'

'How?'

'A heavy load was taken off from my heart and I wanted to rush here and open my heart to you.'

'Well?'

Jackie kneeled down and holding her hands asked, 'Will you marry me Seema?'

Seema pressed him to her body and said in a quiet, yet firm voice, 'Yes, yes. yes.'

* * * * *

Seema and Jackie were married. The marriage was held with pomp and ceremony at the Saxena House. It was a great and solemn occasion for Parvati. With a handful offering of fresh roses, before the portrait of Lolita, she craved her blessings for the young couple, who were going to begin their life together. It was attended by Ram Gopal jee and Maya, Raja and Ranee, Kamal and Jaya and many others, who thronged there to bless the couple and wish them a happy married life.

The most surprised of them was Jaya, who was the best friend of Seema. She was the first to hear the news of betrothal of Jackie to Seema. They were at Hotel Sheraton in Shimla, when the news reached them. *Ma jee* telephoned her and said, '*Beti,* my life's ambition seems to be achieved. You will be glad to know, that Jackie at last is willing to get married.'

Freeing herself from Kamal's arms, she sat bolt upright and exclaimed, 'Oh! *Ma jee*, whom she is getting married to?'

'You know her *beti*, she is Seema.' Jaya's joy and surprise knew no bounds. She telephoned Jackie to congratulate him and said, 'Again, you have floored all of us, Jackie. You know she is my best friend and never believed that one day, she would be my sister-in –law.'

* * * * *

In the hotel suite in Ooty, Seema was busy unpacking her bag. Jackie came from behind and clasped her. She tried to stave him off, but could not succeed. Once in bed, he relieved her of the pair of specs, put them away and just stayed put in looking at her.

'What are you looking at?'

'You.'

'Me!'

'Yes, I wanted to see you, how you look behind those glasses. These pretty eyes, I just want to take a dip in their depth and remain immersed in everlasting bliss and happiness.'

'Jackie, even now, I don't believe that I have got you. In the beginning, it was hero worship, a young girl that I was, I was swept away by your magnetic eyes, gradually the yearning grew in me and suddenly it dawned upon me, that I was in love with you. We were lost to each other, no doubt, but your image stayed with me, ever fresh and enlivening. I could hardly suppress my feelings, when you appeared suddenly in the library, before me. My speech, betrayed my feelings, I had no control over it, but I tell you, when I saw you bewildered and lost at my mentioning, that I have a son, it gave me a sweet pleasure. I realized that, yes, you cared for me and the feeling that I cannot be yours, tormented you. Oh!Jackie, I am really sorry, and I would have lost you forever, had that incident not occurred at the road crossing, which brought us together, again.'

With their passions rising, they were drawn to each other and the room was filled with their body language. Jackie's fingers on her dress to uncover her, put her on fire, which was extinguished only at the end, when they were spent together and slept in each other's arms in utter exhaustion.

* * * * *

It was Ten o'clock in the morning and the date was Twentieth November 1992. *Kaidi* No. 411 was brought before the Jailer, dressed in fresh uniform and shaved. His greying hair and tall handsome figure would have done justice to a military uniform with stripes. The Jailer had a File before him, which he was going through. He was very young and did'nt look the typical jailer, with handlebar moustache and a '*damn you'* face, enough to strike terror in a prisoner's mind. On the contrary, this man was soft voiced and jovial. He raised his face from the File and looked up. Being recently posted to this jail, specially for his expertise in jail reforms, he didn't have time, enough to acquaint himself with his charges. A study of the File of the prisoner, brought to him for his release, provided him with a complete account of the crimes he committed, sentence he served and his behavior during the term and everything else he did in the jail, which was his home for the last seven years. The Jailer got up and did something, which was unheard of before, and caused a ripple of reactions, favourable and unfavourable, amongst the subordinates. He shook the hands of the prisoner and asked him to sit. But the prisoner begged excuse and said, 'Thank you very much sir, for your kindness, but I will not let you do something, which will violate the Regulations laid down in the Jail Manual. The status of a jailer and a prisoner are well defined in the *manual.* '

'So be it, Mr. Saxena. I expected, that you would react, somewhat, in that manner. Would you care, to tell me one thing?'

'What is it ?'

'I read in your File, that you have used hundreds of sheets of paper, to write something. What you have written and where are those papers?'

'You will find them staked in the library shelves, where old and tattered books are kept.'

'I see. This is the copy of your release order. There are two packets here, which, I am going to handover to you. You will find your belongings, you had, when you entered the jail, in one, and in the other there is a gift for you, presented by your fellow prisoners, as a token of their love and affection to you, purchased out of their earnings. As you go out, you will collect an amount of Rupees Twenty three thousand, seven hundred and fifty only, from the cashier, as your wages for the jobs undertaken by you, according to the labour chart. You are now free to walk out of the jail, the warden here, will accompany you, to the gate. Wish you good luck and Happy Diwali to you Mr. Saxena. Today is Diwali, I must tell you. I am sure, your family will be waiting for you, outside the gate.

'Thank you, again, sir, for your kind words. I shall cherish, these few moments, I spent with you, for the rest of my life.' With these words, Saxena walked out of the jail.

* * * * *

Worlds within the world, that is how time manifests itself over the space. The individual is tied to its own limited space and names it, family, society and country. Unknown to him or known to him, another individual functions in his own world. There the similarity ends. If time is a path, distanced by space, and scaled in seconds, minutes, hours, days, years and so on, the individual is bound to traverse, steadily in the scale forward soon after he is born, irrespective of his relative movements in the space. Whether you sit still before your computer at home, or walk along the street, or travel by train or fly in the aircraft and finally return to your computer at home, traversing in space in all directions, yet you have moved in one direction only in the time path, that is forward. If one is capable of observing all the events taking place in any world at the same moment, as if captured by a satellite camera with a huge microscopic lens, the pictures that would emerge, will be anything but sequential. While at one space, there may be *tsunami* waves rising to cause havoc, at another space there may be a peaceful scene at a holiday resort by the sea shore. Apart from these diverse physical manifestations of occurrences, if one, capable of studying the ripples in the mental plane of the individuals, observes, he would come across all the human qualities: sufferings, enjoyments, manifested and experienced by the individuals. The scenes would go on changing from moment to moment, across the backdrop of time.

Seven years is too long an interval in the life span of any body. Parvati's family has grown in the meanwhile. Her sons, Kamal and Jackie are doing well in their own fields. Kamal is now a Professor in the University and Jackie a successful business man. Jaya and Seema, friends before, are now happy housewives and proud mothers of a boy and a girl.

Immediately after the court proceedings and various settlements signed by Saxena, duly Registered, the family Solicitor got busy in working out the details of all stocks and investments held in the names of Kamal, Jackie and Parvati. Shrewd, as he was, Saxena's personal investments were mostly in blue-chips and Government Bonds. The financial status of his family, after he went to jail, was therefore, comfortable. Several of the companies, where Jackie held majority of the shares, were in the red. Though, Saxena resigned from Chairmanship of the companies 'Boards and Jackie was elevated from the Director's post to the Chairman's, the values of shares continued plummeting for sometime, it took years' efforts and manoeuvring, to normalize the situation, before the shares regained their position in the market.

Parvati's position in the family was that of a grand matriarch. Her grand children, Rohit, son of, Kamal and Jaya, and Renu, daughter of Jackie and Seema were very fond of her. Disrgarding the ire of her daughter-in–laws, that she was spoiling their children by over indulgence, she went on showering on them expensive dresses, imported toys and chocolates, on every occasion. Their birth days were celebrated lavishly, at Saxena House every year and became the talk of the society, for their grandiose shows by celebrites and delicious varieties of Indian and Chinese cuisine offered in the buffet. To this, were invited children, who were friends of Rohit and Renu along with their parents. A regular invitee was Loila, a fourteen years old lovely and beautiful girl.

Loila was the adopted daughter of ACP, Pradhan. When Joshi was sentenced to serve rigorous imprisonment for seven years, convicted in two independent cases, one for killing and another for murderous attempt, both the sentences to run concurrently, Loila, his daughter, was barely seven years old and studied in a boarding school at Calcutta, quite oblivious of this development. Pradhan, in charge of the investigations, took charge of the motherless child, with the written consent of Joshi, that in future, he will not claim the girl and will not try to establish any connection with her. Pradhan brought the girl from the boarding school, to his house at Bombay, where he, a bachelor, lived with his mother. The girl was told that, her father was missing when he undertook an expedition to Himalayas with a team of mountaineers. The man who was responsible for bringing him to justice, became a friend of the family of Saxena, in later years. He and her daughter Loila were regular invitees to all family functions of Saxenas.

Pradhan had a good rapport with Parvati jee and kept her posted with news relating to the prison life of Ratan and how he was conducting himself in the jail. Jackie and Kamal visited their father, in the jail, regularly and brought him up to date, how everything was at home and in office. Everytime, his eyes traversed beyond, in search of some one, who never came.

The day of release of Ratan, arrived at last. The family got ready to receive him. Jackie went to the room of Parvati and knocked.

'*Badi ma*, are you ready?'

'Yes *beta*, let's go.'

Kamal had arrived and they went together to receive him. Parvati was silent through out the drive. Pictures appeared before her mind, just as on a screen in a theatre in black and white. She has come a long way, from a nondescriopt village to Bombay, destiny has kicked her like a football, from one side to the other, bringing in its wake tales of sorrow and sufferings, clinging to her like moss to an old tree. They arrived at the gate of the jail and waited.

Jackie and Kamal stood outside, keeping watch over a small gate, through which, their father would emerge. The clock struck ten-thirty, when the gate was opened and Ratan came out. In his hands, were a bag and a small packet. Both of them, went forward and touched his feet. He took them in his arms and said, 'How are you, my boys?' His eyes searched for some one, whom he did'nt see.

Jackie said, 'Come, *dad*, let's go to the car, *badi ma* is waiting for you.'

Parvati looked at Ratan, as he approached the car, through the glass window, he appeared a bit thin and bent, but had the same glint in his eyes. Jackie opened the door and she stepped down and taking a step or two forward, bent down and touched his husband's feet. Ratan was taken aback, he stood still for a moment or two and then raised Parbati by holding her shoulders and said in a choking voice, 'How are you, Parvati?' She looked at him, there was compassion in his eyes. Did she notice repentance and a shade of remorse in his eyes? Is it possible for somebody, to take an U-turn in the evening of his life? Here is the man, whom she loved once and had given herself to him in pure innocence.

'You look so thin, Ratan. Did they not feed you well?'

'There was no dearth of food. I took a little, to sustain myself. The people inside were kind to me. See, what they gave me. It is a gift, a token of love and affection for me.' He gave her the packet. Jackie and Kamal, watched their parents, from a distance. It was a rare occasion for both of them. To Kamal, seeing his *ma*, conversing with someone, who was introduced to him, as his *dad*, for the first time, after twenty two years of his life, made him sad and understanding. Jackie was happy, to see his *dad*, for the first time in a defensive role and someone talking to him condescendingly.

Jackie said, 'Come on, *dad*, let's go home, others are waitng. You sit with *badi ma*, in the back seat, we will be taking the front seat.'

They drove, homeward. Jackie pointed to his *dad*, while passing through certain places on the way, new constructions that have come up, in the meanwhile. At one place, he slowed down and said, 'Look *dad,* at the constructions over there, we got that contract in the last year, outbidding Hindusthan Constructions.'

'Well done, my boy', he said. Many other things, Jackie said, didn't register on his mind, which was preoccupied with thoughts, closer to his heart. His closeness to Parvati, their bodies touching each other, took him years back, when both of them were very young and carefree. Had he not pursued wealth, the life would not have been so miserable. A single action of his, in the right direction, that is admission of his guilt, made his conscience clear. The rest of it was taken care of, by law. He has now, no regrets, nor any axe to grind. He looked forward to meet, his grand children.

As they approached Saxena House, Kamal asked, '*Dad,* what is that gift, they have presented you?'

'Open it, let me also have a look at it.' The packet was unwrapped and every one was anxious to see, what it contained. It was a cute replica of Taj Mahal, in ivory, encased in glass.

'How splendid it is!' Parvati exclaimed.

'Yes, is it not?', Jackie and Kamal, said together.

The car had stopped under the porch. And whom did he see waiting there, with a boquet of freshly cut roses? It was *kaka*, his faithful servant. He came forward, opened the door, presented the boquet and fell down at his feet, sobbing. Saxena lifted him and pressed him to his bosom.

'How are you *kaka*?'

'God is great, *malik*. He has delivered you to us.'

His daughter-in-laws and grand children waited in the verandah with bouquets in hands. He followed Parvati to meet them.

She was introducing, 'This is Jaya, whom you know, is your *badi bahu,* this lovely child is Rohit, your grand son. We have just celebrated his sixth birthday. This is Seema, your *choti bahu* and the baby girl in her arms is Renu, your grand daughter.'

Jaya and Seema touched the feet of Saxena. He picked up both the children in his arms and said, "Parvati, I never expected, that I would live to see this day.' The children looked at their *grand pa* with wonder in their eyes. Their mothers came and took them off, from his arms. To everyone's surprise, he fished out two large size chocolates from his pocket and offered them to the children, who took them with pleasure and murmured, 'Thank you, *grand pa.*'

Saxena kneeled down, embraced the children and said, '*Yug yug jio, mere bache.*'

Entering the hall, his attention was drawn to the lovely portraits of Lolita and Parvati, hung above the mantle piece, on the opposite wall. He went forward, others followed. Standing before the portrait of Lolita, where an oil lamp was kept burning and incense sticks gave rise to coiling fragrant smokes all around, Saxena fixed his gaze on the figure and inaudibly uttered, 'Forgive me, Lolita and bless your children.'

Saxena, then, took out the ivory replica of Taj Mahal and placed it on the mantle piece, under the portraits.

Parvati said, 'Did the other people back there, love you much, to have gifted you this lovely present, Ratan?'

'Yes very much, they used to call me *dada.*' He related, an incident in the first year of his stay. Independence Day was being celebrated in the jail compound. A bigwig of the Police department was expected to come for unfurling the flag. There was excitement all over. Names for certain honorary posts, for the ensuing year were to be announced from among the inmates, such as Mess Supervisor, P. T. Instructor, Library Clerk, etc., on the basis of grades obtained for behavior, leadership, team spirit during the year. My name was announced for the post of Mess Supervisor. All were happy, except one, who desired to continue in the post, which he held since last one year, for obvious reasons. He being a hardened criminal, never expected that there would be a contender and that too, *a green* in their vocabulary. The jailer heard lot of complaints against him, regarding bad quality of food served to the prisoners, unhygienic condition of the kitchen, etc. Since he represented the inmates, it was his responsibility to look into these matters, but the corrupt officials took him in their fold and adequately compensated him, to keep his mouth shut. To improve matters, the Superintendent wanted a change and brought me in. So, that was the background, with which I went to the mess hall, on the evening of the Independnce Day. I found there was no queue and everybody crowded in front of the counters and tried to reach first; the stronger ones were able to get the lion's share and the weaker ones had to satisfy themselves with whatever was left. At the top of my voice, I shouted to stop and pulled down the counter shutters. Kalu, the ex-Supervisor sat at a corner and enjoyed the scene. When he saw me, he stood up, to his full height of six feet two inches, really a giant of a man and came towards me menacingly. Ignoring me, he went inside and brought himself a steaming hot vessel filled with chicken curry, a special dish prepared for the occasion. When I accosted him and asked, what was he up to, to everybody's horror, he raised the vessel and was about to pour the boiling contents upon me and would have succeded, had I not springed back with alacrity but not before a little of the gravy caught me on my shoulder and it singed me. Kalu was grinning, others were silently watching the situation. Without caring for my burn injury, I asked him to clean the floor. He said, "What will you do, if I don't." This fanned the fire in me and I put my entire body weight of eighty kg. behind my punch which landed on his chest. It took the wind out of him and he fell flat backward and lay sprawled on the floor.

Everybody was listening to his account intently, but Rohit with awe and wonder, he said, 'Oh! Grand pa, you are a *super man*, tell us what happened thereafter, did you give him another punch?' He was jumping with excitement and jesticulating, as if he he was giving the punches. Saxena ruffled his hair and continued.

'Yes, I was going to, but seeing him busted and lying there flat, there was no need. His mates were coming to give him a hand to get up, I stopped them and said,' No, let him come to his senses and do the mopping, as I said'. There was tension in the air, the mess warden had joined, in the meanwhile, he stood silently and watched the situation. To everybody's surprise, Kalu the invincible, got up meekly and throwing a scornful look at me, began cleaning the floor. There was clapping all around, I had won the day, The medal, I received that day, I am still wearing.

Rohit said, 'Please show us the medal, *Grand pa*'. Saxena bared his left shoulder and showed a six inches long scar of burn injury on his collarbone.

Parvati smiled to herself, afterall Ratan was not boasting.

* * * * *

EPILOGUE

Years passed. The year was 1995, three years since Ratan returned home after serving his sentence. He had no work to do, Jackie and Kamal, managed the affairs, between them. He was now sixty five years old. He did'nt go out much and spent his time mostly in the garden, under the open sky and helped Renu in her home works, when her mother was busy. In the evening, the family would sit together for dinner and Ratan enjoyed their company and regaled them with tales of his prison life.

Parvati observed that Ratan was getting fat. There was a gym in the house and she dropped hints, a number of times, that he should spend some time in the gym. But he would brush aside her advice with a thin smile and a forlorn look in his eyes. She knew, what was ailing him. His life long drive in quest of wealth, ultimately left him dry and uncared for. She has caught him many times, looking at her with great expectations and looked away when their eyes met. This is the man, whom she loved once, but it was years ago, when the meaning of love was not clear to her. Both of them were young and suffered from rapturous expressions, which ultimately landed them in wedlock. When she learnt that fulfillment of love was in 'to be loved', it was too late. Their remaining together, was perhaps destined to be short lived. It was again destiny, which brought them together. This time, after a lapse of twenty two years, a wide gap reminiscent of memories on either side, some pleasant and some harsh. On such occasions, Parvati's hand would move to her *mangal sutra*, which she wore, as a reflex action. She held it sacred as a sign of her womanhood, which has lent her the status of a married woman. The Hindu way of life, which teaches one, sacrifice and *bhakti*, also inculcates the value of forgiveness.

It was midday, post lunch period. Parvati was alone in the dining room, others had retired to their rooms. She could see Ratan, going towards his favourite spot in the garden, a wooden bench under a *peepul* tree, for his afternoon siesta, through the French window. Ratan told her once, that he felt suffocated inside the rooms, aired by fans and air conditioners. She began seeing in him, the young cowherd, roaming the forest with his herd of cattle without a care in his mind. She was thus engaged in her soul searching, when the silence was broken by the harsh ringing of the door bell. She got up and answered the bell, a courier messenger was at the door. A heavy packet was in his hand.

'This is meant for Mr. Ratan Kumar Saxena', he said. She wondered, who could have sent this. When the courier boy said, that the packet was from the Central Jail, her heart missed a beat. With great trepidation she took delivery of the packet and opened it, when the boy was gone. Inside the packet, there was a book, entitled, 'Diary Of A Prisoner'. There was also an envelope, which contained an official letter. It read.........

Central Jail

Dated, 22nd May 1995

Dear Sri Saxena,

I am pleased to inform you that, the Jail administration have judged to publish the notes, which you left here, on your release, in the form of a book entitled 'Diary Of A Prisoner'. This book has been acclaimed as a pioneer work on Jail reforms. In recognition of your work, the Government is pleased to award you a cash prize of Rupees One Lakh, a cheque for the same is enclosed along with a copy of the First edition of the book.

With regards and good wishes,

Yours ——————

Parvati could not hold back her tears, she let them fall down her cheeks, freely. She held the Book and the cheque in her hand and pressed them close to her face.

Oh Ratan! atlast, you have achieved the real wealth, which nobody can take away from you. I am proud of you. You don't know, how happy I am today. She didn't want to let others know, about this, yet. She rushed to the garden, to give the good news to him, herself and share the moments of joy, with him alone. It would be a surprise to him, when she would handover the book written by him along with the cheque and a greater surprise still, awaited him. She remembered, while awaiting his sentence, he wrote a letter to her, ending with the sentence, *'I loved you once, forgive me, if you can.* 'She realized, that it was she alone, who would deliver him from the agony, he suffered from. She didn't know, how to frame her words, it would be the first time in the last twenty two years, that she was going to speak to him softly in endearing words, as a wife to her husband. She already felt like a young bride going to meet her husband, after so many years.

Spotting him, sitting on the bench under the tree, in the shade, she tiptoed from behind and dropping the book on his lap said, 'Hi'. There was no response. Her heart was chilled, before her eyes and in her arms, he collapsed. It was too late.